Brass Bonanza Plays Again

How Hockey's Strangest Goon Brought Back Mark Twain and a Dead Team—and Made a City Believe

Robert Muldoon

iUniverse, Inc.
Bloomington

Brass Bonanza Plays Again
How Hockey's Strangest Goon Brought Back Mark Twain and a Dead Team—and Made a City Believe

This book is primarily a work of fiction, but based on actual events and real people alongside fictitious and dead characters. Any conversation with or concerning fictitious or dead characters, any interaction with or concerning fictitious or dead characters, any situation with or concerning fictitious or dead characters either are the product of the author's imagination or are used fictitiously. Real events, quotes, commentaries and histories are footnoted wherever possible. The following are fictitious characters: Tiger Burns, Broadway Lawlor, Gracie Farrell, Mr. and Mrs. Schmidley, Frenchie LeDuc, Michel LeGros, Keyshawn Streets, and the Commissioner.

Cover Art by Brian Cipro. Top to bottom: Mark Twain, Rube Waddell, Sam Colt, Frederick Olmsted and Harriet Beecher Stowe.

iUniverse books may be ordered through booksellers or by contacting:

iUniverse
1663 Liberty Drive
Bloomington, IN 47403
www.iuniverse.com
1-800-Authors (1-800-288-4677)

ISBN: 978-1-4502-8105-8 (pbk)
ISBN: 978-1-4502-8106-5 (ebk)

Printed in the United States of America

iUniverse rev. date: 1/5/11

For Mom and Dad,
Fred Muldoon,
John Callahan,
Donald Milne,
Cathy Ryan,
Ray Lis,
Michael Corbley,
Steve Chiasson

...and others who live on always in our hearts

Preface

This book began 9 years ago on a walk with my father when reminiscing about the past I unexpectedly choked up. I realized then how much I missed Hartford and the Whalers. I needed to find someone who loved them as much. Tiger Burns was revealed to me.

From 1984 to 1994 I worked for the Whalers—driving a new car on-ice between periods (moonlighting in the Actuarial Department at Travelers Insurance). Some would say I saw a lot of bad hockey. I couldn't disagree more. It was the most privileged association of my life.

It was a magical time, just out of college, with scores of like-aged actuaries to hang out with. And, of course, there was the Whale. My roommate Brad Peters was a press gofer for the team. One night out of the blue he called, tone urgent, "Get down here! We need someone to work the penalty box." That night, I opened and closed the gate for Hall-of-Famer Gilbert Perrault.

Two weeks later, Brad called again. This time the need was different. When I arrived, his supervisor Mr. Henderson tossed me a pair of keys. Drive the promotional Honda Accord on ice between the first and second period. "On ice?" I gasped. What if the car skidded, rammed the boards and flew into the crowd? I could already see the headlines: DRIVER GOES BERSERK AT CIVIC CENTER. 10,000 LOOK ON IN HORROR. 'MAD DOG' MULDOON UNDER HEAVY GUARD.

It went fine. Next season, incredibly, the regular driver left. These jobs were plums, passed on from father to son. Get your friend, Mr. Henderson told Brad. For the next 10 seasons I drove the car on-ice (first a Honda, then a Buick and last a Cadillac). No headlines.

I wrote a story "View from the Penalty Box" in the Sunday *Hartford Courant* describing the experience. Phil Langan, the Whalers PR Director, invited me to write for *Goal Magazine,* the game program. I cut my teeth with features on the Zamboni Driver, Team Photographer, Team Dentist, Security Guards, Assistant General Manager, and Sky Boxes. Mercifully, at last, he entrusted me with a player.

His name was Shane Churla. A tough guy! Wear a helmet and mouthpiece to the interview, my father teased. Others followed: Sylvain Cote, Paul MacDermid, Randy LaDouceur, Scott Young. No more Zamboni Drivers. Some of the players I profiled became NHL Coaches: Joel Quenneville, Dave Tippett, John Anderson.

I went to grad school in New York City and moved back home to Boston, where for 2 seasons I drove 120 miles round-trip to keep the car-driving gig. In Boston I experienced first-hand how all things Hartford were sneered at: Hartford sucks! Whalers suck! My affections deepened. Who doesn't love an underdog?

On April 13, 1997 I headed down for the last game. PA Announcer Greg Gilmartin snuck me down in to the penalty box where it all started for me 14 years earlier. I watched teary-eyed along with 15,000 others. *Oooooooooooone minute left in Hartford,* Gilmartin said.

After the game, we went to Chuck's for the Irish wake. Beat writers Jeff Jacobs and Alan Greenberg, of *The Courant*, Randy Smith, of the *Journal-Inquirer* held court, as always, but the mood was funereal.

Kevin Dineen scored the last goal—and the players left for Carolina. Hartford was left with bittersweet memories. Five years later, I took that walk with my father—and the memories all flooded back.

Writing this has been a monomaniacal pursuit for 9 years. I've learned one thing: I don't have a glass jaw. Again and again I've been knocked down, dusted off the ice shavings and skated back into the fray.

For a time I had a New York agent (who represented *The English Patient* novel), and she pitched it to a New York publisher, and the pointed response was "Hockey books don't sell!" I tried telling her it was a Rocky book, not a hockey book. An underdog story. A love story. She said in these troubled times publishing houses are closing. I said in these troubled times America needs Tiger Burns and his story of loss and perseverance.

Hockey books don't sell. The epitaph.

So now I take inspiration from fellow Bates alum Lisa Genova who published with iUniverse when she was told Alzheimer books don't sell. *Still Alice* went viral, was picked up and debuted on the New York Times best-seller list at #5. Alzheimer books don't sell, indeed.

###

I'd like to thank Brad Peters for being a friend and making that call in 1984; Bill Henderson for tossing me the keys despite quaking knees; Phil Langan for the magazine assignments and faith. Linda Thornton, Rich Chmura, Rick Francis, Diane Sobolewski, all with the Whalers, were supportive. The ice crew—Charley Tucker, John Weir, Wayne Knight—all rallied around a nervous driver.

Howard Baldwin, Whaler founder, made it all happen. Ron Francis, Kevin Dineen, Ulf Samuelsson and others made the team special. Terry O'Reilly, of the Boston Bruins, was the perfect opponent. Thanks to them all.

Randy Smith, Jeff Jacobs, Alan Greenberg and Jack Lautier chronicled the exploits—and held court at Chuck's Steak House. I learned much pricking my ears and craning my neck. I deeply regret that Randy, Alan and Jack are gone.

Greg Gilmartin, Grace Lim, Mike Onyon, Sheila Callahan, Robert Muldoon Sr., Cindy Bates, Vipada Kasemsri, Lisa Bobak, Marcy Thibodeau, Vince Juaristi, Ted Roupas, Grace Aylesbury, Kit Hoffman and (he claims) Richard Crocker read the book and gave comments. Richard Marek added professional polish. Brian Cipro and Russ Busa lent their talents. John Merola did not scoff. Addie Kim helped me conceive this as something larger than I first imagined.

Warren Muldoon has always been a believer (in the face of all evidence). My mother Joanne has always been steadfast and loving (if not patient). My father Robert was the smartest and funniest man I ever knew. His spirit lives on every page.

Bob Muldoon

November 2010
muldoonbob@aol.com

Prologue

The gnome-sized man pulled his hockey stick back. The hopes of a down-in-the-mouth city, a down-on-its-luck team, and 15,535 beaten-down fans rested on his thick back and the thin blade of his stick.

The rising crowd roared. The small stick rushed forward in a blur and slammed the puck—*Thwack-Clang-Noooooooooooooooooooooooooo...* The echoes of that doleful harmony still ring out decades later.

Single-handedly losing the Stanley Cup, and sending a small city's beloved team into oblivion, is enough to drive a man to rum, ruin—or madness. For Tiger Burns it drove him to pick up trash for untold years in Hartford's Frog Hollow barrio.

But let us begin on a note of *false* hope.

The three greatest trophies in sports—a major league ball club, an NFL team and the Stanley Cup—were once in Hartford's grasp. Yes, unheralded Hartford, in the shadows of New York and Boston, eclipsed now even by Providence, nearly claimed the three greatest jewels in the diadem of sport.

The baseball team, alas, is 19th century history; the football faux-pas has been chronicled; but few know of the last—until now.

It is a tale of betrayal and death played out in the grimy alleys and bridge bottoms of a city scorned—and in the recesses of a tormented mind. For shame, regret and guilt can kill a man as surely as arsenic—only slower and with far more pain.

What causes a man to snap? The chess player Bobby Fischer did, and wandered the squalid streets of Los Angeles in castaway clothes,

1

occasionally sighted late at night in the public library studying games. Unhinged by demons, it was whispered.

The mathematician John Nash did, and for decades shuffled the halls of Princeton in untied sneakers, a phantom-genius scrawling arcane symbols on blackboards. Broken by an unsolved equation, it was murmured.

And the hockey fighter Tiger Burns did, too. Undone by an ill-fated game, it will now be told.

But Fischer came back to play, Nash to receive the Nobel Prize, and Tiger Burns to claim a piece of the Stanley Cup. For in the end, this is a story of redemption: a man's, a team's, a city's—and a star-crossed spirit's.

It is also a love story.

1. "A Lilliput (sic) among Gullivers"

Oh, the rare old Whale, mid storm and gale
In his ocean home will be
A giant in might, where might is right
And King of the boundless sea
—Whale Song

He was perhaps the oddest-looking player ever to lace on skates. Standing five foot—three inches, he weighed 200 pounds, with a barrel chest, wrecking ball biceps, a 21" neck that seemed small under the head, and thick thighs on bowed legs that made skating difficult.

The left eye was lost to the butt-end of a stick. The two toes were gone in a botched attempt to plant a green pennant on Everest. The 500-stitch belly scar came from running (but not fast enough) with the bulls of Pamplona. The cauliflower ears, cartilage-free nose, and toothless grin were the grim memorials of a decade of on-ice tussles.

Sherlock Holmes could deduce a man's profession at a glance, distinguishing bookkeeper from beekeeper, violinist from ventriloquist, by the subtle markings each left. But even the great sleuth, in obeisance to the name, and the remnants of a face, might have mistaken our hockey player for a wild animal trainer unskilled with the whip and chair. Elementary!

To old-timers, his battle-scarred appearance called to mind "Two Ton Tony" Galento, the 5'8" dock brawler who went four rounds with Joe Louis, or "Hack" Wilson, the 5'6" steelworker whose 191 major league RBIs is a record—but they dwarfed him.

Out-of-towners saw him differently. "GHASTLY! The Phantom of the Opera unmasked," harrumphed the New York broadsheets. "A beer barrel on skates," guffawed the Boston tabs. In Montreal, he was (in 2 tongues) "a muscle-bound hobbit in need of face reconstruction."

But on one point, there was agreement: he was not a pretty sight.

In a league where players dated Miss Americas, Olympic ice princesses and super models, he was a misfit. But in a league of Los Angeles, New York and Chicago so too was Hartford. To many he personified town and team. With all his defects he was the *perfect* Hartford Whaler!

When his left eye—the glass one—once popped out, he slapped it past the bewildered goaltender, lighting the red lamp and turning skate-over-helmet cartwheels. It took five minutes of replays, a bench-clearing brawl, and a call to the Commissioner's Office, before the "goal" was disallowed. It would have been his only one that season. Throughout, the organist serenaded him with "Eye of the Tiger".

But it was with his fighting—not his "eye-popping" scoring—that he made his bones (and broke a few). A boxer like Muhammad Ali might have 60 fights in a career; Tiger had 600. Parsimonious as a scorer, as a fighter he was profligate. In a 10-year career, he spent 3,000 minutes in the penalty box—50 hours, enough to watch 100 Seinfelds.

"With that many minutes, he should have had his own contoured chair and reading lamp inside," quipped one wag.

If he had applied himself, Tiger could have mastered Trigonometry—or Latin—from the captive confines of the "Sin Bin." Instead, he did stomach crunches. There were battles ahead to be fought.

Hockey's rough-and-tumble Adams Division was not for the meek. With the likes of Chris "Knuckles" Nilan and Terry "The Tasmanian Devil" O'Reilly running amok, a willingness to scrap was necessary.

The Norris Division was known as the "Chuck Norris" Division after the kung fu expert. The Philadelphia Flyers fielded a line "The Legion of Doom" that *averaged* 6'4" and 230 pounds. Lurking elsewhere were Stu "The Grim Reaper" Grimson, Linc "The Missing Link" Gaetz, and "Bruise Brother" Bob Probert.

He was, noted one observer, "a Lilliput (sic) amongst Gullivers."

But even though you might stand a foot taller, weigh 40 more pounds, have both eyes, and more toes—with Tiger, the whole was greater than the sum of the *missing* parts. He took them on, one and all, and rarely faltered.

When asked how he did it, night after night, knowing the toll it was taking, the emotion of his answer overwhelmed him.

"I never fought for myself—ever," he said, tears streaming down one cheek. "They said a lot of mean things out there—'specially 'bout my mug. I never lifted a finger. But if they ripped Hartford or the Whale…" at that, his raspy voice faltered, "they were in for the fight o' their lives."

After repeated efforts to compose himself, he finished in a whisper: "I love dis place, ya' know."

Although he was small, he was strong. He skated with a city on his shoulders.

To signal his willingness to fight at the drop of a puck, or civic slur, he wore a tiny scrap of a leather helmet—a cross between something worn by Red Grange, the Roaring Twenties football star, and The Red Baron, World War I flying ace. Padded models with face shields were an abomination to him.

"Easter bonnets!" he sneered.

For protection, he relied on natural defenses: calcium deposits that encircled his face like a monk's cowl; shoulders sloping like black diamond ski trails; the neck of a prized boar. Everything about him became adapted to the absorption of blows—and at a pace that befuddled science.

Whereas Darwin's finches developed larger beaks over millennia, Tiger's physiognomy "evolved" over but a few NHL seasons. But his face was no threat to Darwin. On the contrary, it illustrated a central tenet: Nature cares nothing for appearances, except in so far as they may be useful to any being.[1]

But his most unusual feature was this: he loved Hartford and the Whalers.

Tattooed in green on his muscle-slabbed chest was a full-rigged whaling ship. Etched on his biceps was his motto: *Pro Cetus et Hartfordiae.* So what if his Latin was butchered—his heart wasn't. He was a *rara avis* indeed.

Understand that a lot of players in the league – and on the *team*— despised the Whalers. The feeling was that Hartford, the smallest and poorest of NHL cities, was strictly minor league. They mocked the shop-lined arena ("a Mall"), the team song ("dumb"), the jubilant fans ("*assholes*"), anything associated with the Whalers was subject to withering contempt.

When Edmonton's Dave Semenko, Wayne Gretzky's bodyguard, was traded to Hartford on December 11, 1986, he wrote in his autobiography: "Don't cry, I kept telling myself. Whatever you do, don't cry. The plane was getting closer and coach's words kept pounding in my ears. 'I've traded you to Hartford...I've traded you to Hartford.'"[2]

Then another low blow from the tarmac: "When I got off the plane, I was humming that **dumb** Hartford Whalers' theme song."[3] Look it up!

When winger Dave Williams was released, he said this about the team: "They had no class. Never did have any class. Never would have any class."[4]

Coming or going—it didn't matter—players harpooned the Whalers.

But these slurs were as nothing compared to the hue and cry of the hoi polloi.

Hartford had entered the popular culture as a joke. In one episode of The Simpsons, when Homer entered a "How Low Will You Go?" contest, first prize was—a weekend in Hartford.

In 1986, when the city staged a parade to honor a team that had finished fourth in a five-team division, the breach in form forever sealed their fate. To pundits, it was the equivalent of rewarding a "C" in Gym class with a trip to Disney. The Whalers cemented their reputation as "Mickey Mouse."

So what if that team had finished on a 12-3-2 tear, propelling itself into the playoffs for the first time; sweeping first-place Quebec; and extending Champion Montreal to overtime of game seven? Success-starved Hartford had won nothing.

Still there were those who loved "the Whale", as they were affectionately called. When the Hartford Civic Center roof collapsed in the Blizzard of 1978, a caravan of thousands followed them up Interstate 91 to Springfield (MA) during the two-year reconstruction. Dubbed the "91 Club", this group was lampooned as "a gang of rejects from the Gong Show", by *Hartford Courant* columnist Alan Greenberg.

From 1985-90, the Civic Center turnstiles clicked at a clip of 550,000 fans a season. In 1986, Hartford hosted the NHL All-Star game. A year later, the Whale won the Adams Division title, ahead of "Original Six" Boston and Montreal.

At the height of the Cold War, they trounced the Soviet Red Army Team. Captain Ronnie Francis was an All-Star four times, and feisty Kevin Dineen thrice. Celebrities like Roger Staubach, of the Dallas Cowboys, Ivan Lendl, the tennis star, and "Busty" Heart, the burlesque queen, all attended games—as did local meteorologist Brad Fields, who rarely missed one.

For Hartford, it was a time of limitless possibility— truly a golden era. Ask anyone aboard for the ride, the Whalers hitched this sleepy New England city to a rising star. It seemed like it would never end.

2. Tiger's Walk

Hartford is America's File Cabinet.[5]
—Dan Shaughnessy, *The Boston Globe*

At the center of this rollicking romp—and madcap adventures too many to regale—was Tiger Burns, Hartford's pint-sized pugilist. In a city with a charisma deficit—let's face it, "the Insurance Capital of the World" inspires little awe—Tiger brought flair.

Before every game, he led a parade of stragglers and street urchins, whose ranks swelled to hundreds, on the jaunt from his Asylum Avenue home to the Civic Center. For Tiger, girded for battle, it was simply a matter of walking to work. For City Fathers, however, it was a grievous affront to the common civility! The City Council, alas, had recently banned "street performers."

"The Puritans were opposed to fun and we've tried to carry on that tradition, too,"[6] lamented *Courant* columnist Colin McEnroe.

Charles Dickens, in his 1842 American tour, noted as much:

> Hartford is the seat of the local legislature in Connecticut, which sage body enacted, in bygone times, the renowned code of "Blue Laws" in virtue whereof, among other enlightened provisions, any citizen who could be proved to have kissed his wife on Sunday was punishable, I believe, with the stocks. Too much of the old Puritan spirit exists in these parts to the present hour.[7]

Dickens could have penned much the same a century later—but for Tiger Burns. On his daily walk, he turned arse-over-tea-kettle cartwheels delighting shopkeepers lining the road, office-workers gawking down, and his own ragtag brigade of ne'er-do-wells.

"It's a great day fa' Hartford," he proclaimed, in a voice garbled from too many elbows to the throat.

To accommodate sponsors, he wore a satin-green fighter's robe fitted for a heavyweight, the train dragging like a wedding dress. Stenciled on back was "MAC'S MUFFLERS ON ALBANY AVE—$10 OFF FOR EVERY KO." It took a wide back—and fast fists—but Tiger's measured up.

"That's our Tiger!" the crowd roared, engulfing their sawed-off hero as an amoeba does a germ.

Before games against Boston and New York, he hired out the Weaver High Band. When the parade reached the players' lot on Ann Street, the adults having peeled off at the Russian Lady Café, Tiger snaked his ragamuffins through rows of BMWs and Mercedes. At the player's gate, he led them in cheer:

"One-two-three, WHAAAAAAALE," they screeched in accents of all dialects.

Tiger's "Cubs" hailed from every neighborhood in the city: Puerto Ricans and Dominicans in Frog Hollow; Blacks and Jamaicans on Albany Ave; Italians on Franklin Ave. As a farewell, he tossed out tickets like confetti at a Connecticut-Georgetown game.

"Time to rumble fa' Hartford," he explained, and ambled off bow-legged to do just that.

Although short in duration, and confined to 40 game nights, "Tiger's Walk" did not escape the notice of City Fathers—who were not amused.

"It must be smashed with the iron fist of government!" thundered one irate Councilor.

Tiger's Walk, you see, had become a "happening"; worse, it was creating a "buzz"; and, worst yet, Hartford was becoming a "destination." Folks were streaming in from all over—even the suburbs.

"This so-called 'walk to work' is civil disobedience masquerading as pedestrian rights!" railed another. "What's next? Street Mimes? Elvis Impersonators? Jugglers? He walks again over my dead body!"

Not since Alabama Governor George Wallace intervened at the schoolhouse door had politicians taken such a bold stand in upholding the law. Councilors, backed by a battalion of club-wielding cops, aimed to restore decorum. A showdown was set a week hence before a game against the Winnipeg Jets.

Throngs—triple for a Boston game—swelled the route, many waving placards "GOONS ARE PEOPLE TOO!" and chanting "LET TIGER WALK!" Amongst them was a phalanx of skateboarders, and a knock-kneed, third-grader named Keyshawn with a pair of contraband rollerblades.

With the wind at his back, the size 5 blades strapped on his feet, and chants of "GO, TIGER, GO!" ringing in his cauliflower ears, Tiger was slung, "Roller Derby" style, down Asylum Hill, escorted on all sides by skateboarders. Careening on one leg past Union Station, he veered into the Civic Center Garage, screaming on the descent: *Yeeeeeeee-ooooooooooowww!*

"The dragnet's been foiled!" declared a fist-pumping Keyshawn. All of (non-Puritan) Hartford rejoiced.

That night, at an emergency meeting, speeches were made, passions inflamed, and mild-mannered men came near to blows, before a midnight vote was (narrowly) passed: Tiger could walk to work!

"One small step for Tiger, but a GIANT LEAP for Hartford," exulted columnist McEnroe.

Inside the arena, to the rousing fanfare *Brass Bonanza*, the fight song that heralded the Whalers' arrival on-ice, he vaulted the boards, with furiously-churning strides, three of them the equal of one stately glide of the others.

"Ladies and gentlemen, here are YOUR Hartford Whalers."

DAH DAH DAH dadadadada…

As the others skated in lazy circles, Tiger launched a furious frenzy of shadow boxing, launching haymakers at imaginary opponents on all sides. "Visualization!" he termed the unorthodox ritual.

Telescoping the crowd with his good eye, and spotting one of his cubs, he hoisted him onto his shoulders, the two together as tall as the others, and dashed between blue lines. "Blood Circulation!" he proclaimed it a tonic for.

Entering the familiar penalty box ("Acclimatization!"), he pumped out 50 pull-ups from against the glass. Against Boston, he might commandeer a forklift, and circle the ice with a Bruins mascot hanging in effigy ("Terrorization!").

One humid night, when fog lifted off the ice, as if up off London streets, he hopped the Zamboni, startling the driver.

"Three eyes are betta' than two!" he hollered, offering up help.

Finally, as a matter of solemn duty, he never (ever!) left warm-ups until the last of the practice pucks were tossed into the crowd. It was the only time that he ever touched a puck —and *never* with his stick!

"Superstition!" he divulged, with a twinkle of his right eye.

Between periods, he wandered from the locker room to compete on-ice in the "Shoot-to-Win" Contest for a trip to Hawaii. Try as he might; he'd lose to some overweight actuary from Avon.

"CHIN UP, Tiger! You'd win in a fight!" the leather-lungs shouted.

Buoyed by the support, he bee-lined it up to the "Whaler's blimp" hovering high in the arena dropping prizes. When the laser-guided dirigible started behaving suspiciously like the Hindenburg, one thing was certain.

"Tiger's at the helm!" roared the whole of Section 105, diving for cover.

In sum, Tiger spent so little time practicing that it was a miracle if he ever scored—and statistics bear this out. In 10 NHL seasons, he scored 6 goals—less than one per year. Do the Math!

So when he lit the red lamp, pent-up emotions, long suppressed, were bound to come un-dammed. His signature celebration was a series of skate-over-helmet cartwheels, bringing him perilously close to a fractured skull.

"Self-preservation is why he scores so seldom!" cracked one wiseacre.

Then he hurdled the boards, dove into the crowd, and performed the equivalent of Green Bay's "Lambeau Leap", dubbed the "Hartford Hug." When he once scored against Boston, every bar and restaurant in the city had the "winning puck" on display—Tiger having swapped the rare relic for free sarsaparillas. To this day, hundreds of Tiger's "winning goals" are out on ebay at auction.

But fists—not finesse—earned him his spot in the league.

Toughness is prized in hockey. When Linc ("The Missing Link") Gaetz was taken in the 1988 draft, he arrived on stage for the ceremony with two black eyes. The General Manager, who just selected him, took one look and dissolved into tears.

"Can I pick again?" he blubbered. "I want the guy who did that to him!"

The role of enforcer (or "goon") is a time-honored one. Since men first laced on skates, stouthearted players, of lesser ability, have been called upon to "keep things honest" or keep a team from "getting run out of the building." The lexicon of the game is spiced with euphemisms that reflect the enforcer's importance.

In hockey, when players "drop the gloves", it is expected that they will make a good account of it. One night in New York, two guys stood facing each other, circling and circling, without launching a blow. Referee Wally Harris penalized them each two minutes for "dancing."

"It was an insult to call it fighting. Not a punch was thrown," he sneered.

With bodies flying, elbows crashing and sticks slashing, hockey is like no other sport. The feeling has always been that dropping the gloves is the most honorable release. The alternatives could be fatal. Hockey's door has been darkened before by stick-swinging incidents turned tragic.

To keep a lid on it, certain players, dubbed "policemen", are called upon to keep opponents from "acting chippy" or "getting brave" especially toward "skill players." Above all, the goon's job is to protect his team's star.

In Hartford, Tiger was the "bodyguard"—and proud of it! His job, stripped of all pretenses, was to protect Captain Ronnie Francis. Opponents learned the quickest way to set him off was to knock Hartford, the Whale or Captain Ronnie. At times like these, he was a whirlwind of righteous indignation and offended dignity.

His specialty was the body punch. To reach towering opponents, he launched ham-sized fists from tottering ankles, the force of the blow lifting him up off-ice.

"He 'it you low; he 'it you hard," winced tough guy "Frenchie" LeDuc. "He could 'it you no other way."

And when he hit you right, the results were awesome.

"TIMBERRRRRRRRR!" was the signature call of radio voice Chuck Kaiton.

After a knockout, he ripped off his jersey, and thumped his tattoo in a display of bravado that enraged the opposition. On the road, rabid New Yorkers pelted him with cauliflowers ("Tiger's ears") while Bostonians doused him in beer (a "golden shower.")

"MOIDA DA BUM," the Gothamites screeched.

"GO BACK TO HAAAHTFID," boomed the Beantown brethren

Wherever he fought signs like "Trounce The TROLL", "Handicap The HOBBIT" and (in Boston) "Tiger's Mother is a PUSSY" sprang up. Throughout the abuse, he smiled that toothless grin, "Just doin' my job, that's all."

He was that familiar dichotomy: the toughest guy on-ice; the gentlest off it.

"It was the men who loved their wives and children, who were kind to dogs, (who) could leave each other looking like raw meat in the course of a night's work,"[8] explained tough guy Dave Williams.

It is a proverb of hockey that goons have the biggest hearts— "The Grim Reaper" pens children's books; "The Dominator" runs a charity. Described as "stalwart" or "stand-up", their battles are most always on someone else's behalf.

"You looked after your teammates," said Boston strongman Terry O'Reilly. "You didn't leave it up to the referees to find justice out there. It was not manly to turn away from a challenge."

Tiger's brawls with O'Reilly were the stuff of legend. He once challenged the whole New York bench—and none accepted. It gave pride to Hartford fans that their guy could take on Boston's and New York's heavyweights—and win most every time.

"When our little guy beat their tough guys, it meant that we measured up," said one fan, welling up. "We stood taller!"

In a world where Hartford was reviled and ridiculed, Tiger took up its cudgels. Tiger was Hartford's champion.

3. Bear Le Batard

It's not the size of the dog in the fight.
It's the size of the fight in the dog.
—Mark Twain

Born under the red planet Mars, in Canada's Northwest Territories, he was the bastard son of a Scotch-Irish teen and Native American, or "First Nation's" man, as he is called up north. The year of birth was 1964—or 1965. It was not recorded.

Within two years, he was traded to a dog musher and his common-law wife in exchange for a frozen caribou carcass. It was the only trade of his career. A bill of sale, later to serve as a *de facto* birth certificate, recorded the transaction: "the child (to be named) for the caribou (dead)." The thumbprints of his illiterate mother and father sealed the deal.

Years later, when a reporter asked how a mother could give up her first born like that, he dissolved into tears. "She needed ta' eat, I s'pose," he shrugged, biting his fattened lip. It was the only time he walked out of an interview.

Of his mother, little is known but one incongruous fact. "She was beautiful, stunning actually," testified Daniel Sirois, a Royal Canadian Mounted Policeman, the only man alive with a picture.

From her then, the boy could not have received much—perhaps a bit of the pluck of the Scots, whose motto is: "No one wounds me with impunity!"

Of his father, a compact man known as "Half Moose", more is known—little good. Tales of Half Moose Burns' exploits were legendary in the bucket-of-blood saloons and taverns dotting northwest Canada. By trade, he was a gold prospector, who never had much luck, forever seeking the elusive yellow powder—always in vain, never in vein.

"Things didn't pan out," he wryly described his fortunes.

It might have been an epitaph. An aimless wanderer and brawler, he pushed from Yellowknife to Red Deer, Whitehorse to Deadhorse in futile pursuit. All he ever found was whiskey and trouble. On those scores, he hit the mother lode.

"Half Moose Burns was the toughest sonofabitch I ever seen," declared Sirois, of the RCMP, slamming a fist to his desk. "He fought lumberjacks, oil workers, roustabouts, anyone who dared. He knocked 'em out and then hoisted 'em over his head, by Jove. There's a picture of 'im in some tavern holding up Canada's heavyweight boxing champ, a 300-pounder named Cutter Phelps, like a sack of potatoes. He never had no use for people—except those who'd serve 'im a drink or fight 'im. And both grew smaller and smaller."

Sirois continued his narrative: "Half-Moose Burns was the most feared ruffian in the Territories until the day he stepped out of the Red Garter Saloon one night and vanished."

Few tears were shed on that solemn occasion.

"He was a Half Moose, alright—the back half!" griped a barmaid Victoria, who served him his last drink—and was stiffed for it. The last eyewitness to see him stagger out onto Ragged Ass Road, named for an abandoned mine, she said there was nothing unusual about his behavior that night.

"He knocked the teeth out of a fur trapper named Big Elmo," said Victoria, filing her nails and blowing away the dust.

Staggering out into the countryside dotted with lakes and sink holes, he might have fallen through thin ice, or been followed and met his end at the point of a blade.

"A hundred whipped men might a done it," said the barmaid, adding bitterly, "a hundred cheated bartenders, too."

The official investigation shed little light.

"The stomach of a grizzly or bottom of a lake will never give up its secrets," concluded Sirois, dismissing the case. "The investigation was closed quickly."

After a pause, he continued, his baritone voice catching: "Let me add on a personal note, as our paths crossed many times, I have known him when sober, when released from jail of a fine morn, to be happy. He weren't all bad. No man is."

And so there the matter of Half-Moose Burns must rest. The sum total of what this itinerant brawler gave to his castaway son was this: a one-syllable surname, a small body of improbable strength, a bit of the wanderlust perhaps, and, not least, a fighter's chance. And such was life and death in the frozen north for a man who ran his whole life—but never from a fight.

###

In a world ruled by what Jack London called "the law of Club and Fang", perhaps it was preordained that life would be a struggle. The sled musher's wife fled soon after the passing of "adoption" papers. Maybe her will—or nose—had been broken one time too many? It is not known.

From her then, he got nothing—or perhaps her gift was the undivided attention of a man who cared for but one thing in life: the shaping of the unbreakable character of sled dogs.

Pierre Le Batard—everyone called him "Bear", and with fear—loomed 6'5", with a black beard, cruel eyes, a booming voice and a right arm swelled to twice the normal size, from the "training" of sled dogs with a razor strap.

"Spare zee strap, Spoil zee dog," was the principle that ruled life in the log cabin he built with his own hands, above the Arctic Circle, in the Yukon. That simple philosophy, elegant in its framing, and energetic in its execution, was seared into the flanks of every sled dog on the team— and to Bear the new lad was no different.

"Ever' un eez treated equal!" he said, articulating his egalitarian ways.

The boy's role, painstakingly "trained" into him, was to care for the 20-dog pack of malamutes, named after the Inuit tribe *Mahlemut*. But Bear's beasts were not purebred. On cold Arctic nights, they betrayed in chilling chorus the wolf strain running in their bloodlines.

"Zee wolf's blood make zee champions!" bellowed Bear, pounding at his massive chest, as he did for emphasis.

But wolf's blood also made for disposition problems. Wolf's blood meant that fights flared nightly between the lead dog, or "Alpha", and his rivals. And wolf's blood meant that wolf's teeth often pierced the flesh of the stable boy who slept on a straw pallet on the frozen dirt of the wind-riddled kennel. But tears were not suffered lightly.

"No cry or zee strap will stop ya!" snarled Le Batard, snapping the belt down.

And so life with Bear had its rhythms. By day, the dogs needed washing, harnessing, exercising, and feeding. By night, fights needed refereeing. And so the boy's life was a full one! And in time he proved his worth—which meant he could stay. And so, at age six, he needed a name.

Now, Bear had a gift for name-giving. Every wolf-dog had one. There was Devil's Eye, Dagger Tooth and Razor Claw and a score more, each the result of his studied appraisal of their most salient feature in combat. In short, as others sing for their supper, Bear's beasts fought for their names.

"Fightin' reveals zee character!" he declared, thumping his chest.

So when it came to naming the boy, like the rest, he was tossed into a pit with one of the wolf pups and when Bear exclaimed "'Dat boy, ee fight like zee Tiger!" the christening was done. From that day forth, he had a name.

So no longer was it "Boy, do 'dis" and "Boy do 'dat." It was "Tiger, do 'dis" and "Tiger do 'dat." And it gave the boy pride to have his own name.

"Tiger is my name now and forever," he announced grandiosely to the dogs, the only ones to listen. It was a name he was proud to answer to. He had earned it—and that meant something to a boy with nothing else.

Now Bear Le Batard was no great cook, despite his birthright to the sumptuous traditions of French cuisine, but give the hulking sonofabitch his due. He had a clearly-articulated culinary philosophy for the high-protein slop of caribou guts and moose entrails that he stirred in rotting barrels with a splintered oar.

"Zee dogs eat first! Dey are zee breadwinners, dem!"

When Tiger reached the age of seven, Bear left to compete in 1000-mile sled races across Canada. And, as unlikely as it may seem, the absence of his steady hand and guiding wisdom, did the boy no harm. He was free—with the run of the kennel and miles of the frozen McKenzie River.

"Yeee-Haaaw!" he squealed, belly-sliding like an otter down the steep banks.

Freedom meant a lot to one who had never tasted it. He slept late, moped about, and lay flat on his back gazing at the arctic skies. But after a week of such bliss, he was bored—and lonely.

"I miss the dogs, my brothers," he said, shivering alone in the kennel.

Thankfully, in every blessed person's life, there is someone to show the way. He doesn't have to be a major figure; but he must introduce hope and a sense of possibilities, sometimes where there is none. And so in Bear's absence a neighbor named Hank, holed in a shack by the river, took it on himself to look after Tiger, and gave him his first gift, other than a name: a pair of skates, two-sizes too big, and rolled-up newspaper to fill them with.

"WOW, they's beautiful, Mr. Hank!" exclaimed a pie-eyed Tiger, as the stooped, old man stuffed the toes and pulled the laces tight.

Alone without wolves and a brutish taskmaster, Tiger learned to skate. For 12 hours a day, more when the moon was full, he glided on the black ice of the McKenzie. And what joy—and such lumps!—it brought him.

At first, the seat of his canvas britches saw more ice than the rusty blades of his too-big skates. On his first step, his legs splayed, he spun 360 degrees and tumbled. Undaunted, he picked himself up, pirouetted and tumbled again.

"Arse-over-teakettle!" howled Hank, from the cabin where he kept a blanket by the roaring fire for Tiger.

But he kept at it. In a day, he could stand. In two, he could stagger. On the third, he could glide and so was wanting a new challenge.

"I've got something else for 'ya, Tiger," said Hank, shielding a surprise behind his back. Having fashioned a "stick" of spruce, and carved cakes of ice into "pucks," with these gifts, Hank introduced Tiger to Canada's great and grand pastime.

And such was Tiger's joy that when he scored his first "goal", by sliding an ice chunk between two logs 10 feet apart, he spontaneously turned a "cartwheel," lifting his arms to celebrate, then crashing on his head.

"Yee-OOOOUCH!"

Perhaps Tiger would forever associate the pain of that moment with scoring a goal. He seldom did thereafter. But in the years ahead, he would come to perfect the cartwheel as the manifestation of his greatest triumphs and joys.

"That boy—he a gamer!" laughed old Hank, beside the cabin fire.

But bliss such as this can not go on forever—especially in the life of a sled dog musher's stable boy. When Bear returned, bedecked with ribbons, and with city-bought whiskey, there were tired dogs ("Zee champeen dogs!") to coddle and pamper.

"Dey fill my purse wit' zee gold!" said Bear, "and my heart wit' zee pride! You make sure thar' plates are filled, you no-good sonofabitch."

And so life returned to its rhythms. But through the cuffing and chores, the pain and regiments, Tiger had something to sustain him now. All it took was one glide on the frozen Mckenzie to leave behind the life of toil and tyranny.

If Tiger had had the luxury of attending school (he didn't—"Zee school interferes wit' zee chores!"), he'd have penned one of those rhapsodic essays that began, "When I grow up, I want to be a hockey player" and listed a thousand-and-one reasons why. As it was, the unlettered boy carved pictures of sticks and pucks into the bark of pine trees and the drafty walls of his kennel-home.

Like many a boy, there rested deep within his bosom, as a birthright, the belief that the game could rescue him from his cares—and propel him to glory. If he could have put those hard-to-express feelings into words, and polish them up, like he did his skates each night, they would have come out gleaming like this:

"One day, in a faraway place, I'll be great at this game. Mark my words as my back is now marked—one day I'll bring glory to my name and honor to this game."

As it was, all he could muster was defiance: "I won't stop! I won't never stop!"

And so hockey, which brought transitory hope, fleeting freedom, and burgeoning dreams, also brought hellish beatings. "Zee skating interferes wit' zee chores!" thundered Bear, in his blackest rages yet, the smell of whisky on his breath. But Tiger would not stop!

"No—never, I won't!"

In every ill-used boy's life, there comes a time to make a stand. For some it comes early; for others late. For Tiger it came the day when Bear, recognizing that Tiger at 13, already wider than tall, could no longer be "trained" with a strap, and so picked up an ax.

"You'll not skate agin' wit' chores undone, you no-good sonofabitch!"

In a fiendish rage, he swung the flat end at Tiger's head. And to the surprise of both, but especially to Bear, Tiger did not fall. And knowing instinctively, that now was the time to make a stand—or forever lose the chance—Tiger balled his fist and struck back. This time, only Tiger was surprised. The lumbering brute toppled back—stone-cold, knocked-out. Tiger looked down at the bully at his feet and then to his bloody fist in awe.

"Wow."

Perhaps the moment wasn't quite akin to the first time that Picasso picked up a brush, or Twain a pen. But for Tiger his first punch was a revelation. He was a prodigy. He knew then that there was iron in his jaw and dynamite in his fists—and those aren't bad things for a sled dog musher's boy to know.

"Wow," he marveled, staring down at Bear's crumpled body.

At that moment, his boyhood, such as it was, ended. A shade below five feet, but already 190 pounds of muscle and sinew, his face blighted from a diet of moose shanks and entrails, barely suitable for a sled dog. But he was free—and for that, grateful.

So let us close the chapter on the brutish dog musher. Bear Le Batard's story deserves no more stain on these pages. The accounting is complete. From him he got: a first name, a body hardened by ceaseless toil, an inkling that he could take a punch, and most important, deliver one in the name of righteousness.

"I hate you," said Tiger, weeping bitterly and stepping over the hulking bully's body.

As he tramped away, his hockey stick slung over his shoulders like a hobo stick, he looked for all the world like a man with a destination. But really he was only a frightened boy, concealed in a grotesque strongman's body. He was different than other boys, and soon he would find out how the world treats those who are different.

Looking back at the only home he'd ever known, a wind-riddled kennel on the banks of the Mckenzie, his brown eyes filled. With a choked good-bye to Hank, the kindly neighbor who gave him stick and skates, and a wave to the howling pack of wolves, his only brothers, he looked back one last time.

"So long," he cried, the words swept away in the arctic gale under the northern lights.

The road ahead was long, and it was time to push on. Under a Full Wolf Moon, he trudged ahead. But if Tiger had looked back, he'd have seen he was not alone. Behind, at a watchful distance, leaning into the wind, was a stranger clutching a straw summer hat to his head with his strong left arm. His name was Rube.

4. The Scrimgeours

A scout from the plains came down from Saskatoon
Said, "There's always room on our team for a goon
Son, we've always got room for a goon."
— *Hit Somebody,* Warren Zevon

When 13-year-old Tiger tramped into the arena of the Moose Jaw Warriors, and with his first punch decked the resident goon, an 18-year-old who had fired a wad of tape at his head, he was hired on the spot. Niggling details like birth certificates could be handled later.

"A godsend!" proclaimed Coach Stump Peters to pie-eyed assistants. "'Ave you ever seen such a gifted hockey player, eh?!"

After a round of hearty backslaps, followed by the lighting of Cuban cigars, a question was asked, as an afterthought, to complete the hiring process.

"Can you skate, boy, eh?"

Everyone howled again. His fists had spoken. Before Tiger could answer, Coach Peters tossed him a black and red jersey.

"Welcome to Moose Jaw, son. You're gonna fit in fine, eh."

###

Canada's Junior Leagues are pint-sized versions of the NHL. Players are drafted at age 15; play a grueling 72-game schedule culminating in the Memorial Cup—oh, and they can be traded.

16-year-old Tom Martin of the Seattle Breakers was once swapped for a broken-down bus. "Best deal I ever made," boasted the team's owner. For the rest of his career, the lanky Martin was called "The Bus".

At age 12, players were scouted in midget and mite leagues and placed on protected lists, like pork belly futures. Those who lived away from home were "billeted" with local families.

"We're looking to build good teams here, not all that self-esteem jive," explained Coach Stump Peters, speaking to the league's philosophy.

To some, this all might seem a bit mercenary. But, on one point, the league, to its credit, was staunch: all players must attend school—even when it interfered with hockey.

"Rules are rules, eh," lamented one coach. "They may not always be right or we may not agree with 'em, but if we can't skirt 'em, we abide by 'em."

Because this system is uncomfortably close to outdated notions of indentured servitude, players who play one game in Canadian Juniors are ineligible for U.S. college scholarships. Moreover, a whole college program could be put on probation, or shut down with a "death penalty", if a Junior were discovered on its roster.

###

While the Leagues in Ontario and Quebec are reputed as "skill leagues", the Western Junior Hockey League, scattered across four provinces, prides itself on producing tough guys. It's known, in half-admiration and half-disgust, as a "goon pipeline."

WHL lore is replete with tales of brawls and melees, with players charging into the stands, fans charging the ice, coaches assaulting officials, and at least one PA announcer joining the fray. After one particularly ugly episode, the mayor of Victoria coined what might well serve as the league's motto—"This isn't sport—it's barbarism."

After anxious games, visiting teams were known to borrow tactics employed in war zones. "I've got the Red Cross signs on the bus so we can get out of town," divulged one coach.

In sum, courts, jails and police blotters were as much a part of the Western Junior Hockey League as pucks, sticks and protective cups. Since 1966, it has produced players like Dave Semenko, John Kordic and the five Sutter brothers—players who mirrored the rugged terrain, blazing a trail to the NHL, sometimes with little more than a pair of willing fists.

###

Located north of Montana at the confluence of two creeks, Moose Jaw was once a winter encampment for Cree hunters who stalked deer and elk dressed in animal costumes. When Europeans arrived, the city was quick to flourish. From five ragged tents, it spawned a vibrant community with saloons, shacks and dozens of tents.

After the Canadian-Pacific railroad was built, a new prosperity came. Bootlegging, gambling and prostitution flowed from an underground network of tunnels linking the hotels and restaurants. In The Roaring Twenties, celebrities like Al Capone visited.

In short, as every jewel has a setting which shows it off best, Moose Jaw was the perfect spot for 13-year-old Tiger Burns to launch his career as a hockey brawler.

Precious little had changed since those halcyon days and that sparkling day when a weary musher's boy, with blood still dripping off his fists, tramped into town with a stick over his shoulder—and a dream in his heart. Then as now, Moose Jaw was a place where a man with the requisite talents could find opportunity.

Next day's *Moose Jaw Times-Herald* printed the following notice of arrival, read as eagerly as birth and wedding announcements elsewhere:

> The oddest boy ever to put on the Warrior uniform of Moose Jaw was signed to a contract yesterday. Standing 5 foot and weighing 14 stone, he has the physique of Hercules, if dumped into a trash compactor. His face, otherwise nondescript, is covered with dense clusters of suppurating pustules. This lack of comeliness owes perhaps to a poor diet. Under the care of Mr. and Mrs. Scrimgeour, of #27 Caribou Leg Lane, he is soon sure to be clear of that blight. Tonight's game at The Arena against Medicine Hat is set for 7:00 p.m. Last night's game, called on account of the brawl (see **Police Notes**), will not be rescheduled. See this new boy named Tiger Burns. He is 16 years old.

In truth, the Moose Jaw man-child was 13, three years below minimum. But a fighter's apprenticeship like his would not be derailed over so fine a point. After all, soon he was taking on and beating the league's toughest goons—and learning to skate in the Devil's Bargain.

"Looks 16 to me!" declared Coach Peters, appraising him up and down, mostly down, and crumpling the bill of sale handed to him. So 16 he was! But still a boy needs a home.

"You'll need billeting, eh?" asked Coach Peters, the b-word rolling off his tongue, billowing like a cloud, full of airy promise.

"Yes, sir!"

For Tiger the prospect of living with a family was as exciting as launching his pro career. Outside of an ill-tempered ruffian and a pack of wolves, he'd never had a normal family life.

"Any special requirements, eh?"

"Requirements, sir?"

"Sure. A big family or a little family?"

Tiger thought for a moment, then licked his swollen lips.

"Well, how 'bout a home with a mother and a father both," he said timidly, as if placing a special order.

"A mother *and* a father, eh?"

"Yes, sir! The both of 'em!" said the boy, his voice trembling.

"Then that is what you'll get, by Jove! But don't let family life soften ya'," warned Coach Peters. "You've got a job to do here, eh."

"No, sir!"

Next day, after practice, Tiger followed the hand-drawn map the coaches had sketched to the outskirts of town. His first glimpse of the Scrimgeours, of #27 Caribou Leg Lane, was one he would never forget.

Behind a dilapidated fence, the slats spaced like hockey teeth, and an ill-tended lawn, more properly a field, stood a ramshackle house, the shutters dangling at odd angles.

"HOME!" he cried out, his pulse racing.

With turrets and gables, the house appeared like a Gothic Castle—only the windows were broken, sheets of purple paint calved from the sides, and three cats hung limp from a rope outside an attic window.

"MAGNIFICENT!" he appraised, soaking it all in.

Skipping up the path, dodging here and there a rusted car carcass, his heart pounded. Ten feet from the door, he could contain his excitement no longer.

"I'm heeeeere!"

Silence.

"Yoohoo! I'm hoooome!"

Nothing.

"Yo, yo, it's me, Tigerrrr!"

Rapping on a brass knocker, he nudged the door, and it promptly fell off the hinges, crashing into a wall of empty cans, scattering them down the hall in an avalanche. *Now* there was a response.

"THIEF! THIEF! Who the hell is stealing my beer cans?"

Mrs. Scrimgeour was home. Following the distressed shrieks, Tiger stepped gingerly over the cans into a dark corridor of cobwebs and threadbare carpets, where the screams reverberated.

"THIEF! THIEF! Identify yourself this instant."

Owing to the steam from his breath, Tiger advanced like a spelunker navigating a new tunnel, using his stout arms to guide him, occasionally kicking a stray can.

"WATCH IT! They're returnable—and so are you!" snapped a shrill voice.

Painstakingly reaching the kitchen, Tiger pierced a curtain of smoke where two hunched figures sat. Poking his head in, he coughed shyly— announcing his arrival.

"GO FISH!" said the woman, dressed in a purple robe with matching curlers, slapping down two cards.

Mrs. Scrimgeour exhaled a plume of smoke from a cigarette painted red with lipstick. Behind her, on the wall, in a spot other homes might reserve for a "Home Sweet Home" needlepoint hung this:

> "Fish—and VISITORS—Stink After Three Days.
> ~B. Franklin~"

Tiger had signed on for four years. Seated by a pail overflowing with fast food wrappers, the woman peered up. Tiger mistook it as an invitation. Wading through the smoke, stepping over more cans, he presented himself before the pot-bellied man, whose bagged eyes and disheveled hair gave him the wise look of an Einstein, and acknowledged Mr. Scrimgeour's belch with a shy smile.

"Get over 'ere and let's have a look at 'ya," hacked Mrs. Scrimgeour, motioning him over franticly. Tiger scampered over. Surveying his stout body through oversized frames, she offered this spot-on appraisal: "Looks like this one has an appetite!"

Then returning to his face: "But girls won't be a problem!"

Plopping down two more cards, she launched into a review of the house rules, "SLIDE—don't push—the door. Understand?"

"Yes, Mam."

"And don't crush the old fool's cans, understand?"

The man, his belly poking out from a two-sizes-too-small t-shirt, took another guzzle and belched again. Tiger smiled politely at his attentions.

"Yer room's out back!" barked the woman, her cigarette stitching up and down like a sewing needle. "Look at me when I'm talking at 'yer!"

Tiger's neck snapped. A purple polyester robe, flecked with ashes, strained over her porcine body. Her feet were shod in slippers shaped like bunnies. Removing one, she singed a corn on her toe with the cigarette, before sticking it back in her mouth. It was 2:00 on a Wednesday, and the Scrimgeours, who billeted hockey players, were on duty.

"The kitchen's off-limits!" shouted Mrs. Scrimgeour, a hot ash landing on the robe. "If the hot plate in 'yer room is broke, *your* responsibility! Any *more* questions?"

Tiger shook his head vigorously.

"Then be gone with ya'," she hacked, pointing out back. As he scampered in the direction of her pink-manicured fingernail, she halted him with a last piece of business.

"Ooooh boy," she cooed sweetly, "make sure yer' team has the correct address for the billeting fees. Two months in advance are required, do remind them." Then returning to her usual gruff tone: "Now be gone with 'ya!"

Crossing the olive-green linoleum, careful to sidestep stray cans, he turned down a hall like the first, only colder and darker. At the end, was a door with a sign "New Boy."

"MY ROOM!"

Sliding the door, Tiger entered a bleak, windowless cell with cracked plaster affording bountiful quantities of arctic air. A lone 25 watt bulb provided all the light—and what little there was of warmth. A horse hair mattress on a rusted frame, beside a wardrobe with two metal hangers, completed the spartan decor.

Tiger dropped his stick and skates on the floor. The nicotine-colored walls were bare except for a torn photo of Miss Moose Jaw 1976 autographed "To Shane. XXOO, Miss MJ". Tiger carefully removed the tack, replaced it with a Moose Jaw Warrior schedule 1977-78, and marveled at the photo.

"Wow! What a hottie! Maybe someday I…"

Just then, a ruckus in the hall alerted Tiger to someone's approach. Stashing the photo into the toe of his skate, he turned to the door, arms folded guiltily behind his back. Mrs. Scrimgeour, her hair fiery red like her lipstick, poked her head in:

"The old fool collects beer cans for deposit. Leave yer empties on the table once a week, and he'd be obliged." Apparently that fulfilled the league's billeting mandate to 'include your player in family activities.'

Weekly slid under the door was a scrap of suet wrapped in butcher's paper marked "beef" that decent folk wouldn't hang for a woodpecker. It fulfilled the mandate of "regular meals with meat." The rest of the week, cans of pork and beans, stacked up like cord wood, would do. Yes, the Scrimgeours were careful to play by the rules! They had a good situation and didn't want to jeopardize it.

For Tiger, the word "billeting", which had rolled off the tongue full of promise, had come down to this. Say this about the Scrimgeours, they left him alone. Their policy of neglect was royal treatment compared to the abuse at the hands of Bear Le Batard.

Still a boy wants love. Doesn't every boy, even a hockey fighter?

The Scrimgeours, the coaches, and his teammates could never fill his deficits and give him what he longed for. Lying on the bristly mattress in the drafty room, Tiger cried. Burying his head into the pillow-less bed, the tears overwhelmed him.

"Let it out!" he sobbed, as chips of lead paint fluttered down from the ceiling like snow. The intensity of his hurt surprised him, his whole body convulsing. Sure he had dreamt of more from his new family, the Scrimgeours, but he thought he could handle any disappointment. But the pain consumed him as a mishandled cigarette might an old house.

"Let it out!" he wailed into the pitiless mattress, as his whole body shuddered.

For those who have nothing, there is a corollary to something uttered by those who have much, yet long for more: "Be careful what you wish for. You might *not* get it—and you'll be crushed."

Tiger was devastated. For one hour he cried, or close to it given that the clock—like the hot plate—was broken. Then it was time to steel himself for the battles ahead. Rising red-eyed from the bed, he made a fist—and a vow.

"I'll be the best DARN fighter this league has ever seen!" he roared, stretching to his full five feet. "Who needs a family?"

If this was the way life in Moose Jaw was to be, well, he had survived worse. His resolve was gathering like a storm cloud.

"This is nuthin'!" he cried, slamming his fist into the mattress.

In the end, Providence had bestowed him with a sanguine temperament. A lack of love had hardened him—but not coarsened him. Nor did it diminish his hope that one day he might find love.

Just then, he remembered the treasure stashed in his skate. Leaping from the bed, he pulled the photo out, careful not to bend it.

"Maybe someday soon," he said, entranced by its singular beauty.

While cruelly used, he was not without hope, and hope, after all, is the fuel of dreams. And Tiger had dreams. Big dreams! Boy's dreams! Fighter's dreams! So he vowed one more time—with passion:

"I can do without love at my new home in Moose Jaw."

But if it ever came his way, and at age 13 he hadn't *entirely* discounted the possibility, he vowed to return it with a vengeance. "If any one out there ever loves me," choked the sled-musher's boy. "I will never, ever let 'em down."

That was the solemn promise he made that first night. He had trouble putting it into words. What 13-year-old would not? But he could put his hockey dreams into words—and so he did again with fervor.

"I'll be the best darn hockey player Moose Jaw 'as ever seen," he cried out, sending a flutter of paint chips from the ceiling. "You watch and see!"

Just then, a banging on a distant floor alerted Tiger that Mrs. Scrimgeour was awake. He extinguished the lone light and sobbed himself to sleep on the bristly mattress.

5. The Moose Jaw Man-Child

Let each of you discover where your true chance of greatness lies.
Seize this chance! Rejoice in it!
And let no power or persuasion deter you in your task.
—Chariots of Fire

Tiger was as good as his promise that first night. In the days and weeks ahead, he uncoiled on arenas in the prairie towns of western Canada with the fury of a twister.

The son of Half Moose Burns proved well that the chip never lands far from the stump. In towns where the father once raised holy hell in saloons, the son now did the same in small arenas—and after games, he was careful to avoid the old man's haunts. Coach Peters made sure of it.

"Avoid the Killer B's—'ear me!" he warned. "No Booze! No Brawls!! No Broads, eh!!!"

He needn't have worried about the last. The small knot of girls who followed the Moose Jaw Warriors, cheerleaders some called them, with a wink, early made their feelings known.

"He's not exactly what you'd call fetching," said Victoria, speaking for the Moose Javian fair sex.

"Not *fetching*!" shrieked Rebecca. "Why if he were a stick, a dog wouldn't fetch him! He's REE-volting!"

So girls, it seemed, would not be a problem—as Mrs. Scrimgeour, in her prescience, had predicted. But Coach Peters wanted to make sure that his fighting prodigy did just that—but on-ice only. His audition punch, knocking out the team's top goon, had impressed everyone. And soon he was knocking out goons all over the league. Talent like that needed to be managed carefully.

"No more brawling off-ice," Coach Peters warned. "There's only so many good blows a fighter's got in 'im—and we need every one, eh."

"Yes, sir."

"If I hear ye're scrapping off-ice, I'll take ya' away from that family we've got ya' with, understand? And you wouldn't want that, eh?"

"No, sir."

"Besides, we play it rough up here. You'll get your chances."

"I'm 'ere for hockey, sir."

"Atta boy!"

So brawling would be no problem either—which left booze, the bugaboo of many a promising player. But for Tiger, who'd heard the tales of his father Half-Moose, who knew what the smell of whiskey on Bear meant, and what a steady stream of beer did to Mr. Scrimgeour—well, that would be no Achilles Heel, either.

"Can't stand the stuff, Coach!"

"Good boy! Stay away from demon rum! There're a lot of fighters pushin' brooms who could be playin' at the next level but for it. You hear, eh?"

And so Tiger, who desperately wanted to please, obeyed. And for that he was pilloried. You see, a boy who abstains has no place in the social order of Moose Jaw.

"Tiger? Who's he?" feigned a teammate, pretending not to know.

"How the H-E-L-L would we ever get to know him?" shrugged Stu Grimes, a surly defenseman, spelling it out over a cold Molson on the bus. "He don't drink. Not exactly what you'd call sociable, eh?"

Nor did it help that with his first punch, he had beaten up the wrong teammate, the Police Chief's son, with the power to squash speeding tickets and "take care" of underage drinking complaints. Maybe if he had been quicker to claim the mantle of new tough, things may have been different? But he hadn't. And the opportunity was gone forever. A coalition, led by the Grimes Gang, quickly turned against him.

"Any time he wants to pound down a few, he's welcome," offered Grimes, extending an olive branch. "Until then, well, he made his bed!"

When word spread that the punch that had secured him his job was his last without skates and stick, things changed for the queer-looking boy. Tiger soon found that the brotherhood of wolves was preferable to the fellowship of teammates.

While few dared insult Tiger to his face, to clever boys, there are myriads of other ways. Lockers can be vandalized; hockey equipment sprayed with shaving cream; epithets hurled from the rear of buses. The effect was the same: "WELCOME TO MOOSE JAW, MISFIT!"

And when the other players discovered he was billeted with the "bottom-of-the-barrel" Scrimgeours, there was much merriment at his expense.

"Hah! He's in with old lady Cheetskates!"

"She'll suck the life outta 'im, fer sure."

Retreating into the sanctuary of his back room, Tiger found solace—and learned to loathe himself. His face, pocked and pitted, he scrubbed raw. His squat body, built for fighting, grew stouter still. His boyish features took on a pug's hardened look.

Mirrors became a sworn enemy. He danced around polished metal, snapped his neck from clean windows, and side-stepped pools of water. Anything which cast a dreaded reflection, he avoided.

So he shaved in the shadows, combed in the dark, and brushed his remaining teeth with his wide back turned. Observing these habits, the Grimes Gang placed a full-length looking glass by his locker, and howled in unison as he dragged it away, head down, eyes shut.

"Look! HOBBIT HEAD'S moving it!"

Taking cues from the players, in school a whole new class made sport of him. Here there was a new locker to vandalize, new equipment to be defiled, a new bus to hurl insults from.

"Hah! Hah! PIZZA FACE!"

But school, which brought added humiliation, also brought a measure of salvation. Tiger found friends in unlikely places: in books. Assigned to a class of first-graders, he took every mock and jeer from teammates who traveled miles for the delicious sight of Tiger nestled among babes—and mastered the gift of reading.

"Yo! Yo! GORILLA-BOY'S reading Curious George!!"

Books became his boon companions. Inside their pages, he made his only friends. In Moose Jaw, his was a fighting apprenticeship, but with a taste for the stories of other boys with troubles to match his own. For Tiger, it was a fellowship of the miserable.

What right did he have to complain when poor, motherless Huck Finn had a father who "lay drunk with the hogs" and "in the gutter all night", swatted Huck with "hick'ry", "cowhide", anything he could get hold of? A father who made schooling punishable:

> Your mother couldn't read and she couldn't write,
> nuther, before she died. None of the family couldn't
> before they died. I can't; and here you're a swelling
> yourself up like this... if I catch you about that school,
> I'll tan you good. [9]

No one was tanning Tiger's hide. In fact, on the ice quite the opposite was happening. And reading—well, Mrs. Scrimgeour encouraged it, sort of: "Keeps 'im out 'o the kitchen, so I'm all fer it!"

Then there was poor orphaned Tom Sawyer. He attended his own funeral, that one did! Tom lived with Aunt Polly and his half-brother Sid who tattled on him at every turn so that he got licked ("whacked over the head with a thimble") almost as much as Huck. Made a boy grateful not to be burdened with a family!

"What right do I have ta complain?" Tiger asked, devouring the stories by the light of a bulb that Mrs. Scrimgeour slid under the door, wrapped in purple tissue, along with better cuts of meat, when she saw he was a "good boy" who "kept to 'imself" and "weren't no trouble."

At least, Tiger had his hockey dreams. What hope did poor Jim, who set out on a raft with Huck, have? Miss Watson was aiming to ship him down river and sell him for $8000. Heck, in Moose Jaw a boy could always refuse a trade and quit, but Jim couldn't quit being a slave.

"Things ain't *that* bad," Tiger admitted.

The adventures of Huck, Tom and Jim made his own misfortunes bearable. As with many an ill-used boy, reading was a life-line. Tiger was alone—but with distant friends. And for the right kind of boy, with daring and dreams, that can be enough.

Sliding out the autographed photo of Miss Moose Jaw from the toe of his skate, he used his new gifts to cross out one word and carefully insert another:

TIGER
To ~~Shane~~. XXOO Miss Moose Jaw

"*That's* more like it!" he crowed.

Moreover, he had an escape plan. But unlike Huck and Jim who sailed away on a rough-hewn raft. Tiger aimed to do it with rough-and-ready fists. Game-by-game, fight-by-fight, he built his raft.

And four years later, when he was drafted, "the last pick of the last round of a weak draft", he celebrated with the three-mast whaling ship tattoo (in truth it was a triptych, or three tattoos, if you count the main ship, the spouting whale, and the chase boat of harpooners.)

Getting the tattoo was the brazen act of impetuous youth. Soon after the ink dried, Tiger discovered that Hartford was not—nor *ever* was—a whaling port! Egad!

Moreover, Tiger got the "Original Whaler" before tattoos became *de rigeur* among the jock class—decades before Allan Iverson strutted about with 25 (and counting), and Mike Tyson unveiled his ornamental eye mark.

Finally, as the last pick of the NHL draft, he was the "longest of long" shots to ever actually make the club. The NFL has a name for its last pick: Mr. Irrelevance. In hockey, he has a different name: *Horse-Shit*.

"A 5'3" goon? Who are they kidding?" asked one draftnik pointedly. "The NHL ain't the Land of Misfit Toys. The big boys will beat up on him. It's a wasted pick—even for the last one."

Notwithstanding, Tiger liked the tattoo. His status as the "ultimate pick" was a defining moment. He was *someone* now—and, more important, *someone* wanted him. For Tiger Burns, the draft was both the culmination—and beginning—of a long, improbable journey.

He was sailing away to the NHL. To Twain's city, where for two decades, coinciding with the flowering of his genius, he wrote *Tom Sawyer, A Connecticut Yankee in King Arthur's Court,* and *The Adventures of Huckleberry Finn.*

Harriet Beecher Stowe, who wrote *Uncle Tom's Cabin,* lived next door. Lincoln called her "the little lady who wrote the book that started the Great War"

Sam Colt, from a complex on the Connecticut River, invented the six-shooter—"the gun that won the west." According to frontier wisdom, "God created men; Colonel Colt made them equal."

And Frederick Law Olmsted, the Father of Landscape Architecture, lived there, too. Of Central Park, he wrote: "It exerted a distinctly harmonizing and refining influence upon the most unfortunate and most lawless classes—an influence favorable to courtesy, self-control and temperance." [10]

But Tiger knew none of that then—neither that Hartford, once a charter member of baseball's National League, had stumbled.

"Once the nation's richest city, Hartford slipped into the 21st century as a holding tank for the poor. Riddled with drugs and gang violence, tenements and poverty, it was a place people talked about in the past tense, an echo of the city Mark Twain, Harriet Beecher Stowe and Samuel Colt called home long ago,"[11] wrote the *Los Angeles Times.*

The *New York Times* labeled Harford "the most destitute 17 square miles in the nation's wealthiest state."[12]

With his lone bag packed, Tiger was again at a crossroads. Reading had given him the tools now to put into words what had been in his heart since he was an unlettered sled musher's boy quartered with wolves. So he articulated it with feeling:

"If anyone in this world ever loves me and welcomes me to their home, I'll fight a hundred men for 'em," he sobbed, surprised at the depth of his hurt. And as he thought back on Bear Le Batard, the brute, and the Scrimgeours, his guardians, he upped the ante: "No, I'll whup a thousand men!"

As much as there was a rage in that boy that overflowed on-ice, there was a pent-up love, too. And if that ever came unleashed, what a force it would be.

His fighting apprenticeship over, 17-year-old Tiger set off from Moose Jaw, but not without thanks to the Scrimgeours, who fulfilled the billeting requirements of a home with meals, and to Coach Stump Peters, who imparted some last words of wisdom:

"Remember to fight hard, young man, it's the only chance you've got. Never dishonor this great game by giving it less than your all, eh."

For Tiger, his aim was to be a hockey fighter, the best in the NHL. And he would go wherever he must, even to a forsaken spot midway between a rock and a hard place.

But Tiger would not be going alone. An old ballplayer named Rube in a crushed straw hat was watching out for him.

(Dear Reader, If you care not a whit about the small city and team our hockey fighter is heading off to, but only of his adventures once there, then proceed directly to Chapter 8. Otherwise, please turn the page and read on.)

6. A Ship Sets Sail

A Whaler was not a pretty ship. Compared to the sleek lines of a clipper,
it was stubby and sturdy. Its sails were darkened by the soot from the "try-
works"...Because it was not fleet enough to outrun hostile craft, it often
had simulated gun-ports painted along its sides to discourage attack.
—*Travelers Currier & Ives Calendar*

In 1971, Howard Baldwin was young, brash and handsome—in a word,
dashing. With a shock of blond hair and gleaming smile, he had Hollywood
written all over him, and in time he would win an Academy Award there.
But first he would take Hartford by storm.

A graduate of the Salisbury School, he shipped off to Boston University
and the Marines before landing as minor league business manager of the
Philadelphia Flyers. Soon he graduated to ticket manager, but climbing the
ladder was not Baldwin's style. He had his eye on the top rung.

In 1966, the NHL was a six-team league run by, in one pundit's words,
"a tight, little island of close-fisted, inbred standpatters with a stranglehold
on a grand pro game."[13] The average salary, after adding six more teams,
was $22,000.

Pooling $25,000, Baldwin and three partners secured a charter
membership in the World Hockey Association, a renegade league founded
to take advantage of the sport's popularity. These were the high-flying
days of Bobby Orr, Bobby Hull, and bench-clearing brawls. Hockey was
white hot!

At 30, Baldwin became the youngest executive in sports, but funding
was a problem. With characteristic moxie, he approached Boston Celtics
Owner Bob Schmertz. Legend has it that Schmertz, spotting a black,
circular object on the desk, asked what it was.

"A hockey puck," said Baldwin.

Schmertz, who had never seen a game, agreed to invest $350,000
with a million-dollar line of credit. The New England Whalers were born.
Taking their name because "WHALERS" carried with it the letters of
the new league, and something of the region's maritime heritage, the first
logo was a "W" impaled by a harpoon. Jack Kelley, winner of back-to-

back titles at Boston University, was hired as the first coach. Larry Pleau of Montreal and Rick Ley of Toronto signed on. In weeks, 2000 season tickets were sold.

The WHA's big break came when superstar Bobby Hull signed a 10-year $1.75 million contract with the Winnipeg Jets. With a stroke of the pen, Hull became hockey's "Golden Jet". Wayne Gretzky and Mark Messier later began their careers in the WHA.

In October 1972, the Whalers won their first game against the Philadelphia Blazers at the Boston Garden. The ship had set sail. With a league-best 46 wins, the Whalers headed into the playoffs with favorable winds. Before a national TV audience, they beat Hull's Jets 9-6 to win the inaugural AVCO World Trophy. When Baldwin challenged Stanley Cup Champion Montreal to a one-game playoff on neutral ice, he was treated like a child asking to sit at the adult table on Christmas.

Notwithstanding early success, the league was having a rough go of it. In Philadelphia, the Zamboni once fell through the ice. In Boston, many Route 128 defense contractors were laying off after Vietnam. For the Whalers, going against the Bruins in Boston was a losing proposition. With their bare knuckles style, the Big Bad Bruins, led by Bobby Orr, embodied the zeitgeist of the times.

A hundred miles to the south, Hartford was putting the finishing touches on a new Civic Center, Mall, Convention space and Hotel. The goal was to make the capital of Connecticut a global destination for tourists and conventioneers.

For too long, this city of 125,000 had been no more than a urine-stop and ass-wipe between Wall Street and Cape Cod. Since time immemorial, Hartford has craved respect from the world—especially its bookend neighbors. But it just didn't seem to be in the genetics of the small city— nor the dispositions of the hulking neighbors.

Remember the 98-pound weakling who has sand kicked in his face, and his girlfriend taken—that's Hartford! And the two bullies—"The Big Apple" and "The Hub of the Universe." But hockey was a chance to hit back!

Following the same route that founder Thomas Hooker tramped 350 years before "on the earliest western migration in U.S. history"[14], Baldwin left Boston for a settlement on the Connecticut River. Amid fanfare, the **Hartford** Whalers were anointed anchor tenants.

"We were the only professional team ever where the primary reason for our being was to assist in revitalizing a city," crowed Baldwin.

On January, 11, 1975 the Whalers played their first game before a sellout of 10,507, defeating the San Diego Mariners 4-3 in overtime. Boston's castaway had become Hartford's beloved child.

In those early days, some of the most colorful characters ever to lace on skates glided through. With thick glasses and big honkers, brothers Jack and Steve Carlson looked straight out of *Revenge of the Nerds*—but they could fight and later starred in the cult classic *Slapshot* with Paul Newman.

In 1977, the Whalers out-dueled the Bruins for Gordie Howe and sons Marty and Mark. Gordie's wife Colleen negotiated the historic deal, making her the first female agent in sports. Hartford had hit the motherlode.

"There aren't too many professions that you can go on the road with half of your family," chuckled Gordie, who at 50 could still tan the hide of any whippersnapper—and now carried a nasty paternal instinct.

"I remember we were playing Edmonton one year and one of the Oilers got involved in a fight with Marty," recalled Mark. "You know how big Dad's hands are. Well, all I recall, and very vividly, is Dad picking the guy up by his face by burying his index and middle finger in the guy's nose."

The second season a tradition was born that became synonymous with town and team: playing *Brass Bonanza* whenever the Whalers took the ice or scored.

DAH DAH DAH dadadadada…

Over the years, that snappy fanfare has inspired many emotions. To true believers, it sent tingles down the spine. To naysayers, it was nauseating.

"Bombastic," complained *Sports Illustrated*.

When Kevin Dineen was traded to Philadelphia, his teammates hummed *Brass Bonanza* whenever he entered the locker room. In 2005, an ESPN station played it every day of the year-long NHL work stoppage.

An obscure composer had sold it to a record library before departing to Austria, home of Mozart. Somehow it "turned up" on a Whalers' highlights film at a time when "something was missing" in the atmosphere of the building. Fans responded immediately. The rest was history.

Stick Boy David E. Kelley, the son of the first coach, went on to become the Emmy Award-winning producer of "L.A. Law", "Ally McBeal" and "Boston Legal" (and husband of Michelle Pfeiffer). A security guard was the son of the Ugandan Prime Minister who succeeded Idi Amin, the infamous cannibal. Defenseman Russ Anderson married a Miss America. But right winger Blaine Stoughton married a Playboy bunny *and* scored 56 goals.

"Even with all those goals, Cindy was more popular in Hartford than Blaine," said Gordie.

Hartford was drawing interesting, vital and beautiful people. The marriage of hope and necessity was bearing fruit. Then it all came crashing down.

On January 17, 1978, under seven feet of snow, the Civic Center roof collapsed. Tom Wolfe, the white-suited New York author, blamed it on the proletarian design:

> Other American monuments to 1920s Middle European worker housing began falling down of their own accord. These were huge sports arenas and convention centers, such as the Hartford Civic Center coliseum, which had flat roofs. The snow was too much for them—but they collapsed piously, paying homage on the way down to the dictum that pitched roofs were bourgeois.[15]

Piously or not, the 1400-ton roof collapsed in a pile of steel, concrete and broken dreams. Miraculously, no one was hurt. The night before the building had been filled.

For the next two years, all "home" games were played 30 miles up the interstate in Springfield. The "I-91" Club, the 4200 fans who followed the team, kept the ship afloat. In the "land of steady habits" the fans were nothing but steadfast.

By 1979, the NHL was looking to end the war with the rival league that had driven up salaries and stolen away fans. Baldwin, now WHA President, brokered an historic deal. The NHL agreed to a merger with 4 WHA teams: Edmonton, Winnipeg, Quebec, and Hartford.

With Boston casting a dissenting vote, Hartford was welcomed into one of the most exclusive clubs in the land: The National Hockey League. Move over Los Angeles, New York, and Chicago, the city of Twain, Colt, Olmsted and Beecher Stowe was back at the adult table.

On February 6, 1980, under a rebuilt roof, the Whalers defeated the Los Angeles Kings in a "Home At Last" Celebration before a record sellout of 14,460 fans. Since the fall of the building, the Whalers had played 160 "home" games in the dark jerseys of the road team. On this night, the Whalers wore white again.

7. Pride in the Jersey

Clothes do not merely make the man...clothes *are* the man.
—Mark Twain

I stood up at the bench during the national anthem before my first game as a Whaler. I looked down at my uniform and there was this big W on the front of my sweater... I felt like ripping this one off and going back to Edmonton right then.[16]
—Dave Semenko

Two players from the 1981 draft embodied the heart, soul and brawn of the Whale. Ronnie Francis, taken first, embodied heart and soul, while Tiger Burns, taken last, brawn.

The fourth overall pick out of Sault Ste. Marie, Ontario, Francis came to Hartford a wide-eyed, 18-year-old with gobs of talent. By temperament, he was quiet and respectful, not drawn to the bright lights as many rookies are like moths to a flame. The Insurance City suited him fine. Right away people took notice.

"He asked questions and he listened," said Dave Keon, his first roommate, "but it was the way he carried himself that got me. Rookies get caught up in the fame and fortune stuff. Ronnie wasn't like that. He not only wanted to be a player, he wanted to be the right kind of player. There's a big difference." [17]

With 68 points in his first 59 games, he quickly established himself as one of the best, a 6'2" 200 lb. center who could pass, score and defend. Off the ice, he lived with the family of goaltender Greg Millen. And far from resenting such kid-glove treatment, Francis developed a bond with the team and city that nurtured him.

At 22, he was named Captain, and wore the "C" on his sweater. Over the next 9 seasons, Ronnie "Franchise" was the corner stone. By 1990, he had made his third All-Star Game, and led the Whalers to five consecutive playoff appearances and an Adams Division title. A classy center iceman in the mold of Hall-of-Famer Jean Beliveau, he was the gold standard for what it meant to be a Whaler.

Off the ice, while others dated actresses and models, Ronnie fell in love with a girl with this distinction: she owned the "prettiest eyes in Connecticut" as certified by the State Optometrists Association. In Gilligan's Island terms, he chose Mary Ann over Ginger—only her name was Mary Lou. At 25, they married. At 27, they had a daughter Kaitlyn. As the Whale grew, Ronnie grew. The relationship was hand-in-hockey glove.

By 1990, he was on the way to 1000 points, a Hall of Fame benchmark, establishing a tradition in Hartford, and fighting off rear guard revolts from players who didn't want to play there. Every step of the journey, he led by example.

"At a time when professional sports became a destination for the loud, vulgar and selfish, he insisted, first and last, on being a gentleman,"[18] wrote Jeff Jacobs, of the *Hartford Courant*.

He supported State Police "Don't Drink and Drive" campaigns and volunteered for the Special Olympics, inspired by his brother Ricky who would win gold there. Long before athletes did milk commercials for megabucks, Ronnie did them for peanuts.

"He can be dull as Sunday school but at the same time refreshing: a religious man who doesn't beat you over the head with his beliefs, a family man who doesn't wave his three children in front of the camera like props,"[19] *Sports Illustrated* wrote.

One year, not feeling so merry at Christmas, rookie Sylvain Cote was invited to Francis's home. "I told him that since the beginning of the season, I hadn't been happy," said Cote. "There was nothing that really made me feel good. He told me to do the things that will make me happy. He told me to get myself together first and the rest will follow. Ronnie always has the right words to make you feel good." Cote played 18 years.

Francis had grown up in a close family. When Ricky competed in the Special Olympics, Ronnie got permission to see his brother win gold in two skiing events.

"It was like watching Ricky win his own Stanley Cup," he said.

On draft day, Ronnie's father challenged writers to hold his son to the highest standards. They rarely had to. "They never caught Ron Francis driving the wrong way on a one-way street with a blood-alcohol level of .20. They never caught him with cocaine,"[20] wrote Jacobs.

Randy Smith, of The *Journal-Inquirer*, noted: "No player ever bled more plankton than Francis, who genuinely loved Hartford and his lot with the Whalers." [21]

When curly-haired Kevin Dineen was taken in the third round in 1982, it was a homecoming. His father Bill coached the Whalers in the WHA, and a scrawny Kevin had gone to Glastonbury High School. One of five hockey-playing sons, he joined two brothers in the NHL.

"Dineen was a hero the first day he arrived and remained one until his last day," declared Smith.

Scrappy and undersized, he played like a power forward. Swooping in from right wing, he clawed and fought his way to the net—no matter who barred the way. "Kevin Eleven" fans called him in homage to name and number.

"Dineen has more guts than a slaughterhouse," said GM Emile "The Cat" Francis.

In a fight against Boston's Mike Milbury, who once climbed into the stands and assaulted a fan with a shoe, Dineen dropped him with one punch. Teammates had to drag Milbury off the ice.

"Looked like Bambi attempting his first steps," chuckled Dineen.

Dineen was the rare Whaler who fans could mention in any Boston bar and command respect. Hartford's "John Wayne on Skates" could beat you with stick or fists. One of only eight players with 300 career goals and 2000 penalty minutes, Dineen never took a step back in defense of town and team. Like his Captain, he married a local gal named Annie.

"Ronnie and I found a couple of Connecticut gems," he boasted.

Suffering from Crohn's Disease, a debilitating bowel ailment, he became a spokesperson. Like Francis, he showed young players the way.

"I thought the NHL was just about having fun, and whatever happened on the ice, well, whatever," recalled Jeff O'Neill, Dineen's 19-year-old road roommate. "It was a tough transition, to try to become a man and succeed in the NHL at the same time." O'Neill still keeps an autographed photo of his first mentor.

Ulf Samuelsson, of Sweden, was a rugged defenseman with a style that challenged the way many viewed European players. Before Ulf, Swedes, Finns and Russians were regarded as "skill" players who could be intimidated with a well-placed elbow.

The chief advocate of this view was former Bruins' Coach Don Cherry, nicknamed "Grapes", who reinvented himself as a curmudgeonly TV commentator. To Cherry's way of thinking, anyone named Lars, Bjorn or Ville was "soft."

"Chicken Swedes," he called them in his xenophobic rants.

Because Europeans play on a larger, international ice surface, their style, it was true, tended to rely on finesse. But Ulf played in a swashbuckling style that belied his heritage.

"If Ulf had been born here, he'd have been a linebacker," crowed Smith.

An irritant who goaded others into retaliating, then glided away, Ulf was spoke of in the same breath as another "sneaky dirty"[22] European Tomas Sandstrom, known as the "Endangered Species" because everyone wanted a piece of him.

It infuriated opponents that Ulf wore a plexi-glass visor. Helmets so configured protect the eyes, but it is a badge of honor among tough guys not to, as they also have the effect of impeding a good scrap.

A face shield is a signal that the wearer is reluctant to "drop the gloves." The feeling around the league was that someone as chippy as Ulf should not "hide behind" a visor. It was construed as cowardice.

But in Hartford, Ulf was too valuable to fight. He was needed to log 30 minutes a game on-ice, not in the penalty box. Leave it to the specialists to drop the gloves.

Summing up the divisive "Ulf" issue, Ronnie Francis noted, "Everyone hates to play against Ulf, but everyone in the league would love to have him on his club."

Love him or hate him, he had a devil-may-care attitude and toothy smile the equal of Mr. Ed, the talking horse. His favorite thing about America? "Gummie Bears!" The first time at a horse track he bet $150 on a long shot. Before games, he tossed baskets at a makeshift hoop outside the locker room, leading the team in "air balls." In Sweden, basketball is as exotic as ski-jumping here.

Later in his career, he made a devastating hit open-ice on Bruins' star Cam Neely's knee, all-but ending his career. For that, he was reviled like few others. In Boston, there is an old adage: "Only three things matter: politics, sports and revenge." Ulf was no politician, but on those other counts he was despised.

In Ronnie, Kevin and Ulf, the Whalers had a trio who exemplified "Pride in the Jersey." Players with "Pride in the Jersey" will fight for it, bleed for it, rally around it like a flag. The jersey of the Montreal Canadiens is known with patriotic fervor as *"le bleu, blanc et rouge."*

In Hartford, pride was building—even as the logo in front changed. After the original "W" impaled by a harpoon, and a cartoonish whale called "Pucky", the final version came in 1980, the first in Hartford.

"We wanted to keep the 'W' and develop the Whale's tail, the strongest part of the animal," explained founding partner Bill Barnes. Bringing those together, something magical formed inside: "an 'H' for Hartford."

For 17 years the Whale logo was as identifiable with Hartford as *Brass Bonanza*, the hokey theme song. Over time, the Whalers developed a corps of devotees who had pride—and daresay, *affection*—for the jersey. But of all the youngsters who wore the jersey, one stood apart.

8. The Beantown Basher

Never give up, for that is just the time and place that the tide will turn.
—Harriet Beecher Stowe

"I'm Ronnie Francis of the Soo Greyhounds," said the movie-star handsome boy, extending a hand to the beer-barrel shaped one. "You must be Tiger Burns of Moose Jaw. I've heard an awful lot about you."

With those words, two boys, ages 18 and 17, who would change the face of Hartford hockey, met. They made an incongruous pair. The tall boy, in a snappy suit, had an air of confidence; the stout one, in a blood-spattered jersey, had the look of a country rube. Luck (or fate?) had placed them on a connecting flight to a hastily-arranged press conference in the Insurance Capital after the 1981 draft.

Retrieving luggage, a matching set for one and rumpled sack for the other, they left the terminal at Bradley International. As the bow-legged boy struggled to keep pace, a uniformed driver waving a sign "FRANCIS #1 PICK" came into view.

"YOU!" screamed the ball-of-muscle, tugging up at his older companion's sleeve.

The solicitous driver, quick to recognize a fare, grabbed the tall boy's baggage, leading him to a limo stationed curbside.

"WOWEE!" exclaimed the bug-eyed boy lagging behind. "In Moose Jaw, every one drives pick-ups—even 'da Mayor!"

As Tiger looked on—never imagining there might be a driver somewhere waving a sign with *his* name—Ronnie was not so star-struck. Sizing up the situation, he spoke up.

"Driver, help Mr. Burns with his bag!"

Before the driver could protest, certain his docket had called for only one pick-up, Ronnie pushed Tiger's sack forward. Something in the number one pick's no-nonsense demeanor told him to obey. Squeamishly reaching for the blood-smeared bag, he placed it in the trunk, respectfully away from Ronnie's matching leather cases.

"Yes, Mr. Francis."

Slamming the trunk and making the long march up front, the driver opened the door. Craning his bull-neck for a furtive glimpse, Tiger again was awestruck.

"WOW!" For a long moment he gazed, before Ronnie interrupted his reverie.

"What are you waiting for, Tiger?"

"Huh?"

"Get in! Us Whalers stick together!!"

The record books won't show it, but it was Ronnie's first assist. Flashing a Huckleberry Finn grin, Tiger hopped in beside Ronnie, thumping into him like a hockey check.

"By the way, I like the sound o' that."

"What?"

"Us Whalers stick together!"

Ronnie looked over at him funny. "Don't the guys in Moose Jaw all hang out?"

Before Tiger could speak, *Brass Bonanza* came blaring over the speakers. Now was not the time for rehashing old miseries. Basking in the glow of the pre-programmed TV, humming to the surround-sound melody, and breathing the fresh-cut roses, Tiger was on sensory overload—intoxicated by the sights, sounds and smells of a city's embrace.

"No detail has been too small to be overlooked!" he gushed.

Ronnie wasn't so sure of it. Sensing that one *small* detail might have been overlooked, he grabbed the limo phone to call ahead with an update.

"Hi, this is Ron Francis," he greeted Whalers' PR Director Phil Langan. "Tiger and I are on our way."

"You brought a guest?"

"My new teammate Tiger Burns of Moose Jaw," he said, looking over.

On the other end, Ronnie detected what seemed like muffled profanities. In the ensuing chaos, a chair may have been overturned. It was hard to tell; satellite communications were not so clear then. Finally, a missing piece of paper was at last located.

"Ah, YES! Tiger Burns our #311 pick," said Langan, reading from a sheet at the bottom of the pile. "He's coming *too*?"

"We're on our way!"

"How far away are you, Ronnie, this *very* moment?"

"Leaving the airport."

"15 minutes," growled Langan, then cheerily on the phone. "Yes, Ronnie, we'll be ready for both of you. Have a safe trip! And do drive slowly!!"

As the limo roared onto Interstate 91, Ronnie pulled two Cokes from the fridge.

"Here's to winning the Stanley Cup."

"The STANLEY Cup!" yodeled Tiger. "Zowee!"

Feeling strangely at ease, Tiger opened up some.

"Gretzky played with the Soo, eh?" he said, using the shorthand for Ronnie's junior team, the Sault Saint-Marie Greyhounds. "Did ya' ever skate a shift with him?"

"Nah, Gretzky turned pro at 17. Can you believe it? So young?"

Tiger awkwardly changed subjects—and inquired about the Ontario League that many feel is superior to Tiger's rough-and-tumble Western League. Year after year, the OHL thrashes the WHL in the Memorial Cup. As a result, many WHL players arrive with a chip on their shoulders.

"Sure are a lot o' great ones in Ontario, lots o' scorers, huh?"

"You betcha!" said Ronnie, swelling up with pride. But before he reeled off a list, something in Tiger's tone sent him on a different course. "But *your* Western League has just as many! You don't have to fear anyone, Tiger! We're both in this limo 'cause Hartford wants us."

"Gee, ya' think so?" Tiger asked, looking up to the older boy.

"Yes, I do!" declared Ronnie firmly, "Where you come from makes no difference! It's how hard you work, how *bad* ya' want it.

"Draft order means nuthin' either," he said sternly, almost lecturing. "There are lots of number one picks flipping burgers while late round picks are cashing NHL paychecks. Don't ever forget it, Tiger!"

As he patted Tiger's sloping shoulder, the strength of his trapezius muscles surprised him. It was like slapping a rock, and Ronnie was about to say so, when just then the limo crested a hill, and Tiger caught his first glimpse of Hartford, west of the river.

"WOW! Look at all them buildings!"

"Most are insurance," explained Ronnie, sharing what he learned from the guide books. "See that shiny one yonder? It's called the 'gold building.' You can see why."

"Never seen nuthin' like it!" exclaimed Tiger, as awestruck now with Hartford as he had been with the shiny limo. "Lookin' at it makes a fellow glad he has two eyes ta' soak it all in! Ya' haven't seen beauty until ya've seen Hartford, eh!"

For Ronnie, who lived near Toronto, this was all getting a bit much.

"Tiger, haven't you ever been out of Moose Jaw?"

Never one to back down, Tiger snorted. "Yup, ta' Medicine Hat *and* Saskatoon too, so I seen a good bit of planet earth."

Just then, as the limo crossed city limits, blue lights flashed and sirens wailed.

"SPEED TRAP!" yelled Tiger, diving for cover. "BUSTED! Happens all 'da time in Moose Jaw!"

For a moment, Ronnie too looked worried, but then broke into a knowing grin.

"Look! A police escort. They're taking us in!"

The two boys looked on as four cruisers, dubbed "Francis 1 through 4," part of "Operation First Pick", led the limo through thronged streets to the Civic Center. Along the way, horns tooted and green-clad fans waved placards "MARRY ME, RONNIE!" and "RONNIE OUR SAVIOUR!"

"They LOVE us!" exclaimed Tiger, his eyes welling up. "Look!"

As the limo rolled to a stop, the two rookies arrived at a makeshift stage outside The Russian Lady Café. Spanning the stage was a 50-foot banner, "Welcome RONNIE FRANCIS #1 In Our Hearts." While on the far right, like a pilot fish riding a leviathan's tail, was a pennant flapping in the wind "And Tigger Berns, #311."

"SIGNS!" exclaimed Tiger, pointing.

Two state troopers bulled a path to the stage overflowing with dignitaries: Thurman Milner, the first African-American Mayor of a state capital; City Councilors in green hats; the business leaders known as "The Bishops"; and overseeing it all, owner Howard Baldwin:

"RON-NIE, RON-NIE, RON-NIE..." chanted thousands.

"This is grand, ain't it?" exclaimed Tiger, grabbing Ronnie's arm for support through the jostling crowd.

When Mayor Milner presented a "FRANCIS #1" sweater to the first pick, and Ronnie pulled it over his suit, the *Courant* captured the iconic image with front-page headlines: "A KING IS ROBED."

When, unprompted, Tiger rose and ambled over to the Mayor for *his* jersey, there was momentary confusion. Nothing in the pre-printed program—or the Mayor's script—made mention of a *second* presentation. Helplessly the politician looked over to Langan, orchestrating from stage left.

For what seemed an eternity, the beaming fighter stood with arms upright, waiting for a shirt to be draped over his shoulders. Gesturing franticly, and then whistling, Langan at last directed the Mayor's attention to a bag beneath the podium.

"Ah, I see."

Pulling out a t-shirt that looked as if it had been slapped together moments before at the Whaler's Gift Store, the Mayor held it aloft. Like the pennant, it read: "BERNS #311"

Whipping off his blood-spattered Moose Jaw jersey, Tiger unveiled to the world for the first time the full-rigged whaler tattoo, riding atop cresting waves of muscle.

"Good God Almighty!" screeched a woman in front, swooning into a faint. As the Mayor struggled to pull the XL shirt over Tiger's XXXL frame, photographers stood aghast.

"We thought it was an interloper," explained a shutterbug, who'd won a Pulitzer for snapping a baby falling out of a 5-story building, but missed the dead-on shot.

But young fans, drawn to the oddity, clicked away as Tiger burst with pride in his new jersey. When Mayor Milner next presented Ronnie the key to the city, the photographers regained their nerve. When Tiger, comfortably into the rhythm of "what Ronnie does first, I do next" approached with hand out, the Mayor did not miss a beat. Reaching into his pocket, he handed him his house key.

"I present to you the key to the front door of the Mayor's house!" he proclaimed with solemnity. Bowing as if receiving the Nobel Prize, Tiger looked as if for all his life he had been accustomed to such great honors.

"Thank you, your Excellency," he said, kissing the Mayor's ring, and blowing kisses to the crowd, "Thank-you all for coming!"

The audience, warming up to the strange, young muscleman, howled. Back at their seats, the two boys compared keys like a couple of locksmiths.

"Size doesn't matter," whispered Ronnie, his huge ceremonial key dwarfing Tiger's. The two were having the time of their lives.

At last, it was time for the guests of honor to speak. Continuing in the established pattern, Ronnie went first. Pulling out a sheaf from his vest, he expressed his fervent hope that "in some small way" he might help bring the Stanley Cup to "so great and deserving a city."

Above the roar, he concluded, "For my new friend Tiger and I, this is the greatest day of our lives. We promise always to make you proud!"

As police in helmets ringed the stage, the Mayor, no longer hostage to a script, asked Tiger to "step up and say a word."

"THANKS!" he bellowed, and did just that.

As Ronnie had so ably put it, this was the greatest day of his life. At moments like this, when his joy overflowed, he expressed himself in the most eloquent way he knew, cart-wheeling across the stage and crashing into the Mayor's lap.

"Sorry, Mr. Mayor!" he said, as the crowd embraced Ronnie's offbeat friend.

"TI-GRRRR, TI-GRRRR, TI-GRRRR," they growled, overpowering the police guard and carrying the boys off into the limo.

Back at the hotel, when it was discovered, by some oversight, that Tiger's accommodations had been misplaced, Ronnie stepped forward. "C'mon Tiger, you're with me!"

From the penthouse, overlooking Bushnell Park, the two talked like a couple of scouts on an overnighter. At midnight, exhausted, Tiger dropped off to sleep dressed in his green jersey.

Next morning, packing his bag, Tiger's eyes filled, as he turned to Ronnie and said something he'd ached to say his whole life:

"You're my best friend. I'll never forget what you've done as long as I live."

Then reaching into his bag, he pulled out his blood-spattered Moose Jaw Jersey and tossed it to him. "Us Whalers stick together!" he said, and fled in tears.

Next day, at the end of a 25-inch column, every one extolling Ronnie, the *Hartford Courant* added a brief note:

> **Whale Tales**: On hand also at the Francis coronation was the unlikely prospect, Tiger Burns of Moose Jaw, the 311th –and last—pick. A man of action—he performed an acrobatics routine in lieu of a speech—this odd fellow will be the longest of long shots to make the club. But one never knows. In a league where toughness can never be counted out, he may one day crack the lineup. At 5'3" and 200 pounds (*fact check???*), Burns led the Western League in penalty minutes four years running. **Nota Bene:** The Whalers play the Bruins 8 times next season.

#####

When Ronnie and Tiger met again that August in camp, the reunion galvanized them both. Both prospects opened eyes—and Tiger closed a few. Each showcased his special talents: Ronnie his speed and finesse; Tiger his right and left dukes.

Over the course of the month, Tiger leapt like *The Jumping Frog of Calaveras County* over a dozen touted picks, vaulting him from last on the rookie depth charts to just behind Ronnie. The revised scouting report on him read: "Short in height, skill, and ability—but has a BIG punch. There will be a spot for him." The lump of coal was now seen as a diamond in the rough.

At the end of camp, both boys were returned to Juniors for seasoning—but with a warning: "Be prepared to return at a moment's notice." The team trumpeted Tiger's newfound status in a press release: "We drafted Ronnie to save the franchise, but we drafted Tiger to save Ronnie."

After a 3-10-8 start, the SOS to Ronnie came in November 1982 to right the foundering ship. The move paid off immediately, with the team winning four of the next six.

Twenty games later, the ship on an even keel, a second summons was made. The Whalers had a home-and-home series against the bellicose Bruins. Tiger's debut, still talked of, is part of the legend and lore of hockey.

Some say it was jitters—others a ploy— but when Tiger skated on ice without his jersey, Bruins veterans who'd thought they'd seen it all were agog.

"What the hell is *that*?"

Atop tidal waves of rippling muscle, on Tiger's heaving chest, sailed the great green whaling ship. On back, a second tattoo: a Whalers logo. Tiger looked like a tottering, two-sided sandwich placard on wobbly ankles A green Mohawk completed the outlandish ensemble.

"There's a new SHERIFF in town!" jabbered the muscle-bound hobbit banging his armored chest, and calling out Terry O'Reilly, hockey's most feared brawler.

"Is that a MASCOT?" shrieked Radio Voice Chuck Kaiton over flagship WTIC 1080. "No, No, No! It's the rookie from Moose Jaw. My, oh My!"

O'Reilly didn't know what to make of the pint-sized spectacle, careening about on bent ankles. "What the hell is *that*?"

Boston's Gallery Gods were caught unawares, too. The Boston papers had made short shrift of the call-up, noting: "For rookie Left Wing Burns, the move from Moose Jaw to Hartford can only be termed a lateral one—*culturally* at least."

On his second lap, he crossed the center-ice line, a territorial violation in hockey's inbred culture tantamount to war. Crossing the red line is the equivalent, on the Jerry Springer Show, of tipping over the chair of your uncle who's sleeping with your wife. A challenge to fight!

But a bewildered O'Reilly, flanked by astonished teammates, continued to shake his head, "What the hell is *that*?" He would find out soon enough.

Thrashing in turn O'Reilly, Stan Jonathon and Al Secord, Tiger forever rescued his name from the agate type and splashed it across headlines, punctuating each victory by ripping off his jersey and drumming his tattoo in signature celebration.

"GO BACK TO HAHTFID, YA' GOON!" hollered the enraged Gallery Gods, golden-showering him with Harpoon beer.

The invective continued in next day's Boston papers.

"Before last night, we thought the Green Monster was a wall at Fenway. WRONG! It's a thug from Hartford," blasphemed the tabloid.

"Quasimodo without the hump!" sniped the refined broadsheet.

In Hartford, Tiger Burns was the talk of the town at insurance company water coolers. *The Courant* plastered his battered mug atop a 25-inch column, every last word devoted to him, save these: "Oh, we won."

Next night, the Civic Center was jammed to the rafters, all to see the mighty mite who had defanged the Bruins. Before ever he took his first step on ice (a stumble, let it be admitted), a mighty roar echoed all the way to Causeway Street in Boston.

"TI-GRRRR, TI-GRRRR, TI-GRRRR…"

Not knowing how to acknowledge the applause, he turned skate-over-helmet cartwheels. His legend grew. By game's end, only O'Reilly would fight him, the others afflicted with that yet-unnamed malady, the "Tiger Tummy Ache." Over the years, many of the league's toughest goons would be stricken by a bout before a game with Hartford. Curiously, it lasted one game.

After the game, wringing out his beer-soaked jersey, for many Boston fans had made the short trip, he addressed a crush of reporters.

"I did me best," he mumbled, his voice on-edge. "I hope it's enough ta' keep me 'ere."

Let history show the Whalers swept the home-and-home series with the hated Bruins. Young Tiger had found a home at last. All he needed now was a place to stay.

9. The Schmidleys

Kindness is the universal human solvent.
—R.A. M Sr.

As with other young draftees, the Whalers arranged for Tiger to live with a family. But this was no billeting arrangement. It wasn't done with the exchange of lucre, or with "minimum care" guidelines.

It had been done for Ronnie Francis, and would be done for Quebecois Sylvain Cote and Sylvain Turgeon. When Kevin Dineen was traded to Philadelphia, he and Annie carried the tradition there and took in Eric Lindros, the 6'5" 240 pound *enfant terrible*.

So it was only a part of the established order to find Tiger a home— only his situation proved different. Whereas the others accepted homes in tony suburbs, like Simsbury and Avon, Tiger would not even entertain such a heresy.

"I want Hartford," he said, folding his arms across his chest. In that defiant outburst, Tiger had snubbed a millionaire's row of hosts and opted for down-at-the-heels Hartford.

"We're offering him prime rib, and he wants chuck beef," remarked a miffed team secretary. "But the kid's from Moose Jaw, he'll learn."

Alas, Connecticut folk today regard their capital as strictly a workplace. At dawn, the population swells as armies of suit-soldiers report for duty in procession. But at nightfall, all hell breaks loose as these same folks trip all over themselves to get the hell out!

But those in flight leave with their purses stuffed. Hartford's suburbs are the wealthiest in the nation, as lucre flees the city and settles on the gold-paved streets of Simsbury, Glastonbury and Farmington.

Left behind is a residue of poor, ethnic neighborhoods. Hartford's poverty rate is higher than Detroit.[23] Homeownership rivals Newark.[24] Nearly 80 percent of the children are born to single mothers.[25] The population, once 175,000, hovers at 125,000. But Tiger was determined to be a statistic.

"Hartford's my town," he repeated, digging in his heels as when preparing to fight.

When a stalemate seemed inevitable, a breakthrough: a team doctor had a banker, who had a house cleaner, who knew a retired insurance clerk and his wife with a home in the city. And so that is how 17-year-old Tiger Burns, of Moose Jaw, came to live with Mr. and Mrs. Schmidley of Asylum Avenue, named for America's first school for the deaf.

Now the Schmidleys were not the Scrimgeours. The "WELCOME TIGER" banner billowing above the porch proclaimed as much. When Tiger arrived, a bundle of nerves, the couple had already vacated the master bedroom. It was Tiger's now, decorated with pennants, posters, and matching bedspread.

"You'll want to learn something of your new city," said Mr. Schmidley, pointing to shelves groaning with books on Twain, Colt, Olmsted, and Beecher Stowe.

"I called ahead and found you like sarsaparilla," said Mrs. Schmidley, blushing at her forwardness. "I hope you don't mind."

Seating the uncouth boy, sporting a shiner courtesy of Boston's O'Reilly, at the head of the table, Mr. Schmidley gave thanks: "God bless our food, our family, and especially our newest member. May Tiger's stay be long, healthy and happy!"

Folding his mangled hands on the red-checked table cloth, Tiger bowed his head. He didn't want them to see him crying. Mr. Schmidley filled the awkward moment with a family yarn.

"Legend has it that this table we're sitting at is made of Charter Oak..."

And so Tiger learned about the Hartford tree, on commemorative quarters, where the Fundamental Orders was stashed when British troops demanded its surrender in 1687. The document, declaring that authority lies "firstly in the free consent of the people", was an inspiration for the United States Constitution.

On game nights, his hockey mom set out on the table a slew of remedies. The raw steak was labeled: "Apply to black eyes"; the sock with rice "microwave for aches"; the tea bag "to staunch bleeding". If Tiger came home unscathed, he had a three-course meal!

And soon the combination of a healthy diet and family produced an unimaginable effect: his face cleared. For the first time in his life, he did not dodge mirrors. At first, he approached warily, head down, steps small—as if approaching a land mine. But in time, with courage and persistence, he stood before the dreaded object, head up, feet squared. And what stared back—while unsettling—was not entirely displeasing.

"Not bad!" he sang out, the first time he dared open his eyes. "Not BAD at all!"

Absent the pimples, and before the onrush of scarring, Tiger was not *entirely* uncomely. So he was not speaking out of turn as he cried out, "I'm a hottie!" Then diving into the toe of his skate and sliding out the photo of Miss Moose Jaw, he declared into the mirror.

"My time is coming. Yes, it is!" he said, and carefully slid it back.

####

Fighting had always been a source of justifiable pride, but for the first time it troubled young Tiger—and it had nothing to do with vanity. No, Tiger was worried how the Schmidleys viewed his brutal craft. After weeks of happiness, he convinced himself it could not last.

"They're gonna get rid o' me!" he fretted. "Who would want a goon like me in their home? Yup, I'm a goner alright."

Unable to sleep for such thoughts, Tiger wandered down to the kitchen one restless night and there at the oak table sat a startled Mr. Schmidley. "Tiger, what are *you* doing up? You have a game tomorrow against New York."

The old man's soothing voice comforted Tiger. But it was this same gentle spirit that convinced him that soon he would be tossed out on his cauliflower ear. Time to fess up!

"Something's been eatin' me, Mr. Schmidley, and maybe I should just pack up and hit the road now. Make it easy on all o' us."

"Tiger, what *are* you talking about?"

"Well, it has to do wit' livin' here."

"Are you unhappy, Tiger?" the old man asked, disclosing the very reason he could not sleep. "Mrs. Schmidley and I have noticed you've not been yourself of late. Makes us feel we're not doing enough to…"

"Not doin' enough?!" Tiger roared. "I love it here! It's the only home I've ever known. But you're gonna evict me, so I might as well just go now."

The mere mention of a departure seemed to invite the possibility and Tiger broke down sobbing.

"Come, come now," said Mr. Schmidley, rubbing the boy's mangled hands folded on the tablecloth. "Throw you out? Where did that come from?"

"You and Mrs. Schmidley wouldn't hurt a fly and, me, well...I'm just a goon," he blubbered.

Mr. Schmidley wrapped his wiry arms around the boy's bull-neck. For the first time in 70 years, he felt the joy of fatherhood. "It's okay," he said, whispering into the cauliflower ear, and kissing it. At that, Tiger burst anew into tears.

"Why are you crying now, Tiger?"

"No one's ever kissed me," he confided, tears streaming down both cheeks, into a network of scars, and burying his grotesque head in the old man's embrace. Then Mr. Schmidley, with the deft touch of fathers everywhere, surprised him.

"What's my last name, Tiger?"

Tiger pulled out and looked at him strange.

"Is that a trick question?"

"No, quite serious."

"Schmidley, a' course. Why?"

"Tiger, can you imagine growing up a Schmidley?" he asked, rolling the "i" for effect.

Tiger guffawed at the queer-sounding name, but stopped.

"SCHMIDLEY'S not like Smith or Jones!" he continued, voice rising. "Something about it invites derision. To the proud bearer, it can bring great suffering."

Transported to a faraway time, the old man's face flushed. His scrawny muscles fanned. Tiger, too, swept up in the unjustness of it, balled and un-balled his fists.

"To survive as a Schmidley," he continued. "I say, to survive as a Schmidley one either had to be the toughest street fighter in Hartford—or fleet as the wind."

After a pause, he said: "And I wasn't fast, my boy!"

At that delicious revelation, Tiger smothered the old man in a hug. "You're a fighter, too, Mr. Schmidley!"

"Yes, I am!" he affirmed, as Tiger clung tight. "Tiger, Mrs. Schmidley and I know there is no malice when you fight. You are simply striking a blow against bullies. As Schmidleys, we understand. We do."

Grinning from ear to ear, for Tiger it was the magical moment of acceptance. In the company of a fellow fighter, it was time now to talk shop.

"Could ya' swat, Mr. Schmidley?"

"With the best, my boy! With the best!"

For the next half-hour, the two fighters swapped tall tales until the last of the home-baked cookies were devoured. Throughout, a toothless smile never left Tiger's face. At bedtime, the old fighter put a pallid hand on the strapping shoulder of the young one.

"Tiger, can I ask a favor?"

"Sure, Mr. Schmidley, just name it!"

"You know, the name Schmidley *is* a bit cumbersome—even I'll admit. Would you mind shortening it?"

"Sure. How 'bout Mr. S?"

"Well, I was thinking of something even shorter."

"Like?"

"Dad."

That first father-son talk did not bode well for the rest of the NHL. Thereafter, Tiger fought with righteous abandon, and his father and Hartford loved him the more for it.

###

There comes a time in every fighter's life when neither a mother's remedies nor a father's understanding can save him. For Tiger it came the night of April 3, 1982, the last of his rookie season, against the New York Rangers.

No raw steak or tea bag could save a left eye impaled by the viciously swung stick of a beaten opponent. In one horrific instant, Tiger's season—and likely his career—ended. Grisly images of Tiger wheeled off the ice led the 11 p.m. news.

The injury plunged the small city into grief. In the days ahead there was an outpouring of emotion rarely witnessed in the "land of steady habits." Insurance people, accustomed to stoicism, wept. State workers, jaded about everything, huddled. The neighborhoods, bickering and fragmented, united. In short, Hartford rallied around Tiger as if he were an officer fallen in the line of duty.

Every school sent "Get Well" cards, the tear-stained notes revealing the singular connection between the offbeat rookie and the city's children.

Dear Tiger,

At Christmas, you inspired us to never give up, no matter the odds. We pray for you now to do the same.

56

Love, Miss Wellman's Class

P.S. Carlos and Kimbo have surpassed your 63-inch height chalked on the blackboard! But rest assured, your 22-inch biceps remain (temporarily) safe!!

One note, from a music teacher, told of an Austrian pianist, who after the loss of his right arm in World War I, commissioned "A Concerto for the Left Hand." For Paul Wittgenstein, the score heralded a dramatic return to the stage.

"After the first few moments of wondering how the devil he accomplished it, one almost forgot that one was listening to a man whose right sleeve hung empty," hailed the *New York Herald-Tribune*.[26]

But Tiger's doctors were not so sanguine about a return. "A hockey player needs to see the puck," said Dr. Turco, dismissing all talk. "I'm sorry."

But Tiger was no ordinary player. He was a fighter—and a breed apart!

"Doc, those letters on that chart ain't 6'5" and 250 pounds and leanin' right on top o' me. Of course, I can't see 'em!"

A hockey fighter fights at close quarters. Tiger's style was to grab an opponent's jersey, the "Death Grip" they called it, burrow into his chest, and pummel away relentlessly.

"I never looked anyway, Doc!"

But the real objection, the fatal one, was that Tiger no longer had a back-up. The doctors, the Schmidleys, and Captain Ronnie Francis—none pulled their punches.

"Don't be a fool! Hockey ain't worth it!" Ronnie rebuked.

Mrs. Schmidley broached the subject more tenderly—taking Tiger's hand.

"Tiger, your rehab will require a lot of care," she said, choking back tears. "Your father and I are getting old now. When the team asked us to billet a player for a year, we were only too happy. But now that year is almost over…"

She struggled to find the words: "Tiger, your care will take a lot of energy. Your father and I don't have the stamina we once did. It's hard for us now…"

On cue, Mr. Schmidley stood by his wife and held her in a united front for the difficult words to follow. "Your father and I had a long talk last night, and we came to a major decision…"

Caught by surprise at the crackling emotion, Tiger suddenly grew tense. Lying in bed, his eye bandaged, he realized, for good or ill, the next words out of her mouth would make or break him. Bracing himself, he hugged the pillow for support.

"Tiger, we'd like you to think of this as your home. Will you stay with us?"

For this lone castaway boy, once traded for a frozen caribou, he had finally found a home. "YEEE-HAW!" Tiger blurted out, embracing his pillow.

But Mrs. Schmidley was not done:

"Tiger, your father has lots of contacts in the insurance business..."

Tiger's face, joyous moments ago, contorted. He had been hit with a lot of low blows in life—but none as low as this.

"Now, Tiger, insurance may not be what you dreamed of," she said, choosing the next words carefully. "But it's better than a poke in the eye with a sharp stick."

Guffawing, Tiger could see every one stood behind her: Ronnie, Mr. Schmidley and the doctors. It was time to speak up. And so he did now with a fighter's passion.

"Playin' hockey is what I live for, Mom! I love my job. I love my team. I love my family."

Everyone was with him, so he spluttered on: "But the next night, the next fight, I live for 'em. This city and team *needs* me. Don't ya' understand?"

No one did.

"I'm not like the teacher who dreads the sound of the bell or farmer who hates the cock's crow."

It was true. Tiger wasn't like another hockey fighter, found dead in a hotel room, surrounded by cocaine and steroids. He didn't need to get jacked up every night. He fought for something greater than himself.

"If it comes ta' just fightin' for me, I'll skate away!"

There was quiet in the hospital room, the quietest it had been, with every one staring down in dismay.

"People fight and lose limbs for their country every day," he pleaded. "But me—I'm just fightin' for a little spit o' land called Hartford."

Again there was that awful silence until a voice in back broke it.

"He's right!" said Mr. Schmidley, surprising all, and angering some. "He shouldn't give up now!"

The doctors, Ronnie, and Mrs. Schmidley all disagreed, but in the end, with one man's blessings, Tiger over-ruled them all. A week later, from his hospital bed, his eye bandaged, he read haltingly from a hand-written statement:

"I'm comin' back ta' da' sport I love fa' my family, fa' Hartford—and ta' keep Terry O'Reilly and the Big, Bad Bruins from runnin' amok! I accept the consequences that come wit' 'dis decision—whatever 'dey may be. "

For Tiger, his aim was nothing less than a spectacular return for next season's opener against Boston. For the plucky fighter, soon up and walking, he found support at every street corner:

"Keep on punching, Ti!"

"We're with ya', brother-man!"

Dressed in a green jersey emblazoned with "Eye on the Prize", he rollerbladed the blighted neighborhoods, from the Capitol Building to Twain's Mansion, from Park Street to Colt's Armory by the river, peppering the air with uppercuts and exhortations.

"CAN'T stop us! WON'T stop us!"

As the sun set each day, his jersey soaked, Tiger wandered down Asylum Hill across Bushnell Park to squint up at the words chiseled on the pediment of the Bushnell Memorial, Hartford's performance hall:

Life is always insipid to those who have no great works in hand,
No lofty aims to elevate their feelings.

Then he trudged back along the deserted streets—followed by a strange man in a crushed straw hat. Rube was with him.

10. The Public Eye

Better to light one candle than curse the darkness.
—The Christophers

The public was filled with both a tender concern—and morbid fascination—for Tiger's glass eye. And so in time, he decided the best way to both reassure fans—and gratify their macabre urges—was to have fun. But getting there wasn't easy.

Lying in bed those first dark nights, he wallowed in all-consuming pity. How could he not succumb? Everything he had worked for his whole life had ended, it seemed, with one malicious thrust of a stick.

"Everything was comin' together—and now this," he wailed, voice trailing off.

As tears of woe streamed down his right cheek, generating a long, winding stream, and *one* stream only, the immediate awareness of that made him mad. For Tiger, the two-fisted fighter, that wouldn't do! Pawing at the tears, he bolted upright in bed.

"I won't do anything in half measures," he hollered, pounding both fists on the hospital bed, "including crying."

It was an epiphany. As nurses with morphine raced over, they were shocked now to find him cackling maniacally: "The Tiger ROARS as before!" wiping away the tears in grand gesture.

Months earlier, he had agreed to appear at the West Indian Celebration in Hartford's North End, home to New England's largest Jamaican community. Intended as an autograph party, for Tiger, it promised now to be a "coming out" party.

Days later, with reggae music blasting and curried goat wafting in the air, he appeared on North Main Street—as only he could—dressed as a Barbary pirate. With peg leg, hook arm, silver scabbard and *piece de resistance* black patch over his left eye, the diminutive Blackbeard was instantly engulfed by swarming kids.

"SHIVER ME TIMBERS" he bellowed in his best *Ho, Ho, Ho and a bottle of rum* voice. "Where's me ship?"

"There, Captain Tiger!" said a boy, pointing ahead. At the end of a narrow plank, in a pool of sharks, beneath a Whalers flag, sat a ship bristling with cannons. The sign in front read:

Walk the Plank **Blindfolded** and Meet Captain Tiger
for The First Time Since He Lost His Eye In A Duel
Do You **DARE**?

Behind curtains, the battle-ravaged pirate sat stiffly. Appropriately, his public unveiling was intended *not* for the eye—but the touch. Participants were led up the plank and seated before the battle-ravaged Captain.

"Well, shiver me timbers, you must be LaKisha," said Tiger, when the first victim arrived. "Careful! Watch yer' step!"

"Hi, Captain Tiger," said LaKisha nervously fidgeting with the blindfold.

"Let's get down ta' business!" he roared. "Are you ready ta' experience a pirate's death-defying mutilations the up-close-and-personal way?"

"Y-y-yes, Captain Tiger!"

"Well, do ya' dare touch the Captain's peg leg—RIPPED off by a 20-foot shark?!"

LaKisha hesitated, as assistants secured the blindfold tightly.

"O.K." she whispered, her trembling hand led to the shaft of a dinged-up hickory bat.

"COOL! It's wood," she squealed. "I can feel the teeth marks!"

Next, she was invited to touch the captain's hook arm—"SWALLOWED by a 30-foot octopus!"

"Yes," LaKisha gasped, her quivering hand placed atop the curved end of a coat hanger.

"Awesome! It's really a HOOK!"

Next, if she cared, she could stroke the green parrot perched on the Captain's sloping shoulder. Assured now, LaKisha thrust out a hand and caressed the stuffed bird.

"Da BOMB! I feel the feathers!"

"Polly want a cracker!" squawked Tiger.

Now the moment every child feared most.

"You know, LaKisha, Captain Tiger lost his eye in a duel. Said so in all the papers, right?"

"S-sorry, Captain Tiger. We watched it on the news."

"Well, ya' dare touch the patch covering his glass eye?"

LaKisha recoiled at the gruesome suggestion, before meekly acquiescing, "O.k."

At that, her hand was guided to the silk patch atop Tiger's eye.

"Cool! It's soft!" she said, confidence surging again.

And there the "Hands-on Tour of Captain Tiger's Death-Defying Mutilations" might well have ended—but for a last invitation:

"LaKisha, you can walk the plank now," said the Captain, offering escape. "The Captain's removed his patch, and popped his glass eye out. LaKisha, ya' wanna feel the empty socket?"

Now, LaKisha, who incredibly had come this far—through severed legs and dismembered arms—was feeling queasy about removable eyes and empty sockets.

"Empty?" she asked, seeking clarification

"EMPTY!" boomed the Captain.

LaKisha wedged her hands between her knees and mulled the offer over carefully. There was no coaxing, no cajoling. In the end, the decision was hers—and hers alone. Reasoning perhaps that she was past the point of no return—or her friends in line might hear of any chickening out—she declared her firm desire.

"Err, um, well, O.K., I guess."

"Is that a 'YES'?" roared the flinty Captain.

"Yes," whispered an ashen-faced Lakisha.

The go-ahead received, her quivering finger was held inches from the Captain's socket. "Are you *sure*, LaKisha?"

"Yes," she whispered.

At that, the reluctant finger was plunged into a chilled lemon half—and rotated.

"AAAAAAAAAAAAAAAAAAARGH!"

Well, you never heard such whooping and hollering in all your life as after LaKisha yanked out her finger dripping with juice. Ripping off the blindfold and racing down the plank, she dove into the waiting arms of her mother, who'd signed the required waivers.

"Girl OVERBOARD!" howled Tiger, repositioning the patch. "Next victim!"

Tiger's eye provided endless opportunities for hijinks and hilarity. At restaurants, it might find its way to the bottom of a beer mug—or top of an olive dish. At playgrounds, it might show up in a bag of marbles. At a golf tourney, an instructor nearly drove it with a 9-iron, Tiger having obligingly "teed up" for him.

As news of his antics spread, Letterman invited him to appear on a Late Show segment called "Stupid Eye Tricks." Ambling bow-legged on stage, Tiger, who had just arrived from the west coast, was asked by Dave if he took "the red-eye."

"Nope, the blue one!" he deadpanned, and popped it out to show.

Rolling his eyes, and Tiger's in his palm, Dave quipped, "So this is the sort of thing they do in Hartford for fun, huh?"

In time, Tiger's eye became not a mark of disability, but a trademark. Wherever he went, he sported his signature black patch. But when a few fans, reasoning "a patch is like a shirt, and a man ought to have a change now and then", sent him some and Tiger began sporting them, well, you can imagine the deluge. Tiger soon had eye patches to match Imelda Marcos's shoes—in all colors, fabrics and styles!

At Christmas, when he was invited to light the holiday tree on Constitution Plaza, he appeared in red costume, white beard, and festive green patch. The Director of Ceremonies took one look at the oddest, one-eyed Santa Claus ever seen and rebuffed him rudely.

"I'm sorry, Sir. You *can't* be Santa!"

"Why not?" Tiger protested.

Picking from a laundry list of objections, he replied, "You're too short!"

"Am not," Tiger objected, rising to his full 63 inches.

"Are too!"

"Am not!"

"HUMBUG! Santa is a six-footer!" declared the Director, as if it were carved in stone. "You look like an elf on steroids. Children will laugh when they see you in spite of themselves."

Overhearing the row, a crowd of kids, many taller than Santa, which seemed to bolster the point, gathered. The disputed matter appeared to reach a stalemate when a stuttering voice in the back chimed in.

"S-S-Santa was sh-sh-short and I-I-I can p-p-prove it!" said a boy of eight, challenging the Director's assertion directly.

"Who speaks such heresy?" the Director boomed, looking around for the culprit. "Declare yourself this instant!"

At that, the crowd parted and the unlikely defender of Tiger's honor marched up front in untied Nikes and a Whalers hat flipped backwards.

"Identify yourself!" the Director demanded.

"K-Keyshawn."

Keyshawn was the smallest and most timid of Tiger's Cubs who tagged along at his appearances. Indeed, he was the very boy who'd slipped Tiger the rollerblades when City Councilors tried to ban his walk to work. A boy of action, as with the blades, Keyshawn rarely spoke. His teachers thought he might be self-conscious about a small stutter.

"So you think you can prove that Santa is *not* a 6-footer?"

"Y-Y-Yes!" he said, standing next to Tiger, with an arm around him, as the hushed crowd gasped.

"This I can't *wait* to hear! Well, go ahead then. We're ALL waiting."

With 50 people circled around, and 99 eyes on him, Keyshawn's throat went dry. His heart pounded. Seeing his difficulty, Tiger leaned over and whispered, "I believe in you, little buddy."

"B-B-Before I d-d-do, you must make a p-p-promise," Keyshawn piped up.

Again the crowd gasped.

"If I can p-p-prove it, you must p-p-promise to make T-T-Tiger be S-S-Santa *n-n-next* year too."

Keyshawn was talking trash now! The crowd gasped a third time.

"You're on!" said the Director, snatching the bait.

Keyshawn's heart pounded as never before and his tiny palms sweat. But before delivering the *coup de grace*, there was one final preliminary:

"O-O-On whose authority, S-S-Sir, do we know what S-S-Santa looks l-l-like?"

No one had ever heard Keyshawn talk like this! He seemed to be blossoming in front of everyone.

"Well, if you must know, the poem 'Twas the Night Before Christmas' describes Santa to a 'T'," said the Director. "If we appeal to the poet, this impostor's candidacy will be doomed for sure. Santa can **not** be short!! Now quit stalling, kiddo. I need to find a replacement!!"

The trap sprung, Keyshawn cleared his throat and recited without a stutter:

> He was chubby and plump, a right jolly old **ELF**
> And I laughed when I saw him in spite of my self

With that, Keyshawn was swarmed by the whooping and hollering mob. Even the haughty Director acknowledged defeat.

"You have proven your point by appealing to the presiding authority!" conceded the former Scrooge. "The job is his. He is *perfectly* suited for it!"

As Keyshawn was hoisted onto the crowd's shoulders for the best Christmas tree lighting ever, the director's face turned suddenly grave.

"WAIT!" he screeched, halting the parade. "I'm afraid there exists a second—and, this time, fatal—objection."

Every face turned ashen, Santa's too, as the Director delivered these damning words:

His eyes (**plural**!) how they twinkled, his dimples how merry!

"You are one short of a quorum," said the killjoy. "On the basis of that deficiency, you must be disqualified. I'm sorry."

The point was unassailable. Every child—and Santa, too—could see it plainly. Fair play dictated that Tiger turn in his white beard and green eye patch.

"Live by the poem; die by the poem," crowed the Director, as if it were a lesson for all.

With massive shoulders slumped and grotesque head lowered, the oddest looking Santa the world had briefly known trudged away, with a train of dejected street urchins in tow. The sight of the slow retreat moved even the haughty director.

"Wait!" he called out again, this time not so angry.

Then in the spirit of the season, a Christmas miracle: "Your glass eye twinkles in the lights as well! The objection is not fatal! You're HIRED again."

And so amid renewed shouts, Tiger sealed the job as Hartford's Santa for years to come. "Keyshawn's Triumph", as it became known, propelled him to the front ranks of the neighborhood gang.

"Thanks for believing in me," he said, hugging his hero, who wiped away a single stream of tears. "I'll never forget this day."

That summer, Tiger kept his eye on the prize. Each dawn, he pumped out pushups, and each eve played roller hockey with Keyshawn and the gang, and sprinted up Farmington Ave. to the Twain House. In August, he reported to camp at 200 pounds with 3 percent body fat, packed on a 5'3" frame.

When he stumbled on ice for the 1982 opener against Boston, and winked, Keyshawn and the gang went berserk. "Poetic justice!" they roared. After his third fight, a "goon's hat trick", Insurance City fans showered the ice with eye patches in fitting tribute.

"Gutsiest performance I ever seen," said Terry O'Reilly, icing a black eye, after three of the wildest donnybrooks the Mall had ever witnessed.

Even the begrudging Boston papers were moved: "In the kingdom of the blind, the one-eyed man is king. All hail to Tiger Burns, Hartford's mutilated hero."

11. The 37th Stone

Damn the torpedoes...full speed ahead.
—Admiral Farragut, *USS Hartford,* 1864

While a good fight, in hockey lingo, "can get a team going", so too can a body check—and with his low center of gravity, Tiger was a checker nonpareil. Known as avalanche checks, his were the most feared in hockey.

"He hit you like a ton o' bricks," testified Montreal's "Frenchie" LeDuc. "After Tiger hit you, you ache for days—'specially da' knee caps."

With Tiger barreling in, bent on mayhem, moving the puck up ice was an occupational hazard. Unflappable defensemen dumped the puck to brace for the collision. And teammates like Francis and Dineen were the beneficiaries, feasting on errant passes, and potting them for goals. And for all his troubles, Tiger got no credit.

"Zippo!!!" he complained, bitterly.

Alas, like blocking in football, body checking is statistically thankless. As elsewhere, the spotlight shines on the scorer, while the checker toils away in faceless anonymity. But hockey insiders appreciated his value.

"Some games he no score, but I *still* give him MVP," said LeDuc, icing his swollen knees after a game. "And never forget, dat boy he can fight," he added, shifting the ice bag to a purple shiner.

Try bringing a team of finesse players into Boston's Garden or Detroit's Joe Louis Arena. At these and other stops, that would be like leading lambs to the slaughter. A team needed a few players like Tiger—to keep opponent's honest.

"He may *never* score a goal for all I care, but he plays while I'm here," thundered Whaler's GM Emile Francis.

Tiger was old-school. A "throwback" in every sense, except in the way fishermen use it, he was forever slinging muck into the well-oiled machinery of an opponent. On-ice, he was a whirlwind of constant agitation.

"Dat rascal, he always up ta' no good," confirmed LeDuc.

But that all changed on the power play. With the Whalers a man up, the whirlwind stilled. Tiger's role was to plant himself in front of the enemy net—even as Bunyan-sized defense men tried chopping him down.

"I lay some heavy lumber on dat boy but he no budge," recalled LeDuc, shuddering at the gruesome recollection. "Sometimes, he even smile."

Tiger was never happier than when he skated off-ice—with a tooth dislodged or chunk of cartilage hanging—to the joyous strains of *Brass Bonanza*, the Whaler's victory song: "DAH DAH DAH dadadadada…"

On the power play, he was the 37th boulder of *Stone Field Sculpture,* Hartford's controversial public arts project consisting of 36 rocks—and nothing else—by "minimalist" sculptor Carl Andre. After years of trying to remove it from a downtown square, weary citizens and politicians had given up. That was Tiger, impossible to move—even by civic decree! But unlike those 36 reviled stones, this one was beloved.

Now, because of his stature, Tiger did not make the best screen. Every goalie in the league could see *over* him. But he was wide, and it was hard to see *around* him.

Neither was he adept at deflecting the puck. But again he was *wide*, and sometimes the puck ricocheted off him into the net. And by league rule, he was awarded the goal—and launched into celebratory cartwheels.

Of his six career goals, four came this way. A purple bruise on his buttocks, from a blistering shot that drilled him and dribbled in, lingers still.

"My first goal! Against Boston!!" exclaimed Tiger, rubbing the cherished memento.

But when it came to fundamentals, Tiger was as serious as a heart attack. The first on and last off- ice, he labored to perfect his shot—although it generally proved resistant. One observer likened it to a Scud missile—"powerful but misguided." (The Boston papers said the same about his allegiance to Hartford.)

Lining up pucks, he slapped at them until his hands bled. When the goalies left, he draped a plastic sheet over the goal, a "Shooter Tutor", with openings in four corners and between the goalie's legs ("the five hole"). Before retiring, he practiced breakaways, Tiger against the plastic goalie: mano a mano.

"One day I'll get a penalty shot," he swore to anyone still around to listen, "you'll see."

"Sure, Tiger, some day it'll pay off," the ice crew snickered.

In time, Tiger worked himself into a position where, in hockey speak, "he could take a shift." It meant he wouldn't hurt the team when he wasn't fighting.

"Etch it on my gravestone!" he clucked.

After practice, his last stop was the same: Gordie Howe's office. Reverently called "Mr. Hockey," Howe is the Babe Ruth of the sport; setting records eclipsed only by Gretzky. On ESPN's list of the Athletes of the Century, Howe was judged #21, a spot ahead of Joe DiMaggio.

Not only the best, Howe was the toughest. A "Gordie Howe Hat Trick" consisted of a goal, an assist, and a fight. He played in five decades from the 1940s through the 80s, and when a team suited him up for one shift in 1990, the press pilloried him for the stunt. But to pie-eyed Tiger, "Gordie" had three-too-many letters; he regarded him simply as "God."

Each night as he draped his coat on those sloping shoulders, Gordie bestowed on Tiger a parting word of wisdom—from God's mouth, as it were, to Tiger's cauliflower ear.

"When that goalie puffs up like a cobra, giving the illusion he's covering the net, remember there's an opening between the legs. Always go *five-hole*, Tiger. Don't ever forget it!"

Businessmen love rubbing elbows with jocks, and as a Whaler who stuck around summers, Tiger was sometimes in demand. Requests filtered in through the PR Department—at least until Tiger's appearance at the Insurance Roundtable.

When the call came, the request naturally was for Ron Francis. Off sailing in Nantucket! Kevin Dineen? Fishing in Maine! Ulfie? Home in Sweden! Several other names were tossed out before the exasperated secretary shot back, "Well, is there a water-boy available then?"

"How 'bout Tiger Burns?" replied PR Director Phil Langan, nervous but upbeat.

"Does he play?"

"Well, in a matter of speaking...on the power play!"

"Hmmm...there are no others?"

"Nope, just Tiger!"

"Okay," she sighed. "But have him here at 5:00 tomorrow. Sharp!"

To this point, Tiger had done little more than a few school appearances and ethnic street festivals. Fair or not, he was not deemed suitable for something so rarefied as the Insurance Roundtable. But now by process of elimination, he was on the docket to appear before the most powerful moguls in the city, the power behind the throne of government, and naturally he was worried.

"I don't know an actuarial table from a buffet table," he whined. "Can't I jus' do a Show-and-Tell at the schools?"

"Businessmen love jocks!" assured Langan. "Just swap a few locker room stories! That's all."

Leaning over and putting an arm around the skeptical fighter's mountainous shoulders, Langan offered a last bit of encouragement.

"Talk about what you know best. Don't worry! You'll do fine. "

So he did, and he didn't, and, well, you be the judge.

In Hartford, the city takes its personality from insurance. When asked to explain the high turnover of bars and night clubs, one industry executive offered this spot-on analysis.

"Is it any wonder that the bars close?" he asked. "The *wonder* is that they open at all! We have armies of actuaries studying day and night to pass the insurance exams.

"Coffee fuels our industry—not whiskey! Insurance is for sane, sober and serious men, and now we are open to ladies. It is *not* a place for buffoons."

Arriving promptly at the Hartford Club, the three-story brick across from The Travelers, Tiger had not slept well. The Hartford Club was home to "the Bishops", moguls with the power to bury rivers and strangle waterfronts. Headstrong men, with accountability to none, they had razed acres of 19th century architecture to build Constitution Plaza, a concrete fortress walled off from downtown.

Hartford, alas, has some of the world's most magnificent rubble—redbrick fronts, slate roofs, stained glass—the detritus of old world charm hauled away to make high rises and parking lots. Other mutilations included burying the Park River, building one highway gashing Asylum Hill from downtown and another severing the Connecticut River from the city. The effect was ghastly.

Michael Holley, of *The Boston Globe*, quipped: "Hey, yo' mama so busted ugly when she wake up in the morning she look like downtown Hartford."[27]

Membership in the Hartford Club, as at fine golf clubs, required sponsorship. This ensured only the best made it. When Tiger arrived, a lone woman, her hair in a bun, greeted him.

"Ah, Mr. Burns, our keynote speaker," she announced, handing him a nametag.

"That's me!" he said, humming a few bars of *Brass Bonanza* and spinning to reveal his name on his jersey. "Keep the tag, mam!"

Interrupting the boisterous medley, the woman inquired, "Have you prepared a *Power Point* demonstration for the gentlemen, Mr. Burns?"

Tiger scratched his head—before a bulb flashed.

"A *Power Play* demonstration?! Why didn't I think of it before?"

Talk about what you know best!

"Whatever, Mr. Burns!" said the woman towering over the hockey brawler in her black business pumps.

Surging with confidence now, Tiger jostled his way through patrician men in red ties. Besides the white-gloved wait staff, Mayor Thirman Milner, the lone African-American, stood out. Striding past the oak bar to the podium, Tiger faced the austere assemblage.

"You are here for a **Power Play** demonstration!" he bellowed.

Peering into the crowd, his lone eye was drawn to the two largest nametags, Mr. Budd of The Travelers and Mr. Conrad of the Aetna, the lead executives at the largest firms.

"BUDD, CONRAD to the front!"

Startled, the two titans of industry, accustomed to giving orders—not following—obeyed. Something in Tiger's booming voice, and reckless disregard of protocol, sent them scurrying, martinis sloshing over the burgundy carpet and walnut wainscoting.

What followed is a part of industry lore, on a par with Eliphalet Terry's sleigh ride into New York after the Great Fire of 1835 that established Hartford as Insurance Capital of the World.

After a primer on the finer points of the power play, the two men, at the first retort of the whistle, took turns bashing and head-butting each other in front of the podium, overturned to simulate a goal. At the second, the two barons of industry grappled and elbowed each other in a spirited effort to "clear the crease."

As a bonus, the Bishops were taught the rudiments of brawling: to "grab and punch"; pull the coat "over an opponent's head"; and "rabbit-punch" when no one was looking. When the two battered executives shook hands, the shiners around their eyes matched their ox-blood wing tips, and the blood on their shirts rivaled their red power ties.

"Remember, boys, if them bullies in New York and Boston try ta' steal yer' companies, beat 'em back—jus' like I showed 'ya!"

###

Tiger was always happy to do the Olde Towne a good turn. When it came to community service—as with the Insurance Roundtable—he believed in getting his hands dirty.

Before Tiger, the Mark Twain Festival, honoring the city's famous resident, had been mostly about fun—with frog-jumping and yarn-telling inspired by the stories themselves. But one-eyed Tiger saw greater possibilities!

In Twain's words, he had "nothing less than a great, magnificent inspiration." With the help of Mayor Milner, Tiger surveyed several blighted areas of Park Street, Hartford's Hispanic Main Street, and noted: "A coat of paint would do wonders!"

But painting, as Tom Sawyer had famously noted, "wasn't an every day occurrence." The chance to whitewash Aunt Polly's fence had cost Tom's friends a king's ransom. With little sweat, he collected:

> an apple core; a kite in good repair; a dead rat and a string to swing it with; twelve marbles; a piece of blue bottle-glass; a key that wouldn't unlock anything; a fragment of chalk; a glass stopper of a decanter; a tin soldier; a couple of tadpoles; six fire-crackers; a kitten with only one eye; a brass door-knob; a dog collar—but no dog; the handle of a knife; four pieces of orange-peel; and a dilapidated old window-sash.[28]

"If he hadn't run out of whitewash, he'd have bankrupted every boy in the village," remarked Twain.

So the chance to help Tiger clean up Park Street wouldn't come cheap, either. The event was dubbed "WHITEWASHING WITH TIGER" with proceeds going to the UCONN Children's Cancer fund, the Whalers' Official Charity.

One insurance man ponied up $10,000 for the privilege and a Pratt and Whitney engineer matched him. A sixth grade class raised $237.34, while Local # 84 donated the brushes and paint. The Francises and Dineens forked over $1,000, and Channel 3 sent meteorologist Brad Field to broadcast live.

At the end of the day, Park Street sparkled, the charity was $50,000 richer and a slew of people who never tasted a juicy mango at El Mercado

Market had. True to Twain's spirit, Tiger spruced up the city *and* made money.

"Tiger, we're all used to seeing your face spattered in *red,* but today white is most becoming," proclaimed Mayor Milner, holding the huge ceremonial check dwarfing the paint-splattered fighter.

But he kept no mayoral citations, proclamations or awards—only this. On his spartan bedroom wall hung the famous *Life* Magazine photo of Emmett Kelley, the sad-faced clown "Willie the Tramp", carrying a bucket of water at Hartford's Circus Fire of 1944, the war-time blaze that killed 168 spectators, mostly women and children. Some soldiers in the audience reported they had not seen horrors any worse in towns where they had been under bombs.[29] One girl, dubbed Little Miss 1565, after her morgue number, was never unidentified:

> The city that night was in a state of shock…We were outsiders who had come to town and advertised we were in the business of making people happy. And we were Ringling Brothers and Barnum & Bailey—the biggest thing of its kind in the world. It was something that just couldn't happen. But it did.[30]

The circus, with its memories, would not return to Hartford for 30 years. For the next three decades, the circus trains whistled on through at midnight without stopping. Beneath the tattered photo on Tiger's wall, the caption read "The Clown Who Tried to Save Hartford."

12. SWM, 5'3", 200, 1-Eye, Cauliflower Ears

No one knew his first name, and in general he was known as Beauty Smith.
But he was anything save a beauty. To antithesis was due his naming.
—Jack London

After Tiger had found a home in Hartford, he was primed to find love.
But it wasn't so easy. His, alas, was a face for fighting—not beguiling the
fair sex. To succeed, he had to be enterprising. And so early on, he placed
a personal in *The Advocate*, Hartford's alternative weekly. With only 25
free words, he chose these:

> SWM, 5'3", 200 lbs., 1-eye, cauliflower ears, nose
> (absolutely!), shoots left, punches right. Seeks similarly.
> Bruins fans need not apply!

The results, in hockey terms, were a "shutout." The wives, Mary Lou
Francis and Annie Dineen, took up his cause, showering him with fashion
tips ("*That* eye patch goes well!") and arranging blind dates. But as with
the ad, nothing quite panned out.

"Well, she thought you were cute in a rugged kind of way but…"

To outward appearances, he took rejection philosophically, like a
fighter. ("I take my beatings like a man.") But he never lost hope—nor let
on how much he ached inside. Nor how isolated and lonely he felt. For
Tiger, it just didn't seem to be in his planetary alignment to find love.

A man of the people—he was an island. In the midst of many, he stood
apart. The center of attention—he stood at the fringes. Everyone's, but no
one's. That was Tiger—like public property. So close relations eluded him.
With Tiger, every interaction was a command performance—rarely a fair
and equal exchange.

"Take a picture, Tiger?"

"How 'bout an autograph?"

"RIP his lungs out!"

So he posed, signed and fought—and at night, beat-up and weary, the man a whole city loved was alone. But next morning, spirit on the rebound, he hit the streets again with game face on. A struggling city needed him.

One of the familiar sights on a sultry day was Tiger in his shorn-off, green jersey straining over those wrecking ball biceps. Whether at G. Fox or Sage-Allen—the city's Main Street department stores; Hartford National or Connecticut Bank and Trust—its venerable banks; or The Russian Lady—its favorite bar—he rarely took it off.

"Like a kid in a varsity letter jacket," chuckled Clyde, a North End barber.

A decade before XFL players sported monikers on the back of their jerseys, spawning the celebrated "HE HATE ME", Tiger roamed about with "HARTFORD IS FOR FIGHTERS" on back. On-ice, he preferred the more dignified "GOTHAM'S NIGHTMARE" or "BOSTON STRANGLER." The day Charles Barkley infamously declared "I am not a role model!" his jersey that night rejoined "OH, BUT I AM, SIR CHARLES!"

He was a living, breathing placard for his own bare-knuckled and civic aspirations.

When Jane and Michael Stern, the *Courant's* notorious food critics, savaged another restaurant, there was Tiger next day, napkin tucked in over the jersey, hollering "Chow down, every one!"

"With Tiger, a one-star review brought more customers than five stars," claimed one greasy spoon owner.

In Hartford, it meant a lot that an athlete stayed year round. The feeling was that greatness had chosen to live with and amongst them. For Hartford folk, it meant they measured up!

But why did Tiger love lowly Hartford—midway between Boston and New York—when so few others did? Because Hartford loved Tiger! And why did Hartford love misfit Tiger? Because Tiger loved Hartford!

"A chicken and egg thing," quipped a bemused Boston scribe.

With one-eye, cauliflower ears, and 500 stitches, he had been mangled, mutilated, and mauled. Hartford too, between Boston and New York, was missing its share of original parts, plundered again and again for talent and treasure.

Did you know Bill O'Reilly got his start at Hartford's WFSB? Gayle King, Oprah's best friend, stayed for years at Channel 3, until Oprah whisked her away. Even shock jock Howard Stern, the "King of all Media", started in Hartford at WCCC. But Tiger started and stayed!

For years dressing as Tiger was the city's most popular Halloween costume, outstripping Batman and Superman. But dressing as him—or watching him play—was no preparation for seeing him in the flesh. Tots screamed, and teens grabbed at his vein-rich biceps and tousled his raven-black hair. To sanctify awkward moments, he handed out pucks like a parish priest delivering communion.

"He left pucks everywhere but the opposing team's net," remarked one wag.

But no moment was more awkward than when he visited St. Francis Hospital, and some sick kid made him promise to score a goal for him.

"*A goal?!*" Tiger gulped. "How 'bout a fight? I can get ya' 3 tonight!"

The smart-aleck kid was adamant. "A goal! I want A GOAL!"

Seeing he couldn't be talked out of it, Tiger huddled with doctors and set about fulfilling the onerous promise. True to his word, three years and 176 games later, Tiger scored. Scooping the rare relic from the net, he launched into cartwheels before handing the precious puck to the boy, now a young man with the beginnings of a beard.

On summer nights he umpired baseball games at Colt Park, named for Hartford's inventor of the six-shooter. Ever the showman, he drew crowds from far and wide—even the suburbs—with his flamboyant, arm-flapping calls:

"Safe! Safe! Safe! Yer' SAAAAAAAAAFE at Home in Hartford!"

But a hot July eve was never complete until Tiger lit up the skies with a home run- hitting contest. Throngs ringed the field to marvel at the dwarfish oddity, rocketing shots that vanished in majestic parabolas over Colt's blue, spangled onion dome.

Standing at the plate, he had the diminutive stature of Eddie Gaedel, the 3' 7" mite who once drew a walk on four pitches for the St. Louis Browns. But he clubbed homers like the mighty Gehrig, who briefly played for the Hartford Senators, and whom the *Courant* described as "the stealer of Babe Ruth's thunder, the Sultan of Swat, The Behemoth of Bing, the Kleagle of Clout." As the balls faded away into specks, the crowd swarmed their sawed-off hero.

"Hooray! HOORAY for our Tiger!"

One night, spying from his good eye a stray cat trapped beneath a car, he wrestled loose from the crowd's clutches. Grabbing an Escort, he hoisted it by the bumper—and in this unlikely way, car-lifting became a nightly command performance. After every game, a chant, taken up first by a few, then the multitudes, rolled across the field like thunder:

"Taurus, TAURUS, **TAURUS!**"

At last the clamor was so great that the people's will must be obeyed. Ambling bow-legged to the vehicle called out, and spitting on his hands, he bent his scarred knees and gripped the bumper. The expectant crowd held its breath. With sweat pouring from his brows and veins bursting, he let loose a yell that echoed through the Dutch Point neighborhood—and slowly straightened his knees.

"Aaaaaaaaaaaaaaaaaaargh!"

A lift was never deemed official until a gangly kid named Orlofsky ("the Russian judge"), positioned to his right side, gave the "thumbs up." At that, hats and gloves darkened the Hartford skies as passenger pigeons once did.

"Hooray! HOORAY for our Tiger!"

By summer's end, he graduated from Escorts to Tauruses to the cab of an 18-wheeler, his strength progressing as the Greek wrestler Milo of Crotona, who lifted a calf every day until it became a bull.

But a summer evening at Colt Park was never over until, by popular acclaim, Tiger, recited a last, plaintive rendition of "Casey at the Bat," finishing like this:

Oh somewhere in this favored land the sun is shining bright
A band is playing somewhere and somewhere hearts are light
Somewhere men are laughing and somewhere children shout
But there is no joy in Hartford, mighty Tiger has struck out

On that somber note, the crowd dispersed in their Escorts, Tauruses and 18-wheel cabs, and Tiger dragging his bat behind made the long, lonely walk through deserted streets home—followed by an old ballplayer in a beat-up straw hat: Rube.

13. The Cat

You leave that young man alone.
—Emile Francis

Emile Francis arrived in 1983 with the titles of President and General Manager, but everyone in Hartford knew he was the "hockey czar." After four seasons of progressively dismal results in the NHL, each moving the Whalers farther from the playoffs, fans were getting pissed.

"Bums!" was the whisper at insurance company water coolers.

To make a covenant with fans, and establish credibility in the league, Owner Howard Baldwin needed someone with "impeccable credentials." In Francis, he got someone with 37 years in the game, already enshrined in the Hall of Fame. Informed of the hire, Boston GM Harry Sinden uttered prophetically, "Now I have to worry about the Whalers."

A mediocre goalie in the 1950s, Francis made his bones as Coach and GM of the Rangers and then President of the St. Louis Blues. A short, animated man whose reflexes earned him the nickname "The Cat", he had worked miracles before.

The Rangers had missed the playoffs in five of six previous seasons. On his watch, they made it nine straight. In St. Louis, he kept a tottering franchise afloat, and fans from singing the blues, as the team made the playoffs almost every season.

To some, he was the wrong man. In a column advising Baldwin during the "czar hunt", Randy Smith wrote: "Keep it simple, Howard. Pick somebody who has his name inscribed on the Stanley Cup at least once." Francis's was not.

Pressed to explain, the Cat alibied, "Injuries, bad bounces and Bernie Parent." (The latter, a Philadelphia Flyers goalie, had stymied his teams before.) To Smith, it was a loser's lament.

Francis was a monomaniac: he ate, slept and drank hockey. It ran in the bloodlines. His son Rick was Marketing Director of the Whalers. Bobby coached in the NHL. His wife and mother attended every home game.

Given carte blanche, his first move was to hire Coach Jack "Tex" Evans, an old school defenseman from Chicago. His first draft pick was Sylvain Turgeon, a flashy but fragile sniper with Gallic good looks.

Francis would look far and wide—or down the hall—for talent. Before a game against Quebec, he traded Finnish defenseman "Rocket" Risto Siltanen for Nordiques winger John Anderson. The two exchanged lockers that night.

The team improved 21 points his first year. In 1985-86, they roared into the playoffs on an 11-3-2 tear, swept Quebec in the first round, before falling to Champion Montreal in OT of game #7 of the Adams finals.

To success-starved Hartford, it was a magic carpet ride. The giddy city rewarded its fourth-place team with a parade on Main Street, and Francis was named NHL "GM of the Year."

Next year, the Whalers finished with 93 points and clinched the Adams Division—ahead of "Original Six" Boston and Montreal. But even with the success, malcontents were a problem.

The lineage of grousers began when former Ranger Chris Kotsopoulos went on "couch patrol" in 1985 rather than accept Francis's contract. The Cat quickly dispatched him to Toronto.

More often, problems came when a "worldly" veteran was shipped to a place he deemed an outpost. Hartford, after all, was a "small market" team, the poorest in the NHL. So if a certain type of "sophisticated" player was shipped from New York or Los Angeles to, say, Winnipeg or Hartford, then he might not go quietly.

"It was very depressing," Dave Semenko said of his first night. "They were going to open the hotel pool for me, but I didn't want them to find me face down."

In his biography, he admitted, "I couldn't get excited about perhaps winning a Cup in Hartford by beating Edmonton because, deep down, I still considered myself an Oiler."[31]

By the 1990s, the tradition of harpooning the Whale would reach a nadir with veterans Paul Coffey and Brendan Shanahan publicly refusing to suit up and demanding trades—and so turning Hartford into Siberia.

###

But others welcomed coming aboard—like Pat Verbeek, of New Jersey. Verbeek had survived worse than a trade to Hartford. In 1985, on his family farm in Ontario, his left thumb was severed by an auger. His panicked brother raced him to the hospital, leaving behind the thumb. Fortunately, their father located it in a fertilizer bin. After a six-hour operation, the thumb was reattached. Verbeek played 76 games next season.

From 1989-1995, "Beeker" was a vessel for the hopes and dreams of many. As Captain, he had the unseemly task of dealing with "floaters," players who went half-speed. "I gave my best every shift, and in Hartford when I saw someone who wasn't doing the same, I came down on him."[32]

The 5'10" Verbeek played with such fury that *Sports Illustrated* called him the "Little Ball of Hate." Off the ice, he was no choirboy either. In 1994 he was one of six Whalers involved in a fracas at Jim Kelley's bar in Buffalo, garnering national headlines. But when the Whalers played in Detroit, he left tickets for Sister Eileen Marie Hunter, his high school teacher in Ontario.

Over the years, other veterans wore the jersey with pride. But always among them were a few who heard the whispers. Maybe it was the parade? Maybe it was the down-at-the-heels city? Maybe it was the song?

Whatever the reason, some players viewed the green jersey as something odious, to be touched with long tongs. Chief among them was a goalie named Broadway.

14. Broadway

Bad helmet, that one he has a bad helmet.
—Randy Smith

When he was dispatched to Hartford, Sly Lawlor didn't know much about the Insurance Capital, but this much he picked up quick:

(1) A HOOKER founded the city.
(2) Thomas HOOKER arrived with more COWS than people
(3) PODUNK Indians were native, and
(4) The Indian name for Hartford was SUCKiaug (*emphasis added*)

Upon these four pillars of truth, he based his opinions. Hartford was a "puke town." "Twain Town," he called it, dripping disdain. Lawlor fancied himself a "New York talent"—hence the nickname "Broadway." To him, Hartford was "off, off, off Broadway"—nothing could be more contemptible.

In three turbulent seasons, he never bothered changing license plates. Caught on surveillance, he was filmed cuffing a young autograph seeker in a parking garage. Idling nearby was a red Porsche with New York plates "GOALIE1." On the bumper was an "I Love New York" sticker.

He once climbed into the stands to slug a wiseacre who called him "Frog Hollow", after a down-in-the-mouth Insurance City neighborhood. At the ensuing trial, his lawyers counter-sued for "defamation of character." All charges were dropped.

But autograph hounds and leather-lungs got the royal treatment compared to frumps. One in a plaid knee-skirt and braces made this awkward come-on: "My friend offered me $50 to say 'Hi.'"

"The going rate is $100!" he said, pirouetting away to a nearby blond.

In a league where many started at 18, Broadway had a year of college—giving rise to another nickname "Professor." Flaunting his credentials, he carried on about most subjects under the sun, or "celestial orb" as he called it.

But for all his pompousness and peccadilloes, Broadway was one of the best in the league. A tall, stand-up net-minder, he challenged shooters with an uncanny knowledge of angles.

"Trigonometry," he said, when asked his keys to success.

Off -ice, he knew the angles, too, chasing "puck bunnies" in corner bars as much as rubber pucks in rink corners. In the contest between Priapus, Phallic God, and Cetus, Whale Mascot, the choice was not a hard one.

"SEX RULES!" he declared: "I won't serve two masters."

Indifferent to wins and smirking at losses, he was a festering pustule whose attitudes poisoned others. At every turn, he knocked the city and team.

"Hartford puts the SUCK in SUCKiaug," he was fond of elocuting.

But he was careful not to spew this vitriol at Ronnie, Kevin and Ulf, veterans with pride in the jersey. No, his was a rear guard attack launched at rookies and disgruntled veterans. A master manipulator, he specialized in isolating his prey, selecting the weak and vulnerable.

"Culling the herd" he called it.

The effect was insidious. Whereas some teams are fueled by disrespect, fostering an "us against the world" attitude, the Whalers were crippled by it—because it was an inside job. Broadway and his brethren stoked the flames of self-hatred and self-immolation.

###

Goalies have always been flaky. Montreal's Patrick Roy talked to goal posts. Boston's Gerry Cheevers penciled stitches on his mask to show how his face would look without it. New York's Gilles Gratton donned a tiger mask—to frighten shooters. But Broadway was in a league all his own.

After games, he blasted off in his red Porsche with custom plates to his Park Avenue penthouse, a different puck bunny ("puck fuck" in his crude lingo) in tow. Because he judged a city on its nightlife, and nothing else, on that scorecard Hartford was wanting.

What few bars there were closed at 1 a.m. In cities passing muster, "last call" was 4:00—and then "after hour" clubs. In Hartford, bars had trouble staying open not until 1:00, but at all. At one prime Civic Center spot, four came and went with mayfly life spans: "VACANT" outlasted them all.

"There isn't even a decent strip club," Broadway grumbled. "What am I supposed to do go visit that goddamned Twain House?"

A prima donna and party boy, he surveyed the vast wasteland and escaped—as others used it to advantage. Edmonton GM Glen Sather, when playing back-to-back in Hartford and New York, always stayed in the Insurance Capital. He knew where his team was likely to get rest—and therein lay the genius of a Sather, who won three Stanley Cups.

Now Broadway had more talent in his manicured pinkie than Tiger Burns did in his whole bruised body. But the two were cut from different cloth—and the difference was between satin and burlap. His beer-breathed motto was: "Take from the game all you can; it can end any shift."

When a New York glossy *Metrosexual* ran a feature on "Celebrity Bedrooms", his Park Avenue penthouse with ermine bedspread, gold-plated jacuzzi, and Polar bear rugs took top laurels. Visible in the Italianate marble fireplace were the charred remnants of a green pennant.

"Every last detail is placed for exquisite effect," gushed a breathless judge.

(*Ed. Note*: The runner-up, an exiled Saudi emir, was "sent to the penalty box" for being "too besotted with platinum, mother of pearl and Picassos.")

When it came to the rough-hewn Tiger, Broadway was all jibe and jeer, belittling his "bucket of blood" style and "all heart" game, carrying on about the plucky fighter like a Las Vegas lounge act.

"His looks could scare a cat off a fish wagon!"

Badaboom.

"His nose's been broke more times than the pole vault record!" cribbing the line off a LA sports writer.

Badaboom.

"He's built like a Greek statue—but skates like one, too."

Possessed of an ungovernable impulse to mock, he trashed the little fighter at every turn, sometimes by the mere dropping of a vowel.

"How's T-ger? Hey, he's missing an 'i' ain't he?"

Other times, he placed a hand over his left eye: "How is (hand over eye)?"

But Broadway was too craven to do it to Tiger's face. Tiger Burns was the fiercest fighter in hockey. You couldn't observe him rolling his neck at odd moments, and shadowboxing, and not worry that he might go off. But after his audition punch in Moose Jaw, decking the goon who fired a wad of tape at his head, Tiger was no threat to anyone not in skates.

"Off da' ice he just da' sweetest guy!" cooed Frenchie LeDuc.

But Broadway was never quite sure of it. So he erred, as always, on the side of cowardice and pusillanimity. Befitting a man with two nicknames, he was two-faced:

"Hey, T-ger, LOVE the jersey."

"Thanks, Broadway! Donated 100 like it ta' da' Boy Scouts—means a lot ta' da' kids," replied Tiger, flashing a toothless grin.

"That's right T-ger, us athletes gotta give back." But seeing Tiger in the team jersey off-ice enraged Broadway. "That yahoo's a bush leaguer just calling attention to himself," sneered the owner of the fire engine-red sports car with "GOALIE1" plates.

But the players that mattered chuckled about his fashion *faux-pas*.

"Hey, you try finding a 60-inch jacket tailored to a 5'3" frame—off the rack," cracked Dineen. "I defy you."

But Broadway hated him. And because it wasn't in Tiger's nature to be two-faced, or see it, he couldn't detect the condescension. It was a blind spot—a second one.

"Stay away from him!" warned Kevin. "He's no good."

"C'mon Kev, Broadway's a Whaler like you and me."

"Stay out of his clutches!" scolded Ronnie.

"Sure he's a little flashy, Ronnie, but Broadway ain't a bad guy."

Now, the supreme irony in all this was that as much as Tiger was Ronnie's bodyguard, the player he defended more than any was the goaltender. And it had to do with the nature of the position.

In hockey the goalie has a special protected status—like a spotted owl. The guardian of the gate, last line of defense, and only player on ice 60 minutes, the goalie stands alone, an island, singularly focused on the puck. For opponents barreling in, he's a sitting duck.

In a gesture acknowledging his status, teammates tap the goalie's pads with their sticks before and after every period. It's well-known that a "hot goalie" can carry a team.

In his crease, the semi-circle doorstep to the goal, the goalie has safe haven. The crease is a sacred patch of ice—and any infringement is prosecuted ruthlessly. "Run" the goalie, and you must pay!

Some of Tiger's fiercest battles—and ghastliest wounds—came defending Broadway's crease. His crowning disfigurement, the loss of his eye, came when a Ranger speared him as he rushed to clear the crease. Tiger had no regrets.

"I'd do it again, but not a third time—for I regret that I have but two eyes to lose for my goalie," he cracked, but the sentiment was earnest.

In football, quarterbacks shower the linemen who protect them with Rolexes. But Broadway heaped only scorn on Tiger. The two parted ways the moment their blades left ice—Tiger to the trainer's room, Broadway to his vanity kit. After the game, was his time to shine—he loved the ladies.

Truth be told, Tiger did too. It's just that he faced "challenges." As Broadway put it, "He couldn't get to first base in a woman's prison with a handful of pardons."

Ever thoughtful, Broadway offered counsel.

"Hey, T-ger, next time you see some dish, pop that eye out of yours, and throw it to her. Then say, *'Hey, you caught my eye.'* Get it?"

Aside from lust, hatred was his one unadulterated emotion. Everything else came alloyed. In Tiger, he saw something pure and uncorrupted, so he needed to despoil it.

"Stay away! He's trouble," Ronnie warned.

"Aw, he ain't so bad, Ronnie," said Tiger rising to his goalie's defense as on-ice, "I'd just like to get to know him better. Maybe someday I will?"

15. Chuck's

There were no theaters, nor public entertainment, no dancing, little painting,
no sculpture, and no literature except for long-winded sermons... This
environment, coupled with the Puritan ethic, resulted in strict living, and it
was no accident that Connecticut was called the "land of steady habits."[33]
—Connecticut: A History

To celebrate a win or drown sorrows after a loss, Whaler fans fanned out in
every direction. In the Civic Center, Margaritaville was favored for frozen
drinks, Chuck's Cellar hosted live bands, and The Sheraton offered Top
40 dancing.

The Russian Lady, on Ann Street, was renowned for its namesake
statue. Champions Sports Bar sat next door. Just around the corner,
L'Oreans and Le Jardin were discos favored by the gold chain crowd.

But every hockey city has a favorite, and so the well-trodden path
ran across the Civic Center lobby to Chuck's, with views of Asylum and
Trumbull Streets. On rainy nights, fans didn't even have to get wet—*one*
advantage of playing in a "shopping mall." Two bouncers, a linebacker and
offensive tackle from the North End, manned the doors.

"IDs," demanded the linebacker gruffly.

Behind the bar, Stan the bespectacled server offered the occasional
round "no charge." Yes, Chuck's was the place to go. Announcer Greg
Gilmartin hustled over so fast that the echo of his signature call—
"Ooooooone minute left in the game"—still reverberated in the rafters.
Sidling up to "Blue Line" Betty, the bleached blond ticket holder who sat
by the penalty box, Gilmartin ordered the usual.

"One cold Bud coming up!" said Stan, wiping hands on apron.

Goal judges, statisticians and press gophers—the off-ice officials—
arrived next. In deference to their blue blazers with orange NHL crests,
the bouncers passed them in without IDs. "You're O.K."

Fans and factotums congregated in the book-lined hallway leading
to the restaurant out back. Animated talk all around was of that night's
game.

"Lootie came up HUGE tonight!"

"How 'bout that HIT by Ulfie?"

"That was a CHEAP shot!"

But every conversation before 10:30 p.m. was distracted—with one eye on the door. Showering and handling press questions took a half-hour—after a tough loss, with beat writers Jacobs and Smith probing, it could go longer.

The players cut an unmistakable figure. Outside of a raw-boned defenseman or two, the doormen dwarfed them. Still there was something of the supple strength of the elite athlete that gave them that certain "look." "Blue Line" Betty could spot it a mile away.

"STEWIE!" she squealed, as the first passed in. "Great game, Stewie!"

Occasionally a well-built insurance man could "pass", but still there was something about "the look" hard to duplicate. One in a hundred could pull it off. To those who could were granted such perks as moving to the front of the beer line or chatting up a woman out of their league.

On game night, the restaurant out back was "Players Only." To reach it, the athletes had to run a gauntlet of fans. There was no other route.

"Way to go, DEANO!"

"Nice goal, PEE WEE!"

Most pushed through with a nod. With wife or girlfriend in tow, it would be disrespectful to stop—or so the thinking went. For some, the women acted as "human shields", protecting them from unwanted interactions.

"Sorry, guys, the old lady's here."

A few like Kevin, Ronnie and Ulf stopped. Still dinner out back was getting cold. "See 'ya next game, fellows."

But one muscle-bound mite defied all protocols and prohibitions. When Tiger burst in, bandaged after a trip to the trainer's, flashing that toothless grin, Chuck's took on the raucous atmosphere of a German Beer Hall.

"DAH DAH DAH dadadadada," echoed the heralds, as word filtered in, "TIGER'S in 'da HOUSE!"

As he shouldered up to the bar (his stature would not allow "bellying up"), eager fans slapped at his wide back, and poked his bulging biceps.

"Great FIGHT tonight, Ti! Probie won't be back soon after that beating!"

When Stan heard the ruckus in front, he clanged the bar bell and shouted: "Tap that cask of SAR-SA-PA-RILL-A! We got us a SAR-SA-PA-RILL-A Man in the house!"

Everyone knew Tiger's favorite beverage, and soon a foaming mug was thrust into his throbbing hands. If there was a line out the front door, after a Bruins or Rangers game, Tiger never pulled rank or "big-timed" anyone. He waited like everyone else. But celebrity had its privileges.

When word reached Stan that Tiger was stuck in line, the sarsaparillas were passed bucket brigade-style into the lobby. Fifty hands might touch a mug before it reached him.

"Hey, you didn't have to do *that*," he protested, but gulping it down gratefully.

Depending on the line, two or three frothing mugs might be delivered this way. To show his appreciation, he turned cartwheels in the lobby—or walked on his hands up and down the escalator.

"That's our Tiger!"

Once inside, at the sight of the tipsy announcer, Tiger croaked, "We Wooooooooooon!" his raspy squawk in contrast to the dulcet tones of "Golden Pipes" Gilmartin.

In victory, his eye rarely stayed in its socket—finding its way to the bottom of some beer stein. Or top of an olive dish. Once removed, it rarely returned, some fan pocketing it as a gruesome souvenir. His glass eye—like Tiger, you see—was public property. Every felt entitled to a piece.

At midnight, the party in full gear, he slipped out quietly without fanfare and limped bow-legged up Asylum Hill to spend another night alone.

16. A Date with Destiny

… he achieved his masterpiece of exploitation.
—Paul Johnson

The 1990 Stanley Cup playoffs against Boston was the series that Hartford had longed for since it entered the NHL 11 years before. This was the Battle of New England writ large, the first time the rivals had ever met in the playoffs.

For seven games, if that long, they could kick, smash and gouge at each other. For the Insurance City, it meant a chance at the respect that had long eluded them:

> Even in their own building, the Hartford Civic Center, the Whalers have had to suffer the indignity of hearing Boston's boisterous fans whenever the Bruins have visited. A Boston goal in Hartford is often visited with nearly as much zeal as a Whaler goal, which doesn't quite fit the idea of root, root, root for the home team.[34]

Respect is a devalued word, bandied about, but here there were three centuries of bullying behind it—ever since Thomas Hooker escaped persecution in Boston to found Hartford in 1636.

Players, coaches and fans can read the tea leaves. Taking their cues from society, superior airs and condescension became the *lingua franca* when it came to Hartford and its hockey team.

When Tom Wolfe, the New York author, called the Hartford Civic Center a "monument to 1920s Middle European worker housing", mirthful Ranger fans piled on.

"You play in a SHOPPING mall! Let's go SHOPPING!" they chanted.

Their own arenas, they tinged with romanticism. Yankee Stadium was "The House that Ruth Built"; Fenway Park a "lyrical little band box"; Madison Square and Boston Gardens were "hockey cathedrals." But Hartford's Civic Center was a friggin' "Mall."

But Rangers fans were quaint compared to their northern cousin: *Neanderthalis Bruinsis*. When Boston played in Hartford, their fans descended like Visigoths, hell-bent on overrunning Liliput. Dressed in black and gold, with spoked "B" symbolizing "Hub of the Universe", they had a lawless swagger. In roving packs, they tramped from the satellite lots where they parked their jalopies: ululating, cursing, and vomiting the whole way.

"Here we go, BROOO-INZ, HERE WE GO!"

Inside the "Mall", fights erupted, arrests for drunkenness were common, and a stolen Christmas tree was once used as a battering ram. These delightful folk gave English soccer hooligans a good name. When they fled, rivers of urine flooded the streets. But the fans only took their marching orders from above.

Wrote Joe Fitzgerald, of the *Boston Herald*:

> Of course being in the other guys' building would have meant a whole lot more if they'd been playing in Montreal, Philly or New York, rather than in ho-hum Hartford where 15,000 actuaries sat through the evening with their hands folded on their laps, nodding approvingly, as if they were watching 'Man of La Mancha.' Good grief, what a village of nerds.[35]

In interviews, the Bruins brass barely acknowledged the upstarts from the south. After all, Boston was an "Original Six" team and the Whalers were, well, Hartford's.

But all this haughtiness belied what had become a torrid rivalry, the "Battle of New England", a backyard brawl in which from 1984-1990, the Whalers played Boston even, 22-23-3, and on March 5, 1987 trounced them 10-2, a "Boston Massacre" led by six assists from Ronnie Francis. It may be a heresy, but the Red Sox-Yankees rivalry had nothing on Boston-Hartford.

On the ice, the Big, Bad Bruins tried to run roughshod over their smaller foes. No surprise, Terry O'Reilly's single-game record for skullduggery (5 minors, 3 majors and a game misconduct) came against Hartford. But when a scarlet trail ran down the Pike from Boston to Hartford, hockey was the better for it. It mattered.

One incident, in particular, illustrates the contempt Boston held for Hartford. The last game of 1987-88, the Whale had just won 4-2, and Terry O'Reilly, former strongman, now coach, was livid. In icy silence, the Bruins showered and boarded. As the bus idled in an underground lot, a car parked by the exit blocked the way.

"Get it out of there," O'Reilly snapped.

Told that the owner would have to be located, O'Reilly took matters into hand. Plunging a fire extinguisher through the window, he and some burly Bruins pushed it aside. And so like vandals, in a wake of glass, the Bruins left Hartford that night. Practice was early next morning.

###

1990 was the chance to step out of the shadow of its surly neighbor and belt them in the nose. But the Beantown brass begrudged nothing.

"I think the fans have tried to create a Hartford-Boston rivalry," scoffed Boston Coach Mike Milbury. "They want Hartford to be known as a bona fide NHL team." [36]

If it was ever going to happen, *this* was the year. With Francis, Dineen, Samuelsson and Verbeek, *this* was the team. In game one, the Whalers kicked the bullies in the shin, upsetting them 4-3. After the game, scribes up north were suddenly not so haughty.

"There's no doubt: Hartford for real,"[37] wrote Bob Ryan, in his *Globe* column.

In game two, Boston held serve, 3-1, as the series moved south deadlocked. In game three the Whalers spat in Boston's eye, 5-3. A win in game four, in the Mall, and the Whalers could seize command.

Leading two games to one, with Bruins' Hall-of-Fame Captain Ray Bourque injured, the Whalers were on the cusp of greatness. Win *that* series, *that* year, against your age-old nemesis, and it was a clear skate.

WIN! And you are no longer an object of derision.

WIN! And gain a measure of lasting respect.

WIN! And never move south to a faraway city.

But lose *this* game, *this* night, and history will judge this as the moment when your team "jumps the shark", when something good goes bad, and all roads lead downward.

###

Arriving hung-over for the morning skate, Broadway scanned the locker room through bloodshot eyes. His mood was cranky. Stale beer oozing from his pores, he walked over to the equipment manager, right up in his face.

"Where is (hand over eye)?"

"Practicing!" snarled Skip Cunningham, with the team since its WHA days.

"Why bother? That numbskull's good for only one thing!"

"If you worked *half* as hard, Hartford would have a Cup or two by now."

"Hey, I work hard, Skippy" Broadway protested, stifling a yawn. "You shoulda seen me last night at the clubs."

Skip continued folding towels, ignoring the provocation.

"Hey, Skippy, if you see my good friend. Tell T-ger I want to talk with him about our power play. He's been badgering me a long time about it. Maybe tonight, the night before game four, I'll oblige?"

"You, no-good, son of a bitch!" Skip muttered under his breath.

Broadway grinned, showcasing two rows of perfect teeth.

"Yea, old T-ger's been wantin' to talk 'strategy' for awhile, Skipper? Maybe tonight's his lucky night?"

"Not Tiger, Broadway. Not this game. Not *tonight,*" Skip pleaded.

Rolling his sweaty jersey in a ball, Broadway tossed it at the laundry bin. He always made a point to miss. "Ooooh, soooo sorry Skippy! I usually don't miss my marks, you know."

"Son of a bitch," Skip murmured.

"You'll be a good little trainer and pick it up for me, won't you? Us Whalers stick together, right?"

Skip bent down, picked up the acrid jersey and stuffed it in the bin.

Broadway headed for the shower, whistling as he went. He felt good, a little hung over, but that was normal. The season was winding down. Soon it would be done.

"SAY-O-NA-RA SUCK-i-aug!" he sang out, the water jets massaging his tired muscles. "No more trips to TWAIN TOWN!"

Broadway visualized the water washing off the stain of the green uniform. Spirits soaring now, he crooned his favorite scrubbing ditty, an Elvis tune:

I don't want to be a tiger cause tigers play too rough…
Just want to be your teddy bear
Put a chain around my neck and lead me anywhere

Stepping into his thongs, he plodded back to his locker, dropping the dirty towel on the floor. To his dismay, Skip was not around to see. "Poor, Skippy, he'll have to pick this up, too."

The locker room was empty. Tiger was still practicing, and the others were at home resting now. It was rare for Broadway to be one of the last still at the rink. Usually he was the first to go, often begging out altogether with aches and pains.

Glancing at Tiger's locker, he shook his head in disgust at the oversized boxing gloves presented as a gift at the team Christmas Party, one labeled "Ronnie's"; the other "Bodyguard." Hanging on a hook was the jersey Tiger wore to practice stenciled "BOSTON STRANGLER."

"Poor, talent-less bastard! That moron doesn't get it. But tonight old T-ger's finally gonna get it!"

A half hour later, Tiger skipped into the locker room, grinning that goofy grin. The Whalers were in the hunt! Boston was on the ropes! It was the time of his life!

For a moment, he allowed himself to think about the Stanley Cup— and what he'd do with it, when they won. He'd take the Cup to the hospital to the doctors who fixed his eye, to the schools, to the Hartford Club for "The Bishops."

"Hah! Even they'd be impressed! All we gotta do is win tomorrow night." Boston's record, when down 3-1 in a playoff series, was 0-21. "Yea, all we gotta do is win, baby!"

Just then, a tall man in gray Armani interrupted his reverie.

"Hey, T-ger, how 'bout Chuck's tonight? You and me been meaning to get together for a while now."

"Broadway?!" said Tiger, startled. "What're you doin' here? I thought you'd be in New York by now."

"Nah, gotta rest for the big game tomorrow. Staying local tonight."

"Where ya' stayin', Broadway?"

"The Goodwin," he said, casually dropping the name of Hartford's five-star hotel across the street.

"WOW, you always go first class, huh Broadway?!"

"What other way is there, buddy? But since I'm in town, you wanna meet up tonight at Chuck's?"

"But, Broadway, it's the night before game four," he protested.

"C'mon, the power play ain't working. We'll fix it over a beer at Chuck's. Wadda ya say, buddy?"

Tiger never went out the night before a game—ever! His ritual—corny as it sounds—was to sip sarsaparilla, crank out 1000 pushups, and shadowbox to the dulcet strains of *Brass Bonanza*. The song others thought "dumb" sent shivers down his spine.

Draping a towel over his head, Tiger turned his wide back and slumped down at his locker. So Broadway came in from another angle.

"There's a broad been buggin' me to meet 'ya," he said, sitting down. "Seen that picture of you in the paper at Mark Twain Days and been talkin' about 'ya ever since."

"Seen my picture and wants to meet me," deadpanned Tiger, still looking down.

"It was the one covered in paint," Broadway explained. "She's a real cutie, too."

Tiger blushed, back turned, not budging. "How 'bout *after* the game?"

"She's coming to Chuck's at 8:00 tonight. DEAL or NO DEAL?!"

Tiger was surprised at Broadway's vehemence.

"You'll be home by 9:00," he said, softer. "Then you can do your goddam pushups—or whatever the hell you do."

Tiger bent over and scratched his foot.

"Look—it's a one-shot deal!" Broadway said, voice rising. "We've been talking about it all season. Can you make it **tonight** or not? I need to let her know."

Tiger moistened his lips, but said nothing.

"Okay, I'll cancel the whole god-damned thing. Have fun doing your pushups. But she's gonna be real disappointed."

Broadway got up from the bench where he had planted himself, and stomped off to the door.

"WAIT!"

The goalie turned and looked at the anguished fighter.

"I don't have time for games!" he warned. "I'm canceling my hotel room and heading to New York. Cause of you I probably won't get any sleep tonight—sure to screw up our chances tomorrow."

Tiger swallowed hard and looked down.

"I'll see ya' at Chuck's at 8:00."

In the end, as Achilles had a heel, so Tiger had a heart. The opportunity was too enticing to pass up.

"Now you're talking, BUDDY!!" Broadway shouted, trotting back and slapping Tiger on the back so his hand stung. "Ouch, you're a ROCK, man!"

"See those pushups ain't no waste of time after all. You oughta try some!"

"Yea, yea, cut the bullshit now! Here's the deal: meet me in parking level P3, at 8 sharp. You hear? You won't regret it, buddy."

With the little fighter's fate sealed, Broadway left the room, whistling again. At the player's gate, instead of plowing through, as he always did, he stopped to sign autographs, shocking the knot of boys.

"WOW! Broadway *never* signs!!"

"Don't get used to it!" he warned, rolling the Sharpie over the card. "Today's just a good day, ya know?"

"Yeah, Bruins tomorrow night! They're DEAD MEAT! WHALE Rules!"

Striding to his Porsche, whistling still, he spotted Skip unloading the equipment van for tomorrow's game. Putting two fingers into his mouth, Broadway hailed him.

Skip looked over in disgust at the cocky goalie. "So what are you up to tonight, Broadway?" he shouted. "The night of the biggest game in team history. And with who?"

Broadway said nothing—but placed a hand over his left eye, and smiled that pearly smile.

"You, no-good BASTARD!"

Dropping the bundle of clean laundry onto the floor, Skip raced back to the locker room. But no one was there.

17. Suzy

Man is the only creature that blushes. Or needs to.
—Mark Twain

There were three things unusual about the night of April 10, 1990: Tiger was not home on the floor doing pushups; Broadway was not in New York trolling for "puck bunnies"; and the two were together on level P3 of the Civic Center Mall. The tall goalie, in charcoal gray, seemed happy to see the squat fighter, in pressed green.

"How 'ya doing, buddy?" he said, circling an arm around him, as the two walked to the elevator, shoulder-to-chest.

"Nervous," Tiger admitted, rolling his neck. "How do I look?"

Broadway bit his tongue. "Never better, buddy!"

"I haven't had a blind date in a while."

A blind date would be the only kind for you, T-ger.

"What was that, Broadway?"

"You'll do fine. This gal's excited. Running late, though!" At that, he playfully elbowed Tiger. "Wants to look fine for tonight!"

Tiger blushed. "What's her name, Broadway?"

"Her name?" he stammered. "Oh, it's, umm, Suzy. Yeah, Suzy, that's it."

"SWEET!"

Does the trick.

"What's that?"

"Nuthin', nuthin.' You look nervous, buddy," he said, at the elevators.

"I *am* nervous—about tomorrow's game and tonight's date."

As the door opened, the goalie grabbed Tiger's sleeve, holding him back. "Join me for a beer tonight. It'll relax 'ya."

"I don't drink, Broadway. You know that," said Tiger, looking up at him like he was crazy.

"It'll relax you to meet...what's-her-name."

"Suzy!"

"Yeah, and take the edge off about the game."

"Broadway, I can't stand even the smell of beer! Don't talk stupid!"

"Well, then have a little rum in one of those god-damned root beers."

"Sarsaparillas," Tiger corrected, surprised at his vehemence.

The towering goalie wrapped his long arm around the fighter again, surprised at how strong he was. "Holy Shit! O'Reilly musta been nuts to tangle with you! You're an animal!"

Tiger smiled. It was nice to receive a compliment from his teammate, but Broadway returned to badgering.

"C'mon, a drink will loosen ya' up. You're tight as a virgin's pussy for Crissakes! Look at me! A few drinks haven't hurt me."

Tiger couldn't argue with that. Broadway was one of the best.

"Know what's holding you back, buddy? You're not a bad little player, big heart and all, but you're too damned uptight. It's the same thing off-ice and it's killing 'ya."

Presented with an opening, Tiger opened up, his anguish spilling out.

"Broadway, I'd love fa' this ta' work out tonight with Suzy. I'm lonely."

"Dammit then *do* something!" Broadway exploded. "All it takes is one beer. As the Bible says, 'Better to light a fucken candle than curse the darkness.' Leviticus—I think. It'll loosen you up for Boston and the broads. Kill two pussies with one stone, Biblically speaking. Then you can go back to those god-damned root beers."

"Sarsaparillas."

"Your problem is you're fearless on-ice, but a pussy off it. Women can sense fear, you know. They're a lot like animals in that respect," he explained, breaking into a grin: "You don't think all my charisma is natural, huh? C'mon, buddy, join me for one. It'll help, I swear."

Tiger's lip trembled. A tear slid down his cheek. He could hide his pain no longer. "I've been lonely a long time, ya' know."

"Then light the fucken candle! Have *one* drink."

Broadway's counsel ran foursquare against everything Tiger held sacred. Posted on his wall were the words of his Junior Coach Stump Peters: "Never dishonor the game by giving it less than your all."

And he never did—except the night of April 10, 1990 when he allowed Broadway Lawlor to bend his cauliflower ear and twist his muscular arm.

"C'mon," he said reassuringly. "It'll make all the difference."

Tiger bit his fattened lip and fanned his neck. He was on-the-fence, Broadway sensed it—so he went in for the kill.

"C'mon, buddy, us Whalers stick together."

At that appeal, Tiger broke into a goofy grin. "O.K.," he relented, "but just one."

"Now, you're talking, buddy!" he said, slapping his thick back. "OUCH! It's on me!"

The Concourse of the Mall was quiet. A Tuesday night in Hartford drew little foot traffic. In Chuck's, a few stragglers sipped beers.

"Tiger?! What are you doing here?" cried one, startled at the unlikely apparition. "Hey, great game last night! You really kicked 'Mofo' Jones' ass!"

Then spotting the goalie, he did a double take.

"Broadway? In Hartford? On an off night?! Be still my beating heart!"

"Get out of the way," he growled, yanking Tiger by the shirt. "He's mine tonight."

"Sorry," Tiger shrugged, dragged helplessly down the hall.

At the end of the hall, wiping the bar, it was Stan the bartender's turn for surprise.

"Tiger? What the hell are you doing here? Tonight? With *him?!*"

"Not to worry, Stanley," said the swaggering goalie. "Big game tomorrow. We're here to straighten out the power play. Been misfiring lately, don't you know?"

Before Stan could respond to the outrageous claim, Broadway pushed the little fighter out back into the restaurant, returning alone.

"Stanley, I'll have the usual," he said, pausing, "oh, and a sarsaparilla with Bacardi."

Stan's blue eyes flashed. His pink fists balled. In an instant, the burly Irish bartender leaned inches from Broadway's nose.

"I'll make yer goddam Long Island iced tea, Sly, but I won't put *any* rum in Tiger's sarsaparilla—and that's final!"

"He wants it," he said, crossing his arms and smiling.

"Bullshit!" For an instant it appeared he might lunge, before Broadway backed away.

"Hey, really, Stan, I promise."

"I've been serving him straight sarsaparilla 10 years! You don't come barging into *my* bar from god-damned New York and tell *me* what Tiger drinks."

Again Broadway backed down.

"Hey, Stan, it's unusual, I understand. Here, I'll have him order himself."

Sniggering, Broadway walked out back, and returned with Tiger.

"Tell Stanley what you want in your drink!"

Tiger hesitated.

"Tell him!"

"Rum," said Tiger softly, looking down.

Stan stood with mouth agape.

"Really?" he asked, staring at Tiger's downcast eye.

"Tell him!" urged Broadway.

"I didn't ask *you*," Stan said, glaring, then turning to Tiger.

"Yeah," he mumbled.

Stan stood dumbfounded. If he had time, he might have asked a third time, but just then, a group of women arrived. Jostling his way to the front, Broadway placed the order again.

"The usual extra strong, and a sarsaparilla with rum."

"Wait your turn!" snapped Stan.

"Always trust Broadway," he needled. "His word's as good as gospel."

What could Stanley do? He'd heard it with his own ears. He made the drinks. Knowing he had the upper hand now, Broadway whipped out the needle again.

"Damn you're good at what you do, Stanley! Put it on the tab!"

Broadway returned with the drinks, placing the smaller glass in front of Tiger. Seeing his apprehension, he said in a calm voice, "Trust me buddy, it'll help."

As Tiger lifted the glass, inspecting it carefully with his right eye, Broadway proposed a toast.

"Cheers... WAIT! Stop!! That's a bar in Boston, right? We can't have that now, can we?"

Tiger guffawed at the lame joke.

"Strike that from the record! To Hartford and the Whale, long may they thrive."

"That I'll drink to!"

After the two glasses clinked, Tiger apprehensively brought the alcohol to his lips, the two never having touched. After a lusty chug, Broadway slammed down his glass, holding his breath.

"How is it?"

"Just like sarsaparilla!" Tiger declared, flashing a devil-may-care grin. "It's greeeeeeeeeeat!"

Broadway released his breath like a ruptured steam pipe. "Told 'ya! Now drink up before that broad gets here."

"Suzy!"

"Yea."

Tiger did as he was bid—at his usual chug-a-lug pace.

"Does it burn?"

"Nah! Can't tell no difference."

"Atta boy! Must be all those elbows to the throat! Lost all your taste—but not in clothes, I see. Same old green jersey, huh?"

Broadway was regaining his usual edge. Tiger took a third swig, flashed a grin, and slammed the glass on the table, like he'd seen in those old westerns.

"That was gooood, pardnah!"

Broadway smiled. "How 'bout another? The second'll be twice as good!"

"No, No, NO!" warned Tiger, turning serious. "One and done! That's it! Sarsaparillas from here on."

"No problem, pardnah! Straight sarsaparilla this round—but on me again!"

"Thanks, Broadway."

Broadway walked casually up to the bar, looked Stanley in the eye and placed the order: "You heard what he wants, barkeep! Another round! Like the last!"

Stanley glowered at the goalie. But what's a bartender to do? He'd heard it with his own ears; he poured the drinks as before.

"Thanks, Stanley—from T-ger with love!"

Broadway took the drink and held his breath again. He was white-knuckling this one.

"One sarsaparilla for my man!" he said, thumping him on the back. "Ouch!"

"Thanks, Broadway! Let me do the toast this time."

"Go for it, buddy!"

"Hmmm...let's see...To Teammates and Friends!"

Broadway almost gagged, but chugged as Tiger raised his glass, squinted his right eye as if inspecting a jewel, and downed it. Again his face lit up in a cockamamie grin.

"You Okay, buddy?"

"Greeeeeeeeat!" he roared. "Thanks for takin' me out tonight. I feel better already."

What a moron! Still can't tell.

"No problem, buddy! I owe you for all the times you cleared my crease."

Tiger was touched. His face flushed. It was the first time Broadway had ever acknowledged the sacrifices he made on-ice for him. Hoping the remark might spark a conversation, he added: "You're my teammate—nothing's more import-..."

Before he could finish, the goalie spun away.

"I'll get 'ya another root beer, or sarsaparilla. What's the god-damned difference? I feel like a fool making the distinction."

"There's a *big* difference!" Tiger protested.

Confident that Tiger could not tell the difference, Broadway dropped off a third spiked drink and wandered over to the bleached blondes who gathered like rats in a rag closet when he appeared.

"Drink up!" he chided, looking over his shoulder at the forlorn fighter.

"Hey, where ya' going, Broadway?"

"Got some business to attend to here."

One of Broadway's bimbos, knowing how to curry his favor, wrinkled her little nose. "Yuk! What's Beastie Boy doing here tonight?"

"Oh, just a little experiment. One of you won't mind keeping an eye on him? When he finishes his drink, give me a little pinch on the rear," he said, wiggling his butt and sidling up to the bustiest one in the bunch.

"I will! I will!" volunteered the pudgy one who insulted Tiger. "When Beastie Boy finishes, I'll pinch you."

"Thanks, honey," said Broadway, pecking her, and turning his attentions elsewhere.

Each time Tiger finished, Broadway was informed and in this way he was not long without a drink. Beyond attending to his cups, and belittling him to his back, Broadway ignored him, except for the occasional reassurance.

"On her way, buddy—just got word!"

Tiger felt great! Like a million bucks! *Win tomorrow and Boston's done.* He squinted at his watch. 9:00. *Gee, I wonder what's taking Suzy?* Rising unsteadily, he bulled his way to Broadway. Several of the women shot nasty looks, as he passed them.

Noticing the commotion, and Tiger's approach, Broadway cracked, "Hey, you stay at your table! I don't need a eunuch to guard my harem!"

"Hire him!" giggled the one watching Tiger. "No temptation there!"

"You leave that young man alone! He's got a big date tonight!"

"B-Broadway, it's b-been an hour," Tiger stuttered, grabbing the goalie for support, as suddenly he felt dizzy.

"Whoa! Hold on tight, little buddy. She's parking now. Valet—takes a few minutes, I'm sure you know. How 'bout another?"

"B-Broadway, I can't s-s-stay much longer. Just a quick intrah-duction. Big game tomorra'."

"Yea, yea drink up!" he said, shoving him a drink fetched by the blonde.

Tiger sat down, nervously looked at his watch again and considered leaving. But Suzy was parking already. Just one more, he thought.

"Hang in tight, Buddy, just around the corner now."

Just then, as everything hit him at once, Tiger turned morose. Never before had alcohol touched his lips, and you never quite know how it'll settle. For Tiger, anxious about the date, and tomorrow's game, his spirits plummeted.

A few tables away, a small group of women noticed the strange goings-on. They were out celebrating. At the Travelers, whenever someone got a promotion, or left the company, she was taken out. It was insurance tradition!

"Why does that tall guy with the perfect teeth keep passing that little guy drinks and then leave him?" whispered the guest of honor.

With straight, black hair, little makeup, and slacks, she looked nothing like the painted ladies in tight skirts flitting about Broadway. At 5'2"—she was Tiger's height, but half his weight. Glancing over, she was drawn to the odd-looking fellow, not as an object of curiosity, but of growing pity. Tiger caught her approach out of his good eye, half-rose, and extended a mangled hand.

"You must be Shooozy!"

"Oh, no, so sorry—I'm Gracie."

"Oh, um, I'm waiting for Shooozy."

"I'm so sorry!" she blushed, and about-faced.

"WAIT!"

"Are you sure? I don't want to interrupt anything."

Tiger motioned Gracie to sit, then stared straight down into his lap, with his hands folded on the table.

Gracie sat and smiled—but couldn't help staring. She had never witnessed anyone quite like this man. Several teeth were missing, his ears folded in strange patterns, and one eye didn't blink—but was he ever built! And that chest!!

"I wish mine were as big!" she blurted out, brushing into him, owing to the wine she had been sipping. Then laughing, she added, "But if it were, I guess I'd be over there," she said cocking her head over at Broadway's gaggle. They both laughed.

Surveying the odd sight across the table staring straight into his lap, Gracie's mind raced. *What does he do for work? Maybe he trains junkyard dogs? Or toils at a foundry with a poor safety record?* Giggling at her fanciful musings, she inspected him more closely. His hands looked like they'd been through a meat grinder. *A butcher, perhaps?* Judging from the green shirt, he must be a sports fan—and she was about to ask before Tiger beat her to the punch.

"Whaddaya do, Gracie?" he asked, looking up.

"I'm going to be a teacher," she volunteered self-consciously, expecting he might belittle her like the other actuaries at work.

"WOW!" he bellowed, his scars lighting up. "Visited a-a- lotta classrooms in my day and could they s-s-sure use someone like 'ya!"

Captivated by her revelation, and her looks, Tiger perked up, peppering her with questions. *Hmmm, seems to know a lot about schools! But he's coy about his own work. He's so shy, so vulnerable...*

"S-s-sorry," he stammered, as the conversation flowed. "Don' usually squawk so much. Guess I-I'm jes'..."

"No—I've enjoyed it!" said Gracie, interrupting. "You've been so supportive. What do you do for..."

"DRINK UP, everyone!" boomed Stan, clanging the bell. "LAST CALL."

It was 10:55—closing time. Gracie looked at her watch, as Broadway peered up over the blonde heads and smiled. *Sloshed off his gourd! Hah! I love it when a plan comes together.* Leaving with two of them ("low hanging fruit") for last call in New York ("Screw the Goodwin!"), he couldn't resist a parting shot.

"Hey, T-ger, I see you found your Soooooooozy!"

Passing Stan sponging off the bar, Broadway whipped out the needle again.

"Here's a tip for your service, Stanley. Cyclops is flat-out gonzo back there."

"You bastard!" said Stan, ripping the C-note in half.

"Hey, hey, I worked hard for that!"

As Broadway and the bimbos weaved their way out, and Gracie left with her friends, it fell on to Stan to drive Tiger home. He was in no condition to walk. As Tiger fumbled helplessly with the seat belt, Stan reached over and buckled it. Gunning it up Asylum hill, Stan noticed Tiger was asleep. Unbuckling him and pushing him up the stairs, he turned to open the door, and Tiger, unattended, stumbled.

"Are you okay, Tiger?" he asked, wheeling and holding him to keep him from falling. "Gee, sorry about all the rum and cokes. I shoulda known better."

"Sass-pa-rool-o!" Tiger corrected. "But jus' one. It jus', umm, dis-a-screwed wit' me. Guess I'm jus' tired."

Tiger unleashed a yawn.

"Thans fa bein' a fren', Stenly. I'll be fine. Big gem tomorra, 'ya know. Brooooinz."

As Stanley drove away, full of remorse, he passed a man in a battered hat, leaning against a lamppost in the moonlight, with tears glistening. Rube was re-living a century-old nightmare.

18. The Battle of New England

Pressure busts pipes.
—Evander Holyfield

"Where is he?" asked a distraught boy, gazing up at the window.

It was late afternoon on April 11, 1990, and the shades in the small room were drawn. Two terra cotta gargoyles to ward off evil spirits—and an occasional Bruins fan—stood sentinel on the ledge.

"It's not like him," said the boy's father gravely. "Not like him at all!"

It had been hours since the papers up north had unleashed the first salvos in "The Battle of New England." The *Herald's* Joe Fitzgerald had blasphemed Hartford fans as "15,000 actuaries in baseball caps and bowling shoes", before placing the small city in the cross-hairs:

> It's Buffalo with a skyscraper. It's two locals, dressed up as Jake and Elwood Blues, somersaulting at center ice during the first intermission, hoping for that big break which might net them a gig in Leominster.[38]

Boston scribes have long had a tradition of trashing an opponent on game day. The *Globe's* Dan Shaughnessy (who dubbed Hartford "America's File Cabinet") elevated the practice to an art. The *Herald's* Gerry Callahan could always be counted on to mount a campaign of Shock-and-Awe. But on this day the poison pen was Fitzgerald's:

> It's a dangerous town for hockey because it tends to dull the senses…Hartford is not a city as much as it is a sedative.[39]

The crowd beneath the window was growing anxious. Since Councilors, under pressure, had sanctioned Tiger's walk to work, hundreds gathered at a staging area for the short trek to the Civic Center. But it was 6:00 p.m., an hour before game time. Where was the defender of Hartford's honor?

"Why doesn't he *at least* signal?" asked Tyrone, a trombone player from Weaver High, nervously fingering his instrument.

"He *always* signals!" said a drummer, in a plumed hat. "Something ain't right in Denmark!"

"Maybe he's napping?" added some one hopefully. "This game is epic!"

It was true. The Whalers could all but end the series tonight, take a commanding 3-1 lead, and earn the respect that had eluded them.

> [Hartford is] a Cadillac being driven to center ice in the second admission as added incentive for two other locals who will attempt to shoot a dozen pucks through holes in a board that's been placed across the mouth of the goal, knee-slapping entertainment last seen in Mayberry RFD.[40]

"Maybe someone drugged him?" suggested a conspiracy theorist. "Did you read the papers? They're frothing up the Cretans up there."

At that, Tyrone the trumbonist could stand it no longer. Grabbing a fistful of pebbles, he hurled them up at the window, a flying alarm clock.

Inside, bubbles surfaced in a denture jar by the bed. An eye patch swayed in the breeze of a ceiling fan. Several more hung off a tie rack. A personally autographed photo of Miss Moose Jaw was tacked on the wall. The famous *Life* photo of the sad-faced clown "Willie the Tramp" at the Hartford Circus Fire of 1944 completed the spartan decor.

At the center, on a small bed, snored the hobbit-sized man on whose shoulders rested the hopes of a city. Folded neatly on a chair was a green jersey with the brash moniker "BEANTOWN BASHER."

Plunk! Plunk! Plunk!—the scattershot strafed the window.

The small man opened one eye, which took in no light—and a second which blinked. Yawning and shrugging, he flexed his arms and two drumlins peaked, and his neck fanned like an accordion.

Plunk! Plunk! Plunk! A second fusillade pummeled the window.

"Whoa! Wha-, Wha's that?"

Tumbling to the floor, he crawled on all fours, dragging behind the sheets. Pulling the shade, he threw open the window. A blast of cool air rushed in, as the Weaver High Band struck up a chorus of *Brass Bonanza*.

DAH DAH DAH dadadadada…

"Wha', what are you all doin' here?" he called down, his head throbbing as if pelted by the rocks.

"GAME FOUR, TIGER" shrieked Tyrone. "It's TONIGHT! It's NOW!!"

Just then, the bells of a distant church rang with the familiar 16 notes of the Westminster Chimes.

TI-GER YOU'RE LATE!
RUN! RUN! RUN! RUN!
THE GAME'S BE-GUN
RUN! RUN! RUN! RUN!

As the bell peeled seven times, signaling the hour, the urgency struck him like a punch to the solar plexus. Dashing down the stairs, two to a bound, he burst out the door barefoot. On cue, the band played.

DAH DAH DAH dadadadada...

With knees high, and thighs pumping, he broke free of the throng. Racing down Asylum Hill, across I-84, past the Soldier's and Sailor's Memorial Arch, the wind gusted in his face. Rounding Adajian's restaurant, he staggered down into the Civic Center lot—chest heaving. Dodging between the shiny rows of BMWs, he stumbled to the player's gate where Jacobs of the *Courant*, and Smith of the *J-I* awaited, pens poised.

"What the HELL'S going on, Tiger?"

Bulling past without a word, he staggered into the stadium bowels, weaving around the ESPN trucks and promotional Cadillac. In the arena, *Brass Bonanza*—heralding the Whalers arrival on-ice—blared as grim-faced fans scanned the whirling vortex of green below.

"Where's TIGER?"

"INJURED?"

"SCRATCHED?"

Nothing in *Goal* Magazine explained. As pale-faced Whalers warmed up, a murmur swept the stadium. Every lap or so, an anxious player looked over to the gate. Nothing!

"I can't believe he'd pull a stunt like this!" seethed Captain Ronnie Francis, slamming a puck into the net.

"Like going to battle without armor," snorted Kevin Dineen, wearing the "A" of Assistant Captain, as Boston's outsized goons circled with unchecked swagger.

Ulf Samuelsson, usually jabbering a mile a minute, stood mute. But one man, his face behind a mask, smiled.

"Let's go GUYS!" Broadway yelled, scraping the crease with his skates, an old trick to dull the ice. "Tonight's our NIGHT!"

On the other side, first one, then a second black-and-gold goon, brazenly crossed the red line over to the Whaler's side. Several of the smaller Whalers shrank back. Where was the man in green to prosecute such violations? Speculation ran rampant.

In the locker, Skip franticly pulled Tiger's gear on. Everything had been carefully laid out—everything except his jersey.

"Where's your sweater, Tiger?"

"Oh, no!" Tiger gasped, bolting for the door.

"There's NO time!" cursed Skip, grabbing Tiger's suspenders and getting a Nantucket sleigh ride.

Owing to his peculiar habit of wearing his jersey off-ice, Tiger did his own laundry. It was an unusual arrangement, for sure, and now on account of it there was not an XXXL on site. With Tiger's outsized frame, only one other would do.

"Wear Broadway's—I'll send some kid up the street for yours."

Skip pulled on the enormous jersey that makes a goalie in pads look like a handler of junkyard dogs. Moments before face-off, Skip tied the last skate and shoved him out onto the ice. Spotting him with the binoculars he used to ogle women in the upper sections, announcer Gilmartin hit the right note over the public address:

"Ladies and gentlemen, we have a LATE addition…"

With Tiger on the ice, *Brass Bonanza* never sounded so brassy. DAH DAH DAH dadadadada…

With confidence surging now, the fans took up a thunderous chant, "TI-GER. TI-GER. TI-GER…"

The fortified Whalers circled their enforcer, as trumpets and air horns blasted. Only one man did not join; every goalie, after all, is an island. From the innermost ring, Ronnie pressed his lips to Tiger's cauliflower ear, "We're gonna need 'ya tonight! It's gonna be old-time hockey. This game might hinge on your fists—maybe your stick. Be ready for either!"

"Huh?" said Tiger, his head spinning in the maelstrom of motion.

As the players peeled away, Tiger stood alone, revealed for the first time to all. Skating on wobbly ankles, he bee-lined it to the boards, hugging to the dasher. Half-way around, when his glass-eye popped out, as it was wont to, he crawled like a beaten fighter groping for a mouth guard. A few Bruins looked on and smirked.

"What the hell's wrong with you?" snarled Dineen, flicking the eye with his stick into his gloved hand. "Get your HEAD into the game!"

Athletes talk of being "in a zone", when time slows and the action flows to them. Tiger had that feeling—in a fight. But skating now as if mired in molasses, he heard Broadway shout.

"Hey, T-ger, do it for Sooozy!"

A glue-horse among Derby horses, a midget car among Indy racers, for two periods, on heart and fumes, he stayed in the race. And the Whale responded, taking a 5-2 lead into the biggest third period in team history.

In the locker room, as the Coach exhorted the team, suddenly he felt as if on the deck of a storm-tossed ship. Falling to the floor, he crawled to the bathroom where retching rumbled into the room. Coaches stopped mid-sentence, and players shifted uneasily—until one broke the mounting tension.

"Sounds like he won't be much help!"

"SHUT UP!" snapped Ronnie. "It's just nerves!" And Broadway just sat and smirked. Not another word was spoken.

To start the third, the Bruins, desperate to swing momentum, set a trap. On the opening faceoff, "MoFo" Jones slashed Ronnie, and Tiger, as he was conditioned to, sprang into action, arms like battering-rams.

On his approach, one leg buckled, his arms dropped, and "MoFo" caught him clean. Like a knife slashing through a blood bag, MoFo's fist ripped into Tiger's face, and he dropped, a red pool puddling beneath him.

"DOWN GOES TIGER!" boomed Kaiton over the radio. "Hartford's little warrior is DOWN."

Struggling to rise, but with MoFo looming, fist cocked, Tiger, his face rimmed in blood, rolled over.

"He's TURTLING," Kaiton gasped. "Tiger's rolled onto his back. He wants no part of MoFo Jones."

In Hartford, "TIGER LOSES FIGHT" would make headline news, but "TIGER TURTLES" was almost unprintable. He hadn't lost a fight since rookie season—and that was to Terry O'Reilly, not some pedestrian goon like Mofo Jones.

"I can't *believe* it," repeated Kaiton, rubbing his eyes.

Shielding the pitiful figure, Dineen and Francis towered over him. A man of great pride, Tiger wanted to rise—but couldn't.

"Help me, Ronnie, please!"

Grabbing an arm, Dineen and Francis lifted the battered fighter to his feet, but then his legs splayed and he pitched forward like a barrel of rum on a ship deck.

"Keep your blades on the ice, dammit!" Dineen barked.

Lugged like a sack of concrete to the penalty box, Tiger was out of it.

"Bend your knees and sit!" snapped Dineen, positioning Tiger's body into the box. The familiar surroundings seemed to orient him some.

"Did Terry O'Reilly do this to me?"

Reading his lips from her seat near the box, "Blue Line" Betty fought back tears; O'Reilly had retired five years ago. Gilmartin, the announcer, reached for the amber beverage he kept in a bottle marked "Water." On the ice, the Whalers shrank back, as Boston's bench surged. When the penalties were announced, Tiger was assessed an extra two minutes for "instigating."

"GET 'EM!" roared Bruins' Coach Milbury.

Boston exploded like a dam bursting: GOAL, GOAL, GOAL, three in minutes, knotting the score 5-5. For the first time in his career, boos rained down—and cat calls.

"HE'S A PAPER TIGER!"

"GO BACK TO MOOSE JAW!"

Sure he'd heard a lot worse in Boston and New York, but now they turned on him in Hartford. As his penalty expired, Tiger made the lonely skate across ice to a cascade of boos.

"HE'S A BUM!"

"Can't EVEN Fight!"

Slumped on the end of the bench, away from teammates—he was an outcast; worse, a pariah. No one reached over to tap his pads or tousle his blood-caked hair. Tiger sat alone, an island.

But with a minute to go, Ronnie rallied the team. With the puck on his stick, in the slot, he faked a shot, and redirected the puck to a blur of green racing in on the right. Tiger! And there it rested—the puck on his blade, the goalie down. All it would take was a flick!

His eye widened. Adrenaline surged. Long-suffering Hartford fans rose. It was destiny.

The gnome-sized man pulled his stick back above his shoulder. The fate of a struggling team and city rested on his wide back—and the thin blade of his child-sized stick. He swung with all his might.

Thwaaaaack—Claaaaang—Noooooooooooo...

The doleful echoes of that three-part harmony ring out decades later. Disbelieving fans collapsed back into their seats, having witnessed a shot that could kill a team—and crush a man's spirit. At the violent collision of rubber against crossbar, the puck fluttered high above confused heads towards center ice. Jubilant Whalers, arms raised in triumph, reacted slowly.

A cherry-picking Bruin at the blue line gathered the puck, as Hartford players awkwardly reversed. At center ice, 10 feet ahead of the nearest Whaler, he moved in on goal.

At the blue line, five strides ahead of a frantic chase pack, he bore in. A trailing defender thought for a moment about sliding his stick, but that would mean a penalty shot. He held back. The Whalers' fate was in Broadway's hands.

Puffing up like a cobra, the goalie gave the illusion of covering the net. With stick flat and glove fanned at his side, his position was text book. Broadway was master of his domain.

Swooping in on goal, the Bruin forward dipped his shoulder. Forced to respect the possibility of a shot, Broadway dropped to his knees and slid in the direction of the fake. In that instant, the left side was open. All it would take was a flick.

The fans rose, this time in horror. The stick blade, scraping along the ice, kissed the rubber.

"BRUINS SCORE!" shouted Fred Cusack, above the unleashed pandemonium, on Boston's TV 38. "The GREATEST comeback in Boston history! It's 6-5. I can't believe it!"

Broadway did not hesitate. With long, angry strides, he charged from his goal, whipping off his mask. Side-stepping ecstatic Bruins, and racing to the other end, he brandished his oversized stick over the crumpled figure on the ice.

"It's YOUR fault," he raged, raising his stick above Tiger.

And the fans in Hartford, to their everlasting shame, backed him.

"He's a GOAT—not a TIGER!"

"Go back to MOOSE JAW, ya' BUM!"

In the waning moments, the Whalers desperately tried to answer, but when the buzzer went off on April 11, 1990 it was a death knell. The Whalers lost 6-5. Look it up.

"A night that will live in infamy,"[41] wrote Alan Greenberg, in the *Courant*.

Russ Conway, of the *Eagle-Tribune*, compared Boston's win to a Houdini escape:

> Chained and handcuffed here last night, stuffed into the old black bank safe that had been dropped to the bottom of the river with an hour to escape sure death. Only a couple of air bubbles had surfaced when 40 minutes had ticked away.[42]

Back from dead, Boston beat Hartford in seven games, before reeling off 9 wins in 10, en route to the Finals—where victory can change a team's destiny.

For Hartford, the loss marked a slow, agonizing spiral into oblivion. Never again would the team finish above .500. Never again would they draw 500,000 fans—until too late. April 11, 1990 was a tipping point. Over the next seven years, the record was 195-282-64. The eighth was in Carolina.

If Boston had the "Curse of the Bambino"—*trade Babe Ruth and the Red Sox will not win a World Series*—then Hartford had the curse of the Tiger. Only the fate was worse: *lose to Boston and the team will die.*

19. Hockey Hobo

Every one is a moon, and has a dark side which he never shows to anybody.
—Mark Twain

Goats had lost games; goats had blown championships; but never before had a goat plunged a dagger into a team. Tiger was in a Hall of Shame all his own.

Bill Buckner's "wicket" legs cost the Red Sox the 1986 Series. Rube Waddell's "bum" shoulder blew the 1905 Series. Fred "Bonehead" Merkle's base running blunder kept the New York Giants out of the 1907 World Series.

But only one man alive would ever know the feeling of killing a team— and with it, a city's hopes and dreams. At game's end, Tiger dropped to center ice, as if felled by a bullet, the red line on either side of his head like blood from a gangland slaying.

In many ways his life ended. Benched, then cut, Tiger Burns never played another minute. In time, he became hockey's Miss Havisham, the Dickens spinster who, jilted at the altar, spent the rest of her days in a wedding dress. That was Tiger, but in a Whalers jersey. He never took it off.

The Old Guard, Ronnie, Kevin, and Ulf rushed to his side, shielding him from angry onlookers. Gliding by to the showers, Broadway braked, spraying a rooster-tail of shavings over the stricken fighter.

"Hey, T-ger, let's do it again tonight," he needled, whacking at him playfully with his oversized stick.

"You get the hell out a' here!" snarled Ronnie, as Broadway skated away, baiting hecklers all the way.

As the others peeled away to wash off the stench of the worst defeat in history, Ronnie kept a vigil at Tiger's side. A decade ago, the two had arrived together: Ronnie and his bodyguard. Only now the roles were reversed.

"It's not your fault, Tiger," he said softly.

Tiger lay motionless, his small body convulsing. When the Zamboni's engine revved, signaling to clear the ice, Ronnie gestured to Wayne the driver for another minute.

"There's still a lot of fight in us," he said, rubbing Tiger's neck as he might his child's.

Because Tiger was his protector, he had always seemed invulnerable to Ronnie. But now for the first time he saw just how vulnerable he was. When the team won, he was ecstatic. When they lost, he was inconsolable. He lived game-to-game.

"We're all feeling low now, Tiger. You'll come around."

Ronnie hurt too, but he had ballast in his life: a wife, a kid, a home. Tiger had no one. It was hard to keep an even keel in life's storms.

"Come for dinner tomorrow? Will ya', Tiger?"

He would never get an answer. Long after the fans left, the players dressed, and the lights dimmed, Wayne inched the Zamboni out on the ice around the edges.

"Wayne's here, Tiger. I'll leave you here a few minutes, but I'll see you in the locker room. Okay?"

He never would. The scoreboard flashing 6-5, Tiger lay frozen in time. In the end, even the Zamboni swerved around him. When he finally roused, the arena dark except for the scoreboard's glow, Tiger skated off- ice for the last time. Left behind, etched in tears, was a grotesque mask—The Shroud of Tiger, some called it.

Formerly amiable, he took a turn to the morose. The cartwheel, once his signature celebration, ceased. In bygone days, he twirled on ice, in malls and parks and meadows. From that night forth, he ceased.

The eye patch, once a vanity, he wore no more. In his heyday, his left eye was covered with one of a hundred colorful patches. Now shuffling home on Asylum Hill, his dead eye stared out, rolled into his skull.

But Hartford folks, sore at first, could never abandon him. Cut loose from hockey, he had standing offers from the fire department and Union Stage Hands to drive a forklift.

"Tiger, we LOVE you," revelers called out, spotting him wandering late at night.

"Please don't," he mumbled, shuffling into the shadows. For Tiger, the hardest part was to hear kind words. To those who feel unworthy, they cut like stones. "I'm sorry," he mumbled.

Of course, Tiger had no way of knowing then what would come to pass with the team. But he felt it in his bones, the way an old sailor feels a change in weather.

When you betray what you love most, there is only one honorable course: to leave. So one night, unable to bear the shame, he walked down Asylum, his final act penning a note to the Schmidleys:

"I'll never forget what you did for me. Love, Tiger."

He had so much passion for the game—and the Whale. When he lost both, something had to give. Like Fischer, the crazed chess champion, and Nash, the mad mathematician, he came un-moored.

Hartford, alas, had known abandonment before. Olmsted, who built Central Park and Boston's Emerald Necklace, never built a great park for his hometown. His lone project, the Hartford Insane Retreat, was eclipsed by his work at McLean Hospital, Boston's great asylum—and when he went mad, that is where he went to die.

Sam Colt, who built the guns that tamed the west, died young—and so did his company. Today the famous rampant colt weathervane crowns a decaying hulk by the Connecticut River.

Harriet Beecher Stowe, "the little lady that wrote the book that started the Great War", lost a child in that river. Inconsolable, she wandered into neighbor's gardens and into their homes to play sad melodies on the piano. When she died, she was buried near Boston at a school where her husband once taught.

And the great Twain, after a disastrous investment in a typesetting machine with 18,000 moveable parts, went bankrupt. Forced on an arduous lecture tour to five continents, he left behind his home on Farmington Ave.:

> To us our house was not insentient matter—it had a heart and a soul and eyes to see us with; and approvals and solicitudes with deep sympathies... We never came home from an absence that its face did not light up and speak out its eloquent welcome—and we could not enter it unmoved.[43]

After five years, he returned to find that his daughter Suzy had died in the home. He could never live there again

And so, on a gloomy night, Tiger walked down Asylum a last time, turning north on the interstate. From the breakdown lane, he looked back on the city he had defended with his blood for a decade. An 18-wheeler barreling by almost toppled him.

"Get out of the road, ASSHOLE!" yelled a trucker with New York plates.

For two hours, he trudged on. At midnight, tramping into Windsor Locks, he spotted a freighter idling in the rail yard ahead. The smoke from the engine shot high into the air and was whipped away in the swirling wind. Spying an open boxcar ahead, Tiger walked toward it. He had miles to go before he could sleep.

20. Northern Lights

He knew by the streamers that shot so bright
That spirits were riding the northern light
—Sir Walter Scott

Crammed into a Canadian-Pacific boxcar, stacked with scrap metal, Tiger chased the Pole Star. As the freighter slowly gathered steam, every clickety-clack of the rolling steel wheels taunted him:

"Lose The CUP! Lose The TEAM!"

"Lose The CUP! Lose The TEAM!"

Shifting restlessly on the metal bed, seeking the one position where an iron rod did not impale him, he gazed out and up into the sky, his lone eye telescoping on the stars of the Northern Crown. Chasing it was Orion, The Hunter, the one forever in pursuit, the prize destined to elude. Even the heavens mocked him.

The torturously slow freighter rocked and rambled into the night, whistling through Springfield and Burlington, past a sign "Latitude 45 North—Midpoint Equator to North Pole." On and on, Hartford's hockey hobo chugged across the prairies of Canada—debarking in Churchill, on the Hudson Bay, fabled home to polar bear and night sky.

To ease a heavy heart, and idle away long nights, he took up the pursuit of whalers of bygone centuries. Tiger became a scrimshander.

Scrimshaw is the lonely sailor's art of decorating whale's teeth. For whalers of yore, who left hearth and home in pursuit of sperm whale, the scenes were of a distant port, a faraway love or the hunt itself. But Tiger's oeuvre reflected a bleaker journey.

Picasso had two phases: "rose" when all was bright and "blue" when all was gloomy. But Tiger's art had but one: death—a tiger burying its fangs into a whale; a whale harpooned by a hockey stick; a whale and tiger beached on the blood-soaked shores of a river. This last he wore round his neck like a leper's bell, giving fair warning to all he encountered: "Unclean, I'm Unclean."

In summer, the yodels of loons on Hudson Bay hinted that other mad spirits abounded. To subsist, he took up silversmithing, fashioning trinkets that sold in southern cities like Winnipeg and Thunder Bay.

Three hundred nights a year, shimmering shafts of emerald light dance across the sky, making Churchill home to the world's most spectacular Northern Lights displays. Japanese legend has it that fortune will come to a child conceived under the Northern Lights, and so in his wandering Tiger encountered buses of Aurora "chasers."

In winter, he hunted polar bear. When the bay froze, the bears, called Nanook, or "white kings of the North", gathered on the shores. On hind legs, some stand 10 feet, as eco-tourists, in armored vehicles, chase them.

On brutal-cold nights, when the wind kicked up cyclones, Tiger set out across the bay, bow in hand, his beard frozen-white. When once his last arrow did not fell a wounded bear, he toppled him with his fists—adding to his legend in exile, and so mixing bear's with Bruin's blood on his green jersey.

But in hockey-mad Canada, even in the north, Tiger could not escape news of his struggling team. Hockey was the talk of the occasional arctic adventurer cocooned in seal fur pushing a sled. One prospector, on seeing the blood-stained jersey, but not recognizing the hermit within, spoke of the recent sale of the team—"for a whopping $47M, no lie!"

"Gee, who could afford that in Hartford?" Tiger wondered.

Warming his hands by the fire, the old-timer informed him that Peter Karmanos, of Detroit, could—"That rascal could!"

Cutting strips of sizzling meat, Tiger gestured impatiently with his hunting knife for him to speak more. The man would have to sing for his supper!

"What does it mean?" he asked the wizened man whose lined face testified that he had seen a bit of the world and knew its ways.

"Nothing good!" he spat out, the juices dribbling into his white beard, then bolstering it with a bit of timeless wisdom. "Beware of Greeks bearing gifts!"

"Huh?"

"Don't you see?" he exclaimed, bolting the meat down, and cleaning his beard with his wrist. "The money is a Trojan Horse! The barbarians are already inside the gates."

"Huh?" said Tiger, but feeling uneasy now.

The old man's riddles confounded the fighter, so he stated it plainly.

"Your team will leave one day. Take it from an old gold prospector. They will follow the trail of the money."

The man's prophesy shook Tiger. "To where?" he pleaded to know.

"Somewhere that glimmers brighter," he said, waving a gloved hand at the green-shimmering sky.

"Hartford will NOT let it happen!" Tiger protested. "They will FIGHT back! For ten years, I taught them how!"

The old prospector, who could glimpse into the future, wiped his mouth of the juices and shook his head, as the dogs yipped by the roaring fire.

"Without local owners, after a bad season or two, they will join John Paul Jones' footlocker at the bottom of the sea. Sadly, that is the way of the world, my friend."

"Nooo!" Tiger wailed, his vain protest carried away in the winds.

"I'm sorry," said the old man, thanking Tiger for the warm fire and meat, and with a lash of the whip, mushing off in search of distant treasures.

Tiger, who could hear the silent toll of the leper's bell, could hear the death knell to the south. Unable to bear the shame of complicity, he abandoned his wind-battered cabin and ventured across the frozen bay. Pushing out into the wind-swept wild, farther than ever before, he came at last to a floe, at the edge of slushy waters.

"It's time," he said simply.

Dangling a size 5 foot above the slush, one more step and he would sink like an anvil. Dressed in his green jersey, the one he never took off, he looked about a last time, struck now by the crystalline beauty—and swirling green lights, like shafts from heaven.

"You gave me everything I ever dreamed of. A home, a family, a team—and I betrayed you," he sobbed.

Like many a ship-wrecked Whaler before, he prepared to step into his watery grave. Raising his foot, he looked down, when suddenly out of his good eye, 60 feet straightaway, appeared a man, as if he had shimmied down on a shaft of light. The apparition clutched a straw hat in the blustery winds.

"Who the hell are you?" demanded the startled fighter, stepping back.

The wild-eyed man, in billowing flannels, grabbed a hunk of ice, reared back with his left arm, and hurled it at Tiger, striking him on the thigh, an inch below his pocket.

"Hey!!" Tiger howled, rubbing his leg. "You mighta knocked out an eye. Not everyone's got an extra to spare."

Pointing to his pocket, near where the spot he struck Tiger, the stranger dug his hand in and removed its contents, imploring Tiger to do the same.

"Oh, ya' want my silver, do 'ya? Well, all ya' had to do was ask!" hollered Tiger, still sore over the ice ball.

Tiger emptied his pocket of the coins within, watching them roll to a stop on the ice.

"There!" he said, glaring at the stranger 20 yards away. "Now leave me be!"

Again, Tiger positioned his feet for the fateful plunge, but again from the corner of his eye he caught the majestic sweep of the left arm, and a second ice ball struck him squarely on the pocket of his *other* leg. Now, Tiger was pissed!

"Hey, I used ta' be a pretty fair fighter in my day," he warned. "All ya' had to do was ask, I said!"

Although angry, and sore on both legs, Tiger couldn't help but admire the man's arm. Both strikes, twisting into the wind, had curved to within an inch of the pockets he wanted emptied.

"Half my riches ain't enough, eh? Well, here's the rest! Now leave me be!"

Digging into the other pocket, Tiger came up empty, only a ball of lint, which he held up for the stranger to see, and released it into the wind.

But the stranger was not appeased. Adamantly, he gestured for Tiger to dig into the pocket again, *deeper.* His bald-faced greed angered Tiger.

"Ya' think I mighta missed something, eh? Well, I'll show 'ya!"

Reaching deep into his pocket, he pulled it inside out, and to his surprise, a part of the lining almost, was a tattered card. Holding it up in the lights, he squinted and read:

Gresilda Farrell

"Gracie"

Actuary

Hartford, CT

On the back was a still legible address. Looking up, he was surprised that the strapping southpaw had vanished back into the shimmering lights from whence he came.

"Where are you? *Who* are you?" he hollered.

The words echoed unanswered into the arctic night. Was it the guiding hand of Providence or the strong left arm of someone else that rescued Tiger from a watery grave that night? He would never know.

"Thank you, my friend!" he hollered, the words swept away.

That night the dazzling lights of Churchill shone brilliant. The arctic winds kicked up crystal cyclones. Tiger did not sleep in an icy grave. He sat down beneath the Northern Lights, and wrote a letter.

21. The Erstwhile Actuary

Certainly there is no nobler field for human effort than the insurance line of business—especially accident insurance. Ever since I have been a director in an accident-insurance company I have felt that I am a better man. I do not care for poetry anymore. I do not care for politics...But to me now there is a charm about a railway collision that is unspeakable.
—Mark Twain

Hi Gracie,

Remember me, Tiger? Let me replenish your depleted memory banks. It was a long time ago.

From the top— I have one eye, a bashed nose, broccoli ears, and scars. That about covers my face! You probably meet lots of guys like me.

I'm short, but my chest made you squeal out, "I wish mine was as big!" Remember me, Gracie?

We met the night of April 10, 1990 at Chuck's, the last happy one of my life. There was something I didn't tell you then. I'm a Hartford Whaler...

How could Gracie forget? Everything from the offbeat name to the oftbeat face was seared in her memory. Oh, and Gracie knew Tiger's secret.

It wasn't that she was a hockey fan or went to the games; she wasn't and didn't. Gracie was busy with insurance exams, and that left little time for outside interests.

But April 10, 1990 was a milestone! After years of unswerving dedication, she was leaving insurance—for not-so-green pastures. Gracie wanted to become a teacher. Not many left The Travelers like that, especially a rising star like Gracie, who was on a sure path to insurance immortality.

The honors she had accrued were ample testimony: an indoor parking spot; a cubicle near a window; an access card to a wash room with double-ply paper and bulbs encircling the mirror like a Hollywood dressing room. Few had accomplished so much! So quickly!!

"People toil a lifetime for those things," reminded her boss. "If you keep your nose to the grindstone, even greater laurels lie ahead."

The plastic plant in her cube had already been upgraded to a faux bamboo. How far away could a live fern be? Watered daily by the Corporate Green Thumb! Rumor was that a secretary had seen a requisition for a cherry wood desk to replace the standard-issue, metal gray.

In five years, the square footage of her cubicle had doubled, and the walls were higher, almost to the ceiling. How far away could a swinging door be?

"I'll have to knock to visit!" said her friend Rebecca. "Wouldn't that be a hoot?!"

Now, Gracie was not unappreciative of the trappings of success. She enjoyed a padded chair with wheels as much as the next person. But even as she sat ensconced in such splendor, she wrestled with questions that did not seem to trouble the other actuaries.

"Why the heck does any of this matter?"

That question, posed provocatively, arched eyebrows at the lunch table.

"It's not that insurance is without social value," Gracie added hastily, feeling the glares. "All the exam books proclaim as much."

"Truer words were never spoken!" declared Mr. Doe, one of the actuaries, picking his teeth of crab meat with the serrated edges of a pocket protector. "By pooling premium and spreading risk, insurance is specially constructed to be socially useful."

"Who can argue with that?" Gracie conceded, wilting under the heat.

Gracie was out of step with the rest. Their cubicles were festooned with photos of Ferraris and BMWs, like Stars of Bethlehem above their computers. It made her feel self-conscious about the photos of the two children she sponsored overseas in South America.

"Why are you posting pictures from National Geographic?" asked Mr. Doe, dismissively.

She wanted to strangle them all by their red power ties!

Gracie's head was swimming with ideals ("Rubbish!" Mr. Doe termed it.). She wanted to be on the front lines of social change, not hiding behind some actuarial table. To her, insurance was lifeless and soul-deadening— far removed from *actual* people in actual need.

"I want to see the people we're helping—touch them. Is it asking *too* much?"

Yes, everyone agreed, it was. "Go into claims," counseled Mr. Doe breezily. "You could make regional VP in no time—run your own fiefdom."

In quiet desperation, Gracie had toyed with the idea of joining a convent, even spending a cloistered weekend. When the guys in the office heard about that stunt, they were outraged.

"We're not good enough?!" screamed Mr. Doe, throwing his hands up, his Y-chromosome ruffled.

Truth be told, many of the guys had crushes on her. With straight black hair to her waist, almond eyes, full lips that formed an easy smile, she was, many thought, dazzling.

"Not too hard on the eyes!" appraised Mr. Doe over bourbon at The Hartford Club.

At 30, Gracie had not given up on "finding a man", but the quest was on hold. She was fed up with the actuaries, so grim and humorless. To her, their anal natures begged the question: *Are hemorrhoids catching?*

Before settling down, Gracie first wanted a satisfying career. April 10, as it happened, was the first step. That night, she was out celebrating the gut-wrenching decision to leave insurance—for teaching.

For Gracie, it was a chance to be on the front lines of the day's greatest social battle: improving "inner city" schools. In Hartford, the state had taken over the schools and the troubles were all over the papers. Undaunted, Gracie was ready to make the leap.

"The timing is right!" she told herself, but doubts lingered.

Then a funny thing happened on the way to the chalkboard: She met Tiger. It wasn't his looks that immediately attracted her—but the importance of this next can not be overstated: they did not *repel* her either.

"I like a man whose 'rough around the edges!'" she confided to Rebecca. "Shows character! Look at that tall guy with the perfect teeth he's with. He's *too* smooth."

Gracie, it seemed, was always out of step. Tiger, for his part, was thrilled to meet someone born in Hartford—and living there still.

"The fish that got away!" he joked, slapping his muscular thigh. "The one that slithered through the trawler nets of New York and Boston!"

Shy and respectful, he attracted her right away. The actuaries all preened like peacocks whenever they passed an exam. *Look at me,* they shouted, puffing out their puny chests.

"What's the big deal?" she wanted to scream.

Not once did he even hint that he was a star on Hartford's only pro team. She wasn't accustomed to modesty like that—and found it becoming! Here was this athlete with legitimate yodeling rights and all he said—and reluctantly—was he had started a foundation to help city kids. *That* impressed her!

"If I can help in any way, please call," she offered, handing over her last business card.

As she shared her dreams, unlike the actuaries, whose faces glazed over, Tiger's lit up!

"You'll be a GREAT teacher!" he boomed. "It'll be hard! I gotta be honest—I been in a few classrooms. But if you have patience—'specially wit' yourself—and if 'ya show the kids you care, *really* care, they'll respond. I promise 'ya."

All the actuaries had belittled her. She wanted to hug him then and there. When she left Chuck's that night, she felt at peace. That was Tiger's gift to her.

And so she desperately wanted to learn more about the odd fellow with the improbable physique, who artfully steered the conversation away from himself that night. How could such a fellow have his own foundation? What does he do? How on earth did he achieve that outré look? Those nagging questions would not elude her long.

Twenty minutes later, on her porch, feeding feral cats, as was her nightly custom, when she bent down to pick up the *Courant*, staring up from page 1 was Tiger beating a Boston Bruin to a bloody pulp.

"The PHILANTHROPIST!!" she shrieked, sending a three-legged cat flying off the porch.

Beneath the gruesome photo, the caption read: "Another masterpiece painted in scarlet by Tiger Burns, Hartford's fistic impresario."

"FISTIC IMPRESARIO?!"

Feverishly flipping ahead, she read where he had won three fights, before "earning" a game misconduct and "serenading the Gallery Gods with the bare-chested flagellating of his full-rigged sailor's tattoo."

"SAILOR'S TATTOO??"

Gracie's head was spinning with the onrush of vivid imagery. Sitting herself down, she struggled to process it all.

"Take a deep breath. Get a grip now."

Now Gracie could never condone mayhem and violence. She was an insurance person, after all. But she hadn't spent her whole life in Hartford without absorbing this: "Those Bruins are rascals! Serves 'em right, I'm sure!"

By the end of so tantalizing a story, Gracie had a strong urge to attend her first game. The story noted that game 4 was tomorrow night, and if the Whalers won, they could seize a 3-1 lead.

"The most important game in team history," the story concluded.

"Maybe I'll see for myself!" she mused, dropping off to sleep to lurid visions of sailor's tattoos and fistic masterpieces.

April 11, 1990 was her last day at work, and she slipped out to snap up a ticket. And such was her naiveté that she actually believed she could—hours before a Stanley Cup game against Boston.

"Sold out for months!" laughed the ticket-seller.

Obviously Gracie knew little of the rabid atmosphere surrounding the Hartford-Boston rivalry—otherwise, she wouldn't have bothered. Dejected, she wandered out to Asylum, the usually quiet street thronged with black-and-gold rowdies. Gracie hadn't taken two steps when a cigar-chomping man in a "Cam Neeley" jersey accosted her.

"Need a ticket, sweetie?"

An angel of mercy!

"Yes, I do. But it's a sellout I'm told."

The cigar-chomping man folded his beefy arms and addressed the issue head-on:

"Honey, in life there are three kinds of people. Those who make things happen; those who watch things happen; and those who wonder what happened."

Then pausing for effect: "Sweetie, you have before you a category #1 guy. How many do 'ya need?"

Fanning out five ducats, each picturing a Stanley Cup looming above the Hartford skyline, he added, "Behind the penalty box—so close you could spit on that goon Burns who practically lives in there."

Holding them up, he belched out a plume of smoke.

"How much?" she coughed.

"Two-Hundred-Fifty, and a steal at that!"

Now Gracie hadn't spent years poring over actuarial tables to be bamboozled by some category-1, rip-off artist from Boston. "That's OUT-rageous!" she cried pointing at the clearly marked $25 price after the cloud cleared. "You ought to be ashamed!"

"Look, sweetie! I didn't drive down here to gawk at the insurance buildings. Take it or leave it!"

A quick trip to an ATM and the fleecing was completed. Gracie was going to her first game—but without a hotdog or program. From the highest, nose-bleed seat, right beside the Category #1 guy, who sloshed beer, puffed cigars, and hurled insults, Gracie's first game was one she'd never forget.

Like the rest of Hartford, she thrilled to the early play, with the Whalers staking a 5-2 lead, and *Brass Bonanza* playing like a broken record. But then in the third things went awry—horribly awry!

On-ice for four unanswered goals, Tiger lost a momentum-changing fight and clanged a "bunny" off the cross-bar that would have sealed victory. At the final buzzer, when he collapsed at center ice, she cried out, but her feeble voice, on account of the great distance and irritating smoke, fell short.

"Tiger, I'm here!"

Lingering with the last suffering fans, she wound her way down from the 300s to the 200s to the 100s. On the concourse, she pleaded with security guards pushing fans out into the streets.

"That's my boyfriend down there," she said, pointing to Tiger down on the ice. "He needs me!"

"Sorry, Mam, that's Tiger," said veteran guard Juan Ortiz, "He's got no girlfriend. Everyone knows it," and ushering her outside where Boston fans were already laying siege to The Russian Lady.

Returning to the one place she had ever known him to be, she huddled with shell-shocked fans at Chuck's and waited—and waited. At 1:00, Stan the bartender stated the obvious.

"Don't think he's showing, Mam. That was an awful tough one."

She read where he was benched, and later cut. A 10-year career linked with the greatest moments in team history snuffed out like a candle. For the first time since rookie year, he left Hartford—and vanished.

Gracie followed her dream and became a teacher where she learned first-hand how Tiger was revered, as her students wore his jersey, posted his pictures, and dressed as him at Halloween. The memories die hard.

Gracie's sorrow matched any kid's. Will he call? I gave him my last card. As the weeks and months passed, it seemed unlikely.

"I'm lucky to have met him once," she consoled herself. "What girl wouldn't be?"

But she yearned to learn more. Trudging to the library, she dug into mountains of yellowed newspapers. And what they reported no longer surprised her: "Boy, that dude fought a lot!"

But story after story chronicled his work with children—and always there was mention of cartwheels. On ice! In streets! At Malls! Was there a place where that zany guy was not twirling head-over-heels for Hartford?

"What a peculiar habit!"

Yet she had not observed a single one! Turning it all over, he seemed a man of contradictions: happy-go-lucky outside, yet pained inside— tragicomic. From their lone conversation, it was obvious *to her* he was lonely. For that, she had a keen eye, a caring eye, a *woman's* eye.

Pondering it all over, he seemed like sort of a civic treasure, a statue to snap a picture with, or an icon to sign a puck. But at the end of the day, when everyone went home, he was alone—with no one to lean on when things got tough.

"It's terrible," she sobbed, wishing she could reach out one last time.

22. Tiger's Proposal

> Give me a lever long enough and a fulcrum on which
> to place it, and I shall move the world.
> —Archimedes

News of a dispatch from Tiger Burns would have made headlines the world over. It had been four years since anyone had news of hockey's vanished hero. With trembling hands, Gracie opened his second letter:

Can I propose to you?

"He's PROPOSING!" Gracie's heart leapt from her chest. Carefully reading:

> *Here's my proposal—I need someone to run my charity. My life savings are in it—every penny. It's my last bequest to Hartford and amounts to...*

"MY GOD!"

Gracie was thunderstruck. Tiger lived frugally, she had read, and hockey players made good money, everyone knew, but that little guy had amassed $1 million dollars for his foundation. As for the rest of his paltry belongings:

> *Sell everything! But keep the photos of clown with bucket, and Miss Moose Jaw. Put all money in my account in Hartford National Bank.*

Alas, since Tiger left, Hartford's bank had been taken over by Shawmut of Boston, then Fleet, and Bank of America. Gracie knew that sort of plundering irked him. She read once where he once gave a talk at the Hartford Club urging them to fight back. Tiger never tired of standing up for Hartford on-ice and in the board room. Maybe she should move the account? Already she was thinking like an Acting Director!

> *The foundation needs a name. I was going to call it "Tiger Tracks", but a New York firm that makes dune buggy tires issued a "cease and desist" order. Ruined my plan them bullies! So I was planning to hold a contest in schools...*

Gracie was swept off her feet by Tiger's proposal. Here was a chance to do good on a scale that she never could have imagined. "A million dollars can bring a lot of smiles!" Moreover, it wouldn't interfere with teaching, and best, it would put her in regular contact with Tiger.

"Win! Win! Win! I accept your proposal, Mr. Tiger Burns!"

Gracie responded immediately to the P.O. Box in Churchill. True to his spirit, her first action was to move the money to a local bank. Next was the contest. As incentive to name Tiger's charity, Gracie decided the winner should get two season tickets to the Whalers.

"Another way to support the home team," she said, quickly getting the hang of the new role.

Entries flooded in. It had been years since the kids of Hartford had an opportunity to interact with Tiger, if only by proxy, and Gracie read every last one:

'BRAWLERS for SCHOLARS',

'TATTOOS for TOTS',

'ONE EYE on HARTFORD' ...

On and on they went in this vein, until bleary-eyed Gracie wanted to scream.

"They're all missing the point! Can't they see? Tiger's *not* just about fighting and deformities."

In a pique, she tore up stacks of entries, tossing the shreds into the air. As colorful confetti rained down, Gracie stated her case plainly: "Yes, he fought—A LOT! There's no denying it! But Tiger stood for more than that!"

Shaking the paper shreds out of her hair, Gracie stood firm. By executive fiat, she rejected all 5,000 submissions, 500 from one boy alone.

"I won't make a mockery of his legacy! Maybe I'll have to fight those dune buggy folks in court? 'TIGER TRACKS', at least, shows that he left something behind. Yes, it's the best of a bad lot!"

Gracie was feeling the heat now. With each passing day, the media was badgering her for results. And she had nothing to show. Maybe she'd have to re-open the contest—claiming her cleaning lady tossed out all the entries? She needed a name—fast.

"Okay, Smarty Pants, let's see what *you* can come up with?" she challenged herself.

It wasn't so easy! Like the kids, she fell into the obvious traps:

"CAULIFLOWERS for KIDS",

"The GENEROUS GOON FUND",

"STITCHES for STUDENTS"...

"Even I'm missing the point!" she wailed, tossing her hands up. "And now I've ripped up all the entries."

Panicked, she tried piecing them together, but it was no use. She had mismanaged Tiger's contest. Gracie was a failure!

Sobbing, she tossed and turned through a restless night. The contest was consuming her.

"Why did I take this on? It's killing me!"

Rolling from one side of the bed to the other, back and forth, over and over, the answer to her worries suddenly struck her like an avalanche check.

"CARTWHEELS! I've been turning them all night! 'CARTWHEELS for KIDS.' Eureka!!"

To Gracie, nothing symbolized Tiger like his cartwheels. Those simple, joyous movements, a pleasure to all, spoke eloquently to his exuberance for town and team. People just loved seeing that small brute turn head-over-heels like a child's jack. What a sight to behold it must be!

"Maybe one day I'll see myself?" she thought, a shy smile forming on her lips as she dropped off to sleep.

23. The Teacher

In the first place God made idiots. This was for
practice. Then He made School Boards.
—Mark Twain

Schools were tripping all over themselves to get people with "real world" experience. But before Gracie could fulfill her "Welcome Back Kotter" dreams of teaching at home, she first had to contend with the opposition: the Boston Public Schools were making a run for her services.

"You can live *very* comfortably on the salary we're offering," said the Superintendent on his first recruiting call. "And remember quality of life is our greatest asset up here!"

By the third call, Gracie's starting salary in Boston was above the Math Chair in Hartford. Caught up in the whirlwind, she felt herself buckling.

"I'm leaning to Boston," she confided to Rebecca, her friend.

It was blasphemy! As a girl, she had skated at Bushnell Park, smelled the roses at Elizabeth Park, and shopped at G. Fox at Christmas. For decades, she listened to Bob Steele on WTIC-AM. Gracie was Hartford through-and-through, yet here she was chucking it all away—for filthy lucre, no less.

She wouldn't be the first. J. Pierpont Morgan learned to prepare balance sheets on Asylum Avenue while selling tickets for childhood shows. "Pip", as he was called, was sent to Boston for polish and then New York for prize.

Marcus Camby, the basketball prodigy from Hartford High, played college at UMass, and pro with the Knicks. As with Morgan, greatness was born in Hartford, seasoned in Boston, and "cashed" in New York.

Bill Rogers won the Boston and New York Marathons four times. In Faneuil Hall, a plaque proclaims Hartford's native son "Boston's Billy." Again and again, the bullies use Hartford as training grounds, then plundering fields—and dumping grounds.

Before signing the contract, Gracie asked herself a last troubling question: "What would Tiger do?" She knew damned well! As a free agent, he had refused double-salary to play up north, noting simply "I prefer Hartford." And no amount of broadsheet bullying ("Hub Bids Moron Adieu") could sway him. In the end, he called it a "no-brainer"—and for once the Boston papers agreed.

Inspired by Tiger, Gracie tore up the contract. But teaching at home would not make it easier. Like many new teachers in crowded schools, Gracie was a "gypsy", without a home room, rushing from class to class, with books, in the three minutes allotted. Stationed on the front lines of Colt's hometown, she was given little ammo.

First period, she had Kevin Karl, known in the teacher's lounge as "one to keep an eye on." Every teacher with seniority had passed on him—and so he landed in Gracie's Algebra class.

"Good Morning, Miss Farrell!" he greeted her first day, cherub-like.

"Good Morning, Kevin Karl!" she replied, sure that this fine, young man had been given a bad rap.

At the bell, she sprang into action, scaffolding from a short history lesson into the subject at hand:

"Renee Descartes, the French philosopher, who famously uttered *Cogito ergo sum* ('I think therefore I am'), invented what today we call the Cartesian Plane."

Turning to the board, she traced a vertical y-axis and a horizontal x-axis (*Thwack! Thwack!*) and labeled them.

"The intersection point where both axes meet is called the origin."

Thwack!

"Class, the x-coordinate, or ordinate, is the first element of the ordered pair...."

Thwack!

"The y-coordinate, or abscissa..."

Thwack!

Every time she added a point to the Cartesian plane, Kevin Karl removed a dripping wad of gum from his mouth and lobbed it up at the TV screen above the teacher's desk. If Gracie heard anything, she mistook it for the crackling synapses of 45 eager students. *Thwack! Thwack!* At period's end, 24 gobs of saliva-ridden gum plastered the screen and Gracie hadn't a clue.

The gum gone, Kevin Karl pulled out a screw driver and removed the screws holding his desk together, lending it the stability of a house of cards. (His summer detention had required him to assemble hundreds.) At the bell, dismounting carefully, he bowed and praised her for "the best lesson of the year, so far!"

Moments later, when the Math Chairman arrived, his eye zeroed in on the saliva oozing from the TV. "What kind of custodian of *my* room are you?" he roared, sending her students into fits of giggling.

As Head of the Union, he resented Gracie as one of those "real world types" brought in to clean up the "mess" career teachers had made of the schools. Well, he'd show them a mess! Taking out a camera, he took a step back and aimed at the TV.

Click. Click.

Angling for a better shot, he brushed Kevin Karl's desk and it flattened like a pancake. Wheeling around, he snapped that, too—*Click. Click.*—as Gracie dashed off in tears to her next class, across a courtyard and up three flights of stairs.

In his formal report, the Math Chair described the TV screen ("a veritable Petri dish for the breeding of typhoid"), the desk ("looking like a suicide bomber had alit thereupon"), before summing up with this damning indictment: "My Honors Students were appalled!"

Gracie was so discombobulated when she arrived breathless at her next class, after the bell, she made the classic rookie mistake.

"Good morning class, my name is Gracie Farrell." At that benign utterance, her face turned ashen. "Wait! It's Miss FARRELL. Miss FARRELL is my name."

Too late! The Pandora's Box was opened—and by her own hand.

"Good Morning, GRACIE!" the class sang out in unison.

"Miss Farrell!" she pleaded. "Rhymes with barrel, carol, stylish apparel! It's FARRELL."

"Wassup, *Gracie?*"

For the next month, around every corner, at assemblies and athletic events, from the cafeteria back and auditorium front, the cry rang out: "Hi GRACIE!"

Old guard teachers, appalled that her students addressed her with such "familiarity", icily called her "Miss Farrell." They were the only ones.

But eighth period Geometry took top honors. Jackie, the new boy from Boston, arrived in the district with a suspected, but not clinically diagnosed, case of Tourette's Syndrome. Jackie was the talk of the teacher's lounge, supplanting even Kevin Karl.

"I read his file and almost died!" gasped a secretary.

Tourette's is a mysterious syndrome of involuntary tics, movements and vocal reproductions. A snippet from the World Health Organization appeared in Jackie's folder:

> Common simple vocal tics include throat-clearing, barking, sniffing, and hissing. Common complex vocal tics include the repetition of particular words, and sometimes the use of socially unacceptable (often obscene) words (coprolalia), and...

According to his thick dossier, Jackie was a barker (*Rooof-rooof*), a hisser (*Hissssss*)—and, most regrettably for the new teacher, a vile and unrepentant coprolaliac. *Fuck Gracie!* One beleaguered teacher wrote it was like having "a dog, a snake and a truck driver" in the room at once!

Every teacher who had reviewed his file ("a compendium of filth to make a muleskinner blush") passed when the decision came down from the School Board to "mainstream" him. That decision, based on the opinion of one lone-wolf psychologist, would bedevil Gracie for months:

"I may be wrong, but in my opinion Jackie is just an 'attention getter.' His is a case of *faux* Tourette's."

Alas, for Gracie it was all too real. *Fuck Gracie!* Rooof-rooof! Hisssssss...

But to the special mortification of the new teacher, young Jackie was a hockey fan with the usual provincial biases—and so other sentiments fouled the air.

"Hartford SUCKS!"

"Whalers SUCK!"

At the end of her first day, all Gracie could mutter was "Teaching SUCKS!" That night, exhausted and beaten down—she burst into tears. "What have I gotten myself into?"

The other teachers were not sympathetic. Documenting her failures, the Math Chair zeroed in for the kill, boldly predicting she wouldn't last a month.

"Hah! Won't even make it out of probation! Another real world bites the dust!"

Gleefully he marked the day on his calendar in precise, mathematical notation: "Evaluation Day= Farrell's Last" and tracked her down the day before.

"Tomorrow's D-day; good luck to you, Miss Farrell."

Then flashing a devilish grin, "Oh, did I mention I've chosen eighth period? That is the one with the boy from Boston, no?"

As he waltzed away, she swore she heard barking under his breath. *Roof-rooof!*

That night Gracie prepared as never before. If she was going to go down, to borrow a fighter's adage, it would be swinging from the heels. At the bell announcing eighth period, she took a deep breath to steady herself.

But all her preparations would have been for naught, had she not carelessly left a letter in her previous class, before dashing across court and corridor moments *after* the bell. Sitting in back, in his best "hanging" suit, the Math Chair marked an "X" on the evaluation form next to Punctuality. *Strike One!*

Dropping her books, Gracie launched into the carefully-crafted lesson of the day to the steady background beat of eighth period Geometry:

Hartford Sucks!

Whalers Suck!

Roooof Rooof!!

The Chair made three marks next to "Maintains Classroom Order." She hasn't spoken a word and it's almost over, he thought. Ten demerits and he could shut her down!

"The congruence of these triangles can be proved by SAS, Side-Angle-Side," she gasped, catching her breath. "This is not to be confused this with Angle-Side-Side, which thankfully does not exist!"

"Nice math humor, Gracie!" screeched a voice in back. "That's the ASS theorem."

The Chair smiled and placed a mark by "Inculcates Moral Virtue."

"Hartford SUCKS! Whalers SUCK!"

Seven demerits! The Chair was feeling giddy. Just then a loud tap-tap-tap interrupted the faltering lesson and the door slowly opened.

Estrella in front gasped. Ricky's pen dropped. Others stared bug-eyed. At that moment, filling the door frame was Keyshawn Streets, flanked by teammates Trey Washington and Carlos Rivera. In the same hand that days before had tossed the winning touchdown against cross-town rival Weaver, he held a letter.

"Special Delivery!"

Every student sat up. The Chair adjusted his tie. Geometrically speaking, it was a 180 degree turnabout. When Gracie spotted Tiger's letter, her face flushed.

"Oh, I'm so, so s-s-sorry," she stammered. "I must have left that in my last class."

"Don't be so forgetful, Gracie!" shot out a voice in back.

"Hartford SUCKS. Whalers SUCK."

If the Chair were scoring, those three demerits made ten, but like every star struck teen, his eye was on the Quarterback. Calmly striding to the board, Keyshawn handed Gracie the letter. With Tiger's name conspicuously in front, her secret was out! Blood draining from her face, she collapsed into her chair.

Leaning over, Keyshawn whispered, "I marched in his parades. He gave me tickets every game. You tell him, Keyshawn—the boy who recited the Christmas poem—says he was the best Santa we ever had."

Turning and facing the class, Keyshawn Streets, the idol of every boy, crush of every girl, and envy of the Math Chair, spoke:

"It's OVER. Do you hear? From this moment, it ENDS. She's cool. She's with Tiger."

More gasps followed and pens dropped—until Keyshawn Streets put his finger to his mouth, quieting the class.

"Sorry for the interruption, Miss Farrell," he said, and addressed a student. "Hey, Willie, let me know how it goes at practice today."

For a long moment after Keyshawn left, there was quiet in that room, the quietest it had been all year. Gracie, a nervous wreck, opened her mouth but Jackie in back fired first.

"He's a GOOOOOOOON!"

On any other day, the class would have erupted.

"Shhhhhhhhhh," rebuked the girl beside him, and others turned and glared, as Jackie slowly slunk into his chair.

The room was again quiet, every student facing forward. The Chair looked down and counted 9 X's, one more and he could shut her down.

Gracie stood tongue-tied. Eagerly the Chairman located the row "Uses Time Efficiently" and clicked the stopwatch hanging from his neck. In 10 seconds, the last hangman's mark could be added. Just then, a sophomore football player named Willie, seeing her distress, spoke.

"Miss Farrell, please tell us more about triangles?" and opened his book loudly.

Other books followed until forty-five were open. Sensing what is called in the literature "a teaching moment", Gracie spoke with moments to spare.

"Angle-Side-Angle is a second theorem…"

For the next 45 minutes, the rookie teacher delivered her best lesson of the year by far, concluding with a primer on Pythagoras and his famous theorem. At the bell, every student stood and applauded.

Word spread in the halls like wildfire. Overnight the word went from "Gracie Sucks" to "Miss Farrell is DA BOMB!", and in the teacher's lounge from "Miss Farrell is a disgrace" to "Gracie is a promising teacher." At Christmas, her students, especially the girls, lavished her with gifts: stuffed tigers, carved tigers, glass tigers and posters.

"Miss Farrell, when are you going to get a Tiger tattoo?" asked Estrella, at Math Club after school.

On rainy days, she let them watch tapes of Tiger's games. If they aced an exam, she passed around memorabilia. At year's end, to the surprise of few, Gracie was named top first-year teacher in the district.

"Rookie of the Year—not even Tiger pulled that off!" crowed the Headmaster.

Throughout that year, the correspondence to Churchill flourished. Gracie was the lone filament to a place Tiger still held dear. Over time the letters evolved into flowing missives. For Tiger's part, he always wanted to hear more about the fate of the team he left behind.

24. Death Spiral

I will go down with this ship
And I won't put my hands up and surrender
There will be no white flag above my door
I'm in love and always will be
— Dido

Scholars may debate the fall of the Roman Empire, but there is little debate what killed the Whale. The Boston game of April 11, 1990 was as fatal as a harpoon.

Within a year, Captain Ronnie Francis and Ulf Samuelsson were traded to Pittsburgh where they led the Pens to the next two Stanley Cups, with Ulfie scoring the Cup-clinching goal in '91, and Ronnie in '92. Look it up!

"Worst trade in the history of hockey," Owner Richard Gordon ruefully admitted.

Of Ronnie, sportswriter Randy Smith wrote: "He was a class act in the beginning, the middle and the end. You either had to be blind or (GM) Eddie Johnston not to see it."

Kevin Dineen was dealt to Philadelphia. With those cruel cuts, Johnston, the former Boston goalie who replaced Emile Francis, gutted the Whale. What was needed, after the Boston loss, was the slice of a scalpel. But Johnston hacked away like a deranged butcher—or worse:

> In the same fashion a demolition worker goes about an assignment and sticks dynamite in strategic points to raze a building, Johnston had the green light to blowup whatever ties the hockey team had developed over the years.[44]

Without moorings, the Whalers spiraled out of control. When Johnston was fired, ending his three-year "Reign of Error", the next GM stayed all of 52 games. Coach Paul Holmgren, the subject of a *Courant* investigation for driving with a suspended license, was elevated to Coach-GM—despite no front office experience.

In March of 1994, six players including Captain Pat Verbeek, 19-year-old Chris Pronger and an Assistant Coach made national news when they were arrested in a 4 a.m. brawl at Quarterback Jim Kelley's Buffalo nightclub.

"Knowing them, they lost," quipped a disgruntled fan.

Shots of handcuffed Whalers doing the "perp walk" played the country over. Days later, Holmgren was arrested in his driveway, charged with driving while intoxicated, after plowing over neighbors' mailboxes. The team renowned for family values had lost its moral compass. Holmgren checked into the Betty Ford Center.

Owner Richard Gordon, a decent but overmatched real estate man, had seen enough. Rocked by scandals, and reeling from a bad market, he cashed out for $46.5 million. Thus began the era of Detroit's Peter Karmanos.

By now, the green uniforms had turned blue, and *Brass Bonanza* was replaced with three blasts of a fog horn after goals. Time-honored traditions were being trashed; sacred things tossed out; stable things overturned. The old Greek saying, "A fish rots from the head down", rarely seemed so apt.

Captain Verbeek and cornerstone Chris Pronger were traded, the latter for Brendan Shanahan, a 50 goal scorer in St. Louis, who was elevated to Captain. "B.S.", as he was called, responded by demanding a trade.

After a year of "B.S.", the Whalers traded him for Paul Coffey, who with four Stanley Cups, begged out, too, forcing a trade after a desultory 20 games.

"Paul Coffey, Brendan Shanahan and some other big-time blowhards—turned Hartford into Siberia," wrote Jacobs, of *The Courant*.

Hartford, never fully embraced by the fraternity, was sliding into oblivion—and Karmanos would give the final shove. On March 26, 1997, after challenging fans to buy thousands more season tickets, and watching them do it, he raised the bar. Rejecting a $150 million arena and $50 million in guaranteed revenues, he announced he was leaving—but where?

St. Paul was an early front-runner but the NHL deemed its ancient stadium "unfit for hockey."[45] An abandoned airplane hangar in Columbus was considered. In the end, Raleigh with a TV market ranked #29 (Hartford is #27) won out. It was like being dumped for another woman in the plastic surgeon's waiting room, also needing a nose job.

Raleigh's arena, under construction, would not be ready for three more years. The first two seasons would be played in Greensboro, 90-minutes away.

When a team leaves, sometimes as a token of respect it keeps its name, even if the old name is incongruous with the new location. Thus, we have the Utah Jazz in homage to New Orleans; the LA Dodgers in deference to Brooklyn; the Memphis Grizzlies as a bouquet to Vancouver. Boston's Braves kept their name through *two* moves. And the Whalers?

"Ladies and gentlemen, meet your Carolina Hurricanes!"

Not everyone was blown away. The new logo, formed by interlocking "C"s, reminded some of "25 years of Whalers history swirling down a drain." Bitter fans railed at Governor John Rowland for not doing enough to keep the team. Years later, he would go to extraordinary lengths to keep the Greater Hartford Open for the "morale and spirit" and "visibility" it brought. Was it a case of closing the barn door after the prize thoroughbred had bolted already?

On NHL Commissioner Gary Bettman's watch, franchises were shifting to places where ice had previously only been found at the bottom of a glass: Atlanta, Phoenix and Nashville. Good Riddance to Hartford, Winnipeg, and Quebec—only Edmonton from the WHA remains.

Some fans took the high road, wishing the Canes well, and echoing the words of the poet: "To you from failing hands we throw the torch."

For the rest, the sentiment was: "Rot in hell!" For them, Karmanos had secured a spot in Hartford's Hall of Shame beside Victor Gerenas, the Brinks robber who swindled $7.4M in an armed heist. Gerenas stole Hartford's money, Karmanos its team.

And how did the hockey fraternity treat Karmanos? After his first season in Carolina, he was awarded the Lester Patrick Trophy, "for outstanding service to hockey in the United States." Look it up!

Across the border in the Big Apple, Broadway Lawlor, the prima donna goalie, watched with keen interest the failing fortunes of his former team. After years of grousing and mailed-in performances, he had been granted his wish: a trade to the New Jersey Devils.

"Hartford is best seen from a rear view mirror," he proclaimed, gunning it out of town in his red Porsche with New York plates. When the Whalers announced they were leaving, he took out a full-page ad in the *Courant* offering condolences.

"Ta Ta **TWAIN** TOWN...
...Say-o-na-ra **SUCK**iaug"

The last game was scheduled for April 13, 1997, almost seven years to the day after the fateful Boston game. From his home in Michigan, Karmanos announced he would not be able to attend.

But one man, thousands of miles away, knew he must. Stowing away inside a Canadian-Pacific boxcar filled with timber, bound for some loft in SoHo, or bookcase in Beacon Hill, Tiger wound his way uncomfortably home. After years of isolation and wandering, it was time to affirm the truth of the great proverb:

> *If you love something, set it free.*
> *If it comes back to you, it's yours.*
> *If it doesn't, it never was.*

Tiger was coming home. The man who once led the Circus into town on an elephant returned, as he had left, in a box car. For seven years, the struggling Whale had thrashed and been in the throes of collapse. It was time to watch them die.

25. The Death of Kings

Ooooooooooooooooooooone minute left in Hartford.
—Greg Gilmartin, PA announcer

Following a team is an affair of the heart. Old-timers still sit on Brooklyn stoops and pine for "their" Dodgers a half-century after the last pitch. When Cleveland's Browns left, fans in the "Dawg Pound", dressed in rubber snouts and collars, pelted them with bones. Baltimore's Colts fled like thieves in the night, the moving vans stealing away under a cloak of darkness.

On this night Hartford's Whalers would be buried in the graveyard of dead teams— alongside Brooklyn's Dodger's, Montreal's Expos, Seattle's Supersonics and Hartford's Dark Blues, of an earlier century. At center ice, encircling the logo was a memorial: "To Our Whalers, Thanks for memories. 1972-1997." Fans from across the country came to pay respects.

"One last look, you know," said Ulf Samuelsson, gazing in at the dark arena on his final road trip. "I grew up here. It's sad."

Few things in life have a greater claim on people's loyalties than their team. The bonds of marriage are broken. Brother will turn against brother. But the bonds to a team are binding. Betrayal in the form of strikes and lockouts won't sever them. A century of failure and futility won't.

Rapturous in victory, crestfallen in defeat, fans live—and die—with each bounce of the ball. On April 13, 1997 in Hartford, the puck stopped here. The PA announcer's call that night left no doubt:

"Ladies and Gentlemen, Here are THE Hartford Whalers." No longer were they *yours.*

John Mitrano, in the *Sociology of Sport Journal,* writes that losing a team is akin to losing a loved one. As people go through stages in accepting death, fans experienced those same stages.[46]

> The tears started as soon as I saw the Hartford skyline. They came again when my dad arrived and sat down next to me. [47]

This is the third saddest day of my life only ranking behind my mother dying back in February and my father passing away 8 years ago.[48]

A team is a civic treasure, greater than the sum of employment and revenues. When IBM skips town, the talk is of economics. When a team departs, a piece of the heart goes.

A decade after the Whalers left, websites serve as shrines, sealed vessels, or graves at which to place a flower. One went dark. Others pledged to leave the light on. Remembrances still flutter in:

Let me sit upon the ground and tell to you my sad story of the death of kings...It all began in 1979. I was all of three years old, and for some reason my father took me to my first hockey game...I don't remember the team the Whalers played, or even who won, but none of that matters now. What I DID feel was an emotional and spiritual attachment to a group of men, clad in ivy green, who represented my birthplace. They represented me... As the years progressed in Connecticut, I felt widely varying emotions: triumph with every victory, depression with every loss. But never did my devotion waver to this team...Fast forward to the summer of 1991. My family is preparing to leave town after Connecticut Bank and Trust folds and my father loses his job. We're headed to Northern Virginia...Listening from a new radio in my bedroom, I catch a very faint signal...Another jump in time takes us to early 1997...I was studying at McGill University in Montreal on a semester abroad program. I had consumed my first legal beer at a Whalers-Canadiens game January 6...The April 4 game in Montreal was to be my last Whaler game. Ever. As I watch a large chapter in my life close, the memories...came flooding back all at once. Dineen not merely a link to those years but rather a human embodiment of those happier times... The final game against Tampa Bay was something I will never forget. I watched from a sports bar in the middle of Montreal. As the game started, one man sitting

next to me said, "Ce n'est pas Juste."...He repeated, in
English, "It's not right."...I watched the cameras pan the
crowd...I read all the signs, saw all the people crying,
and remembered how close I had felt to my father and
my younger brother when the Whalers scored and Brass
Bonanza was blaring. God I love that tacky song...As I
staggered out into the cold, I was caught in the embraces
of other hockey fans, mostly Hab fans, who had come
out to pay their respects...that sense of loss I know we
all feel won't ever really disappear. And I hope it never
does...I never want to forget what the Whalers meant to
me. They are a part of my soul...always.[49]

As the seconds ticked down, announcer Gilmartin uttered the last
words no one was prepared to hear: "Ooooooooooooooooone minute left
in Hartford."

"Grown men were crying," observed the DJ Jimmy Patterson from
his aerie above the ice. "Everyone wanted to hold on to the feeling and
memories and make a hockey game go on forever."

Patterson's choice of music captured the fan's hopes ("All I Need Is A
Miracle"), fears ("Final Countdown"), and rage ("You Dropped a Bomb
on Me.")

"I let Karmanos know in song that we were pissed!"

At game's end, as was his custom, Patterson played the short 30-second
version of *Brass Bonanza*. But as players poured out of the locker room,
tossing sticks, gloves and shirts to the crowd, he played the three-minute
version of the singular fight song that forever joined town and team.

"The fans knew it was a Long Good-Bye and held on to every last note.
I looked over my ledge and saw people crying and hugging, hundreds of
them."

No one quite knew how to end it. As fans and players awkwardly
milled about, it was left to Kevin Dineen, Hartford's John Wayne on
Skates, who scored the last goal in team history, to take the mike and say
good-bye. Later, he would say:

I have competed in a couple of great playoff series. I've
had a bunch of hat tricks, I had a four-goal game against
the Chicago Blackhawks and I've managed to reach
a few personal milestones along the way. But I would

guess that of all the big games in my career, the last game played in Hartford is the game I'll never forget.[50]

Players continued tossing equipment into the stands. Defenseman Adam Burt signed his shirt "Never Forget." The plucky city that had survived a stadium collapse in 1978 would not survive Karmanos and his "Hole in the Mall" gang.

> I couldn't clap at the end of the game, couldn't cheer, I just stared through the tears, knowing this really was the end of one of the most beautiful memories of my life. We sat until the police asked us to leave. Leaving that seat in 105 was like leaving your dog behind to be put to sleep.[51]

At the final horn, somewhere in the Atlantic, a whale rose, breached magnificently a last time, and submerged to its grave. On April, 13, 1997, The Whale would sleep with the fishes.

###

From the highest nosebleed seat, overlooking the scene of his greatest triumphs, and failures, Tiger, swaddled in a filthy Indian blanket, looked down. A scrimshaw whale's tooth had been bribe enough to slip him in. Placing his hands mangled from 600 fights over his cauliflower ears, he tried to block out the wailing around him, but the grief was too much.

"It's MY fault!" he screamed, startling fans. "Forgive Me!"

In spite of the hard hat pushed over his face, and hair and beard not clipped in seven years, a forlorn fan recognized him. "Look! Up there! Tiger!"

Mortified, his face a mask of wild emotions, he bolted upright. Overcome by primitive feelings of "fight or flight", Tiger for the first—and only—time in that building chose the latter.

Racing down stairs, dodging dazed fans, he escaped into the night. Sprinting down Asylum, over Main Street, up and over Constitution Plaza, his bowed legs churned furiously. At last, on the banks of the Connecticut, he could run no further. Falling to his knees, he collapsed at the base of the Bulkeley Bridge.

Kevin Dineen called April 13, 1997 the most memorable night of his life. Tiger Burns spent it under an old bridge.

26. The Bulkeley Bridge

A tiger suffers for its own reasons.[52]
—Colin McEnroe

Completed in 1908 when bridges were still monuments, not mere spans of steel and concrete, the Bulkeley was the last, longest—and most magnificent—of an era.

Made of pink and gray granite, in nine Classical arches, it spans 1,192 feet—one "Shaq" short of four football fields. For inspiration, the Chief Engineer studied ancient European aqueducts.

But the gay-colored stone masks a dark history. Four workers perished in the construction, and the stress pushed Chief Engineer Edwin Graves to a breakdown, a brilliant career cut short at 41.

Called the Hartford Bridge, in 1922 after the death of Morgan B. Bulkeley, the former Mayor, Senator, Governor and first President of the National League, the bridge at last had a worthy name. Bulkeley lent stature to America's pastime at a time when ballplayers were considered disreputable. On his watch, gambling was prohibited in the stands and players prohibited to drink at games.

Founded in 1876, with "Original Eight" teams in Boston, Chicago, and New York, the National League is baseball's senior circuit. The Hartford Dark Blues came in third that season, and one of its players, Candy Cummings, invented the pitch that ever after thwarted the ambitions of many an aspiring big leaguer: the curve ball. After one season, the team moved to New York—to be called the Brooklyn Hartfords.

Like the bridge above, the river below has seen tragedy. Meandering from the Canadian border to the Long Island Sound, and taking its name from *Quonehtacut*, for "long estuary", the Connecticut River forms the long boundary between New Hampshire and Vermont, and short one between Hartford and East Hartford.

In 1857, Harriet Beecher Stowe's son Henry drowned in the river while at Dartmouth College. In 1876, the steamboat *City of Hartford*, confusing a light on shore for a bridge, crashed at Middletown. Rebuilt as the *Capital City*, it wrecked again off Rye Beach, New York, never to sail again.

Tiger found shelter that night in a refrigerator box. With winds whipping at the cardboard and granite ripping into his back, he could not sleep. But on this night the best suite in the Goodwin Hotel would have provided little comfort.

At midnight, an owl broke the eerie silence with taunting questions across the ink-black waters: "Whoooo lost the team? Whoooo lost the team? Whoooo…"

"STOP!" the tormented fighter screamed, the outburst scattering his demons momentarily. But soon again they re-gathered.

"Whoooo lost the team? Whoooo lost the team? Whoooo…"

A few miles up the road, as they had for the past 6 years, the Schmidleys kept a light on.

"I can't live like this!" he cried, cupping his hands to his mutilated ears. "STOP! Please!"

Why should they? Had not Prometheus stolen fire from the gods and been damned? Why shouldn't the man who stole hockey from Hartford have his own agony to endure? Across the river, roosting crows cawed: "FRAUD! FRAUD! FRAUD!"

With the Whalers gone, he had ruined the one constant in his city's life—and his own. For that he must pay. The liberating thought of his own demise gave him a sudden rush, spiraling away the demons again.

Intoxicated by these thoughts, he crawled from the bridge bottom, the jagged rocks and glass ripping into his knees. With powerful shoulders, he grabbed the stone outcroppings, and muscled his way up the bridge. With a surge, a hundred feet above the river, he flipped over the rail onto the walkway, the lights of an 18-wheeler illuminating his crumpled figure.

Clutching the steel rail, he moved to the bridge center. Looking back to the city, his eye was drawn to the glow of the Travelers Tower. The light sparkled in the haze like an impressionist painting. To Tiger, Hartford at night was as dazzling as Paris. And now Hartford and Paris had something else in common; neither had a hockey team. For that, he must go.

Choking back emotion, he looked back on the city he betrayed. "You gave me everything: a home, a team, a family. I'm sorry…"

Good-byes said and forgiveness asked, his release was 100 feet below. Placing a small foot on the rail, he turned to the misty waters. One push and it would be done.

27. Rube and the Straw Hat

He had more stuff than any pitcher I ever saw.
—Connie Mack

George Edward "Rube" Waddell was the most star-crossed athlete that any sport has ever known. Ken Burns, producer of "Baseball", called him "the strangest man ever to play." It might have been an understatement.

Pitching for the Philadelphia Athletics, he led the American League in strike outs each season from 1902-07. The first hurler to strike out the side on 9 pitches, he once motioned all his outfielders to sit, then struck out the side.

In 1905 he out dueled Cy Young in a 20 inning thriller that captured national attention. In days, the "actual" ball from that game began turning up in bars and saloons, Waddell having swapped "it" for free drinks. Over 50 establishments would later lay claim to owning the priceless memento.

When the black pitcher Andrew Foster once bested him in an exhibition, he was christened "Rube" in honor of the feat. Andrew "Rube" Foster went on to found the National Negro League.

According to one account, Waddell began the 1903 season in a firehouse in New Jersey and ended it tending bar in West Virginia. In between:

> He won 22 games for the Philadelphia Athletics, played left end for the Business Men's Rugby Club of Grand Rapids, MI, toured the nation in a melodrama called "The Stain of Guilt", courted, married and became separated from May Winne Skinner of Lynn, MA, saved a woman from drowning, accidentally shot a friend through the hand, and was bitten by a lion. [53]

On a bet he could fly, he once jumped out of a hotel window, ending up in the hospital. Waddell was the first of whom it was said "He has a $100,000 arm and a 10-cent head."

149

He wandered off in the middle of pennant races to go fishing, delayed games for a round of marbles with kids outside the park, and often showed up minutes before a game, jostling through the stands, removing his shirt, roaring "Let's get 'em."

His manager Connie Mack remarked: "When I got to the ballpark, I'd look first to the flagpole to see which way the wind was blowing, and then to the dugout to see if Waddell had showed up."

On days he pitched, teammates had to escort him to the field, so enthralled would he get by fire bells. Given to heroic impulses, he once prevented a fire in a department store by picking up a blazing stove and tossing it into a snow bank.

"He always wore a red undershirt," said Mack, "so that when the fire bell rang he could pull of his coat, thus exposing his crimson credentials, and gallop off to the blaze."

He wrestled alligators, rode ostriches, pretended to be an automaton in store windows, and was frequently jailed for non-payment of alimony. But when he was happy, he did handstands on the mound. Branch Rickey, who signed Jackie Robinson, observed: "When Waddell had control—and some sleep—he was unbeatable."

But sleep was a problem. Back then, players bunked two-a-bed. Ever the oddball, Waddell munched animal crackers to lull himself to sleep. This habit so infuriated his catcher and bunkmate Ossee Schreckengost that he threatened to quit.

"I don't mind the flat ones so much, but those with horns bother me," he griped.

The dispute ended only after Mack put a clause in Waddell's contract prohibiting him from eating crackers in bed. (Note: Schreck later saved Rube from drowning himself over a love affair gone bad.)

Manager Connie Mack, 66 years in the game, summed him up best: "I have seen them all…I have seen Wild Bill This and Screwy Sam That, but in his heyday the Rube made them all look like amateur night…[But] when he was right I've never had another who could touch him."

Boston was his unlucky town—and not just because his 44 scoreless inning streak ended there. His third wife lived there. For two seasons, whenever the A's pulled into South Station, constables were on hand to arrest him for non-support.[54]

Banned in Boston, he was a sensation in Hartford. Barnstorming the city after the 1906 and 1907 seasons to raise funds for a tuberculosis hospital, he was mobbed. Page one of *The Courant* reported "immense" crowds awaiting him at Union Station.

"There he is, that's the Rube!"[55] shouted overjoyed fans.

The largest Hartford crowd ever, including the Governor, the Mayor and Senator Bulkeley, witnessed him strike out a record 16 Washington Senators, including fanning the side in three consecutive innings.

"**Rube Waddell was it**," crowed the *Courant* on page 1 in bold. "It was the greatest exhibition ever seen on the grounds."[56]

The Hartford Times noted:

> Members of both teams admitted that they had not seen him pitch so great a game at any time during the season. It is one of Waddell's peculiarities that he is likely to loaf and pitch 'bum' ball in a regularly scheduled game before 20,000 people and then go into a small town and throw his arm off. At any rate, the Hartford crowd saw the great twirler in one of the best games of his career.[57]

Despite the success, he never played in a World Series. In 1905, his A's won the pennant and went to the Series—but without Rube. A straw hat kept him out.

Back then, men wore hats throughout the summer. Typically one was bought on Decoration Day and discarded on Labor Day by punching a hole in the crown. So when teammate Andy Coakley appeared on a train platform in Providence on September 4, *after* Labor Day, with his hat still on, well, Rube's eyes got big as saucers.

Bounding from the train, he seized the hat and in the ensuing struggle injured his left shoulder. Despite a league-best record of 27-10 and 287 strike outs, a straw hat kept Waddell out of the World Series. The A's lost. For the rest of his life, he would be dogged by rumors that gamblers had paid him to miss the series.

By 1910, he had drunk himself out of the big leagues, and the "Sousepaw", as he was called, began a nomad's life. In 1912, wandering into a small Kentucky town, beset by winter floods, he plunged into icy waters and stacked sandbags for 13 hours.

But the heroism exacted a toll. By 1913, he contracted tuberculosis. The star-crossed hero born on Friday October 13 died on April 1, 1914 in a sanitarium in Texas at age 37, and was buried in a pauper's grave. In a cruel twist, his catcher Ossee Schreckengost died months after. Decades later, a group of major leaguers led by Connie Mack, learning of Waddell's fate, replaced the small wooden cross with a 6-foot granite marker.

Despite a 191-145 record and election to the Hall of Fame, Waddell is a man forgotten, his records long broken, his antics a vestige of a bygone era. Still there are some who believe his spirit lives—as a patron saint to "goats" and misfits like himself.

Bracing with hands mangled from hundreds of fights, for the final push into the abyss, Tiger caught—from his good eye—an apparition dancing along the bridge rail as if it were a tightrope. A strapping man stopped 60 feet away, tipping his hat.

"Hey, who goes there?" Tiger shouted, hopping off the rail.

The stranger tip-toed like a gymnast. Rearing back with his left arm, he tossed a stone into the waters below—and pointed.

Tiger craned his neck. Out from the splash's center, he saw what appeared like a raft with four figures. Straining for a better view, he spotted a man with a white suit and hair and droopy moustache. Beside him were two boys puffing corn cob pipes and a barefooted black man. The white-suited man looked up and shook his head, as if to say, "No."

"TWAIN!" exclaimed Tiger, turning to the stranger, heart pounding. "Do ya' see? With Tom, Huck and Jim!"

Turning back to the water, Tiger saw the rock's expanding circles, but the raft was gone. The stranger lifted his arm again, and hurled another stone, this one towards the rotting factory with the blue onion dome.

Peering into the grasses where it landed, Tiger spied the silhouette of a man with two silver objects aimed skyward. As the clouds parted, he made out two six-shooters in the moonlight. Lowering the guns, the man looked up to the bridge and shook his head, "No."

"SAM!" yelled Tiger. "COLT! Can ya' see him?"

Again he looked up to the stranger, and when he turned, only tall grasses were blowing.

The stranger heaved a third stone to the other shore where there appeared a small woman on her knees crying into the river. She too looked to the bridge and shook her head, "No."

"HARRIET!" cried out Tiger. "Beecher Stowe! Her son drowned in the river."

Next, the stranger flipped two stones over the ledge and a figure with a surveyor's tools emerged from beneath the bridge.

"OLMSTED!"

Like the rest, he shook his head, and out of the mists paraded three others with shovels over their shoulders, and a fourth clutching blueprints. All shook their heads.

"The bridge workers and Engineer Graves?! They died building this bridge!"

Turning to the man with the magical arm, Tiger noticed the staved-in straw hat on his head. Dressed in itchy wools, the stranger reached around to scratch his backside, lost his balance, and then steadied himself on the rail. Suddenly, Tiger remembered.

"Hey, you're the fellow who stopped me from jumping in the waters in Churchill! WHO are you? WHY do you keep saving me?"

The man said nothing—but winked, pirouetted on the rail and danced off in the direction of distant fire bells.

28. Park Street

The only difference between me and a madman is that I am not a madman.
—Salvadore Dali

For the next several years, the Bulkeley Bridge was Tiger's home: Cross Beam #3, Arch #1, West Bank—to state the address precisely. In body and spirit, he resembled little the fighter of yore.

His muscles, once the scourge of the NHL, had atrophied. His hair, once trimmed in a "fade", tumbled to his waist. His beard, flecked with gray, cascaded over the tattoo on his chest. Crowning his enormous head was a battered, hard hat.

His dead eye, once covered with fashionable patches, stared ahead blankly. Around his neck hung a scrimshaw of a beached whale. As a vestige of prouder days, he still wore the green jersey. Black and threadbare, he wore it inside-out, "half-mast." Like the wearer, it too was unrecognizable.

In this way, he quietly added his name to the rolls of Hartford's homeless: next to the opera-singer who dug lunch out of barrels; the poet who penned verse on pizza flyers; and the wild-eyed woman who shrieked "Aliens are among us!" unsettling the insurance folks. To many, he was simply the "bridge troll."

People who had watched him play a hundred times rushed past with nary a glance. Others who had once chanted his name muttered, "Get a job" or crossed the street warily.

Determined to serve the city he betrayed, he was clueless as to how. Beyond hockey-fighting, he had few skills—what Talent Managers call a "limited" skill set.

For a week, he did not leave the bridge, rousing only to wash at the river's edge. But on one trip, stooping to retrieve a can, he peered into the waters and spied a shopping cart. Wading in to his waist, he found more: a radiator, a bicycle, and a safe. Gathering them on the shore, he gazed at the motley collection and his mission hit him with the jolt of an avalanche check.

"I can clean this city as well as any man alive!" he roared.

From that day forth, the man who once fought for Hartford on ice stages around the world quietly picked up trash along Park Street, in the spine of its Latino corridor.

Originally called Malt Lane, Park was once separated from downtown by the factory-lined Hog River. French-Canadians settled there first, followed by Irish and Greeks. Side streets lined with brick, six-unit apartments, called "Perfect Sixes" stand today.

When the mills closed, and the early immigrants fled, waves of Puerto Ricans and Dominicans moved in. And so on Park Street, and the surrounding "barrio", Tiger became part of the landscape, beat-up and pockmarked like the rest.

At dawn, before the buses disgorged their cargo of office workers, he trudged into town carrying an old gunnysack and sawed-off hockey stick, a goon's trash bag and litter stick. Like the trolleys that once lined city streets, he ran on rails.

Left on Columbus, up State Street, down Prospect, past Calder's Stegosaurus, onto Main and then Park: home to Hartford's most blighted streets. Boarded-up buildings "tagged" with gang graffiti, vacant lots overrun with weeds, and fences overtopped with razor wire—a *Courant* editorial summed it up: Eyesore, Eyesore, Eyesore.

But in a city with a crying need for vibrancy, Park Street was teeming with it. Salsa, the music and sauce, and exotic fruits, like plantains and juicy mangos, gave Park a distinctive sound, smell, and taste. *Piquante!*

On his beat, merchants waved and mamas pushing strollers thanked him, *Gracias, Senor*! One bodega owner, on watching him slap at a can with a broom, as if batting at a puck, and whiffing, smiled. On some corners, he was known in hushed whispers as "El hockey loco."

But on Park Street Tiger's secrets were safe. Some reporters would have paid a fortune for news of his whereabouts. The scuttlebutt in newsrooms was that there might be "a Pulitzer in it." Since he vanished, Tiger had spawned a cottage industry of reporters tracking him down. But always he stayed a step ahead—a ghost in a ghost town.

For years now, he has been a spectral apparition in Hartford's underbelly, rising at dawn, returning from to his bridge at dusk, vanishing into the shadows when rumors flared of the homeless hockey fighter collecting trash as a penance. Like Sisyphus who pushed a heavy rock up a hill each day only to find it at the bottom the next, he toiled until the streets were clean, only to find them filthy the next.

Early on, he reached out to the one who had been his lifeline during the lost years in Churchill. When Gracie first saw the mangy, disheveled man at the door, reeking of the odor of the homeless, awkwardly tugging at his shirt, her heart burst.

"Dear GOD, Tiger! What's happened to you?"

His hair was a rat's nest; his blood-stained jersey tattered; his once-sloping shoulders curved like bunny hills.

"Tiger, this is MADNESS!" she wailed, when she sat down gingerly on the pile of old newspapers he used as a makeshift stool under the bridge. Scattered on the floor were gray-and-white pigeon droppings like a Jackson Pollock painting.

"Tiger, you DON'T have to live like this! PLEASE, PLEASE, PLEASE come home with me!"

But Tiger shook his head, as if to say "No—I must suffer as others have been made to suffer."

"It's INSANITY, Tiger! You'll DIE out here!!"

He shrugged as if to say "So be it." Stepping over the headless, hawk-killed pigeons, she pleaded with him. "Tiger, you MUST come home with me. I'll take care of you. Life will be good again."

But Tiger would not yield, as he never did on-ice. And Gracie, just as stubborn, would never abandon him. So theirs was not a reconciliation of joy, but an unspoken acknowledgement of mental illness and its debilitating effects.

Early on, concerned for his safety, she bought him a knife, her first gift. "Please have this," she pleaded, awkwardly holding it out in her hand.

Tiger took one look and bristled. "Don't you know who I once was?" he said, the words laced with pain. "I can protect myself!"

For a decade, he had taken on the game's toughest goons in cities across North America, with bare fists alone. What protection did he need walking his hometown?

"I'm sorry," he said, seeing her tears. "It's just that…"

"I CARE about you!" she cried out. "Don't you GET it, Tiger?"

Looking down to the glass-strewn floor, and away to the river, he hoped she wouldn't notice the tears sliding down his right cheek, separating into a network of scars, and rejoining.

"I just want you to be safe! Can't you see that?"

And so Tiger discovered, like others, that a woman's love is a grace. Absent betrayal, there is constancy to it. A woman keeps the flame of relationships, nourishing it when it is but a flicker, tending to it in chill winds. Tiger had done nothing to deserve it, yet here now it was his.

"It's Okay," she said, dabbing at his tears and caressing his mane.

Women are not ambivalent. They are either with you 100 percent or against you the same. They stake no middle ground. Through the wandering, the pain and isolation, Gracie had kept the embers. In her heart, she could never abandon him. Even if he stayed under this filthy bridge his whole life. But she never stopped trying to reach him.

"Tiger, you're a *millionaire* for God's sakes! You DON'T have to live like this!"

Truth be told, it wasn't all a mission of mercy. Tiger had helped her more than he would ever know in her early turmoil as a struggling teacher. "But for him, I'd still be rotting away in the insurance company—knee-deep in mahogany and misery!"

But there was more! That crazy, little man had a charisma to him, even on his darkest days. Millions of hockey fans had seen it and now Gracie did, too. Watching his old tapes, and observing for the first time an avalanche check, she joked to her confidant Rebecca:

"Wow! With a little coaching, a guy like that could really rock a woman's world!"

"You go, girl!" she screeched, slapping high-fives, as women are wont to after a saucy comment. But Rebecca, while sympathetic, averred. "Gracie, you can't spend the rest of your life like this! You're happy in your job. It's time to settle down now."

Once again Gracie was out of step with the rest. She wanted to pull her hair out and scream. "Why are you persecuting me? There are women who marry death row prisoners and are celebrated on Oprah. This man needs me! I *believe* in him! Don't you see?"

Even under his bridge, he showed stirrings. One day picking up a coin off the ground, a Connecticut quarter with the Charter Oak on back, the wheels turned—even as the tires were flat.

"Gracie, these coins should have a Whaler symbol above the inscription 'Save the Whale.' There's too much Charter Oak here already. Twain was right! Am I right about that, Gracie?"

Yes, that Tiger could make her smile. At night, when the sun set beneath the bridge, and the swallows skimmed the water, there was no place else she'd rather be than beside him.

When he lightly brushed her hand pointing to the rose-hued horizon, she felt protected. Tiger was *her* bodyguard now—and nothing felt better.

When a curl of a smile came on his lips and his eye narrowed, her hopes surged. He seemed in those fleeting moments at peace. For Gracie, the teacher, she never let them pass.

"Tiger, no matter how many times we stumble, if we get up ONE more time than we fall, then we are champions. Tiger, you are a champion! I believe it with all my heart!"

Nodding politely, he smiled. But soon the faraway look returned—and his dead eye rolled into his skull. As the sun dipped, and Venus rose in the sky, Tiger stood up, stepped over the dead pigeons and reached for his litter stick leaning against the bridge.

"Tomorrow will be another busy day," he sighed, twisting a piece of gum off the rusted spike.

On cue, Gracie got up, squeezed his hand, whispered something brave, and returned home in tears, with less hope in her heart than before.

29. Mr. O'Reilly's Night

Hockey is not religion. Sports are not war.
But retiring a number is something special.
It's a sports version of canonization. It's the ultimate Medal of Honor.
—Jeff Jacobs, *The Hartford Courant*

Of all the men Tiger fought, only Terry O'Reilly, Boston's Tasmanian Devil, gave as good as he got. He was Ali to Tiger's "Smokin'" Joe —only these two punched their dance cards more often. In the course of their careers, they fought 100 times—thrice a game, eight games a season, until the obligatory "game misconduct" banished them both for the evening.

"It was as natural for these two to have a go as for water to run downhill," noted one observer. "They both had so much pride in their jerseys."

Now, Gracie knew but little of hockey, but this much she knew well: Terry O'Reilly was a scoundrel!

"Despicable!" she proclaimed, ticking off 100 reasons, one for every fight.

So imagine her dismay when that loathsome name resurfaced in the news, 17 years after his last game. The Bruins were retiring his number 24. The thought shot a quiver down her spine—and puzzled her.

"Wasn't he *just* a goon? They don't retire goon's numbers, do they?"

For a proper explanation, she'd have to go to Tiger. But she'd have to approach carefully. Hockey was understandably a sore subject, and news of the ascension of his mortal enemy might set him back. Yes, she'd have to broach the odious topic of Terry O'Reilly delicately.

Arriving at the bridge at dusk, armed with two anchovy pizzas and a six-pack of his favorite sarsaparilla, Gracie let the food settle, and the sun set, before proceeding cautiously.

"I know you don't like to talk hockey," she began, seeing him wince, "but there's something you should know of."

Pacified by the food, and entranced by the sunset, Tiger stared blankly out over the waters. So Gracie forged ahead boldly.

"That scoundrel O'Reilly's number is being retired in Boston tomorrow night!" she announced—and the reaction came fast and furious.

"WONDERFUL!" he exclaimed, his scarred face lighting up. "BEST news I heard in years!"

"Tiger, did you *hear* what I just said?"

"Terry O'Reilly is bein' retired in Boston," he repeated. "But don't call Taz a scoundrel! He's a class act all da' way."

"A class act?" she gasped. "He broke your nose four times, knocked out six teeth, sent you to the emergency room God-only-knows-how-many times. What's so classy about *that*?"

Now, Tiger was upset. "Well, I got him a few times too, ya' know!" he said, sore at such a one-sided accounting of their battles.

Gracie guffawed—but Tiger's respect for his rival was hard for anyone but another fighter to understand. Tiger could see it.

"Terry loved his Bruins, same as I loved my Whale. Can't ya' see, Gracie?"

She couldn't. All she could think about was all the nasty things he had done—on and off the ice. "What about that windshield he smashed getting out of Hartford, as if it were Dodge City? What was *that* all about?"

Rising to his rival's defense, Tiger offered weakly: "Well, the car musta been in the way." Then with more conviction: "But if I were with him, we'd have lifted it out a' the way together."

Tiger looked up at Gracie, and whispered these words ever so earnestly.

"I don't hate Terry O'Reilly. I love 'im! He was everything I aspired ta' be."

With 204 goals and 492 assists to go with all his penalties, O'Reilly could play the game some. His style was all his own. "As smooth as a stucco bathroom," appraised Bobby Orr.

Two decades after he retired, O'Reilly still holds the all-time Bruins penalty record. When the old Boston Garden was demolished, he was presented with the penalty box as a personal memento. No one spent as much time inside.

O'Reilly played by a strict code of honor. The relationships he forged with the men he fought were rooted in mutual respect. He once protected Dave Williams, a frequent adversary, when an enraged Bruin teammate kicked at his head after O'Reilly had wrestled him to the ice.

"Put your head under my body, I'll shield you,"[58] he whispered.

Sensing her astonishment, Tiger spoke at last with beseeching passion. "Don't ya' understand, Gracie? I need ta' be there ta' honor him. Taz is my friend. "

For the first time since returning, Tiger prepared to leave Hartford. Hopping a southbound train at Union Station, he switched at New Haven before debarking at South Station, back in the belly of the beast.

Crossing the Boston Common, past the Hanging Elm used to execute Quakers and witches, through the cobblestone streets of Beacon Hill, he arrived at North Station, home of the old Garden, where he had his memorable introduction to O'Reilly's fists. A lot had changed for man and building.

In the place of the old Garden stood a gleaming arena, the Fleet Center; and in the place of the frightened boy from Moose Jaw stood a washed-up bridge troll. Building and man had taken opposite roads.

Approaching warily, Tiger was astounded to spot ahead, swept along in the pre-game foot traffic, none other than O'Reilly himself, walking to his own ceremony. True to his blue-collar roots, he was still the lunch bucket hero of Boston's Gallery God's.

"Terry!" cried out Tiger, impulsively bulling his way through the crowd. Standing below him, he thrust out a mangled hand: "Mr. O'Reilly, can I have your autograph?"

For an instant, O'Reilly, looking down at the gnome clutching a scrap of paper swiped off the ground, almost lunged—before regaining his composure.

"Sure," he said warily, then with pity surveying the bum. "For a moment there, you reminded me of someone…Aw, never mind."

Something about the hermit's mutilated ears and lazy eye had aroused his instincts. Stuffing the signed paper in his pocket and mumbling thanks, Tiger scurried off. Following his bow-legged gait, O'Reilly called out.

"HEY! Do 'ya need a ticket for the game?"

The tears streaming down the right side of his face was answer enough.

"Here, be my guest," he said, then being swept away in the crowd. "God bless 'ya."

The night of October 24, 2002 was a glorious celebration of the competitor who played 13 seasons—and coached three more—with unparalleled passion.

"I don't think there ever was a player who wore the uniform of his team with more pride than Terry O'Reilly," said Bruins President Harry Sinden, to the crowd's roar.

When O'Reilly took the mike, he dismissed all the tributes and acknowledged what some that night, no doubt, were thinking.

"I think we would all agree that this is a deviation from the norm,"[59] he said, pointing up to the retired numbers of Bobby Orr, Phil Esposito and Ray Bourque. He laughed at comparisons to Montreal's silky Guy LaFleur. "I had trouble breathing following his exhaust."

Then abruptly O'Reilly turned serious. When his brother Jamie died of leukemia in 1969, Jamie's widow Bernadette entered a convent in Winnipeg where she lives to this day.

"I want the whole world to know she inspires me,"[60] he said, his throat catching.

Next, he called out Joe Howard, a promising player who lost both legs in a train accident at 16, but went on to win a gold medal as Captain of the U.S. Olympic sled hockey team.

"Joe Howard inspires me!"

People who kept faith with the covenant they had made, no matter the obstacles—those were O'Reilly's people. Standing in the penalty box one last time, he thanked the fans.

"You were patient with me as I stumbled and slipped through my first few years and my last few years. I loved playing hockey for you and this will always be my home."[61]

With the help of his two sons, he hoisted the #24 banner to the rafters.

"Next to mine protecting me again," said Ray Bourque, in tribute to his old bodyguard.

On a night when O'Reilly's jersey was hoisted to the rafters in Boston, his rival Tiger Burns hopped a southbound freighter and slept under a bridge in Hartford. There was trash to pick up next day.

30. A Pox on Your City

One of the first things you notice about the city is that you
can drive and walk a while without seeing people.
—Michael Holley, *The Boston Globe.*[62]

After O'Reilly's night, Tiger kept a wary eye on the sports pages. Hockey, for sure, was still a sore subject, but now and then before spearing a newspaper with his litter stick, he snuck a peek—and learned what had become of old friends.

Captain Ronnie Francis returned to his old team, a bittersweet "homecoming" in Carolina, to fulfill his early promise and join the company of legends. With 20 consecutive seasons of 20 goals, he matched records set by Gordie Howe. The world couldn't help but notice.

"In a sports era that celebrates the loud, the lewd, the boorish and the belly-pierced, Francis has quietly slipped through the cracks and into the record books,"[63] wrote *Sports Illustrated*.

Off the ice, he and Mary Lou, with three kids, started the "Night Out with Ronnie" program that brought sick children to a game in a limo, with roses for mom, and a visit to the locker room. The NHL honored him with the King Clancy award for "noteworthy humanitarian contributions."

Kevin Dineen, after stints in Philadelphia, Ottawa, and Columbus, retired as one of eight NHL players with 300 career goals and 2000 penalty minutes. He and Annie had four children—enough for a team.

Ulf Samuelsson played on in Pittsburgh, New York, Detroit and Philadelphia. In one incident emblematic of his career, Toronto's Tie Domi knocked him out with a sucker-punch. In Vancouver, the entire dressing room applauded at the news. In Boston, they all but declared a holiday. Ebay could hardly keep up with the demand for photos.

Howard Baldwin journeyed to Hollywood to produce films, among them "Mystery, Alaska" and the Oscar-winning "Ray."

And what became of the little city that brought them all together and launched them to greatness? Hartford fulfilled the destiny of those who all along insisted it was strictly minor league, hosting the Wolf Pack of the American Hockey League in 1998.

Today when invaders descend from the north, no longer do the Montreal Canadiens wing in on jets; the Manitoba Moose roll in on buses. Gone are the Pittsburgh Penguins; in are the Wilkes-Barre Penguins. Out with the New Jersey Devils; in with the Worcester Devils. The Wolf Pack plays the likes of the Albany River Rats, Lowell Lock Monsters, and Grand Rapids Griffins. Oh, but the Bruins still visit— the Providence Bruins.

The Civic Center—bustling in its heyday with Chuck's and Margaritaville—is home to high-rise condominiums today. Can you imagine the chortling over that?

You play in Condos! You play in Condos!

On streets where royalty once roamed—with Gretzky, Lemieux and Howe—today only minor leaguers and faceless conventioneers trickle in. For 17 years, the city had danced in the heavens, hitched to a rising star. Alas, the hold was not strong enough, the grip failed, and the star went shooting away—to North Carolina.

The little city crashed, surrounded here and there on scorched earth with stardust, a glittering residue of what once was. The rest of the world, far from dissatisfied, could only sneer—"Told you so!" A city of 125,000 never deserved a team in the first place. Overreaching Hartford should thank its lucky star that it was able to dance in the heavens for even a short while.

When the Whalers fell, outsiders moved in quickly. At center ice, where the logo stood, reads "Hartford Civic Center Managed by Madison Square Garden." It is as if a lion has marked the territory of a fallen rival with urine. The Wolfpack is the minor league team of the New York Rangers.

Brass Bonanza, the beloved theme song, was plundered, too. Today the Boston Red Sox play it at Fenway Park and the Boston Bruins do the same. It is as if Colt's trademark rampant horse weather vane had suddenly appeared atop Faneuil Hall.

Kevin Paul Dupont, of *The Boston Globe*, provided an epitaph for the Whalers when he dubbed them the "Forever .500s"[64]. With that flourish of the pen, he memorialized the team as standard-bearers of mediocrity. A decade later, the *Globe* still mocks the Whalers as the "Forever .500s".

And of course the stain of "the Parade" lingers on. That misbegotten day, when giddy Hartford celebrated fourth place with floats and marching bands, will never be forgotten.

164

But one wonders if Boston, for all its haughtiness, doesn't miss the Whale. The rivalry was a torrid one, the "Battle of New England" on ice. In no other sport did Boston have such a natural geographic rival.

Down in Carolina, attendance the first year averaged less than 4000. "The sparse crowd looked like a reunion of normal, well-adjusted Kennedy cousins,"[65] wrote *Sports Illustrated*.

Black curtains draped from the rafters covered thousands of empty seats. Lonely fans waved signs: "Great Seats Available. Heck—Great SECTIONS Available." In NASCAR country, the nuances of hockey proved confounding. Twenty-nine games were televised on "educational" TV. Hillbilly hockey, fans dubbed it.

"I heard somebody say, 'Here comes the Zam*boozi*,'" sniffed Goalie Sean Burke.

In a story titled "Natural Disaster", *Sports Illustrated*, summed it up:

> They are like some down-on- its-luck country band playing in front of small crowds, in a small city, with no home and no hope. Their nickname, the Hurricanes, is the only thing about them that makes sense, because thus far the NHL's incursion into tobacco country has been a natural disaster.[66]

In Hartford, a malaise gripped the once-proud city. A 2005 American City Business Journal Survey labeled Hartford "the most troubled city in the US", ahead of Newark and East LA. 30.6 percent of the population lives below the poverty line. Mark Twain Days, the three day celebration, was cancelled for lack of volunteers.

The Hartford Club, home to the Bishops, struggled. In their heyday, it was said of The Bishops, "if you touched their hand, you were saved." Now, a white-knight suitor was being sought to stave of foreclosure. "One more nail in the coffin of downtown Hartford," said a dejected member.

The Insurance City that rushed like the cavalry to the rescue after every hurricane, earthquake and flood was stumbling. Who was there to catch Hartford when it fell?

###

Stooping to retrieve a wind-blown newspaper against a fence, Tiger came face-to-face with the headline: "DEVILS DRINK FROM CUP!" Fighting the impulse to pull away, he read on:

"Sipping champagne from hockey's Holy Grail, Broadway Lawlor roared above the celebration, 'For all the time I spent in that puke town Hartford, I deserve this like no other. I'm kissing Stanley now, but they can kiss my ass back in Twain Town."

Their lives had taken opposite trajectories. The floater who never respected the game was cradling Lord Stanley's Cup; the fighter who always did was picking up trash. Broadway was rank, selfish, and duplicitous—and his name would forever be etched on the Cup.

The Stanley Cup is the most famous trophy in sport—and easily the most accessible. In a singular tradition that separates hockey from other sports, every member of the winning team gets to spend a day with it—which makes for some outrageous adventures.

"The Cup has been lost, hidden, stolen, dismantled, left on the side of a road, chucked in a graveyard, and drop-kicked into Ottawa's Rideau River," writes *Sports Illustrated*.[67]

"Stanley" has floated in Mario Lemieux's pool, appeared on the Letterman show, and in the Kentucky Derby winner's circle. It has been to church and to strip bars.

Tearing the paper to shreds, Tiger stormed away from Park Street glancing up on the way home at the words chiseled on the Bushnell Memorial:

Life is always insipid to those who have no great works in hand,
no lofty aims to elevate their feelings.

Lying under his bridge that night, Tiger felt something stirring. For the first time since April 11, 1990, he did pushups. Right there on the banks of the Connecticut River.

31. Gotham and Gomorrah

…That great cesspool into which all the idlers and
loungers of the Empire are irresistibly drained.
—Arthur Conan Doyle

For several days, Tiger did not rouse from the bridge. Some merchants on Park Street, fearing he drowned, dropped flowers by the sidewalk. In two days, a small shrine rose up. Gracie, too, noting the change in habit, was troubled.

"Tiger, what's gotten into you?" she asked, rubbing his neck as it rolled back and forth. "I've never seen you so agitated."

He told her what he'd read, quoting Broadway's broadsides verbatim. "He still loathes this town with all his heart. A leopard never changes his spots!"

"Nor a tiger his stripes!" Gracie shot back. "You still love it with all yours."

Cradling his head in her pipe-stem arms, she caressed his flowing hair, silently awed at the power in his heaving back. "It's okay, Tiger."

As always when comforted, he pulled away—launching instinctively into the tired refrain that had so long clouded his life. "It's my fault! I blew the game that ruined everything!"

But this time Gracie wouldn't let it pass.

"Can I ask something, Tiger?"

Tiger nodded, brushing away tears.

"Why did you drink so much the night we met? I've never seen you touch a drop since, but…"

"What do you mean?" he interrupted, shooting her a look. "I had one."

Gracie could see he was serious. "Tiger, you were drunk. You musta had 10."

"NO!" he insisted. "The *first* had rum, but the others were sarsaparilla. I told him."

Gracie looked down, understanding now for the first time what happened that long ago night. "He betrayed you," she said, her black hair framing her pretty face.

"Don't say it, Gracie!"

Gracie sat beside him on the ground covered in droppings. Gently caressing his hand, she patiently went over the events of that long ago night when his world irrevocably changed. Hearing her first hand testimony, he resisted at first.

"No, I don't believe it, Gracie!"

But as she continued, comforting and explaining, it made sense: why Broadway, who had rarely bothered with him, was suddenly so attentive. Even when he walked away, the drinks kept coming. But Tiger had blocked it all out—everything except Gracie. But for the first time now, he could see.

"What a FOOL!" he wailed. "I believed him."

"He was your teammate! You trusted him! There's no shame in that!" she scolded.

"They all told me ta' stay away—Kevin, Ronnie, and Ulfie. What a FOOL!"

With greater vigor than since his fighting days, Tiger rose and paced. The once-great muscles on his scrawny neck fanned out—frightening Gracie, who'd never seen him like this.

"I'm not leaving you alone tonight. You're too upset!"

Seeing her distress, he stopped.

"I'll be okay, Gracie. It's jus' a lot of bad memories flooding back," he said, feigning calm. But Gracie wasn't buying it.

"Let it go, Tiger! It wasn't *your* fault! You're better than that!"

Tiger smiled, his dead eye rolling into his skull.

"I'll be okay. I-I-I jus' need ta' get back ta' work, ta' Park Street, that's all."

"What's done is done!" she scolded. "But I want to stay with you tonight. You're too upset!"

"No," he said, mastering his emotions. "You're right! I shouldn't dwell on it."

"But I want to be with you."

"I appreciate it, Gracie. I do," he said, moved. "But really I'm okay now."

Gracie sighed, squeezed his hand, and rose slowly. It was no use arguing.

"Umm, can I ask something else then? I mean, since we're talking about things."

"Sure."

"Who's Miss Moose Jaw?" she asked, arching a brow.

Tiger, no longer the master of his emotions, blushed.

"Umm, umm, how do ya' know about her?"

"I saw her picture when I cleaned your room. You mentioned her in a letter, too. Remember?"

"Oh, yea, I forgot."

"She's beautiful," Gracie remarked, twisting her shiny black hair and looking down.

Tiger was embarrassed and flattered at once. "Gee, do ya' think so??"

"Gosh, who wouldn't? I mean she's a beauty queen!"

Tiger shrugged goofily, but felt gratified that Gracie thought him worthy of Miss Moose Jaw.

"Was she your girlfriend?"

"Umm, yea, of course" Tiger mumbled, fibbing.

Gracie stood silent, still twisting her long hair and looking away.

"Well, I guess you're used to dating girls like that, being a hockey player and all. Goes with the territory, huh?"

Fearing exposure now, Tiger panicked. "Well, that was a long time ago," he blurted out, dismissing the probes. "I can barely remember it now!"

Rebuffed, Gracie spun and strode away.

"WAIT!"

Tiger's heart pounded. His legs felt like jelly now. Nervously he wet his lips as she faced him. Looking to the ground, he kicked at a stray piece of glass.

"Ya' know, the one good thing that come a' that night was meetin' you."

Gracie took a deep breath. "I miss that old Tiger! I really do!" she sobbed and ran off to her car.

Tiger tried to sleep. But the stirred-up memories, mixed with unresolved feelings for Gracie, were too raw. Over the course of the night, like a clam closing in on an irritant, he sealed off the pain that had for so long crippled him, and at dawn, the pearl of a plan was born.

Stuffing his sawed-off hockey stick into his gunny sack and leaving behind a note, Tiger spotted a chunk of coal on the ground. Picking it up, he penned two words under the bridge, joining them like this:

TIGER

+

GRACIE

Turning to the river, he rifled the stone across the water. Seven skips! A lucky stone! Climbing the hill into town, passing the 36 rocks of *Stone Field Sculpture,* he crossed Bushnell Park, by the old carousel, to Union Station and hopped a southbound freighter.

Two hours later, at Penn Station, his synapses crackled. Was it the explosion of stimuli—the sights, smells and sounds of the booming metropolis? Or something dawning? Tiger felt alive again!

At Madison Square Garden where he once out-slugged Lefty Lyons of the Rangers, earning tabloid raves "TIGER TAMES LYONS", he squinted up at the tall buildings. Even now, 15 years later, he could vividly recall the famous Nike banner with a Mount Rushmore view of Gotham's Sporting Villains: Michael Jordan, standing 10-stories tall; Roger Clemens, 9-stories; Joe Montana, 8-stories; and Tiger Burns, 3 stories—barely.

Within days, a "human-fly" scaling the facade had covered Tiger's face with scars. All of New York had chuckled over that—especially the tabs ("SCAR-Y UGLY!"). Tiger smiled at the happy recollection.

At every corner, on billboards and kiosks, the Citigroup Red Umbrella arched over bits of smarmy wisdom: "The best blue chips are the ones you dip in salsa." Tiger wanted to gag. Stolen from Travelers, he thought bitterly.

Bounding about in that bow-legged gait of old, firing uppercuts, he ambled down the great concrete corridors. At night, he bedded down in Central Park, Olmsted's masterpiece, and churned out pushups as of old. After a week of comings and goings, a plan was taking shape—save one detail.

For the first time in over a decade, Tiger, whose hair tumbled to his waist, and beard tickled his belly, walked into a salon at 36th and Broadway and sat—but not long:

"GET OUT! GET OUT this instant!" exploded a man called Christophe, brandishing a blower and scissors. "Stay away, you FILTHY beast!"

Tiger walked up a block, sat again and got the same bum's rush. Every few blocks, similar rows occurred, until at last at 125th and Broadway, a barber named "Mac" sat him for $100 bucks—"and a god-damned steal at that!"

Slumping into the chair, Tiger stared into the mirror, as behind their morning papers, regulars poked each other and smiled. As the razor whirred like a chainsaw, Tiger's long hidden face slowly emerged. With each falling clump, like ice sheets calving from a glacier, deep lines to match his scars were revealed. Tiger stared ahead.

Like an old house cleared of vines and ivy, his once-stout body appeared now gaunt and decrepit. Tiger grimaced. The man who once struck fear into opponents looked into the mirror and a wimp stared back.

Ripping the sheet off his narrow shoulders and dumping his money onto the chair, Tiger kicked through tumbleweeds of hair. Crossing Broadway, nearly getting sideswiped by a cab, he entered a park littered with needles and vials. Right there, he dropped to the ground, groaning as he struggled to do 25 pushups.

A group of bums, swigging from a bottle, looked down and laughed. But at every small park and playground on the way back, he did the same. At night, dropping on the grass beside a bench in Central Park, he bombarded his muscles more—but to little avail.

Physiologists speak of "muscle memory" wherein neglected muscles regain their bulk under intense training. But Tiger's, alas, suffered from amnesia. After five days, and ten thousand of pushups, they stubbornly refused to remember. But on the sixth day, there was an inkling; and the seventh, half-a-clue. In two weeks when he flexed his biceps, his sleeves tightened.

But his mind, shrouded by a decade of fog, was not so resilient. Unlike the other park bums who slept together in a colony, Tiger kept to himself. Dozing fitfully one night, far away from the rest, he awoke to voices, repeated over and over, as if from above:

Hey, Tiger! Play it and they'll be in the cheap seats!

Yea, way up in the nosebleeds—you'll see!

"What the devil are 'ya yakking about?" he hollered, so loud he startled the other bums.

"KEEP IT DOWN! Civilized people are trying to sleep over here!!" a groggy vagrant called out from a distant knoll.

Burying his face in a newspaper, Tiger dozed fitfully, attributing the strange voices to the hard bench, far from his familiar bridge and river. Maybe he'd have to sleep under the Brooklyn Bridge to feel at home? But next night, just to be certain, he moved to a different bench—farther from the hobo colony. Soon, the voices taunted him again:

Hey, Tiger! Play it and they'll be in the cheap seats!

Yea, way up in the nosebleeds—you'll see!

"Play WHAT?" he yelled, bolting upright and shaking a fist skyward. "WHO'LL I see?"

His angry rants startled the other bums until even they thought he was crazy. Then, mysteriously, the voices ceased—and Tiger could sleep again and carry on with his business.

By day he bombarded his muscles and by night trolled the upscale clubs of the Upper East Side. And each morning he scanned the Society Pages—until one day, the following notice appeared:

> Sylvester Lawlor, of the New Jersey Devils professional Ice Skating team, will host a gala celebration with the Stanley Cup at the Vicar's Club tonight. Better known by the *nom de patin* Broadway, Mr. Lawlor led the New Jersey Pond-Skaters to Lord Stanley's Sterling Cup, first awarded in 1892, with his stellar play in tending the goal. Proceeds from the bacchanal will go to Mr. Lawlor's favorite charity Cigar's Unlimited, a political action group working to overturn the U.S. embargo on fine imported Cuban cigars.

Crumpling up the paper, Tiger fired off a telegram—along with money for a train ticket. That night, as directed, Gracie arrived at Penn Station in a black halter emblazoned "Foxy" with silver sparkles, a red mini-skirt, and stiletto heels that could pierce an olive. Hailing a cab, she caused a brawl between two turbaned drivers fighting for the fare.

"The Vicar's Club," she directed to the winner.

Tossing him $20, she undulated to the front of a long line snaking behind velvet ropes. Whispering to the pony-tailed doorman, he smiled and lifted the rope. Inside, at the center, a cigar in one hand, a Scotch in the other, and the most coveted trophy in sport at his feet, sat the goalie. At Gracie's bouncy approach, Broadway, craning his neck, ogled her from crotch to breasts.

"SWEETIE!" he called out, thumping aside the blonde on his lap. "Don't I know you from somewhere?"

"Actually, I think you do."

"I do???" he fumbled, surprised a throwaway line hit the target.

"From Hartford, remember?"

He didn't—and the association was not pleasant.

"Well, I ain't no fan of Twain Town. Let's get that straight up front!" he stated, staring at her sparkled top. "And I do like things up front."

Gracie blushed at the crude joke.

"Well, you're in the Big Apple now, kiddo" he said, propping his Bruno Magli-shod feet on the Stanley Cup. "And if you play your cards right, you just might get to stay."

Groping the exposed flesh of her waist, he pulled her in, snapping at the waiter as he did. "Maximillian! Two shots for me and the lady here!!"

Gulping the drink, he caressed her neck, admiring her legs, down past her calves, to her ankles, where suddenly something unnerved him.

"Hey, what the hell is that?"

"Oh, that? Just a little tigger," she cooed.

Bumping her from his lap, Broadway inspected the tattoo more closely. Slowly it dawned on him: "Now I remember! Chuck's? You were there that night, right?"

Broadway's smile revealed two perfect rows of teeth. "Well, you sure as hell, didn't look like this then," he said, blowing a plume of smoke.

"That was a work night!"

Looking at the tattoo, he eyed her suspiciously. "You didn't take up with…", at that he instinctively placed his hand over his left eye. "I hear that MO-Ron hasn't been seen in years."

Exhaling another plume, he chuckled. "It wouldn't surprise me if old T-ger did himself in after Twaintown lost its team."

Gracie bit her lip—enduring his gropes and insults. Occasionally an admirer walked by to touch the trophy, but Broadway shooed her away with his cigar. After one such rebuff, he pushed Gracie's lips towards his, but she turned, and he brushed only her neck.

"Hey, loosen up, honey! I'm slumming it tonight with the likes of you, ya' know! MAXIE! Two more shots!"

Gracie nursed her drinks, annoying him more.

"Drink up! Drink up!"

Whenever his gropes strayed, she moved his hand—irritating him still more. But again and again, he kept returning to the one subject he just couldn't stay away from.

"So what do you think became of him?"

"He was *your* friend. How would *I* know?"

The more champagne he guzzled, the more he ripped "T-ger" and "Twain-town", at last admitting to his betrayals, until it begged the question.

"So why did you do it?"

Looking directly at her, he twirled his fat cigar in a most self-satisfied way. "What was it that horny President said about screwing the fat intern? 'Because I could!' That's why! It was too damned easy."

Smirking in the smuggest way, he barked out, "MAXIE, two more shots!"

At 4:00 a.m., Broadway hustled the Cup, Gracie, and a purloined bottle of Dom Perrignon into the waiting limo. At his Upper East Side penthouse, he winked at the doorman, ushering Gracie inside. Juggling the champagne and Stanley Cup in the glass elevator, they at last reached his 30th floor apartment with panoramic views.

"That ain't Bushnell Park down there! Look at it and weep, honey!"

Ushering Gracie onto the red leather sofa by the Italian marble fire place, he began his preparations, as well-choreographed as a power play. Lighting the scented candles, adjusting the soft music, uncorking the chilled bottle, he was already unfolding the ermine spread, when a sharp knock interrupted.

"You no-good sonofabitch! I told you…" he raged, springing to the door, poised to unload on the impertinent doorman.

But when the door opened, and light flooded in from the top half, and only the top half, Broadway gasped and staggered backwards. Filling the lower half of the frame was hockey's most feared fighter.

"Tiger?! How ya' doing? We-we-we were just talking about you."

Broadway's agile mind raced. His unblemished face was masked in horror. Words rarely failed him, and now desperately he sought to string a precious few together now.

"Hey, Tiger! Us Whalers stick together, remember?"

Uncoiling from wobbly ankles, Tiger Burns let loose with the best punch of his life—catapulting the 220-pound Broadway across the Persian rug and into the gold andirons of the fireplace: *Thwaaack—Claaaang—Uuuuugh…*

As Broadway landed heavily, dozens of blue diamond pills from his pocket scattered across the floor, as Tiger instinctively pounded his tattoo, and positioned his hands for a cartwheel.

"TIGER! THE TROPHY!"

Tiger stopped. Scooping up the Cup, he and Gracie stole away into the night. With the trophy strapped in back beside Tiger, Gracie peered into the mirror in sudden amazement.

"My God, you look so handsome!!"

As the car turned onto Park Avenue, Tiger looked into the mirror, right into Gracie's eyes, and flashed that toothless smile.

"'Bout time you noticed."

32. The Stanley Cup

I take the war list and run down it—
Name after name which I cannot read,
and which we who are older than you
cannot hear without emotion.
—Chariots of Fire

Hockey's oddest fighter, his fists awakened, was speeding off to Hartford, no longer with a team, the Stanley Cup in tow, having beaten up a teammate to seize it. Nothing in the chain added up. Yet every link was true! If Tiger's destiny had led inexorably to this moment, he had but one question: What next?

With trembling hands, scarred from a thousand fights, he held the trophy. It was the closest he had come to it since April 11, 1990 when the Whalers were perhaps a goal away. Reading down the rolls, he felt a reverence for the game and its time-honored traditions.

Offered in 1893 by Lord Stanley, Governor General of Canada, the Cup stood a mere 7.5 inches. Like a tree, many rings and inches have been added over the years to make room for the many teams and players that have won it. Today at 3 feet tall, the Cup spends 300 days a year on the road, unconstrained in both dimension and location.

Like the one-eyed gnome cradling it, the Cup is not without flaws. Winners in 1972, the Boston Bruins are misspelled "Bqstqn." One name (Basil Pocklington, the mischievously added father of Edmonton team owner Peter) has been slashed out. No name appears more than Jean Beliveau—17 times with Montreal.

Reading down the hallowed rolls, Tiger's throat lumped. He knew that some men toiled decades, others a lifetime, in futile quest for immortality. Jean Ratelle, Gilbert Perreault, and Emile Francis ("Injuries, Bad Bounces and Bernie Parent!") always came up short.

But for others, whose names he now lingered over, Tiger could close his eye and see them—blazing on-ice in a blur of green and glory.

Pat Verbeek, Hartford's Captain, won in Dallas. Bobby Holik, the savior from Czechoslovakia, won twice in New Jersey. Scott Young, fresh from the Olympics, won in Pittsburgh and Colorado. And of course, Ronnie and Ulf, Hartford's favorite sons, won twice in Pittsburgh.

"Hartford's fingerprints are all over the Cup!" Tiger fumed.

Owner Howard Baldwin was on—as Chairman of the Penguins. Even Eddie Johnston, the scoundrel who traded Ronnie, was on. As he continued his misty-eyed reverie, Gracie interrupted.

"So what's next, Tiger? That's the one part of this crazy escapade you haven't filled me in on yet."

Tiger looked into the mirror at Gracie's pretty face. Her brows were knitted in concern.

"We're bringing it home to Hartford," he said smartly. "It's the final act of redemption!"

Tiger looked up at her reflection for approval, but Gracie's face was flushed now.

"Tiger, that's REVENGE—not Redemption!"

The remark hit him like a punch to the solar plexus.

"Huh?"

"C'mon Tiger, it means nothing! You've got to win it—not **steal** it. You don't have to be a hockey player to know that!"

Gracie's words shook him at his core. How stupid could he be? He'd been so fixated on getting the Cup for Hartford, at any cost, that it hadn't mattered how. His half-baked plan had been to use Broadway's remaining time as a gift to his aggrieved city—to salve old wounds and mete out frontier justice. But Gracie was right! It meant nothing!

"Oh, what a fool I am!" he groaned, placing his battered face into his gnarled hands.

The emptiness of everything he'd so carefully plotted for weeks—the thousands of pushups, the scouting around, the endangering of Gracie—overwhelmed him. Gracie's simple truth pierced the veil of his elaborate folly. Collapsing onto the back seat, the Stanley Cup rolled away from his grasp, just as it had the night of April 11, 1990.

Maybe his life would never have meaning? Maybe he was destined to die under an old bridge? The man who killed hockey in Hartford: that's all he'd ever be.

33. Fire Bells

I'm not crazy. I'm just a little unwell.
I know right now you can't tell.
But stay a while and maybe then you'll see…
a different side of me.
—Matchbox 20

As the car lurched onto Park Avenue for the silent drive home, out from nowhere, a man in red jumped out into the road, waving his long arms.

"Watch Out!" Gracie hollered, slamming the brakes, as the car skidded to a halt. On the horizon, where the apparition pointed franticly, a fireball lit up the sky. Fire trucks with screaming sirens and flashing lights arrived that instant.

"No, Tiger, Nooo!"

Too late! He was on the run, the wild-eyed man on his heels.

At the police line, flashing a badge, Tiger hurdled the yellow tape, the red-shirted man at his side.

"Family trapped on three!" hollered the Captain, mistaking the badge, as flames leapt from the top of the brownstone. "Door ain't budging! Fucken code violation!"

Two to a bound, Tiger took the stairs, the homeless man in stride. Although short, Tiger still had an athlete's spring, and so did the other man. Shoulder to chest, they rounded the stairs up to the third floor where black smoke billowed beneath a door. Two firemen with axes flailed away helplessly.

"We're screwed!" one cried, his hands blistered. "Mahogany—like fucken' steel!"

"STAND BACK!" Tiger ordered. "I'm going through!"

"You Nuts? Power saw's coming!"

"Out a' the way!" Tiger ordered, the strapping stranger flanking him.

Dipping his shoulder, Tiger launched his wrecking ball body as if delivering a check, beside him the indigent. Slamming into the door, they crashed inside, shards flying everywhere.

"THEY'RE IN!"

With blood streaking their faces, the two men slithered like snakes, the stranger in front now. Ten feet in, on a flame-engulfed sofa, they came upon two bodies.

"The boy!" coughed Tiger, his throat seared.

Scooping the 200-pound man over his shoulder, Tiger staggered to the door through tongues of leaping flame, as the stranger cradling the boy collapsed at the threshold.

"HAUL 'em out!" hollered the Lieutenant, jumping into the fray.

Two to a body, the firefighters lugged the four downstairs into the street pulsating with sirens and lights.

"The BOY first!" screamed a paramedic, as water cannons blasted the top windows.

As rescuers thumped at his chest and blew into his blackened face, in a few frantic moments, the boy coughed. "He's breathing!"

"How's the father?" roared the Captain, moving down the triage line.

"Responding to oxygen, sir!"

"How 'bout the others?!" he shouted, moving to the rescuers, last in line, and noticing for the first time Tiger's badge. "Hey, what the fuck is the HVFD? Is that the Hamptons?"

Wrestling with paramedics, the gasping father cried out for his son. "Billy? Billy?"

As paramedics clamped oxygen to his face, he continued calling out.

"Calm down, buddy! He's okay!"

Weeping as he was wheeled to the ambulance, the father turned now to the scorched face of the little man who had saved his son's life. "How's he?"

Peering through a tangle of hoses, just as medics cleaned the man's face, the father suddenly flew up from his gurney as if he'd seen a ghost.

"TIGER BURNS. My God! He's alive!"

"What? Who's he?" asked the Captain, subduing the man, thrashing wildly now.

"Our missing hockey player!"

"What missing hockey player?"

"From Hartford!"

At that, the Captain, no fool he, put his hands on his hips—and sneered.

"Don't be a wise ass! Hartford doesn't have a hockey team!"

"It's Tiger Burns. I swear to it."

"Never heard of him!" scoffed the Captain, certain now the man was delirious—but with a follow-up just to be sure. "Well, then who the hell are you to recognize him?"

"The Commissioner," he said softly, and the ambulance door shut.

And so in a blur of lights and sirens, the Commissioner, his son, the missing hockey player and the red-shirted hero were rushed to Columbia-Presbyterian. Wearily reaching for his pen, the Captain began the paper work he so dreaded.

"What'd he say that name was again, lieutenant?"

"BURNS, Sir! No word of a lie."

Next day, from his hospital bed, the NHL Commissioner requested a face-to face with his long-lost player. When Gracie wheeled Tiger in, his bandaged face could not mask his astonishment.

"Mr. Commissioner! What happened to you, sir?"

"Never mind me! We've been looking for *you* Tiger Burns since '91," he said through breathing tubes. "I can't imagine a better time to have found you, or you me, as the case was. You saved our lives."

Tiger looked down. He never wore the mantle of hero comfortably.

"We have a lot to talk about, you and me, Tiger. For starters, the league owes you a pension, you know that?"

"Keep it," he mumbled, head down.

"It's not okay. We're going to settle up with you. Oh, and where's that other rescuer, your friend there?"

"No idea," shrugged Tiger, looking to Gracie for help.

"He flagged us down on the road," she explained. "Never saw him before."

"Well, he's in the hospital, isn't he?"

Tiger shrugged again.

"*Was* in the hospital," Gracie corrected.

"Discharged already?"

"Well, not exactly," said Gracie. "The scuttlebutt from the nurses is that he bet a nurse he could fly, then jumped out the window, intra-venous tubes and all. Security's been hunting him down since last night."

"What??"

"Well, his room was on the first floor, so it wasn't so big a deal."

"What kind of screwball would do something like that? What's his name?"

Gracie shrugged. "No one seems to know."

Glancing at Tiger, the Commissioner sighed, "Birds of a feather, I guess," before turning serious: "Tiger, this game owes you a lot more than just your pension."

Tiger hung his head low.

"Anything we can do! Name it."

Tiger shook his head to say "nothing", but Gracie grabbed his hand and spoke up.

"Keep the pension, Mr. Commissioner! But grant Tiger his long-held wish."

Looking at Tiger's eager face, and tattered jersey, and guessing where this might be going, the Commissioner nipped it in the bud.

"Look, I can't bring back your team, if that's where you're going here. I'm sorry."

"It's all I really want," Tiger mumbled.

"I'm sorry. Anything else, just ask."

"Anything?" Gracie chimed in.

"My God! He saved my son! If it's within my powers, the League will do it. But I *can't* undo the past. I'm sorry!"

Tiger suddenly remembered the stolen trophy. Maybe police were onto him and getting ready to arrest him? Maybe he could get absolution for that stunt?

"Can we bring the Stanley Cup to Hartford, Mr. Commissioner? Maybe for a day. I mean, to the schools, hospitals, the insurance companies even?"

"Absolutely! Take a week! I think that goalie from New Jersey has it now, if memory serves. We'll get it from him and send it up to Hartford."

"It would mean so much!" said Tiger, turning guiltily to Gracie. "Don't ya' think?"

Gracie stood with arms crossed. "It's not enough!"

Tiger and the commissioner stared. "Well, what would be enough?" asked the commissioner, all huffy.

Gracie didn't miss a beat.

"A game at the Civic Center between the Stanley Cup Champs and Hartford's minor league team—with Tiger as coach!"

"At the MALL?" the Commissioner gasped.

"Yes, Mr. Commissioner! With a chance to win the Stanley Cup—where it counts, on-ice!"

"Against a minor league team?!"

"Yes! That's all we got, Mr. Commissioner! And if the Hartford boys win, Hartford *earns* the Cup for a day."

Only a hockey idiot would make such a request!

"The Player's Association will *never* agree to it," he said, dismissing the matter out of hand.

But Gracie was not done.

"All monies will go to the UConn Children's Cancer Fund, the official charity of the Whalers, and Cartwheels for Kids, Tiger's Charity."

The commissioner sucked deeply from his breathing tube. His ashen face went paler.

"You blithely ask for something unprecedented in the annals of sport. A championship trophy has *never* been put on the line in such an exhibition as you so cavalierly propose. It's preposterous!"

"Well, your life has *never* been saved by a man who sacrificed his, and lives in a city that had its hockey team stolen on *your* watch," Gracie fired back, like a Colt revolver. "You ought to be ashamed!"

Tiger and the commissioner were dumbstruck.

"I don't know what to say," he fumbled.

"Say, 'Yes!'" said Gracie, wheeling a grinning Tiger out of the room.

At the nurse's station, Gracie remembered something. Unlatching a large steamer trunk, she removed the three-foot silver trophy and returned.

"Oh, by the way, here's your Stanley Cup, Mr. Commissioner! Tiger and I are heading back to Hartford now."

34. The Public Watch Dogs

One dead fireman in Brooklyn is worth 10 dead English bobbies,
who are worth 50 Arabs, who are worth 500 Africans.
—Cynical Journalist's Rule of Thumb

"COUP FOR THE CUP!" trumpeted *The Hartford Courant* with jump headline, "MAUL AT THE MALL!"

Next day, from his hospital bed, a weary commissioner announced that the Player's Association, after contentious, all-night negotiations, had approved the unusual game. Reading from a statement, and citing the rarely-invoked "welfare of the game" clause giving him "discretionary powers", he spoke wanly:

> These are extraordinary circumstances, indeed, when a player of Tiger Burns's stature, our all-time penalty leader, resurfaces after a decade.

> Moreover, in doing so, when in an act of valor, he rushes into a burning building, not knowing who lay trapped inside, this league is prepared to take unprecedented action.

> In war, the Congressional Medal of Honor is awarded for conspicuous acts of bravery; in hockey, we have no such medal. Our highest award is the Stanley Cup, a trophy that can be won only in battle. And so it must always be!

> And so as a commendation of present valor, and in recognition of past wrongs and as a partial redress for them, let me proclaim:

> By the powers vested in me by the Board of Governors, and with the consent of the Player's Association, over

the strident objections of the league's liability insurers,
I hereby authorize:

That the Stanley Cup be placed at stake, a week hence,
with the Champion Devils to defend it against the
Hartford Wolf Pack at the Civic Center Mall.

At that, a breathing tube loosened and a high-pitched whining emitted.
Gasping for breath, the commissioner soldiered on:

In the event of a Hartford victory, the Cup shall stay
in that city's possession, under the auspices of Coach
Tiger Burns, for one full day, not to exceed 24 hours.
At the end of such time, the Stanley Cup will return to
the Devils, the current and rightful holders.

At the conclusion, the commissioner, under considerable strain, sagged
into his bed.

And so it was official: The New Jersey Devils were coming to the
Insurance Capital for a one-game playoff against the Hartford WolfPack,
with the Stanley Cup on the line. As might be imagined, the hue and outcry
from the guardians of the game was both immediate and indignant.

"A CHEAP publicity stunt!" bellowed the pundits on ESPN. "If the
NHL can't win in the marketplace of ideas, it resorts to gimmickry time
and again. It's a tired, old hat trick."

The commissioner's press release had trumpeted several "innovations"
to be used in the game—a red-glow puck for increased visibility, white
skates on both teams, and when the puck was shot over 50 mph, a "comet's
tail" would appear in its wake for TV.

"Every slap shot will appear like Halley's Comet!" the release
announced.

To attract fans, the NHL has often been willing to tinker with the
game. Alas, hockey has always been the "weak sister" of the major sports,
never quite able to land an elusive network deal. One recent Stanley Cup
was televised on the Outdoor Life Network between bass fishing and boar
hunting shows. The Commissioner, critics railed, was using "personal
tragedy to showcase the game."

But even with all the carping and high-minded outrage, a funny thing
happened: the public became enchanted. Caught up in the personality of the

shadowy figure at center stage, sports fans—and hockey moms—wanted to know more. And so the belly of the media beast needed feeding.

People Magazine put Tiger on its cover, along with special 3-D glasses to enhance his grotesque features. The edition sold out overnight.

"Put this gruesome guy on the cover and magazines fly off shelves," explained Media Analyst Nigel Redding.

The clamor to learn more grew insatiable: Where have you been all these years Tiger Burns? What brings you back now? How did you achieve that *outré* look? Inquiring minds wanted to know!

The Hartford Courant drove the story. It was their story, after all, and Tiger was their long-lost goon. The plucky, little paper scooped the *New York Times* and *Boston Globe* with a series of investigations on the fire—enraging the Broadsheet Bullies. Again and again, *The Courant* scooped them—breaking ground every day, save one notable omission: the identity of the red-shirted hero. On that score, everyone was stymied.

"Interview every god-damned crack addict and windshield washer in the city," fumed *The Times* editor. "But find that homeless bastard now!"

And so the hounds were unleashed to hunt the story down. And the poor nurse who treated him last was treed and in the cross-hairs.

"I didn't even get his blood pressure," she pleaded outside her Queens flat, shielding her invalid father from cameras.

"TELL us what he looked like?"

"WHAT was he wearing?"

"Please, leave us alone!" she begged. "Can't you see what this is doing? Stop combing through our garbage!"

The cameras panned in closer.

"Okay—I'll repeat: He was tall, left-handed and leaped out the window claiming he could fly—oh, and wore a funny hat. That's all I know! Pray have mercy!"

As the vigil in Queens continued, one enterprising Hartford reporter was piecing together the kind of story that has editors whispering the dreaded p-word hanging ominously over every newsroom in the country—"Pulitzer" (not plagiarism.) Josie Sweaney had dreamed of winning one since she was editor of her high school paper—only now she got a break.

As a cub reporter, Sweaney had done a story on "Rookie Teachers in a Troubled System" and shadowed Gracie. It was a time of stress for both—one writing her first story, the other teaching her first class. Bonding over the experiences, the two met "off record" for dinner. It was then Gracie dropped the scoop of a lifetime in Josie's lap.

Like others, Sweaney had heard the rumors of the homeless Whaler living under bridges—only she was granted access. With Tiger's blessing, she retraced his steps, piecing together the tear-stained trail of a fallen hero. But until Tiger's go-ahead, the story was spiked. Months and years passed. The story yellowed in a folder.

But the day after the Commissioner's announcement, "Tiger's Tormented Tale" was sprung on a world eager to sop up every detail. Lifting the veil on a tortured life, Sweaney's lead began:

> Like a World War II Japanese survivor hiding decades after the last shots were fired, Tiger Burns has emerged from a bunker beneath the Bulkeley Bridge in full regalia—a tattered Whaler jersey—for one final shot at glory.
>
> His emergence is the latest chapter in a decade of wandering that began the night of April 11, 1990 with one errant shot—a tragic misfire that altered the course of a man, a team and a city.

Charting every torturous twist and turn, she laid bare Tiger's suffering, illuminating his loyalty to a team and city. The blockbuster touched off a media firestorm.

"Where Have You Gone Tiger Burns?" sang out the cover of *Sports Illustrated*. *ABC News* made Tiger "Person of the Week" for "fidelity to a cause and a people, borne of a deep and unfathomable grief." Nationally, he became a symbol of hope. Caravans of satellite trucks camped outside the Civic Center, where once The Russian Lady stood.

At his first press conference, the decorum that generally prevails at these affairs deteriorated quickly. In an ill-fitting Macy's suit, strangled by a 21-inch collar, Tiger was besieged by journalists, from as far as Japan:

"Did you SLEEP under the bridge last night?"

"Will these pliable rules be amended to allow coaches to FIGHT?"

"Show us your TATTOO! C'mon take off your shirt!"

Tiger struggled to express his inner feelings, his head poking just above the podium festooned with microphones. "Umm, it ain't easy switchin' allegiance, even to another Hartford team..."

"Will you FIGHT Broadway Lawlor again?"

"How many polar bears did you SLAUGHTER in cold-blood? And a follow-up, please: Are you aware it's a VIOLATION of the endangered species act?"

The public watchdogs were nipping and baying, and now Tiger was in the cross-hairs.

"The game is for Hartford," he pleaded, loosening his collar. "The city deserves this..."

"Answer the question, GOON!"

"Yea, the public has a RIGHT to know!"

For the media, it was a carnival, worse, a freak show. But for Tiger, this game meant everything. Driven from the podium, he passed by a seal with the city motto "After the clouds, sun", the cameras catching every step of a very public meltdown.

From his home in North Carolina, Ronnie read the stories, watched the press conferences and felt sickened.

"He's kept the weight of the world on his shoulders all these years," he said to Mary Lou, "and no one knew."

Like everyone, Ronnie had not been in touch with Tiger since the fateful Boston game over 10 years before. Reading of his tortured life, he berated himself as you would when you learn an old friend has died and you hadn't reached out in time.

"Why didn't I at least make an effort?"

How many times had Tiger bled for him? Stood up for him? Protected him? But how could Ronnie have known?

"How could I *not* have known?" he wailed. "He was my friend and teammate. What's more important than that?"

Ronnie needed someone to talk to, and so he turned to another teammate. Kevin Dineen and Ronnie had remained close, even as trades and growing families kept them apart. He punched his number on speed dial, getting him on the second ring.

"Hey, it's me! Did ya' see..."

"Tiger! Caught it on ESPN. Can you believe it! What the hell happened to him?"

Ronnie paced back and forth, raking his brown hair with his hand. "I don't know, but know what? He's back and he needs us!" Ronnie's voice cracked. "You remember how he always had our backs?"

Kevin chuckled. "Yeah, remember how he went after Frenchie Le Duc for sticking you? It took six guys to pull him off! Good ol' Tiger."

At that fond recollection, Hartford's John Wayne on Skates teared up, too.

"He needs us, Ronnie. No one's ever been there for him!"

"He seemed so indestructible, Kev. I always knew he had a big heart. I just never knew it could break like that…" Ronnie's voice trailed off.

"We've all been so busy, Ronnie! But he never forgot us—or the Whale."

Ronnie stopped pacing and slammed his fist down on the counter.

"That's exactly what I'm talking about, Kev! Tiger is always putting himself on the line for the team. It's our turn to pay him back."

After a few more minutes, Ronnie hung up and smiled. *Hang in there, Tiger. We're coming.*

35. Lights in the Sky

I came in with Halley's Comet in 1835.
It is coming again next year (1910),
and I expect to go out with it.
— Mark Twain, 1835-1910

Storming out of the press conference, Tiger exited the Civic Center and headed up Asylum. At Union Station, crossing a tourniquet of ramps, he passed the statue for America's first deaf school. At last, he reached the familiar Victorian.

Two weather-beaten gargoyles still kept sentinel on the upper ledge. Rapping with a tender hand and staring down at the "Welcome" mat, in minutes, a stooped man fumbling with the latches opened the door.

"Been a long time, son."

Tapping his cane to the floor, the old man led Tiger back to the oak table. In the twilight, arranged neatly on the counter, Tiger noticed the yellowed bandages and dusty remedy bottles.

"She knew you'd return," the old man said, following Tiger's eye, "even if she weren't here to greet you."

Resting his mangled hands on the table, Tiger looked down. The old man clasped a pallid hand atop Tiger's fist.

"She died five years ago."

Tiger looked up, and a single stream flowed down his right cheek.

"She was so proud of you, Tiger!"

A tear tumbled onto his muscular chest, then trampolined to the floor. His father squeezed his hand.

"We prayed for you every night."

Pulling Tiger's enormous head to his shoulder, he whispered, "You brought us so much happiness."

Desperately, Tiger tried to explain.

"I was such a failure. I let everyone down. I had to go."

"NO!"

The old man embraced the fighter with surprising strength. "No one did as much! You cared too deeply. This is your home."

189

Tiger again struggled to explain.

"Every night, I walked up the hill to see you were safe. I kept an eye on you."

"Only one?" the old man asked, arching a brow, and breaking the tension—then it dawned on him. "The flowers at the cemetery?"

"Yes," Tiger confirmed.

Leaning back and slapping his thigh, the old man shouted, "Who else could it have been? But she'd been so kind to many. What a FOOL I've been! "

"No, I'm the fool, Dad."

"NO, Tiger! You taught this city to fight for itself, and now this game is the biggest thing to happen, well, since you left. No one else could have pulled this off!"

Tiger looked away. He always had trouble accepting kind words.

"Why don't you stay tonight? In your old room. Your mom wouldn't touch a thing knowing this day would come."

Uncomfortable now, Tiger fumbled for an excuse.

"Dad, it's been so long that I've slept in a bed I don't think I could. I'm used to the sounds of the river, and a bridge above my head."

"Tiger, sleeping in a bed is *no* adjustment!"

"I thought so too, but sleeping on the benches in New York, I heard voices."

"Voices?" asked the old man, alarmed now.

Tiger nodded. "I hope you don't think I'm crazy."

"Well, had you ever heard them before?"

"Never!"

"Hmmm…maybe it was just the change in atmosphere. I wouldn't worry about it," he said, adding slyly, "But, if you hear voices in your bed, you can block them out with a pillow."

Both men laughed. It felt good to be together again.

That night, surrounded by things familiar, Tiger relaxed. It felt like old times—everything, except his role. Other nights, he played—and fought—next day. But tomorrow he would be coaching against the Stanley Cup Champs backboned by Broadway Lawlor. It gnawed at him.

A Boston writer's disparaging words rattled about in his cavernous head: "Tiger knows fighting, but he don't know coaching! His players will be standing around like the rocks of *Stone Field Sculpture*—Hartford's ridiculous civic monument."

It would have been easier to sleep under a bridge. All night, he was awakened by the sounds of a city in the thralls of anticipation. Blocking his ears, he fell into a fitful slumber—before awakening to shimmering lights. Stumbling out of bed, he staggered to the window and pressed his nose against the pane.

"Wow! The Northern Lights! Just like Churchill! But I've never seen them so bright!"

Craning his neck, Tiger saw, amidst the swirling green, white flashes with streaking tails.

"Meteors and comets, too!!"

Marveling at the celestial fireworks, Tiger at last glanced over at the clock. It was 3 a.m.

"Got to go to sleep," he yawned, pulling the shade, as colors flickered across the white canvas. Back in bed, irksome thoughts rattled in his head—and the damnable voices returned, but with a caveat.

Yup, they'll be in the cheap seats...BUT they'll need tickets, Tiger.

Yea, way up in the nosebleeds—BUT don't forget the tickets!

"Leave me ALONE!" he hollered, burying his face in the pillow to escape the taunts. "I'm going NUTS!"

Blinded by lights and bewildered by voices, Tiger retreated to the kitchen, where to his surprise, his father sat, not at all surprised to see him.

"Only so much a coach can do, son," he said, pouring some milk and sliding it over.

"I'm having nightmares, Dad. I don't want to mess this up again."

A silence followed.

"Tiger, can I ask you a personal question?"

"Of course!"

"Do you have a girlfriend?"

Tiger's face flushed. The milk went down the wrong way. He choked.

"Your mother wanted to see you happy and settled. It was her dream, you know?"

"She did??"

"She wanted to see you loved. It was always her wish to her dying day."

Tiger blushed again, then ducked, an old fighter's ploy.

"Dad, there were lights in the sky outside my window," he reported gravely.

"Spotlights, you mean?"

"No, the Northern Lights—but mixed with comets and streaking meteors."

"Man-made lights, they were?"

"No, no, no up in the heavens."

"Tiger, are you *sure*?"

"Positive, Dad!"

The old man rubbed his chin pensively.

"Well, doth thou think that the heavens rejoiceth or protesteth?"

Tiger guffawed— "Oh, and the voices are back."

"Oh, no!"

"In Central Park, they said *'Play it, and they'll be in the cheap seats.'* But tonight there was more!"

"More?! Oh gosh, let's hear it."

"*'BUT they will need tickets!'* Dad, I don't know what to do. I'm at my wit's end!"

"Tickets?!"

"Yup."

Mr. Schmidley rubbed his gray-stubble and pondered. "Well, you have no choice then."

"What should I do, Dad? Tell me."

"Leave tickets!"

Tiger guffawed. "So logical, Dad—typical insurance guy."

They both laughed.

"Okay, but who do I leave them for?"

"Hmmm…address the envelope 'Tiger's Friends.' That should do it!"

"But, Dad, I don't know them!"

"Then put 'HARTFORD'S FRIENDS.' Good night, son. Get some rest now!"

36. Destination City

On that day the anointed eye saw the crowd of spirits that mingled with the procession in vacant spaces…and the far longer train of ghosts that followed the company, of the men that were before us…the long winding train reaching back into eternity.
—Ralph Waldo Emerson

Spotlights streaked across the sky from building tops. Banners festooned lampposts up and down Main Street. Fireworks exploded over the Connecticut River. Pranksters even placed a replica of the Stanley Cup smack dab in the middle of *Stone Field Sculpture*. Hartford looked like a destination city—and now it was for the biggest spectacle to hit the Insurance City in decades, "The Maul in The Mall", as the press was calling it.

Yes, weird things were going on! The night before, meteors stormed over the capital city—in combination with celestial lights.

"Never seen anything like it!" marveled Professor Russell, a veteran sky sweeper. "Very localized effect—not sure what to make of it, to be honest?!"

"Smog mixed with traffic lights produces that effect," scoffed Harvard University Astronomer Robert Noyes. "They're not used to much traffic down there."

Indeed! There wasn't an open hotel room for miles. Canadian Hollywood like Jim Carey, Michael J. Fox, and Alan Thicke arrived in limos the length of a city block. Hockey royalty like Gretzky, Lemieux and Gordie walked the red carpet. Caravans were even making the "reverse commute" from New York and Boston. Yes, weird things were going on—very weird!

It was like Oscar Night in Hartford, only the trophy was not some palm-sized, mass-produced statuette but the towering, one-of-a-kind, sterling Stanley Cup! Not since the 1986 All-Star Game had this much excitement and celebrity focused on Connecticut's Capital.

On hand also was a special group in vintage costume. The Hartford Whalers Alumni had returned for the first time since April 13, 1997 for a charity game. "Gang Green" was back to scrimmage the local firefighters.

Years after they left, Hartford fans continued following their boys with proprietary interest.

"The Hartford Whalers, whose presence is still felt, like the phantom leg of an amputee, six years after the franchise fled for North Carolina,"[68] wrote Steve Rushin, in *Sports Illustrated*.

A tumultuous green sea swamped the Mall, with thousands sporting old jerseys, many taken out of cedar chests alongside family heirlooms. Mothballs—and a whiff of greatness—perfumed the air.

"I never wore a wedding gown, or a prom dress, so my green jersey is the most sacred article of clothing I own!" declared Blue-Line Betty, from her old seat by the penalty box. "I'll be buried in it!"

Faded posters still adorned walls in the Connecticut River valley. Pulses still raced whenever Chris Berman, on ESPN, harpooned *Brass Bonanza,* the hokey theme song. For years, the fans had endured all the jibes and jeers—but kept the faith.

"RO-NNIE, RO-NNIE,"

"KE-VIN, KE-VIN,"

"ULF, ULF, ULF…" boomed the chants, until everyone in turn was serenaded.

Many of "Our Boys" had gone on to greatness elsewhere. Chris Pronger won the Hart Trophy, as league MVP—in St. Louis; Joel Quenneville won Coach of the Year there, too. Ronnie won the Lady Byng Trophy for gentlemanly conduct three times—twice in Pittsburgh and once in Carolina.

"We knew there was greatness in them," crowed Blue-Line Betty. "Heck, we saw it first. We nurtured it!"

Some had performed on Olympus, like Mark Johnson, of the 1980 "Miracle on Ice" team. Others who cut their teeth here as pups—Bobby Holik, Scott Young, Ray Ferraro, Sylvain Cote, Adam Burt, Sami Kapanen, Jean Sebastien-Giguere—waved to the crowd. Mid-career veterans—Pat Verbeek, Torrie Robertson, Mike Liut; and Whalers in coaching—Dave Tippett and Quenneville—all displayed their colors. Hartford had spawned some of the best brains in hockey.

"A coaching factory," Dineen termed it.

Founder Howard Baldwin, making Oscar-winning films, stick-boy David E. Kelley with actress-wife Michele Pfeiffer, and Hockey Czar Emile Francis, all acknowledged the thunderous cheers. And the ink-stained wretches—Jeff Jacobs and Randy Smith—were there to jot it all down.

Behind the bench in a green dress nervously sat Gracie with Mr. Schmidley in a suit still fitting from his days at the insurance company. A wreck, Gracie clutched Mr. Schmidley's arm for support.

But at the center of all the hype, hoopla and swirling emotion was Hartford's prodigal goon dressed in an ill-fitting brown suit and choking in a 21-inch collar. Tiger Burns alone was charged with taking a ragtag bunch of "no-names, never-weres and might-a-beens" against the Stanley Cup Champs.

Vegas odds were 999- to-1, and might have gone higher if tote boards added a fourth slot. And standing front and center, dipping his wicked tongue in vitriol, was Broadway Lawlor. In the days leading up, he spewed the little city:

"What did the noble savages call it again? Ah, yes, SUCKiaug!"

On the Wolf Pack:

"It's fitting we're playing a bunch of minor leaguers. The Hartford 'Failures' (rhymes with Whalers) were always strictly minor league. Thank God, we won't have to hear that damn song *Brass Bananas* (sic)? "

On Tiger:

"That goon couldn't coach a dog out of a storm with a T-bone steak."

Broadway's every *bon mot* was sopped up, jotted down and satellited around the globe. In one fit of bravado, he predicted a shut out—offering $10,000 to charity if the Wolf Pack scored. When one feisty journalist scoffed, he upped the ante:

"Geraldo, if those donkeys score, I'll dress down in a goddam green jersey and pose in front of the freakin' Twain House for the Chamber of Commerce."

But on game morning an investigative piece in *The Courant* turned the tables. Never-before-told details of Broadway's early life were splashed on the front page under the headline "A Goalie Un-Masked."

An exclusively-obtained birth certificate showed that the cosmopolitan playboy was born in Deer Entrails, Alberta—not Toronto as he claimed. A high school yearbook photo showed a buck-toothed geek who was "Treasurer of The Slide Rule Club 1,2,3,4." A college transcript revealed that the man who answered to "Professor" had flunked out.

"Broadway couldn't even spell trigonometry!" sniffed the *Courant*.

As he led the Champs on-ice, boos rained down and some yahoos in the cheap seats even tossed a gutted deer carcass onto the ice. Fans quickly picked up on the chant.

"You're from DEER ASS, DEER ASS…"

"That rag's got it all wrong!" Broadway lashed back, brandishing his oversized stick: "And that broad on the bloody rag messed it up. Period!"

"Still a 'Class Act' all the way," announced Chuck Kaiton, on hand to call next day's charity game on WTIC-1080. "Broadway hasn't changed a bit."

As Broadway jawed away, an avalanche of applause rumbled down from the rafters. Feet stomped, chairs clanged and a symphony of horns played—as Tiger Burns and the Wolf Pack took the ice.

Few gave the Hartford boys a chance. But that did not temper the enthusiasm in the "Old Mall", the calumny that Broadway had dusted off at press conferences. Walking gingerly onto the ice with mincing steps, Tiger clutched to the dasher for support. The roped veins on his 21-inch neck looked to be strangling him.

"What has Tiger Burns gotten himself into?" asked Kaiton, from the booth. "Leading a bunch of ham-and-eggers against the Stanley Cup Champs? MY! OH, MY!"

Many of the old Whalers on hand wondered the same.

"Wouldn't it be nice if the Hartford boys could keep it respectable?" Ronnie whispered to Dineen. But Dineen spoke not a word. His eyes locked on old teammate Broadway Lawlor, stifling an exaggerated yawn and flipping off fans.

As spotlights cris-crossed the arena, illuminating the faces, an eerie, almost-other-worldly glow cast from one section high above the ice. Up in 399, a half-dozen faces, as if powdered with phosphorous, looked on. Nestled between rogue groups of New Yorkers in 398 and Bostonians in 400, a white-haired man in a white suit, smeared in what appeared like animal blood, gestured madly.

"What's up with you panty-waists? This is Hartford! WHEN WE WERE KINGS, this place rocked!"

A dainty woman tossed missiles of half-loaded beer cups at the rowdies to the left and right.

"Go back to BEANTOWN! BIG APPLE, say's who?!"

A man with six-shooters fired away as if at an Afghan wedding. Had *Brass Bonanza* ever been played before as a dueling duet of .45s?

BANG BANG BANG bang-bang-bang-bang-bang…

Orchestrating the madness was a goofball in scratchy wools waving a battered hat as if it were a lasso. Yes, weird things were happening in that maligned building in that God-forsaken city. All around were ghostly faces not seen in a century!

All tallied, there were 10 Stanley Cup rings, 5 League Trophies and 6 Olympic Medals in those stands. But there were more: Great Books, Royal Medals, and Presidential Honors, too.

And moments before the face-off, the strangest apparition of all slinked in. Looking awkward and out of place, the ruddy-faced figure sat down stiffly in the last remaining seat. Could it be? Could it *really* be? Thrice a game, for years, they had belted and battered each other, and now his crooked fingers nervously rolled a game program.

Hartford had become a destination city of specters, spirits, southpaws— and one unlikely goon.

37. The Drop of the Puck

> It was a ramshackle affair, dragged along by a knock-kneed, broken-winded
> somnambulist, which his owner, in a moment of enthusiasm… referred to as a horse.
> —Jerome K. Jerome

Anthony "Red Shoes" Harrington belted out "The Star Spangled Banner."
In a blue blazer, reeking of mothballs, Greg "Golden Pipes" Gilmartin
manned the familiar mike. All the old faces were back—sure with a few
more wrinkles and grays, but everyone brought his "A" game.

Late into the night before, Gilmartin had croaked his signature lines
into the mirror. It was Prime Time now—and again he was at center stage.
At the drop of the puck, a thousand cameras flashed.

NHL hockey was back! In the Mall! Alas—as soon was apparent, in
half measures only.

Controlling the opening face-off, the Devils advanced with passes as
precise as if Euclid had traced them. Moments in, the play took on the
look-and-feel of a game of "keep-away." In the rare instant that a Hartford
player touched the puck, he caromed it wildly off the boards like a "hot
potato."

"DEE-fense!" screeched the overmatched coach, in a raspy voice barely
carrying over the crowd's groans.

When the play was in Hartford's end, as it mostly was, Broadway
taunted the crowd from his goal mouth.

"Told you he was a BUM!" he boomed out, regaining the upper hand
with fans.

Dineen, Ulf, and Francis who had done so much to lend class and
dignity to the old building, shifted uncomfortably in their seats.

"He's making a mockery of it," snarled Dineen, the fiery Irishman.
Ulf, the happy-go-lucky Swede, looked somber, and Ronnie, the Classy
Captain, seemed plain miserable.

When the Champs scored three quick goals, the last on a behind-
the-back, give-and-go, that great sucking sound was a good bit of the
enthusiasm departing the arena.

"TOLD you I'd shut 'em out!" gloated Broadway, bowing like a virtuoso and gliding off-ice, the score 3-0 after one period.

Down in the locker room, as assistants bombarded Tiger with advice, much of it contradictory, all at once, the coach just shrugged. All his life he'd led with the big hit that electrified the crowd, the toe-to-toe fight that lifted fans out of their seats, or the zany antic that made everyone loose. Called to lead with words, he had none. At last, a callow boy named Blatt, seeing his difficulty, tossed out a suggestion.

"Coach, how's about we switch to the zone trap on 'D'?"

Tiger's eye bugged out. The veins on his neck tightened. All his life he led with hard hat and hammer, blood and guts, passion and fire. X's and O's were the detritus of a tic tac toe game, for all he knew. His fists spoke most eloquently.

"Huh?"

Taking pity, a defenseman named Chabarek, bleeding from the nose, chirped in, voice high-pitched and ardent.

"Coach, if we control the center-ice, we can disrupt their attack and counter-attack. Whaddaya say, coach?"

The lads looked up at him for something. Anything! A wink! A twitch! Hell, a fart would do! Many had followed his career as boys and he commanded their respect. When at last he opened his mouth, nothing came out. Then at last something: a tear trickled out, separated into a network of scars, reconnected at the jaw, and plopped to the floor. It was happening. *Again!*

Hartford was playing the nation's fool—and it was his fault again. Folks in New York must be doubled-over laughing. Plucky Providence must be strutting around like a bantam rooster. And the rest of the world, blissfully ignorant, well, now they knew, too:

"Hartford Is A JOKE!"

The knot of Boston fans in section 400 spelled it out gleefully:

"D-E-B-A-K-L-E...It's a DEBAAHKLE in Haahtfid."

No! Not a nickname game! Please, no! *The Debacle in Hartford!* When a game acquires a nickname, it takes on a hellish life of its own. Like the *Easter Epic* that the New York Islanders lost in four overtimes. Or the *Too Many Men on the Ice* game when Boston blew a lead with 74 seconds left in Montreal. Nickname games are never forgotten!

"Oh, what a FOOL," he wailed, giving voice at last to what every overmatched boy in that room was thinking.

A few older ones, 20-year-olds Merola and Roupas, stepped up to shield the blubbering mess from the rest. "Win it for Tiger!" rah-rahed Merola, gamely rallying the troops.

"Yea, Tiger deserves our best!" echoed Roupas. "He never took a step back!"

A half-hearted amen chorus joined, as players desperately tried to latch onto something. But those innocent words, like a shock, jolted Tiger, galvanizing his thoughts.

"NO!"

Every never-was, might-a-been and never-would-be looked up.

"Look, boys, Broadway's right. I don't know a darn thing 'bout coaching."

Tiger was speaking the truth, everyone knew it. "But I do know that this city has been lookin' fa' something to pick it up fa' a long time. Farther back than any of you realize. And you boys can be the ones ta' do it!"

"Let's do it!" came shouts from the back.

"Whadda ya say we throw out that first period. Forget it, toss it in the garbage, and play 'em even this period?"

"Coach's right!"

"Can we do that? Can we hold 'em for one period? Maybe find a goal in there somewhere ourselves?" Tiger implored.

"Yes!" a lone voice shouted.

"YES!!" sang out more.

His coaching wisdom spent, Tiger stretched out a mangled hand, and every boy in that room leaped up to join it.

"One, two, three Hartford," Tiger shouted, from the center of the jubilant ring.

"ONE, TWO, THREE HARTFORD!"

When the huddle broke, Tiger led his troops out, with 25 whooping teenagers in tow—and a few even believed!

As Tiger was struggling in the locker room, up in section 399, the man in the white suit, shouting through a battered megaphone last seen at a turn-of-the-century Yale game, orchestrated a wave.

A man with a rake, pontificating about green jerseys and "green space", brandished it menacingly—"RAKE 'em over the coals," he growled.

The little woman was engaging the rowdies on either side with half-full beer cups. And the stocky man with the six-shooters fired away to his favorite tune.

BANG BANG BANG bangbangbangbangbang...

"Get off your ARSES!" the white-suited fellow exhorted. "WHEN WE WERE KINGS, this city stood up and was counted."

And the Hartford crowd stood and roared as never before—even the actuaries and insurance folk.

38. The Dead Shall Rise

The past, the present and the future are really one: they are today.
—Harriet Beecher Stowe

Stepping out gingerly onto the ice, Tiger gazed up high into the nosebleed seats. Telescoping his eye, he spied a cluster of empty seats. Maybe they won't come after all, he thought? Well, it won't be because they don't have tickets, he assured himself. He had made sure of it.

In section 400, the party-crashers from Boston, waved their banners with homespun wisdom: "HANDICAP THE HOBBIT" and "TIGER'S MOTHER IS A PUSSY." In 398, the rogue band of New Yorkers chanted, "You play in a SHOPPING MALL! Let's go SHOPPING!" Between them yawned an empty gulf.

But something in the spirit of the building had changed. For the first time in a century, Hartford believed. Down by three, applause drowned out the New York and Boston naysayers. Gracie from behind the bench, with Mr. Schmidley, banged furiously on the glass, as Tiger winked and gave a furtive "thumbs up" signal.

And Tiger's speech helped—until a nifty give-and-go left a Hartford defenseman faked out of his jock. Fans, on their feet, plummeted like stones. The old Whalers—Francis, Dineen and Ulf—slunk deeper into their seats. Gracie and Mr. Schmidley bowed their heads low. The score was 4-0—another humiliation for the Olde Towne.

"It's getting awfully quiet here," reported Kaiton. "The fans are starting to lose inter-... HALLOA!"

Eluding security, a fan in green shirt and eye-patch, hooked a powerful left arm over the glass, scaled the wall, and tumbled to the ice. Running in baseball cleats to center ice, he ripped off his jersey, unveiling a tattoo like Tiger's: the three-mast ship, the whale, even the boatload of South Seas harpooners.

"What the HEY?" hollered Kaiton.

As pot-bellied guards gave chase like Keystone Cops, the screwball executed a series of the worst cartwheels seen in these parts in years.

Eluding hapless guards, he flashed a grin—and tipped his straw hat, apparently crushed from the fall to the ice.

"Get out the straight-jackets!" laughed Al Michaels, of ABC-TV.

The Mall erupted at the offbeat antics—even Tiger managing a tight-lipped smile. As the buffoon waved to the crowd, the fans took up a chant, first a few, then more, until again the building shook:

"TI-GRRRRRR, TI-GRRRRRR, TI-GRRRRR..."

Somehow this tribute, performed by a lunatic being fit in shackles, stiffened the team's resolve. For the next 15 minutes, the Wolf Pack played the Stanley Cup Champs to a stalemate.

"That goofball was just what the doctor ordered!" diagnosed Kaiton.

Then with two minutes left, something unimaginable: a quirky carom on a routine dump preceding a line change squirted off a defenseman's stick, skipped like a beach stone, through a crevasse of bodies, and landed in the last place anyone ever expected: in the net behind Broadway. For a moment there was bewilderment—then eruptions.

"GOOOOOOAL!" shouted Kaiton. "A FLUKE! 4-1. It's the divine hand of Rube Goldberg at work! But the Pack is on the board!"

The goal was credited to the last player to touch it, 20-year-old Merola, who dumped it in 60 feet away. Sweeping the puck out from the net, an apoplectic Broadway shattered his stick over the crossbar, firing the handle at the poor defenseman who had inadvertently deflected the puck.

"There goes the diva," said a disgusted teammate, turning his back on the petulance.

"Broadway couldn't find the high road with a map, compass and GPS," sniffed Kaiton. "But he knows every pot hole, rut and crack of the low road."

As Broadway skated to the bench, even the equipment manager turned away. Grabbing a stick, he slammed the gate, upstaging the rookie defenseman every angry stride back.

"Vintage Broadway," snapped Kaiton.

The Hartford fans, from the rafters, serenaded him.

"LOLLY, LOOLLY, LOOOLLLY..."

In the last minute, the champs peppered the Wolf Pack goalie "Lumpy" Onyon with a fearsome barrage. But somehow, with Houdini-like contortions, he kept the net clean. At period's end, the Hartford boys had done the impossible, playing the Champs to a 1-1 deadlock in the second. The fans, on their feet, screamed for more.

"Now, we GOT 'em!"

"They're OURS in the third!!"

But none of the old Whalers smiled. They could see what fans could not: an angry dam was about to burst. Staring straight ahead, Ulfie grit his teeth, Dineen balled his fists, and Ronnie chewed furiously on sunflower seeds. It was hard for them to watch what was happening to the city that nurtured them, and adored them still.

"HARTFORD WHALERS— STILL OUR BOYS" proclaimed the signs.

Kevin looked up at Ronnie.

"Are you thinking like I'm thinking?"

"You betcha, Kev!"

"Ulfie, you in?"

"Bet your ass!"

"Let's roll then."

The three stood. Others in green did the same, until the whole row was on its feet. No one said a word, but every eye squinted hard and narrow.

Down in the lockers, Blatt was doubled over a barrel, Roupas wiped the blood from his nose, and Merola was cherry-red, as if sucking carbon monoxide from a tailpipe.

"Just ONE more period!" exhorted the Coach, standing before his charges. "You can do it, boys!"

Every head hung low, a few others over barrels. The boys had played the period of their lives. Nothing was left. Every man knew it—save the littlest one in front.

"Four goals is NUTHIN'! Piece a' CAKE!"

Retching echoed from the barrels. Others whimpered as if a dentist were pulling teeth without gas.

But even he, surveying the wounded, weary and decimated before him, did not believe. So again he spoke with his eloquent eye, first in a trickle, then a rivulet, and last a river. When his lips moved, the words flowed now—in a torrent to match the tears.

"I'm sorry, boys. This game shoulda never happened. Never! I wanted ta' right a wrong committed when you was just lads. You shouldn't have ta' suffer for our mistakes. I just wanted ta' make things right, ta' bring back something that was dead, and you can't do it…."

Just then, in the hall, a din arose, cresting like a wave about to break. When the door flung open, in streamed a sight not witnessed in years: the Hartford Whalers led by Captain Ronnie Francis.

"Your work's done, boys!" said Ronnie, patting the shoulder of a boy slumped on all fours. "We here, your elders, have some business to take care of."

Behind Ronnie stood Dineen, Samuelsson and the rest in town for tomorrow's charity game against the firefighters.

"The hose boys'll have to wait," said Dineen, grabbing the stick of a keeled-over player.

Just then, a remarkable alchemy occurred. Lead-footed players were transformed into gold. Guys named Merola, Blatt and Roupas handed sticks and gloves to legends named Francis, Dineen and Samuelsson.

Led by Francis, fourth in NHL history with 500 goals and 1000 assists; Dineen, one of eight with 300 goals and 1000 penalty minutes; and Pat Verbeek, 25th all-time in goals—it was as mighty a collection as had ever gathered outside of an All-Star Game.

"Gee! This is a bunch even I could coach!" exulted the little fellow in the ill-fitting suit whose 3000 penalty minutes placed him atop history's trash heap.

"Ohhh, no you don't!" snapped Quenneville, a former Coach of the Year, with proprietary interest. "That job's mine and Tippy's."

"Start stretching!" barked Dave Tippett. "You're skating tonight."

Tiger stood silent and confused, until Ronnie approached concealing something behind his back.

"Us Whalers stick together," said the Captain, tossing him a green jersey emblazoned with "TIGER KO" on back. Above the heart, was a "C" for Captain. "Suit up, buddy, we're gonna need ya."

Looking down at the vintage sweater, Tiger balked.

"The 'C' is yours, Ronnie. I-I-I could never fill it."

"You're the man tonight, Tiger. This game is your baby."

Every player, from legend to lightweight, applauded. With Ronnie's assist, Tiger pulled the jersey over his rolling shoulders, and a goofy grin lit up his face.

"How do I look fellas?"

"Better than in that damn monkey suit!" snapped Ulf, as everyone roared.

Ripping off the suit, he flexed the great Whale tattoo riding atop waves of muscles and thumped it. "Can't stop this ship, baby!" he roared, and again everyone laughed.

Dropping to the floor, he pounded out 100 piston-like pushups, then bounding to his feet, punched away at shadows until a strong arm on his shoulder intervened.

"Not tonight," said Torrie Robertson, an old enforcer.

"Tonight we got your back," seconded Shane Churla, another grizzled tough. "You're here to play."

Tiger looked confused, as just then a fog horn voice cut through the revelry of renewed camaraderie.

"Listen Up!" barked Coach Quenneville. "Here's the lineup. Lootie in Goal. Ulfie and Pronger on 'D'. First line: Francis, Dineen and Beeker."

With over 1300 goals, 2000 assists and 3 Stanley Cup rings, few could equal that front line—only there was a slight problem.

"Coach, Dineen and I both play right wing," interrupted Verbeek.

"Oh, right," said the embarrassed Coach. "Okay, Ray Ferraro move to Ronnie's line!"

No drop-off there—substituting one top-50 career goal-scorer for another.

"Ah, Coach," interjected Pee Wee, "I play center, remember?"

Quenneville was getting annoyed. Surveying the hodgepodge of players, he cried out. "Doesn't anyone in this goddamned room skate LEFT wing? Or do I have to suit up one of the minor leaguers here?"

On the floor, placing his glass eye into the socket, was the only left winger in the room. Quenneville looked down, as the delicate operation proceeded. Every man and boy held his breath.

"BURNS!"

"Huh?"

"Left wing on Ronnie's line!"

The room erupted. 300 stitches and 3000 penalty minutes had just replaced 400 goals and 500 assists—and the Coach was hailed a genius.

"Now that's a hockey line!" ballyhooed Dineen, as 20 players swarmed the muscle-bound mite who had brought them all together. With players mussing up Tiger's newly-shorn hair and tapping the great tattoo, Coach Q angrily interrupted the reunion atmosphere.

"Now, WHALERS," he yelled, then smiling. "That does have a nice ring to it, no?"

"TIGER"S TEAM!" one hooted, as others massaged his back.

Suddenly Quenneville grew intense. "Cut the bullshit now! Listen up."

The room fell silent. Every eye, an odd lot, looked up.

"We're here to WIN! Dammit! We didn't come all this way to lose."

"No fucken' way," someone yelled.

"First line! Make sure Ronnie gets the puck in the slot where he likes it—just like old times. Kevin, Tiger, got it? Oh, and one more thing…"

Just then, the door to the heavily guarded room burst open—and a few toughs instinctively stepped toward it. For at that moment, in walked the last person on earth you'd expect at a Hartford Whaler reunion: Terry O'Reilly, the skunk at the garden party. As Robertson and Churla moved in to intercept him, O'Reilly faced them down.

"I'm with you boys tonight."

"Huh?"

Turning to his old dance partner, O'Reilly spoke softly, almost tenderly: "I'm here because I respect you. You were always a gentleman out there."

Tiger looked down.

"You never took a cheap shot. There was many a time you could a'. But you never did."

The wall of muscle parted as O'Reilly walked up to embrace his old rival, leaning over to do it. "Besides, I owe you one, pal," he said, whispering into the cauliflower ear.

"You don't owe me nuthin', Taz," Tiger protested, fumbling with his eye.

"You came to my ceremony last year. For a week, it drove me crazy. Who was that little goofball beggin' for an autograph? Then it hit me—like one of your shots. I just couldn't recognize you with unclenched fists."

The guys all howled. The two respected each other in a way that only men who'd left each other's faces looking like raw hamburger could possibly understand.

"Take a photo! That's the first time those two ever touched without drawing blood!"

"How 'bout a fighter's pose?" cracked Ulfie. "Tiger stand up! Oh, you are."

The affection and camaraderie between men who'd went to war together was spilling out like blood. Reaching up, Tiger pulled O'Reilly's head down. "Means the world to me, Taz."

But Coach Q's booming voice cut him short. "Enough of old home week! O'Reilly's on our side. That's good! But we got a game to play."

Quenneville looked to O'Reilly, his newest coach, for a last bit of advice.

"Coach, what do ya gotta say to the boys here tonight?"

"No STOOPID Penalties!" O'Reilly barked. "We're down 4-1. But Hartford has always been up against it. Just play old-time Whalers hockey."

39. *Brass Bonanza* Plays Again

Outlined against a blue-gray October sky,
the Four Horsemen rode again.
In dramatic lore, they are known as
Famine, Pestilence, Destruction and Death.
These are only aliases. Their real names are...
—Grantland Rice

Francis, Dineen, Ulf and Tiger milled on the runway for their un-scripted entrance. Peering beneath the canopy, Gracie's eyes bulged.

"My God!" she shrieked, tugging at Mr. Schmidley's sleeve. "Look!"

Fans, on the other side, saw too, the announcer for one. Spilling the contraband beer he sipped to moisten his vocal chords, Gilmartin soaked his notes.

"Shit!"

Throughout the arena, a buzz was building. "Blue-Line" Betty, the 17-year season ticket holder, looked over and screamed. As excitement radiated upwards, horns blared and feet stomped. Holding the soggy tape at last, Gilmartin banged it in with such force that it almost broke. At the first note, the Mall erupted to words he had ached to say for years:

"Ladies and gentlemen, here are YOUR Hartford Whalers."

DAH DAH DAH dadadadada...

At Ronnie Francis' first glide, seismic waves rocked the old Mall. Feeling the rumble on the concourse, fans stampeded in from beer lines. One vendor hopping his counter, knocked over tip jars, scattering coins and bills, but in dreary Hartford, something better than free money was happening:

Brass Bonanza was playing—and the Hartford Whalers were taking the ice.

Hockey fans, owing to Al Michaels' famous call "Do you believe in Miracles?" had always believed in the impossible. And now it was happening—in Hartford. In the Mall. The dodo walked the earth again.

###

"Holy Shit!" swore a Devils assistant, sneaking a butt in the hall, glancing out at the ice. Racing back to the locker, he breathlessly reported what he'd just witnessed.

"YO! YO! Heads Up! Francis, Dineen and Samuelsson are out there now with the rest in green. All locked and loaded. The baton has been passed."

Players lounging about playing cards looked up. Others reclining and reading papers were slower to apprehend. "Oh, and it don't sound like 'a Mall' out there no mo'," he added.

The herald's report took a moment to sink in. Before the coach could address it, a skate flying above the card sharps crashed into the chalkboard scrawled with: "Relax and Enjoy—One More Period!"

"BULL SHIT!" shouted a glowering Broadway. "That ain't in the contract!"

Before the Amen Chorus sure to greet any call to mutiny followed, the young defenseman who'd been dressed down after the Wolf Pack's goal piped up.

"What's a matta, Broadway, you afraid of the Hartford Whalers?"

As Broadway raised the other skate to eviscerate the impertinent rookie, two players grabbed him. After a brief scuffle, the scout continued:

"Oh, and Tiger Burns ain't coachin' no mo'. He's on ice in green with the rest of 'em."

At that intelligence, a few of the enforcers nervously rolled their necks. With 600 fights—100 against Terry O'Reilly—Tiger was a legend. Although he hadn't fought in over a decade, the time away had done little to tarnish his image. Sleeping under a bridge is not apt to soften a man much.

"Relax, fellas" said the rookie blue-liner, looking over at the anxious goons. "Word is that Tiger is gunning for one guy—and one guy only. And that's our fearless leader here—trying to herd us all onto the getaway bus."

A few players snickered. The room fell awfully silent. Every eye now shifted over to the goalie.

"You impudent son of a bitch," he thundered and lunged again.

Intercepted, Broadway smoothed the wrinkles on his jersey, and gathered his composure. He chose his words carefully.

"That FU-cking, NO-talent, LO-ser. I rid this league of him once. I'll do it again! I ain't scared a' no one."

And with that, the battle was joined. The Wolfpack-Whale down 4-1. One period to go. The Stanley Cup on the line.

40. The Dodo Sings

Neither shall there be any more pain. Rev.
—Ether Monument, Boston Public Garden

On the ice, the Hartford Whalers basked in an orgy of appreciation. Waving, bowing, pointing at old friends, they reveled in the moment. Who could ever have imagined it?

But in one man there was an uncharacteristic resolve. The man once called "a beer barrel on skates" skated now as if one were strapped on his back. Pitching from side to side, huffing and puffing, he appeared a candidate for double-blades. A dozen years of rust is a lot to kick off in a few twirls around the ice.

Boos, epithets, and entrails rained down when the Champs joined them on ice. What had gotten into these boisterous fans? Suddenly this wasn't your usual Hartford anymore.

Both teams observed a strict territorial code. Against the Wolf Pack, Jersey's goons had brazenly crossed the center line each revolution, a sign of disrespect. But now both teams stayed on their own side, a dime's width between two whirling cyclones in green and red.

At every turn, two hulks seemed on the verge of a harrowing collision, until at the last instant, an elbow was tucked to allow safe passage. It's the territoriality that comes when a goal must be defended. Full-scale brawls have ignited over the placing of a toe over the red line. And this third period had suddenly taken on a very combustible feel.

"You WANT us? You GOT us!" snarled Dineen, eyeing an outsized Devils' goon, in the charged atmosphere.

The terms of the contest had shifted. An exhibition had turned into a chance for redemption. And some men will do anything for that chance. The feeling was that at least one out there was willing to die for it.

Every fan's and player's gaze fixed on Tiger Burns. Just what was this tightly-coiled ball of muscle and wounded pride capable of?

"He's looking a lil' ornery," observed Kaiton, on the radio. "But did anyone sharpen his skates? He ain't moving around too good."

And what passions were stirring inside the likes of Francis, Dineen and Samuelsson who'd watched the team of their youth stolen away?

"None of those fellows liked the way things went down here," Kaiton reminded listeners. "They'll be skating with a chip on their shoulder."

And there were other questions: Could the team in green play a lick after all these years? Could the Champs contain a force that they barely understood yet felt palpably in that building? And just what was the ever-volatile Broadway capable of? Tensions ratcheted upwards.

"My! OH MY! Is that Terry O'Reilly?" shrieked Kaiton, noticing the incongruous figure behind the bench. "Things sure are getting interesting here in the Mall."

On his first lap, Broadway made a show of skating by Tiger. But when Tiger looked up, he quickly dipped behind a few burly enforcers.

"I ain't scared of that little puke," he yelled, behind a red wall of muscle.

The two goaltenders made a study in contrasts. Mike Liut, "Lootie" in his day, took a back seat to none. A 6-footer with a stand-up style, he was once runner-up for the Vezina Trophy, signifying goal-tending excellence. Broadway, at the other end, flopped around like a fish out of water. His success he attributed to "Trigonometry" and who could argue? He had Vezinas stacked up like cordwood.

With Francis, Dineen and Tiger on first line, Ulfie and Pronger on "D", and Lootie in goal, the Whale had 80 years, 4 Stanley Cups, and, owing to one man, untold penalty minutes. At stake was the honor of a city, a team, and, at least one man.

"I believe in you," Gracie mouthed, when Tiger looked over. He nodded.

At the drop of the puck, in the glare of a thousand flashes, a hulking goon "Meatcleaver" Mulroney shot an elbow into Tiger's face, sending his Red Baron helmet sledding across the ice.

"Welcome Wagon!" he sneered, and waited for the gloves to drop.

"No Dice!" grimaced Tiger, absorbing the blow.

But from the corner of his eye, he saw something not so easily forgiven. A second Devil sent Ronnie to the ice with a two-handed spear. Racing to the scene of the affront, and dropping his gloves, he pounded away with righteous abandon, as Francis from the ice shouted. "No, Tiger, NOOOOO…"

Too late.

"TIIIIIIMBERRRRRRR," bellowed Kaiton, dusting off his signature call.

As the senseless brute was carted from the ice, the referee relayed the call to the announcer, who breathed deep and clicked the mike:

"At 19:54 of the third period, five minutes for fighting, Burns."

It had taken Tiger all of 6 seconds to land himself in the "Sin Bin". In the confusion, the ref had missed the initial provocation, but caught the retaliation. With a three goal lead, the Devils now had a 5-minute power play.

"STOOOOOOPID!" hollered Dineen, jabbing at his helmet. "What the hell are you thinking?!"

Skating to his familiar spot in the box, Tiger slumped down on the hard bench, cradling his oversized head. "Same old Tiger!" needled a Devil, skating by for the power play.

Even O'Reilly, from across the ice, yelled, "Use your HEAD! DOWN by 3."

Shaped by a lifetime of experience, Tiger had responded in the only way he knew, beating the tar out of a bully. Incapable of governing the primitive forces that caused him always to defend those he loved, his reaction now had jeopardized the game. In other circumstances, the impulse might have been forgiven, even lauded.

But not *here*. Not *now*. Everyone was giving it to him.

"A TIME and a PLACE!" scolded Blue-Line Betty, banging on the glass and pointing furiously to her dyed-blonde mane. "Use your head!"

Ronnie rarely upbraided Tiger. After a fight, he almost always tapped Tiger's shins with his stick, in solidarity. But this was a 20-minute game now, and Tiger had just squandered five.

"I'll fight my own battles," he snarled, shifting to the penalty-killing unit to take the face-off.

Derisive chants from the small Boston crowd in section 400 summed it all up:

"MO-RON, MO-ROOON…"

But Hartford fans closed ranks. He was their moron, after all, and soon the Beantown hooligans were shouted down:

"TI-GRRRRRR, TI-GRRRRRRR…"

Tiger settled into his familiar seat. After a decade, he could identify nearly every scarlet smudge and splatter in the penalty box—the lion's share his own. Dineen, still fuming, skated by one last time.

"We're going to kill this one off, but that's the *last*, o.k.? You're on a *scoring* line, remember! Torrie'll handle the rough stuff."

Tiger slumped down, but the fan's applause rocketed him to his feet. Lootie made two saves, gloving a slap shot and blocking a wrist shot from the circle. As Dineen skated by, doubled-over, he pointed at Tiger.

"That was for you! Now help us score."

The team was with him! 15,535 fans were with him! His confidence surged. Gazing up to the highest reaches of the stadium, up in the nosebleeds, he could not believe his eye.

"They're HERE! In the CHEAP seats!!"

Hoisting the penalty box attendant by the lapels, Tiger pointed in amazement. Up in the nosebleeds, the most ragtag, rowdy bunch seen in centuries was clanging bells and firing guns—and it was catching on.

"What's a matter?" hollered the white-haired man through the battered green funnel. "This is Hartford! FUN is allowed!"

BANG BANG BANG bangbangbangbangbang...fired the man with the six-shooters.

As the rally degenerated into a missile-tossing fracas between the misfits and the interlopers on either side, the white-suited man fingered the woman beside him for blame.

"That's the little old lady who started the war up here!"

"I knew they'd come!" cried Tiger to the penalty keeper. "The crowd's going ballistic—and it all starts up there!"

"You NUTS?" he said, following Tiger's crooked finger to an empty camera platform in Section 399. "No one's there!"

"Can't you see 'em? Twain, Colt, Olmsted and Harriet—in the nosebleeds!" he implored, pointing.

All was quiet in 399, the only quiet spot in the building.

"It's EMPTY, for God sakes, Tiger!"

Tiger looked at him, amazed. The rest of the crowd seemed strangely oblivious, too. The one-eyed man could see what no one else could.

"C'mon, Tiger! Get a grip! Your penalty's about up!"

Tiger, who had entered the pen as docile as a veal calf, was bucking now like a bronco. Jumping onto the glass, he churned out 15 pull-ups, before launching into a blizzard of jumping jacks.

"He's BAAAAAACK!" shouted a leather-lung in 105. "That's OUR Tiger!"

With a minute to go, and the Champs hell-bent on scoring, the puck squirted out of the Whaler's zone to the blue line right where Ronnie was cheating. Gathering it along the boards, there was nothing but open ice ahead.

Racing to center ice, outpacing a chase pack of defenders, his head was up, stick down. Crossing the blue line, he only had Broadway to beat. Ten feet out, he faked left, and when Broadway, obliged to respect the possibility of a shot, committed—at that instant, Ronnie seized control. With Broadway on his knees, Ronnie flipped the disk up over his shoulder in the upper right corner. At the twinkling of the twine, 15,535 fans unleashed a mighty roar. And music played—punctuated by gunfire.

DAH DAH DAH dadadadada....

BANG BANG BANG bangbangbangbangbang...

"THE WHALERS SCORE! THE WHALERS SCORE!! THE HARTFORD WHALERS SCORE!!!" thundered Kaiton, on WTIC 1080. "Words I never dreamed I'd scream again—save in hockey heaven! It's 4-2."

Floodgates of joy, dammed for years, came to a burst. Ten thousand Dutch Boy's thumbs could not have contained the jubilation. And up in section 399 shots fired, missiles flew, and the white suit roared.

"I came in with Halley's and went out with it—but I ain't leaving this time 'round without one of them Stanley Cups! No, sir, I ain't!"

Things got so unruly that the ballplayer doing handstands on the rails was thought to be inhaling laughing gas.

"Nah, he'd act like that whitewashing a fence—or at his own funeral," said the man in white, approvingly.

What had come of that stultifying old Puritan spirit? H.L. Mencken had called Puritans those folks with "the haunting fear that someone, somewhere may be happy", but these folk were having more fun than a city ought. From the box, Tiger took it all in, and Gracie, peering across the ice, smiled.

"He's getting ready!" she yelled, tugging at Mr. Schmidley's sleeve.

With 30 seconds left on the penalty, the Whalers still had a last storm to weather. Scoring short-handed on the Champs had wounded their pride—but Lootie thwarted the desperate barrage with every part of his armor.

SKATE Save!

"Oooooooh!"

BLOCKER Save!

"Oooooooh!"

PAD Save!

"Oooooh!"

From the penalty box, Tiger did somersaults, pantomiming each save. With seconds left, the fans and Gracie counted down.

"5-4-3-2-1…"

Like a circus cannonball, Tiger shot from the box, and five strides out, the Whalers having cleared the puck to release the pressure, it landed on the last place any Whaler fan wanted it: Tiger's stick, with clear ice ahead.

"Nooooo," fans wailed, and others averted their eyes, as Gracie grabbed Mr. Schmidley's arm for support.

With 10 yards on the nearest Devil, Tiger got his bearings, and churned his legs. Crossing the blue line, five yards ahead of a chase pack, more fans covered their eyes, Gracie too, as Tiger bore in, him against Broadway.

But as Ronnie had done moments ago with a surgeon's skill, Tiger now did like a crazed axe murderer. Faking right, his legs splayed out wildly. Tumbling to the ice, he reached helplessly for the puck, sliding past the goal, head-first into the boards, the puck resting on Broadway's stick. On a clean breakaway, he hadn't even managed a shot!

"Unbelievable!" hollered dismayed fans—Gracie among them.

With Tiger flat on his back, Broadway flicked the puck crisply to his defenseman. As fans followed the attack up-ice, Broadway saw his opportunity. Wheeling around behind the goal, he cudgeled Tiger's skull with his stick. *Crack!*

The blood streaming down his face, Tiger half-rose to retaliate. But gurgling in his ears were words from Gracie that stopped him: "No! That's revenge not redemption!" Tiger fell back to the ice.

Enraged Whalers charged from the bench as one, and soon a cudgel-wielding mob surrounded Broadway. Not one teammate moved in to defend him. In the midst of a vigilante mob, Broadway shrank back into his crease. As Torrie Robertson rifled his gloves down, Tiger hollered out in a raspy voice.

"NO, Torrie! NO!!"

At the last instant, Torrie veered away, with Broadway smirking as if he alone had single-handedly fended off the stick-wielding mob.

"Get out of my crease!" he barked.

As the scrum slowly cleared, Broadway still jawing away, Tiger was dragged to the bench. Referee Kevin Collins signaled his verdict with a karate chop to his forearm. "Two minutes slashing." In hockey, as the goalie is rarely obliged to serve his own time, a proxy was delegated. With a man up, it was left to the power play to mete out the last bit of justice.

The Whalers had not practiced in a decade, but Ronnie, Kevin and Ulf had logged thousands together. After a few miscues, the kinks worked out, the power play started to sing. From Ulf at the point, to Ronnie in the slot, to Kevin knifing in on right wing, the band played on—and six-shooters saluted.

"DINEEN SCORES!"

DAH DAH DAH dadadadada…

BANG BANG BANG bangbangbangbangbang…

"Hartford has clawed its way back, 4-3! A story is unfolding here," shouted Kaiton, leaping wildly in the booth.

With arms flapping in disgust, Broadway upstaged the penalty-killers in front of him. "You're playing like PUNKS!" he yelled, grabbing a veteran defenseman, who skated out of his clutches.

Forced to burn a timeout, the Champs gathered round their coach, every player facing forward but Broadway, jawing from the edge of the circle at fans.

"HARTFORD'S A DEAD TEAM!" the coach screamed. "A bunch of PHANTOMS! It's like losing to the LOCH NESS MONSTER or the ABOMINABLE SNOWMAN. They don't exist!"

It was the truth—every player knew it. "Remember, you're the champs now. TEAM on three!"

The players languidly joined hands, those on the outskirts not bothering.

"1-2-3, Team," a few mumbled.

At their bench, doubled-over but attentive, the Whalers huddled tight. The message was crisp and focused, in bursts. "Their pride is wounded! They're gonna make a run! The next five minutes will be a test. They'll throw everything they have. If we survive, we can counter punch. Can you take their BEST shot for five minutes?"

It was a rhetorical question, meant only to challenge, but one man took it personal.

"Yes!" Tiger shrieked.

Ronnie followed, "Yes!"

"Yes!" cried Dineen and others, "YES!"

"'Whale' on three," shouted coach Q, placing his arm like a maypole and being joined by all.

"One-two-three, WHAAAAAAAAAAAALE."

The arena was in a boil. The maestros in the rafter were orchestrating a tidal wave, cresting and crashing, round and round, as the players skated to their positions. The rhythmic chanting and stomping sent chills down Tiger's flesh.

"Here WE go, WHALERS! Here WE go!"

Stomp! Stomp!

"Here WE go, WHALERS! Here WE go!"

As the coaches prophesied, the champs stanched the bleeding—and attacked. With pinball precision, they moved the puck and fired, two passes and a shot, over and over.

Pass-pass-CRACK!

Pass-pass-CRACK!

With each save, first with a skate, then with a pad, the crowd roared louder. Fighting for a rebound, Ulf wrestled the enormous Michel Legros into the crease. For an instant, Lootie lost sight of the puck. Too long! A defenseman at the circle blasted it glove-side above the tangle of bodies, lighting the red lamp.

"Noooooo," groaned the crowd, collapsing into their seats. The score was 5-3—the game surely over.

With bodies emerging from the crease—red in jubilation, green in protest, Referee Collins did not hesitate. Flailing his arms wildly like a man fending off hornets, he waved it off.

"NO GOAL! NO GOAL!" he screamed, an angry mob of red shirts tailing him.

"Interference with the goalie!" he explained to Jimmy, the official scorer, "Man in the crease. NO GOAL!"

Arguments raged on with red-faced Devils having a go at Collins, his arms folded resolutely across his chest.

"Fucking Ulfie pushed him, Collie!"

Collins looked down.

"Fucking Ulfie pushed him in the fucken' crease!!"

Collins looked away.

"Don't you fucken understand that fucking Ulf dumped him in the fucking crease?!?!"

Standing stoic in the face of the vilest personal insinuations, Collins calmly explained the call.

"The player, of his own volition, entered the crease, interfering with the goalie. That's NO GOAL!"

Was it a "hometown decision" to pacify the maddened thousands? If so, Hartford had rarely commanded that kind of respect before. Rabid Whaler fans pummeled the glass, yelling at the top of their lungs.

Broadway, disgusted at the call, shattered his Victoriaville over the crossbar, the fourth stick to meet a similar fate—three goals and now a "God-damned rip-off" call. The Devils continued protesting, as the Whalers circled tight around their coach.

"They're on their heels now! Counter Punch, Counter Punch!! I want my five best skaters out there. Beeker take Tiger's spot on Ronnie's line."

Tiger sat down on the bench. Appreciating his efforts, several players laid hands over him, covering his jersey like a pest-strip. Others whacked his shin pads with sticks as if he were a piñata.

"Atta boy, Tiger!"

"Way to go!"

At the whistle, spirited play went back and forth. Broadway, give him his due, stonewalled the Whalers twice—once on a Francis rebound, after thwarting Dineen point-blank. Wisdom has it that a "hot" goalie can carry a team—and both men were sizzling like skillets. The score stood 4-3.

For the Whalers, the line-jiggering helped. Locked and loaded, the line of Francis-Dineen-Verbeek was as potent as a Colt revolver. All three had worn the Captain's "C." Throw in Ulf on "D", under Coach 'Q', in front of Lootie, and, in the words of one scout, "You'd take your shot against anyone."

So when Lootie deflected the puck to the corner; and Ulf bounced it up to Dave Babych, who head-manned it to Ronnie; who crossed the blue line, wingers in tow, and dropped the puck to Dineen, who feathered it across to a streaking Verbeek, who blasted it over a sprawling Broadway. Who could really be surprised?

The rush left red shirts littered all over the ice, defenders who dove in vain or been deked out of their hockey shorts. As jubilant Whalers circled Verbeek, Ronnie's voice rose above the celebration.

"We didn't come this far for a tie," he said, challenging every man.

Against all odds, the Whalers had knotted the game, 4-4. For Tiger, the unbridled joy of once again being a Whaler in Hartford seized him. For 12 long years, the last six under a bridge, he had yearned for this moment. It was too much to enjoy sitting on his ass.

Catapulting the boards, and staggering on-ice like a drunk, he executed three near-stellar cartwheels before the fourth landed him on his ass.

"The Showman is back!" roared Kaiton. "We've seen Tiger the fighter tonight, but not *this* Tiger. I gotta say, though, he's a bit rusty."

Behind the bench, Gracie rocketed up from her seat. For lo' these many years, she had yearned to see Tiger bust out his signature celebration. It was a thing of near ethereal beauty.

"This is what our city needs," crowed the revival leader in section 399 through his battered megaphone. "Can I hear an AMEN?"

As Tiger lay sprawled on-ice, rubbing his buttocks, the fans at once took up a spiraling chant.

"TI-GRRRRRRRR, TI-GRRRRRRRR, TI-GRRRRRRRR..."

From the crown of his grotesque head to the soles of his mutilated feet— the little fighter basked in this his moment of glory. From the bottom of a filthy bridge to center ice bathed in spotlights, what a journey he had come. For the Whalers, too—from a dusty footnote in history, to one goal from the Stanley Cup—what a ride it was for them.

Taking theatrical bows, Tiger drank in every intoxicating syllable before a sudden realization disgusted him. This was not his moment. It was the fans' moment, the team's moment, Hartford's moment. Mortified at his antics, Tiger slashed at his throat, signaling "CUT! CUT!"

The crowd, wondering if this was his newest dance, growled louder.

"TI-GRRRRRRRR, TIGRRRRR...", but as he slashed away more maniacally, the message slowly dawned on them: Tiger wants to speak.

"QUIET!" yelled a leather-lung in Section 107, and the call was picked up by rows, then sections, until at last the whole Mall was eerily quiet. The rolling silence had taken but seconds.

The crowd stilled, Tiger from center ice, in a raspy squawk that hardly carried, hollered "HARTFORD" and pointed east to Colt's armory. Then pirouetting, and stumbling, he pointed west over to Twain's mansion, yelling "WHALER."

"HARTFORD"–he jabbed east.

"WHALER"–he jabbed west.

After a few times, those much-maligned fans in that much-maligned building picked it up, too. Using his child-sized stick as a baton, the muscle-bound maestro conducted:

"HARTFORD....WHAAAAAAALER"

"HARTFORD....WHAAAAAAALER"

Ringing out as loud as Colt's 1863 factory explosion that rocked the city, the chant was enough to stir the dead. Satisfied at last, Tiger skated to the end of the bench. For the final 2:30, the deafening roar sustained the weary Whale, against a last withering assault.

"Looks like we're going to Overtime," announced Kaiton on the radio. "My! Oh My!"

41. Tiger's Speech

He conquers who suffers.
—Sam Colt

For a decade he had lived in the shadows, his natural luminosity dimmed. For a decade he had lived in eclipse, where all was muted and gray. But something deep inside was dawning. Standing among friends and teammates in a familiar place, the light burning from inside pushed the shadows to the edges. Five overtime minutes remained to decide the fate of a team summoned from the dead to play for the Stanley Cup.

Now there were plenty of voices in the locker room, each searching for the right note to lift a tired team to victory. But no one had prepared for this moment. How could they?

One old defenseman pulled out a book thrust into his hands by fans, "Every Man A Tiger" by Tom Clancy. "This is what it will take!" he declared, waving it high. "Every one must play like Tiger!"

"Damn right, Dana! You got it, brother."

Another spoke of a Special Forces unit "Team Tiger" in the hunt for Bin Laden. "That is what we must become 'Team Tiger'," MacDermid shouted.

"Way to go, Dermie!"

But again it fell short. Something was missing. This locker room had been assembled in the most improbable circumstances. Sure Tiger was an inspiration, but more was needed now to bind them.

And so the smallest among them waddled to the front. He said nothing. But the shadows were receding, the luminosity returning. And so he pointed to his green jersey, the one they all wore for tomorrow's exhibition, and spoke, haltingly at first:

"A-a lot of people have, umm, spat on this jersey, umm, stomped on it and ridiculed it. And that includes, umm, a few who wore it. Look around! There is guys who could be in this room that ain't..."

Tiger was finding his voice.

"There was never no shame in dragging this jersey through the mud. One of 'em that done it is in the locker room next door..."

"No BS!"

"Him too!" yelled someone, referencing the initials of another malcontent.

"They buried this jersey six years ago and everyone thought it was done! Over! Well, they was wrong now. Ain't they? Here WE are!"

"Damn Straight!"

Tiger continued, more sure. "This jersey deserves better! Always has! It made me feel on top o' the world puttin' it on. Lettin' it down killed me..." he said, his voice faltering.

"Ya' never did, Tiger! Ya' always done it proud!" barked Dineen.

Tiger nodded.

"We all played for a city that, like the jersey, has been kicked around more than a place ought 'ta. And why? Why do the people out there deserve any less than the folk in Boston or New York?"

No one had an answer.

"I never wanted nuthin' more than ta' make 'em feel worthy. I fought for 'em, spilled blood for 'em, even sacrificed my good looks, I dare say."

A few players chuckled, but none interrupted.

"And now there are five minutes—one fighting penalty —ta' do what I always wanted ta' do. Win the CUP! In the MALL! For HARTFORD!"

Cheers echoed in the distance.

"If we can be the fellows who brought back the Whale, even for a night, that would be the greatest accolade of my life. Ya' could etch it on my grave!"

"We're already back," someone interrupted. "Look around! We're all here!"

"It ain't enough!" snapped Tiger. "We've got ta' WIN! It's all or nothing. How this team and city looks at itself is at stake. I'd rather this game never was played if we lose now."

Tiger's nostrils flared. His fists balled. No one dared interrupt.

"Look at the people here. Ronnie won twice with Pittsburgh. But he married here, had his first kid here, took his first steps as a pro here. Don't 'ya think Ronnie wants ta' win?

"And Kevin! A few years ago, Kevin had the grim duty of standing before them fans to tell 'em it was over, their team was leavin' 'em. Don't 'ya think Kevin wants to win?

"Look at Ulfie and Beeker! They won Cups. Why not *here*? Why not Hartford?"

The room was silent, but something was building inside.

"Look at me! Everyone knows my story. I never advertised it, but it's out there in, wha'd they call it, the public domain?"

"Nice *Newsweek* cover!" Ulfie razzed.

"Missed my good side!" Tiger deadpanned. Then reaching to his waist, he pulled the shiny green jersey over his head, revealing the blackened, threadbare one he wore at his last game, when the Whalers were on the cusp of greatness.

"I never took it off," he said softly, tears spilling out. "It ain't much to look at, like me. But it stayed with me through times you would never believe."

A few of the players gazed down at their jerseys.

"If they let me play in OT, I'll give my last drop a' blood to win. But coach'll make that call. No matter, I'm wearing this old jersey out there, and no matter what happens, it comes off tonight. I'll have done my part."

A few of the tough guys teared up as Tiger bowed, as if praying for a chance.

And so now the coaches had a difficult decision. Would Tiger play in the all-important overtime? Quenneville, Tippett and O'Reilly huddled in the hall for a final, frank discussion and voices were raised.

"He's not *good* enough, dammit! He doesn't give us the *best* chance to win."

"But we owe it to him for what he's done to get us here."

"Sentiment won't rule this!" screamed the first, slamming a fist into the wall. "The five best must play."

In the end, it was left to Terry O'Reilly, his old nemesis, to break the deadlock.

"He plays. No one'll fight harder."

42. Overtime

It's one thing to be rough, but to be rough and crazy means the other
guy is never going to get the last hit. If someone got me, I'd play
with him, tease him, but he knew sooner or later he'd pay.
—Gordie Howe

Like a charwoman at the ball, Tiger in his dusky jersey stood at center ice.
Five lonely minutes remained in an unlikely quest. If the game ended in a
tie, the Cup stayed with the Champs. Every muscle taut, except his ankles,
which never quite locked, Tiger looked over behind the bench.

"I believe in you," Gracie said, mouthing the words and clasping her
heart with both hands.

Tiger nodded. His jaw, like his body, was strong. His high cheekbones
were chiseled. If you overlooked a few scars, he really wasn't bad looking.
His shoulders sloped, his legs oak, his waist granite, a "six pack" they call
it today.

Tiger looked down to the spot where ten years ago he had cried tears
so bitter that some swore a grotesque image remained. All he saw now was:
"Hartford Civic Center Managed by Madison Square Garden", a bitter
reminder of who had moved in.

Huddling below the circle, the three Whalers gathered one last time.
It was Ronnie who spoke.

"Win or lose, we three here must do it. No line changes! The Whale
lives or dies in these hands. Put 'em together, now."

Tiger joined his mangled hand to the two that more than any others
had guided the helm of the ship.

"1-2-3 WHALE," they shouted, assuming their face-off positions:
Kevin to the right, Tiger the left. Every fan, every player, every ghostly
shadow stood. Gracie, embracing Mr. Schmidley, whispered "This is it."

Ronnie won the draw, and the puck squirted over to Tiger. Like a
bowling ball flattening pins, he trampled over two bodies attempting
to screen him. Gathering the puck, he flipped it towards Ronnie, but it
skipped wide of the mark.

Each possession was precious; each mistake costly. The other coaches glowered at O'Reilly. Fortunately, the backline of Ulf and Babych had not cheated forward.

"BACK on 'D'!" hollered the bench.

Defense had always been an unfathomable mystery to Tiger. His primitive understanding of it was to knock down any opponent near the puck, but the elusive New Jersey forwards passed and pirouetted, passed and pirouetted, with Tiger hitting only air.

"Play the *point*! Not the man!" O'Reilly hollered, feeling the glares of those who felt Tiger did not belong out there.

Tiger moved to the point, sweeping his stick like a metronome, forcing the Devils to set up like the number five on a dice. A minute had passed. The Devils were feeling the pressure.

With the whole world watching, giving up three goals to a team of ghosts was embarrassing. From the other end, Broadway, ever impulsive, screamed.

"SHOOT the goddam puck!"

Follow his command, or incur his wrath, a defenseman wristed a shot at Lootie, who deflected it behind the net. 4:00 remained.

Ronnie swooped behind and took the puck. Stick-handling past one defender, he muscled by a second. A third, he turned inside-out. Ronnie was at center ice, the puck on his blade, where every fan wanted it.

"Better than Sex!" hollered Blue Line Betty, who could only imagine.

With Dineen on his right and Tiger lagging left, Ronnie crossed the red line. His mind was a computer, calculating 100 options at once. And he didn't discount any. Deep down, Ronnie believed in Tiger, that if given the puck in the right spot he could get the job done.

"It's all in the pass," he once said. "That's why they call it an assist."

But a lot of water had passed under the bridge. Tiger was past his prime, and his prime had not amounted to much. Ronnie's mind raced.

Looking left, he flicked the puck ahead to Dineen, Hartford's "John Wayne on Skates." If Hartford needed a big shot, Dineen was the one to take it. Racing up to the pass, he wiggled under a thunderous check on the boards, and turned on the jets, one defenseman to beat.

"GO Kevin! GO!" yelled Blue-Line Betty, on her feet.

Curling his left arm around the defender, Dineen burst in on goal. But Broadway reacted instantly—charging with one, two, three giant strides from his goal. Once again, he was an island.

Diving, stick extended, Broadway closed the 15 feet between him and the puck in a split-second. A cobra could not strike quicker! It was a play one in a hundred goalies could make, maybe one in a thousand. But fewer would dare.

Poking the puck, before Dineen could muster the half-second needed to uncork a shot, or dodge the flying goalie, Broadway had challenged and won.

"Ooooooooooooooooooooh," groaned fans, collapsing in their seats.

Fluttering high in the air, the puck spiraled above Broadway and Dineen entangled on the ice. Jostling for position, Tiger and the enormous Michel LeGros battled like rebounders. With his low center of gravity, Tiger jammed his hip into LeGros's knees and tossed the 240-pounder aside like a rag doll. Alone now he stood under the puck, LeGros on his back.

Placing his glove like an outfielder, he cradled the falling puck and in one motion brought his arm from a Statue of Liberty position to the ice. The journey from above-head to ice had taken but a second. Every fan was astonished at the grace of it. The puck rested on the ice. Flat. Still.

On padded knees, Broadway began the mad clamber back, his face masked in terror. Ten feet from the empty goal, the puck resting on his stick, LeGros down, Tiger began his backswing.

As the arcing stick reached its zenith, LeGros reacted—whipping his stick like a boomerang. Coming forward, Tiger paused to recalibrate, and that instant, LeGros released. A hundred flashes captured the grisly image of the stick whirling in flight, like an unhinged helicopter blade.

As Tiger's stick kissed the puck, LeGros's slammed into his head, and he dropped as if struck by an assassin, the puck at his feet. Disbelieving fans recoiled at the gruesome thud. It wasn't supposed to happen like that in hockey. That's why they dropped the gloves.

Ronnie arrived first, followed by Dineen, a vortex of green in tow. The trainers, pulled along by skaters, arrived next. Ten seconds had passed. Tiger hadn't moved. With 20 players looking on, the kneeling trainer opened his left eye.

"He's DEAD!"

"WRONG one, Skip!" snapped Dineen.

Embarrassed, the veteran trainer put his thumb and index finger to Tiger's right lids and lifted, and the eye blinked with the onrush of light. By now, Gracie was at the player's gate, nose pressed to the glass.

"How is he? PLEASE, please tell me!" she screamed. No one knew.

As trainers worked feverishly, several Devils moved to the outer edges of the circle. Some pushed to the center. Hockey's game of territory no longer mattered. Something greater was at stake.

Away from the tangle of concerned players, stood Broadway, hands on his hips, with LeGros, visibly shaken. On instinct, without malice, he had committed a hockey felony. From the earliest ages, players are taught never to throw their sticks; the consequences can be deadly.

Tiger's crumpled form flashed on the Jumbotron. Those not sickened, or mortified, looked up, as cameras panned in. For several long minutes, he did not move. Then suddenly, the left eye twitched, and the right blinked. When his toes, visible after his skates were removed, wiggled, hopes surged. When ice at last was rubbed on his roped neck, and that toothless grin flashed, a wild applause swept through the arena.

Before Skip could pose the timeless question asked of every fallen fighter ("Do you know where you are?"), Tiger beat him to the punch with a rapid one-two.

"Did I SCORE? Did we WIN?"

Reading his bleeding lips, fans answered in a chorus of groans.

"Noooooooooo!"

At that, Tiger's head dropped to the ice and his eye rolled back into his skull. His stout frame was built to absorb physical punishment—but the emotional kind always devastated him.

With Tiger conscious, it was time for the other skate to drop, and every fan knew it. Torrie Robertson, who pledged to watch his back, had a promise to keep. As he peeled away from the ring of players, and skated for LeGros, all heads turned, even Tiger's.

Ten feet away, and closing, Torrie rifled his gloves off, issuing the challenge. LeGros flipped his off, accepting, and raised his fists, elbows tucked at his side. With righteousness on the other side, LeGros was not long for his feet, or his senses: the former knocked out with a left, the latter separated with a right. Shouts of quenched bloodlust rattled from angry fans' throats.

"Ya' DONE right, Torrie!"

The promise kept, Torrie gathered stick and gloves and skated to Tiger for a benediction.

"Thanks, Torrie," he mumbled, patting his head weakly.

As Tiger was wheeled off the ice, it was an anxious time, no less for the assessment of penalties than for word on his health. After the initial assault, Hartford stood to receive a power play. But had Torrie's promise balanced the scales of justice?

Every fan and player waited nervously, as the officials huddled. Only in the most dire of circumstances would a referee award a power play in overtime. Carefully, Collins and the linesmen unraveled the chain of events.

A minute later, matters untangled, he skated to the scorer's table. The scorer nodded and relayed the decision. All was quiet as the announcer's words echoed:

"Five minutes, fighting, Robertson of HARTFORD."

"Noooooooooooooo…"

"Five minutes, fighting, LeGros of NEW JERSEY."

"Yeeeeeeeeah…"

The announcer took a deep breath.

"In consideration of the throwing of a stick on a shot into an empty net…the Hartford Whalers will be awarded a PENALTY SHOT."

43. The Last Shot

A Whaler sailed unchartered waters from the arctic regions to the
tropics; and, even though it might take two, three or even four years,
it usually returned to its home-port with a valuable cargo.
—-*Travelers Currier & Ives Calendar*

The Hartford Whalers had the opportunity to win the Stanley Cup in
the most dramatic way, shooter against goalie. In section 399, a barrage of
missiles pelted the interlopers on either side.

"Damn Straight! The zebras made the right call!" yelled the white-
mustached man, adding mischievously, "for a change."

"A BANG-UP call!" cried the man brandishing six shooters.

But amidst the glee, there was a technicality to be sorted out. The
referee skated over to the Whalers bench. Pointing to the ice, he and the
coach appeared to be discussing some matter of gravity. When both were
in agreement, he skated to the official scorer who relayed the message.
Gilmartin, the announcer, clicked on the mike:

"Due to injury, Tiger Burns is unable to take the penalty shot awarded
to him…"

The crowd hushed.

"As an alternate …"

The noise suddenly cranked up.

"The Whalers have selected…"

The volume cranked higher.

"…from the players on the ice…"

Bedlam ensued.

"…At the time of the infraction…"

In a night of eruptions, the next was the loudest.

"…Ronnie Francis."

Ronnie Francis, beloved Captain and standard-bearer, would take the
shot in Tiger's stead. It was the storybook ending everyone in the building
had dreamed of—especially the boy from "The Soo", Ontario.

Resigned to their fate, the Devils shuffled off to the bench, heads
bowed. No one skated over to the goalie to tap his pads or linger for a

reassuring moment. Once again, Broadway was an island, as every goalie must be. But his was an emotional as well as a physical island.

The Whalers, by contrast, mobbed their Captain, raking off his helmet and tousling his hair. As Jimmy the DJ cranked up "Celebrate Good Times", every man in green was with him, every fan, too.

Down in the trainer's room, two ammonia capsules jolted Tiger's senses. His head recoiled violently.

"Whooooa baby!"

"Relax, Tiger. Your work is done," said Skip, the trainer.

"Where am I?"

"You took one for the team, Tiger, but Ronnie's got your back," he said, his voice soothing. "It's okay."

The fate of the team was in Ronnie's hands. As the Whalers slowly cleared the ice, blessings bestowed, two lonely figures remained: the goalie and the scorer, a match of equals.

In his crease, Broadway furiously scraped the ice with his blades, sweeping aside the shavings. Dulling the ice is an old trick that gives a goalie traction. This was *his* moment, after all, to stick it to old Twain Town. Broadway was ready!

At center ice, inside the logo, Hartford's favorite son anxiously tapped the puck. It gave him a feel for the hard rubber that would soon do his bidding. This was *his* moment, after all, to vindicate team and city. Ronnie was ready!

It was hockey's perfect moment—until it was ruined.

As Collins raised his whistle, a ruckus on the walkway between the two benches gave him pause. Un-puckering his lips, the whistle fell to his striped shirt. Turning to the disturbance, his eyes bulged.

Holy Christ!

Weaving unsteadily to the ice like an uninvited commoner at a coronation was Tiger Burns. He hadn't read the damned script! Mortified players on the bench stood and gasped. Ray Ferraro screeched, as if protecting an overmatched fighter rising up from the canvas.

"Stay Down! God Damn it!"

Others, turning from the most perfect specimen ever to grace a green uniform to the bow-legged, one-eyed hobbit shouted.

"DUCK! Don't let them see you! For Crissakes!"

Tossing aside a guard barring the gate, he moved unsteadily toward the ice. This, after all, was **his** moment. Fumbling with the latch, he stepped out onto the ice, stumbled and fell.

"STAY DOWN! STAY DOWN!"

But Tiger Burns of Moose Jaw was a fighter. It wasn't in his DNA to stay down, and so he rose clumsily. Leaning on his stick like a crutch, he dug in one toe and pirouetted, a cockamamie grin on his face.

"If they see you can skate, they'll give you the shot! Don't you understand?"

Others picked up on the plea, Blue-Line Betty among them.

"FALL! FALL to the ice!"

With each faltering step, hockey's perfect moment was ruined.

"No! Nooo!! Nooooo!!! "

At last, with gnarled fingers broken a hundred which-ways, Tiger reached up and tapped Ronnie's shoulder, breaking his straight-ahead focus. Now, if Ronnie had pulled back, looked askance, or hesitated in the least, there might have been an insurrection in that building. For as much as those fans loved Tiger, they loved Ronnie equal—and with the game on the line, they loved him a good deal more.

"Tiger?! What are *you* doing here?"

Tiger looked up into the bigger man's eyes.

"You don't have ta' stand in for me no more, Ronnie."

Make no mistake, Ronnie was not thrilled to see Tiger—not here, not *now*.

"Tiger, you don't look so good."

Tiger flashed that cockamamie grin again.

"It's okay, Ronnie. I'm ready. I am."

Ronnie looked down into Tiger's eye.

"Tiger, you always had my back. Now I've got yours. I can make this shot."

But the little fighter did not waver. He reached up to his Captain's shoulder.

"I know you *can*, Ronnie. But I **must**."

Looking down into Tiger's eye, he saw no fear.

"Okay, Tiger, if I can't take this shot, there is no one I'd rather have than you. I mean it. Now go do it! And let's get this damn thing over with!"

And with that, the torch was passed from the greatest goal-scorer the Whalers had ever known to the worst. Before leaving, Ronnie bent down and said something he had ached to say for years into that cauliflower ear.

"I believe in you, Tiger, and I love you."

233

Tapping his shin pads with his stick, Ronnie exited center ice with the grace of a champion. It was Tiger's shot, after all. 15,535 appreciative fans rose, and teammates swarmed him.

"Class act all the way, Ronnie," said Kevin, embracing him, "even if it costs us."

"He can make it!" Ronnie said evenly.

Kevin looked at him like he was nuts. At the changing of the guard, some of the Devils high-fived and whooped it up on the bench. Broadway, heretofore the picture of determination, pantomimed a gesture of relief, removing his mask and wiping his brow.

"That one-eyed, two-bit GOON can't score," he yelled to hecklers pounding away on the glass. "I could lie down and he couldn't even flip it over me."

Like everyone else, DJ Jimmy Patterson was caught off-guard. A master at hitting the right note in song, he had the crowd swaying to "We Are The Champions" for Ronnie's shot, but Tiger needed his own song. Dipping into his bag, he spotted an Eminem rap and jammed it in the drive.

> Look, if you had one shot, or one opportunity
> To seize everything you ever wanted-One moment
> Would you capture it or just let it slip?

> Yo, His palms are sweaty, knees weak, arms are heavy
> There's vomit on his sweater already, mom's spaghetti
> He's nervous, but on the surface he looks calm and ready

At center ice, inside the logo, Tiger looked small, much smaller than Ronnie, unequal to the task. Removing his mask, Broadway placed his hand over one eye and slashed at his throat, universal sign language for: "Cyclops is gonna choke!"

Over the radio, Kaiton's voice trailed off— "I'd like his chances in a fight, but..."

But Ronnie knew better! Although Tiger wasn't the fastest skater, best shooter, or slickest passer, when it came to one-on-one, against a goalie, unhindered by defenders, he was as good as any.

"He can do it!" Ronnie repeated.

Over the years, Tiger had practiced his breakaways tirelessly. Long after others, including Broadway, *especially* Broadway, had left the ice, Tiger draped the net with a canvas "Shooter Tutor", and drilled away. Yes, his fighting had always overshadowed his skills, but Ronnie knew that Tiger could "take a shift."

So now he had to sell 15,535 crest-fallen fans on his unlikely view. Lifting his stick high, he let it crash to the ice, and began a rhythmic drumming. Every Whaler followed his lead.

Seat by seat, row by row, section by section, reluctant fans joined in. Along with stomping and clapping, some added their voices, until this too caught on, and soon the chants rumbled like rolling thunder.

"GO, TIGER, GOOO!"

"GO, TIGER, GOOO!"

"GO, TIGER, GOOO!"

Lying under his bridge, he'd visualized this moment. Glancing up to section 399, the rickety platform where pitched battles had been raging all night, he spied the motley crew. Where others saw only empty space, Tiger could see them. Every one!

The man in white with the unruly shock of hair nodded.

"Twain!" said Tiger, his heart racing.

The small woman clasping the book did, too.

"Harriet!"

The man with the six-shooters and one with the rake raised their instruments in salute.

"Colt! Olmsted!"

And the zany ballplayer in wool flannels removed his beat-up hat and twirled it like a lasso.

"Huh? He's here, too?!"

44. Release

Succeed and further develop the work of previous generations.
—Chinese Proverb

Four Hartford's greats—and one screwball—had given him the go-ahead. Looking to Gracie behind the bench, she blew him a kiss and clasped her bosom. Then looking down at the spot where a tragic mask was etched into the ice, Tiger smiled: Time to wipe that look off the city's countenance forever.

With the hopes of a city on his thick back and the thin blade of his stick, Tiger churned his bowed legs and addressed the puck— *Thwack!* Cradling it, backhand to forehand, he crossed the blue-line, with 15,535 screaming fans riding with him. But Tiger heard nothing. He was in a zone.

Crouching five feet above the crease, Broadway skated backwards, eyes riveted to the puck. Coming to rest at the heart of the net, he clanged his stick on both posts, assuring himself of his position: master of his domain.

Fifteen yards away, Tiger glanced up. Sensing the puck with his stick, he advanced deliberately. Ten yards away, the goalie puffed up like a cobra, giving the illusion of covering the net. For Tiger, five yards away, and swooping in, it was time.

Shifting his gaze, he moved the puck to his forehand, the most lethal position. As he dipped his shoulder, the goalie shifted, and for a split-second, was off-balance. In that moment, Tiger had the advantage.

With a roll of his wrist, he slid the puck backhand, and in one flick, flipped it between the goalie's sprawling legs. *Five Hole!* 10,000 flashbulbs froze the moment of Tiger lifting his small stick in jubilation.

DAH DAH DAH dadadadada…

"HARTFORD WINS! HARTFORD WINS! HARTFORD WINS the most unlikely Stanley Cup ever played," exulted Chuck Kaiton, above pandemonium. "*Brass Bonanza* never sounded so beautiful."

Dancing a wild jig, and pumping his stout arms, Tiger twirled on one leg like a 200-pound ballerina, as Broadway, stick shattered, exited stage right with defiant strides.

As he bent to leap into the embrace of fans, a frenzied mob from the bench buried him in a green avalanche. Hartford's "Mall" had become the scene of hockey's greatest underdog story, and *Brass Bonanza* played on and on.

Dancing spilled out onto Asylum and Trumbull Streets and radiated into neighborhoods. On Albany Avenue, it was like nights of yore when Joe Louis won. On Park Street, tricked-up cars honked into the night. In the south end, champagne geysered like at an Italian wedding.

Fireworks exploded high over the river. The lights on the Travelers spelled "WHALE." On this night, even Carl Andre's 36 stones glittered like diamonds. And up in Boston, in one of those corny civic bets, the Mayor had delivered 1000 Boston cream pies and 1000 gallons of chowda.

"Dump it all in the Harbor!" roared the white-suited man in 399.

Amidst the jubilation, the Whalers and Devils lined up for the traditional handshakes. Ronnie, Kevin and Ulf, who had led a ragtag team from the grave, led the line. While up in the stands hugging, mugging and kissing everyone was Tiger.

"The Cup, Tiger! The CUP!" alerted Blue-Line Betty.

Winding his way down, Tiger assumed his position at the rear of the line. The Champs, give them their due, accepted defeat with grace.

"It's our Cup, but we bequeath it to Hartford," said the red-shirted Captain, handing it to Ronnie. "The Whalers won it, fair and square."

When Ronnie thrust the silver chalice skyward, the promise he and Tiger had made as teens was at last fulfilled. Pressed against his green jersey, with Kevin and Ulf by his side, the Cup never glittered so bright. It was a scene many had dreamed of—but repulsed others.

Leaving behind the carnage of the locker room he had just trashed, Broadway intercepted the Commissioner en route to the ice for the presentations—and blasted him with both barrels.

"You're pissing on the grave of Lord Stanley! This is a god-damned disgrace! Hartford can't have the Cup. They're not even a team!"

"The Union agreed, Sly," the Commissioner said, breaking away from the deranged goalie.

"What are you an asshole? We didn't sign up to play Francis, Dineen and the others. That wasn't in the agreement," he screamed, arresting him by the lapels.

"When you took the ice for the third, it signified tacit approval," he said, in a lawyerly way, struggling to break away. "You should have aired your grievances then. It's water under the bridge. Sorry."

"You spineless jellyfish!" raged the berserk goalie, jacking the Commissioner up against the wall, before fast-acting cops subdued him. Tasered, shackled and fingerprinted, Broadway was booked for a night in the Morgan Street lock-up.

Surveying the chaos on-ice, Tiger realized something was missing. Locating the PA announcer, he shouted: "Hey, Golden Lungs! Call down the Wolf Pack! It's their victory, too."

Looking down to the ice, Tiger noticed something else missing. Where once was etched a grotesque mask of pain, now the ice sparkled clear and blue.

"Gone!"

Ronnie noticed, too. Curling an arm around Tiger, Tiger buried his face into Ronnie's embrace. *Sports Illustrated* would capture the iconic image for its "Sportsmen of the Year" cover.

"I was never happy the way it ended here," Ronnie explained into 100 microphones, kissing the Cup for cameras. "This one means as much as the others. Maybe more."

Bound forever by Hartford and their youth, Kevin took the glittering trophy from Ronnie and together they toured the ice, the Cup aloft between them. As the Cup passed from man to man, at last there were two who had not touched it—and one flat-out refused, recoiling as if it were a chamber pot.

"Not unless Boston wins!" O'Reilly smiled, shrinking away. "The last time was 1972. Hartford's a great hockey town. But I still bleed black and gold."

And so at last the Cup came into the hands of the man who had dreamed of this night like no other. Cradling it like a child, Tiger raised it, as O'Reilly and the others looked on with emotion.

His mind flashed to his boyhood: to Bear Le Batard, the dog musher, and the pack of wolves he bunked with; to Moose Jaw, and fighting his way up; to the early years in Hartford, the happiest of his life, when at last he found a home. Winning the Cup takes a team, but for each man the memories are personal.

And so now the microphones were lowered, and the words tumbled out, raspy but joy-filled: "When last we gathered here, Kevin Dineen said good-bye. Well, I'd like ta' say 'HELLO!' We're back and we brought a little somethin' with us."

Lifting the Cup over his head, eye-level to the others, the little fighter shouted: "This is for YOU, Hartford! Ya' never stopped bleeding and believing."

DAH DAH DAH dadadadada…

Brass Bonanza that "dumb" tune sent chills down his spine, but never more than now. When the noise quieted, he continued: "All I ever wanted ta' do in my career was ta' show Hartford how ta' have FUN…"

"WE ARE!"

"…to FIGHT for itself…"

"WE WILL!"

"…and BELIEVE…"

"WE BELIEVE! WE BELIEVE!"

And for the first time since Twain, Colt, Beecher Stowe and Olmsted roamed the streets, they truly did.

"And I'd like ta' thank two people fa' believing in me."

Arm-in-arm, Gracie and Mr. Schmidley came onto the ice—and Gracie in the spirit of the moment launched a cartwheel, skirt tails flying, landing awkwardly into Tiger's embrace.

"You GO, girl!" hollered Blue-Line Betty, pounding the glass.

Mr. Schmidley extended his trembling hand for a dignified handshake.

"Your mom is looking down now, I promise you that, son."

"I love you, Dad," Tiger said, hugging the old man.

"I know that, son! But does this beautiful woman know how you feel?"

In a night of great assists, Mr. Schmidley had just delivered the best. Holding Gracie in one arm, the Cup in the other, Tiger whispered: "I've got the two greatest prizes in the world with me here."

Then putting the Cup down, he kissed Gracie for the first time.

"I love you," he said bashfully.

"Woooooo! Hoooooo!" hollered Blue-Line Betty, pounding the glass, this time with both fists.

"Umm, do ya' love me too?" Before she could answer, Tiger pressed his finger to her lips.

"Wait! Don't answer! I swear I can kiss better. My first girlfriend wasn't much into smoochin'."

"Miss Moose Jaw?

"Yea, and it takes practice. Like a penalty shot!"

Gracie laughed nervously, and looked down.

"So do ya' love me too, Gracie?"

"You know I do!" she cried, tears cascading down her cheeks as she pounded his massive chest with her tiny fists. "I've loved you since the night you said 'Suzy? Is that you?' You just made it an unforgettable ride."

For years now, he had been beset by demons—demons of his own making. Sure he'd been born with a "bat or two" in his belfry, but over the years his head had become a great roost. Just then, there was a release, the demons spiraling away in an endless river.

Pulling off the blackened jersey, the one he never removed, he spied the banner of the Booster Club, the green-bleeding true-believers once blasphemed as a "gang of Gong Show rejects." They'd never disbanded.

"This is for you," he called, tossing the jersey into their midst.

Passing the Cup into the crowd, Tiger and Gracie led it on a grand tour of the Mall. To firefighters, Gracie's students, and, not last, to his ragtag brigade of street urchins, all grown up, many waving diplomas.

"We always believed!" they hollered, as Tiger, humbled, wept.

Gracie pointed up to Keyshawn Streets, the boy who read the Christmas poem and later rescued her career. He was a colleague now, Math Chair and Coach, on the way to Principal. From the lowly ranks of Tiger's Cubs had sprouted lawyers, engineers, even actuaries. In homage, Tiger bowed, arms forward, signaling "I'm not worthy."

Passing one raucous section, Tiger chuckled at the sign: "Insurance Round Table Salutes Its Favorite Coach!" It was The Bishops, the business leaders whom Tiger had taught to fight in a memorable visit to the Hartford Club.

"Don't let 'em push ya' around!" he growled, flexing his biceps.

As the tour wound down, the stadium was empty now, the celebration pushed out to the streets. But off to the side, resisting entreaties to leave, stooped an old man with the outlines of a once-formidable figure, waiting for an audience. Tiger tensed involuntarily.

"I'm sorry, young Tiger," the old man mumbled, looking down.

Tiger tensed more but still was not sure.

"I'm so sorry, young Tiger," he repeated, looking Tiger eye-to-eye, so much had the great frame bowed with age and care.

Now Tiger looked away, lip trembling, as Gracie rushed to him.

"I'm Pierre," he said, removing all doubt. "Long time 'go dey called me Bear."

Tiger's face blanched and eye filled, as Gracie shielded him in embrace.

"I'm not dat man anymore," he pleaded, seeing the pain. "I jes' come all dis way to say dat I'm so proud a' you and so shamed a' me."

The old man shuddered in a way that was heart-breaking. "I won't cause no mo' trouble. If it's too much ta' ask fer you ta' fah-give…"

His voice broke off, and the stooped man shuffled towards the exit where the guards were pushing him.

"Pierre," Tiger called out.

Taking small steps to turn, he faced back, his gray-beard soaked in tears. Impetuously, Tiger rushed him like he might swing, but instead locking him in a hug. "You gave me my name and the courage to fight. I forgive you, Pierre."

The pathetic man kissed Tiger's cheek. "Yer, always wuz a good boy, Tiger. Dis moment is a blessing. I can die now, thank-you."

The stadium was empty now, except for some guards.

"Tiger, you should join your team," said Gracie. "It's midnight already!"

"Wait!" he said, remembering. "One last group!"

Surveying the cavernous stadium, Gracie looked at him like he was crazy.

"Tiger, everyone's gone! Can't you see?"

"No! They're here—I left tickets!"

Bounding up the stairs with the Cup, past endless expanses of empty rows, Tiger pushed far into nosebleed country, until at last he reached section 399. Huffing from the exertion, he raised the Cup and smiled a kingly smile.

"We did it!" he cried in triumph. "Thank you all for coming!"

To those with two eyes, he faced nothing but a rickety camera platform. But Tiger could see them. Every one!

"HURRAH!" they cheered, and only the man with cauliflower ears heard.

In life, each had abandoned this city, but now they were all back! Passing the trophy up into the motley group, Tiger smiled as each beheld it. The landscape architect, who designed Central Park and Boston's Emerald Necklace, but nothing in Hartford, waxed philosophical.

"Sure a great park can bring a city together, but so can a hockey team!"

The man with the great guns never left—but his company did, rotting by the river today.

"I've won medals from Princes and Presidents, but nothing so grand as this," he proclaimed, kissing the Cup.

The little lady who wrote the book that changed history died at home, but is buried near Boston.

"Some things truly are worth fighting for!" she said, rubbing the trophy.

Finally the writer, who'd fled his grand home on Farmington Avenue after his daughter's death, whispered, "In my heart, I never left." Looking over to the hockey player, he asked, "So what do you think of your little city now, my friend?"

Overcome, Tiger fumbled for words, "Well, I-I-I really like this place, sir. I-I'm honored jus'…"

The great writer, always a stickler in these matters, reproved him none-too-gently.

"Choose your words carefully, my fine fighting friend! The difference between the right word and *almost* the right word is, as one genius warned, the difference between the lightning and the lightning bug."

"I LOVE this place!" Tiger exclaimed, flashing that Huckleberry Finn grin.

And with that, the motley crowd of ghosts, specters and poltergeists applauded. The one-eyed, little fighter had spoken for all: inventors, writers and visionaries.

"HURRAH! HURRAH!"

"Yes, we all love Hartford, but that ballplayer over there has been coming to your rescue at the drop of a hat," said the writer. "He's been keeping an eye on you."

Tiger walked over to the southpaw in the crumpled hat. The two embraced.

"You saved me twice. But why? I never did nuthin' for ya."

The ballplayer, his face a mask of wild emotions, took the trophy from the fighter's hands. In life, he'd injured his shoulder fighting over a straw hat, blowing the 1905 World Series and forever wearing the goat horns. Holding the great Cup, his expression turned serene, as if a storm had passed.

Embracing the trophy, the greatest in sport, the man who once rescued a town from floods, had at last saved himself. Removing the battered hat, he flung it over the ledge with that magnificent left arm. As it whirlybird-ed to the ice below, his face lit up in a goofy grin. Rube was free!

"Now that's what I call a hat trick!" marveled the writer, and the band of misfits cheered.

Spitting a stream of tobacco juice into his hands, the star-crossed southpaw slicked back his brown hair, and smoothed down a century-old case of "hat hair." After a last hug of the trophy, the hatless ballplayer handed it back to the shirtless fighter, bowed and trotted off towards distant fire bells.

"Who is he?" asked Tiger, filled with awe and wonder.

"Who knows? He ain't one for talking," said the spokesman in white. "But that Pudd'nhead sure knows how to have fun!"

"I'm sure gonna miss him," said Tiger, looking to Gracie and the Cup. "I owe him so much."

Spotting a rusty nail on the platform, Tiger had a sudden inspiration. Resting the Cup upside-down on its bowl, he inscribed with a steady hand from his silversmithing days in Churchill the Whaler's logo on the Cup's bottom, so small you'd have to squint—even if you had two eyes.

"Right where it belongs!" he declared.

With those strokes, Tiger elevated Hartford from a dusty footnote in the annals of hockey to forever-etched on the Stanley Cup. Collecting a thimbleful of the silver dust, he sprinkled the filings on the floor by the camera platform.

"The rest of the world can laugh all they want, but a little bit of hockey history will always reside here. "The 'Mall' is hallowed ground!"

In recent years, when people approached, he skulked into the shadows. But on this night, he smiled that great toothless smile and crowds swarmed again. And he signed autographs—until his tender hand throbbed. And so Tiger at last moved on. And if he had once lost the Cup—a maybe he had gained something greater. He forgave himself.

And so now there remained one last piece of business. In his exile in Churchill, he'd witnessed couples under the Northern Lights. Japanese Legend has it that a child conceived under the spell of the Lights will be fortunate in life. Digging into his pocket, he found some remaining specks of silver dust. Just enough for a silver band, he thought.

Just then, the lights in the Mall flickered, like a meteorite flashing across the sky. The writer who once remarked "I have long ago lost my belief in immortality—also my interest in it" pulled out a pocket watch.

"Getting late! How 'bout we all stroll on over to Chuck's for a good cigar and some strong beverage to fortify us for the road ahead. Some of us have to be leaving soon, you know."

"Closed!" said Tiger glumly, before brightening up. "All the old spots are. But we'll find some fun. It's Hartford, after all!"

Just then, somewhere in the Atlantic, a whale breached, rising out of the water, its head heavenward, spinning and twirling, a cetacean cartwheel, before crashing into the ocean depths.

Endnotes

1. Charles Darwin, "The Origin of Species", Gramercy Books (New Jersey), 1979, Chapter IV on Natural Selection, p.132

2. Dave Semenko with Larry Tucker, "Looking Out For Number One", Stoddart Publishing (Toronto), 1989, p.136

3. Ibid, p.136

4. Gary Mason, "Oldtimers: On the Road with the Legendary Heroes of Hockey", Greystone Books (Vancouver), 2002, p. 225

5. Boston Globe, "You Could See This Call Coming", Dan Shaughnessy, May 1, 1999, p.G1

6. "Between New York and Boston", Written and Directed by Kenneth A. Simon, Broadcast on CPTV in 1992

7. Charles Dickens, "Pictures From Italy and American Notes", Harper and Brothers (New York), p. 277

8. Tiger Williams with James Lawton, "Tiger: A Hockey Story", Douglas & McIntyre (Vancouver), 1984, p.16

9. Mark Twain, "Huckleberry Finn", Wordsworth Classics (Hertfordshire), 1992, Chapter 5

10. Lee Hall, "Olmsted's America: An Unpractical Man and his Vision of Civilization", Bulfinch Press (Boston), 1995

11. Los Angeles Times, "Wish Upon A Rising Star", David Lamb, June 15, 2003

12. New York Times, "Poverty in a Land of Plenty: Can Hartford Ever Recover?", Paul Zielbauer, August 26, 2002 p.1

13. Jack Lautier and Frank Polnaszek, "Same Game, Different Name: The History of the World Hockey Association", Glacier Publishing (Southington, CT), p.2

14. Samuel Eliot Morrison, "Oxford History of the American People", Oxford, 1965

15. Tom Wolfe, "From Bauhaus To Our House", p.82

16. Semenko, p.137

17. Journal Inquirer, "Ronnie's Reward is Hartford's Penance", Randy Smith, October 20, 1992

18. Hartford Courant, "Final Chapter: Raising of No. 10", Jeff Jacobs, January 4, 2002

19. Sports Illustrated, March 23, 1998, "Captain Class", Gerry Callahan, p.36

20. Hartford Courant, "Ley's Bungled Move may cost Whalers", Jeff Jacobs, December 9, 1990

21. Journal-Inquirer

22. "Players: The Ultimate A-Z Guide of Everyone Who Has Ever Played in the NHL", Andrew Podnieks, Doubleday Canada, 2003, p.759

23. Los Angeles Times, "Wish Upon A Rising Star", David Lamb, June 15, 2003

24. Los Angeles Times, "Wish Upon A Rising Star", David Lamb, June 15, 2003

25. New York Times, "Poverty in a Land of Plenty: Can Hartford Ever Recover?", Paul Zielbauer, August 26, 2002, p.1

26. Chicago Tribune, "Rediscovered Score Pianist's Last Legacy", Howard Reich, August 11, 2002

27. Boston Globe, "Some Give-It-A-Chance Encounters in Hartford", Michael Holley, November 23, 1998

28. Mark Twain, "Tom Sawyer" , Wordsworth Classics (Hertfordshire), 1992, Chapter 2, p.13

29. Emmett Kelley, "Clown", Prentice Hall (New York), 1954, p.221

30. Ibid, p.223

31. Semenko, p. 139

32. Ibid, p.185

33. Connecticut: A History, David M. Roth, W.W. Norton Co. (New York), 1979

34. Boston Globe, "NHL Playoffs Get a New England Rivalry", Kevin Paul Dupont, April 5, 1990, p.1

35. Boston Herald, "B's Don't Know Meaning of Quit", Joe Fitzgerald, April 17, 1990, p.80

36. Ibid

37. Boston Globe, "There's No Doubt Hartford's For Real", Bob Ryan, April 5, 1990, p.25

38. Boston Herald, "Hartford's Hard to Hate", Joe Fitzgerald, April 11, 1990, p.100

39. Ibid

40. Ibid

41. Hartford Courant, "A Wrong Turn Into Twilight Zone", Alan Greenberg, April 12, 1990, p.B7

42. Lawrence Eagle-Tribune, "Only Houdini Could Have Matched This", Russ Conway, April 12, 1990

43. Mark Twain: An Illustrated Biography, Geoffrey Ward, Dayton Duncan and Ken Burns, Alfred A. Knopf (New York), 2001

44. Jack Lautier, "Forever Whalers", Glacier Publishing, 1997, p.41

45. Ibid, p.55

46. Sociology of Sport Journal, The "Sudden Death" of Hockey in Hartford: Sports Fans and Franchise Relocation, John R. Mitrano, Vol. 16, No. 2, 1999, p. 134-154

47. Ibid, p.138

48. Ibid, p.148

49. Scott M. Wiggins, "Stories of Hartford Whaler Fans", http://whalers.hart.net/story3.htm

50. Chris McDonell, "The Game I'll Never Forget", Firefly Books, Toronto, 2002, p.38

51. Mitrano, p. 138

52. Hartford Courant, "Tiger Woulds and Wouldn'ts", Colin McEnroe, October 12, 2003

53. Account of Lee Allen, Baseball Historian at the Hall of Fame, Cooperstown, NY

54. Alan H. Levy, "Rube Waddell: The Zany, Brilliant Life of a Strikeout Artist", McFarland and Co. (North Carolina), 2000, p. 231

55. Hartford Courant, October 8, 1906, p.1

56. Hartford Courant, October 9, 1906, p.1

57. Hartford Times, October 9, 1906

58. Williams, p.16

59. Associated Press, "Bourque Calls O'Reilly the 'Ultimate Bruin'", October 24, 2002

60. Ibid

61. Ibid

62. Boston Globe, "Some Give-It-A-Chance Encounters in Hartford", Michael Holley, November 23, 1998

63. Sports Illustrated, March 23, 1998, "Captain Class", Gerry Callahan, p.36

64. Boston Globe, "Whale of a time for Diehards", Kevin Paul Dupont, June 2, 2002, p. D13

65. Sports Illustrated, May 26, 2003, "Natural Disaster", Gerry Callahan, p. 65

66. Ibid, p. 65

67. Sports Illustrated, July 25, 1994, "Heeere's Stanley", Franz Lidz

68. Sports Illustrated, May 26, 2003, "Resident Alien in Red Sox Nation", Steve Rushin, p. 19